Secrets of Innocence

Book Two in the Series

The Perils of a Reluctant Psychic

Secrets of Innocence

A Novel

V. & D. Povall

This is a work of fiction. Names, characters, organizations, places, events, and incidents are either products of the author's imagination or are used fictitiously.

Publisher: Dragonfly Media
ISBN (paperback): 9781642374926
eISBN: 9781642374650
Library of Congress Control Number (LCCN): 2016918052
DragonflyMedia, Oceanside, CALIFORNIA

Writing never happens in a vacuum.
Many are those who help in different ways.

Thanks

To the Okanagan County Sheriff's Office for their assistance and particularly to Sheriff Frank T. Rogers for his warm welcome, guidance, and advice on multiple procedures and locations.

To Michael D. Billing, CEO of the Okanagan Mid-Valley Hospital, for his help and to his Assistant Becky Corson for her insights into psychic experiences.

A Special Thank-You

To Jennifer Silva Redmond, our exceptional editor,
for her invaluable advice and her unique ability to elevate our prose while honoring our voice.

Contents

C H A P T E R   1

Sarah spotted the blood first. A red spatter marred the snow that glistened under the weak winter sun.

Then she caught sight of the man sprawled on the side of the road.

She pulled off the highway and dialed 911 to report the incident. Cell phone in hand, she sprang from the car, knelt down, and instinctively placed her hand on his chest. "Help is on the way," she told him. "Can you hear me?"

His eyes were swollen shut, his cheeks and lips scraped and torn. Blood oozed from a gash above his temple. He tilted his head and his eyelids fluttered, but remained shut. He reached out for her.

She took his blood-soaked hand and held it close. "It's all right, don't try to move. The paramedics are on their way. You'll be all right."

He struggled to open his eyes again, but his body wilted and his breathing became labored.

"Stay with me; stay with me." She reached for a handful of snow and carefully patted it on his forehead.

The man stirred once more. "Sarah," he whispered.

"Yes."

"Sarah," he muttered again.

"Yes, I'm here. Stay with me. Please. Help is on the way."

His body went limp as he slid into unconsciousness.

Conrad Thompson rushed down the hospital corridor in a desperate search to find his wife. He spotted her at the end of the hallway, covered in blood. "Sarah!" He raced to her and held her at arm's length, searching for injuries.

"I'm all right; it's the man's blood. I should've asked you to bring me some clean clothes."

"What madness possessed you to drive this far from home?" Conrad pulled her toward him and wrapped her in his arms. "The road over the pass is always treacherous in the snow." His voice held a mixture of anger and despair.

Sarah shook her head and shrugged. "I can't understand it myself. I'd finished baking some bread when I had this uncontrollable urge…an overwhelming awareness that someone desperately needed my help."

Conrad released her and sighed. "Angela again? I'd hoped she was finally resting in peace."

"No, no. Not your grandmother. This time it's someone else."

"Who?"

Sarah shrugged. "Maybe the injured man?"

Conrad's eyes widened with bewilderment. "Are you saying you sensed the living?"

"Don't look so shocked. It's not impossible. I could do it when I was little."

"Yeah, but you haven't had these type of premonitions since then. Have you?"

"No. Years of denial did lots of damage."

"So why now? Do you know this man?"

"No."

"Then what?"

"I have no clue. It's very odd. For a year now, I've had no premonitions, no sensations, no images whatsoever…until today." Her eyes were troubled.

Conrad pulled her to him again and held her tightly. When she lifted her face, he kissed her. "We'll figure it out."

In the year since their wedding, Sarah hadn't changed much—in his eyes she grew more beautiful and desirable with each passing day. At fifty-seven, she carried herself with a youthful energy and charm that Conrad found irresistible.

He caressed her cheek. "I take it you want to hear all about this man once the doctors are done with him."

She nodded. "I do."

"Okay. C'mon then; let's sit down." Without releasing her, he guided her to the waiting room. They retreated to the farthest corner of the empty room and sat. He wrapped her hand in his. "Let's unravel this puzzle. Tell me again how this all began."

"I'd taken the bread from the oven and placed it on the counter to cool, when I felt compelled to leave the house and drive north as fast as possible. I knew someone's life was in danger. I had no idea where I was going or what I'd find. Only that someone desperately required my help and that there was no time to waste. So I took off, as if someone were guiding me. I completely lost track of how long and how far I drove." She paused. "Then I saw him, the injured man, lying there on the side of the road. When I rushed to his side, he moaned, so I knew he was still alive."

"Thrown from his vehicle?"

She shook her head. "There was no crash, no vehicle…only him lying in the snow. I suspect he was assaulted or thrown from a car or something. His face was a bloody mess, eyes swollen shut, and his cheeks cut and scratched. I spoke to him, and he tilted his head toward me—I think he could see me. He tried to smile, but his lips were too swollen and lacerated. He looked dreadful…his head was bleeding…it was awful. Poor man. I kept asking him his name, but all he did was whisper my name."

"Your name? How did he know your name?"

She looked startled. "I could've told him. The blood horrified me so—I don't recall exactly what I said."

"Are you sensing anything else about him now?"

She looked into Conrad's eyes then slowly shook her head. "No. Maybe… I'm not sure."

"You're not used to dealing with all this psychic stuff yet. It was hard enough when Angela thrust you into our lives. But this—"

"Strangely enough I'm not frightened."

Conrad smiled. "That's a good sign I suppose. What's the difference between how it felt when my grandmother connected with you and now?"

"Well…with Angela I tuned into the past. She'd been dead so long. And she used the old photos in the attic to reveal the secrets of our twin houses. She eased me into accepting my psychic abilities, and by the time I realized your grandmother was orchestrating it all, I couldn't go back. I'd accepted that I could communicate with the dead."

"So you're saying that now the sensations are in the present? Is that it?"

She shrugged. "That isn't clear yet. It feels like the present, and yet…not entirely."

"You mean a bit of both? Past and present?"

"Yes. Maybe."

He squeezed her hand. "Well, then be careful what you do and how you react until we're certain, because it sounds to me like you're dealing with the living this time."

Conrad stood as a uniformed sheriff stepped into the room and made his way directly toward them. He was in his mid forties, well muscled, with a permanent frown etched onto his face. He removed his hat to reveal a baldhead, smiled, and stretched out his hand.

"Mrs. Thompson?"

Sarah stood and shook his hand. "Yes, nice to meet you, Sheriff Williams."

The man tilted his head, clearly taken aback. "You know my name?"

Sarah hesitated. "The paramedics must've told me. This is my husband, Conrad."

Conrad shook the sheriff's hand and placed a protective arm around Sarah's shoulder.

"Good to meet you both." Williams nodded at Conrad, then turned back to Sarah. "Mighty decent of you, ma'am, to stop and help this man. Lucky for him you were driving by. May I ask where you were going?"

"To find him," Sarah said matter-of-factly.

The sheriff stared at her, then Conrad, then back at her.

"You mean he called you?"

"No, not exactly. I…" Sarah vacillated for a moment. "I had a feeling that someone's life was in danger, so I got in my car and drove this way."

"A feeling?" Williams asked, unable to suppress a snort of disbelief.

"Yes. A *feeling*," Conrad said. "She gets them. She has good instincts."

Sheriff Williams nodded condescendingly at the couple then took a small pad and pen from his breast pocket.

"Okay…so where were you when you had this *f-e-e-l-i-n-g*?" He stretched the word to ensure his sarcasm wasn't lost on them.

"Home," Sarah answered.

Williams squinted at Sarah as if trying to determine if she was serious. "Okay," he said at last and then flipped a couple of pages back in his notebook, obviously looking for the address that Sarah must've given to the paramedics. "And that's down south, toward Winthrop, right?"

Sarah nodded.

Williams glanced at each of them in turn. "I see."

Sarah and Conrad remained silent.

"And then what?" Williams frowned with impatience. "Go on."

"I got in my car and headed north across the pass," a serene Sarah continued, "and found him lying on the side of the road. That's all, Sheriff."

"You're sure about that?"

"Of course she's *sure*. Why wouldn't she be?" Conrad's annoyance with the sheriff wasn't subtle.

Williams raised his eyebrows, clearly gratified at getting a rise out of Conrad. "Doing my job, sir. Need to get to the bottom of what happened."

"Any idea who he is or what happened to him?" Sarah cut in.

"Not at the moment. I'd hoped you could shed some light on that."

"I'm sorry I can't be more help."

Williams flashed her a condescending smile. "You mind telling me more about this feeling you had? It sounds a little strange, if you don't mind me saying."

"I'm sure this all sounds very odd to you, Sheriff, but like my husband said, I do at times have"—she glanced at Conrad as she searched for the right word—"these intuitions."

"So let me see if I got this right. You were minding your own business when, for no particular reason, you had this 'intuition' and took off across the pass in the middle of a winter storm."

"That's it. Nothing more than that," she said with conviction, her eyes challenging Williams's mocking stare.

"You don't say." He smirked, unable to contain himself.

"Sheriff Williams," Conrad said as he stepped forward, "I realize that it's a bit unusual, but there's no reason for you to treat my wife as if she's guilty of something. She's simply a Good Samaritan who helped an injured man. At some risk to herself, I might add. Nothing more."

The sheriff eyed Conrad without turning his head, then shifted his gaze back to Sarah. "Okay. Let's say that I buy this story of yours—"

"That's it; I've had enough. We're leaving," Conrad said as he ushered her toward the exit. Sarah smiled politely at the sheriff.

A doctor stepped into the waiting room, blocking their departure. He smiled at the Thompsons. "Mr. and Mrs. Thompson, I'm Dr. Lawrence."

"Dr. Lawrence." Conrad shook his hand.

"A pleasure to meet you," Sarah said.

Dr. Lawrence nodded at Sheriff Williams. "Hi there, Billy."

Williams sauntered toward them.

Dr. Lawrence had a calm demeanor, which, combined with his thick, curly white hair, bushy eyebrows, kind smile, and metal-rimmed glasses that rested on the tip of his wide nose, resulted in a placid and reassuring presence.

The doctor cleared his throat. "Mrs. Thompson, the man is very lucky you found him when you did. He received a severe beating, and his injuries could have been fatal."

"Is he going to be all right?" Sarah asked.

"We've patched him up as well as we can, and I believe his physical wounds will heal over time. There's quite a bit of internal bleeding in his brain though, and we're concerned about that. All we can do now is keep a close eye on him and wait. Is he a friend of yours?"

"No. I'd never seen him before."

"Did he say anything when you found him?" Dr. Lawrence asked.

"My name."

"How did he know your name?" interrupted Williams.

"I suppose I told him."

"You suppose?" Williams's mordant tone wasn't lost on Dr. Lawrence who placed a friendly hand on the sheriff's shoulder.

"Now, Billy, you're better than that. Thanks to Mrs. Thompson this man is alive. It's rather miraculous, if you ask me."

"Once you hear the rest, Doc, you'll admit this is all pretty weird. First she gets this 'feeling,' then she drives north from around Winthrop to find a guy who's been beaten all to hell and back, and now she can't tell us a thing about him? And we're supposed to buy this—tale?" Williams's eyes came to rest on Sarah, and he made no attempt to hide his sneer.

Conrad stepped in. "What exactly are you implying, Sheriff?"

Williams's eyes stayed locked on Sarah. "Like I said, just doing my job, sir."

"Please, Billy," Dr. Lawrence cut in, "there's no need for this. We should be very thankful that, for whatever reason, this woman found him when she did. Now, look at her: no injuries whatsoever—no bruising, even, nothing on her but blood from the injured man. The 'clear evidence,' as your daddy would've said, tells you that she didn't do any harm to this man. She simply rescued him."

Williams flinched at the mention of his father and frowned like a scolded child. "No need to bring my daddy into it, Doc. This whole story doesn't sound right to me. That's all."

"Thank you, Doctor," Conrad said.

"Well," said Dr. Lawrence, "it's not often we get this type of case in these parts, so it makes us all a bit jumpy."

"What could've happened to him? Who would beat him like that?" Sarah asked.

"That's for Billy to figure out," Dr. Lawrence turned to Williams. "Did you find anything of his at the scene?"

"Nothing. He was all alone, no vehicle, no ID, no money, no rings, no watch—nothing. We found a keychain a few feet from him. That's all. Not even sure if the keys are his. We're processing them now, and we'll find out soon enough." He glared at Sarah, but when she didn't react, he turned to Dr. Lawrence. "Can I talk to him?"

The doctor shook his head. "He's sedated now. You can talk to him tomorrow if he's alert. But you can't push him; he's in very bad shape."

"Was he able to tell you his name?" Sarah asked.

"No, he couldn't, which isn't surprising given his condition." After a pause, Dr. Lawrence added, "He might be suffering from amnesia."

C H A P T E R   2

Without warning, as if a movie were playing inside her mind, Sarah saw the words *Secrets of Innocence* come into focus over a stunning landscape of mountains and forest on a bright summer day.

The words slowly faded, leaving behind the vista of the forest with a smattering of white clouds against a clear blue sky.

The image shifted to a 1976 Illinois license plate attached to a mud-spattered Jeep as it raced along a dirt road through the woods, bouncing over rocks, exposed roots, and broken branches, leaving a cloud of dust in its wake.

The vehicle burst from the woods and careened onto a paved two-lane road with no regard for oncoming traffic, leaving cars swerving in its wake.

The Jeep sped toward a picturesque town nestled in the pines. A sign by the road read, *Welcome to AMARAY, Population 2,345*. Beyond it, a distant lake reflected a perfect blue sky.

Slowing as it approached the town, the Jeep cruised down the two-lane road as Sunday worshipers emerged from a quaint little church. Some approached the minister, while the rest milled about in groups, made their way to cars, or strolled away with their children.

The Jeep rolled by them and turned onto the town's main street.

"Sarah!" Conrad called.

Puzzled, Sarah stared at her husband. "What?"

"Are you all right?"

Sarah glanced around. They sat at their kitchen table finishing breakfast. "I…I was watching a movie…in my head."

"A movie?"

"I must've disconnected completely." She looked perplexed. "Were you talking to me?"

"Yes, I was," he said. "All of a sudden your eyes glazed over, and you were gone."

"Really? For how long?"

"Not long, a few seconds, maybe. But you definitely went somewhere else."

She nodded. "I sure did. Into a movie."

"Like in a theater?"

"No. It simply played before me. It felt as if I were the camera, and the story played before my eyes only for me. I could watch the images on the screen and also hear—no…no…not hear, *sense* the words on each page of the screenplay as they described what I visualized. Words and images in tandem, showing the film on the screen of my mind."

"No kidding, words and images at the same time. What's it about?"

"It takes place in the summer, or close to summer. The year appears to be 1976."

"1976? Where? Here?"

"No. It didn't look like our Cascades, although it showed a stunning landscape of dense woods and a huge lake.

"How about back where you grew up near Boston?"

She shook her head. "No. It's set in a small town called Amaray. I suspect it's a made-up place somewhere in an idealized Midwest."

"That's lots of specifics, considering you tuned out for such a short time. That's a new one for you."

"New one?"

"Playing a movie in your head. It was photos last time."

"You think someone is communicating with me like Angela did?"

Conrad shrugged. "What else could it be?"

"Perhaps it's my imagination."

"It's possible." He rose and carried his plate to the kitchen sink.

"Don't bother washing the dishes. I'll do it," Sarah said distractedly. "You don't believe it's my imagination do you?"

Conrad turned toward Sarah. "No. You disconnected. Completely. I've seen that look before. Something, or someone, pulled you away." He nodded toward Sarah's empty plate and she handed it to him.

Sarah cleared the table and joined him at the sink. "You've never told me I glazed over."

"I figured you were aware of it," he said, as he rinsed a coffee cup.

"Conrad, for crying out loud, how could I be, if I'm elsewhere?"

He nodded as he dried his hands. "You've got a point there. Anyway, you used to get that same look when you stared at the old photos from the attic, as if you'd gone somewhere else."

"Wow." Sarah crinkled her brow.

Conrad smiled and embraced his wife. "Nothing to worry about. You simply need to figure out the meaning of it." He gazed into her eyes. "It is rather curious, though. First, there's this guy you found, and now, out of nowhere there's this movie. I'd say you've stumbled upon a new puzzle to piece together."

Sarah took the towel from him and reached behind him to dry one of the dishes. "How can you be so cavalier about this?"

"*Cavalier?* Wow, fancy word, Madam Teacher." He chuckled, but the look of concern on Sarah's face demanded serious attention. "Listen, don't let yourself get all worked up over this. The fact is you're a psychic. Like it or not, that's who you are. You have a remarkable gift, and now it would appear someone is in need of your help. Simple as that."

Sarah dropped the towel, then plopped onto a nearby chair and sighed. "You're certainly more comfortable than I am with this blasted *gift* of mine."

Conrad drew close and caressed her hair. "C'mon, Sarah, there's no question it's a gift."

She smiled at her husband. For a tall, rugged man, her husband's touch was always gentle. "Anyway, what were you saying when I glazed over?"

"I'd asked if you were going to the hospital to visit him. Your reaction suggests that he and the movie may have something in common. In any case, you're going to try to lend a hand."

"How can you be so sure?"

"Oh, call it an educated guess. That's who you are. You did run out in the middle of a storm to save him, didn't you?"

She nodded.

"There you have it." He looked sternly into her eyes. "All I ask is that you be careful. This man's alive, so it's not like my grandmother's ghosts. So use caution until you learn a lot more about whatever or whoever is playing this movie in your head."

Sarah heaved a deep sigh and shook her head. "It's confusing."

"That's exactly my point. C'mon, walk me to the door." Conrad made his way out of the kitchen and down the hall.

She followed.

He snatched his sheepskin coat from the wooden rack by the door. "You'll figure it out in time." He lifted her face to his and smiled. "Whatever you do, don't rush into anything."

"How you can be so at ease with this?" Sarah helped him on with his coat.

"I grew up aware that Grandma had a sixth sense, and whenever she got that same glazed look, we all knew she'd be doing something for someone."

"You never told me that's what she did." She handed him his hat.

He leaned in to kiss her. "It's not something I find strange or unusual." He lifted her chin toward him. "The only difference is that she'd managed it all her life. You, on the other hand, are just getting reacquainted with it. So don't do anything rash, like driving over the mountains in the middle of the night."

"I promise."

"I take it you'll be going to the hospital," he said as he stepped onto the porch.

Sarah grabbed her coat and followed him. "Yes, earlier rather than later."

"I'd prefer you stay home. The man isn't going anywhere. He'll be in the hospital for a while."

"I have to go…I *need* to go," she said, pulling on her coat.

"I figured as much," he said, shaking his head. "Make sure you call me when you get there, and again when you're on your way home. Those icy roads are treacherous and I need to know you're safe."

"I will. You expect a busy day at the store?" she asked, caressing his hair.

"No, it's too cold, and folks—prudent folks, that is—don't like driving in this much snow and ice." He smiled and kissed her. "If you keep doing that, I won't be able to leave."

She laughed. "It's the salt and pepper around your temples. You look so debonair."

"There you go again with the fancy words, Madam Teacher, but flattery won't work." He kissed her again. "I'd go with you, but Tom has arranged a phone conference with six of our suppliers." He looked into her eyes. "You could stay home and wait for me."

"The Cascades in winter are spectacular and—"

"Dangerous. Plus you'll be going over the pass and down to Okanogan and—"

"It's been plowed by now. I'll be okay. Anyway—"

"I get it, I get it; you *have* to go." Conrad said as he made his way down the porch steps.

"I'll be careful. Please don't worry. I'll call you."

"You'd better." Conrad climbed into his truck and, with a wave, drove off through the crunching snow. Sarah remained on the porch as her unhappy husband crossed the small valley that encircled their home.

Back inside, she slid into her boots, grabbed her hat, gloves, and purse, locked the front door, and made her way through the snow to her car. She turned on the ignition and allowed the car to idle a few moments before turning the heater on.

"He's right, Sarah," she whispered, rubbing her gloved hands to keep them warm, "you shouldn't be driving across the mountain pass in this weather. Why this irrational urge to help a total stranger?"

Moments later the movie resumed playing in her mind.

Amaray appeared as an all-American town right out of a postcard with its well-maintained pastel storefronts and a dash of red brick here and there.

Symmetrically pruned trees adorned the streets along with perfectly man-icured flower blossoms in matching planters. Not a single piece of trash could be seen.

The Jeep came to a halt across the street from the country store. A cloud of cigarette smoke poured out through the passenger window.

The store, a renovated barn painted white with red-and-green trim, occupied an entire block. Barrels filled with fruit, vegetables, and knickknacks crowded the entrance.

Through the cigarette haze, the driver studied a handsome, freckle-faced fifteen-year-old boy with brown hair covered in natural blond streaks. Dressed in his Sunday best, he rode his bike in deliberate circles, keeping a watchful eye on the entrance to the country store, completely unaware that across the street the Jeep driver's eyes followed him intently.

The stranger, an intense, alluring man in his late thirties, with penetrating charcoal eyes and thick, uncombed black hair, was attractive yet repellant in equal measure.

The driver's eyes shifted as he spotted a beauty of fifteen emerging from the store, a bag of groceries wrapped in her arms. She was a perky little thing with an exquisite blossoming body and long blond hair blowing in the breeze.

Having also spotted her, the boy sped to catch up. He jumped off his bike and fell easily into step alongside the girl, the bike at his side.

"Hi," he said, blushing.

She turned her sky-blue eyes on him. "Hi."

He nodded toward the grocery bag. "Need any help?"

"No, thanks. I can manage."

Through the filthy windshield, the stranger observed their interaction, then started the car, and followed slowly, at a safe distance.

"How do you like it?" the boy asked.

"What?" She looked at him. His deep-green eyes were kind and intelligent.

"Amaray. It's been five months and three days since you moved in."

She chuckled at his precision. "Oh, it's okay, I guess."

"Good."

They continued to walk in awkward silence.

The man realized with amusement that the girl captivated the boy to such a degree that he had trouble speaking to her.

The boy turned to say something, but noticed the girl's small round breasts as they gently rubbed against the grocery bag. His eyes widened; then he blushed and quickly averted his gaze.

The man followed the young couple onto a small street lined with white picket fences and houses set flawlessly among impeccable landscaped lawns, trees, and flower beds.

"Got any plans for the summer?" the boy asked at last.

"Plans?"

"Yeah, like going away somewhere or doing something."

"Oh… No. Why would I leave when I just moved here?"

"I figured you might go to your grandparents or cousins or something like that for summer break."

"Oh, right. No… Maybe."

They strolled in silence, unaware of being followed.

"I was wondering…uh…we're all going to catch a movie after the swim meet on Friday, and I was wondering if you'd like to…well…come along."

She turned to him with a quizzical look. "Friday? Let's see…I have—"

"Hey, if you're busy—"

"Well, I—"

"Yeah, I figured you were. You're pretty popular at school. I get it. No big deal. I mean…you should be busy. It's Friday and…well…I get it."

The girl turned away, biting her lip to keep from laughing.

Minutes later, they reached her house. She swung open the small gate in the picket fence, sauntered through, and kicked it closed behind her.

"Bye," she said with an honest smile. When he didn't respond, she turned and climbed the porch steps.

"What? Oh, uh… Bye."

The boy sighed with frustration as she disappeared inside the house.

He jumped onto his bike, shaking his head, and raced past the Jeep, imitating himself. "No big deal…it's Friday…you're busy. What a dope!"

The stranger laughed out loud, unable to contain his amusement. Through the dirty windshield, he kept an eye on the boy as he sped away. Then the man scribbled something on a notepad as another cloud of smoke bounced off the windshield and flowed out the passenger window.

The image faded away.

"Oh, my God!" A dumbfounded Sarah sat in her car. She was parked in front of the hospital, the engine idling, her hands clamped to the steering wheel. "This isn't right. How in God's name did I get here? I can't disconnect like this."

She took a few deep breaths to calm herself, got out of the car, and made her way into the hospital.

After inquiring at the information desk, she went upstairs to the injured man's room.

"I'll be back tomorrow, and I can read the—" a woman was saying as she backed out of the room and bumped into Sarah. "Sorry, I should look where I'm going, especially walking backward. Hey," she said with a broad smile, "you must be Mrs. Thompson." She grabbed Sarah's hand and shook it vigorously.

"Yes, I am. Please call me Sarah."

"Very, very, nice to meet you. I'm Elisabeth Ralston, candy striper par excellence," she said in a flurry.

Sarah couldn't help but laugh.

Elisabeth appeared to be somewhat younger than Sarah, plump yet shapely, with vibrant azure eyes and a contagious smile. "It's incredible that you were able to find him and save his life. He's very lucky."

"How is he?" Sarah whispered.

Elisabeth smiled and nodded toward him. "Ask him yourself; he's awake."

Sarah tiptoed over to the man's bedside. He stared up at her. "Hi, I'm Sarah Thompson."

"He knows all about you," Elisabeth whispered from behind Sarah.

Sarah smiled. "Dr. Lawrence tells us you'll be all right."

The man tried to speak, but the swelling in his lips and face made it difficult to understand him.

"He said 'thank you.'" Elisabeth translated.

Sarah turned to her in disbelief. "You can understand him?"

"Go figure." Elisabeth smiled and took the man's hand in hers.

The man tried to smile, but it became a grimace.

"Don't smile," Elisabeth told him. "It pulls the stitches."

"Do you remember your name?" Sarah asked him.

He slowly shook his head.

"Here," Elisabeth gave her the man's hand.

Sarah took it in hers and felt him tighten his grip.

"That's his way of saying thank you," Elisabeth offered.

Sarah looked into the man's face and smiled. "You must be in terrible pain now."

The man shook his head and groaned.

"Meds." Elisabeth nodded toward the drip going into the man's arm. "Only hurts when he tries to laugh or move."

"Ah," Sarah smiled. "Well, soon you won't need the medication, and when the shock wears off, I'm sure it'll all come back to you."

The man sighed.

"Elisabeth's been reading to you?"

He nodded.

"I found this great old book about Daniel Boone," Elisabeth said. "I love to read, so imagine how great it is for me to be able to spend my days reading to patients. The best volunteer work in the world."

"I'm sure the patients appreciate it."

"Sarah," the man whispered.

"Yes, I'm here." She leaned closer to him.

"Sarah," he said again.

"Yes. Do you need something?"

"He likes saying your name. He's been repeating it over and over and over," Elisabeth clarified. "Maybe it's his way of giving thanks for being alive."

Sarah tightened her grip on his hand. The man sighed, closed his eyes, and drifted off.

"He's asleep," Elisabeth whispered. She helped Sarah slip her hand out of his, walked her out of the room, and closed the door behind them.

"He'll rest for a while now. It'll help him recover faster. How about a cup of coffee?"

Sarah nodded.

"C'mon, there's a coffee shop next to the lobby."

"You've learned quite a bit about our mystery man, yet he's been here less than a day."

"I have, haven't I? No idea why. I met him this morning when I did my thing."

"Your thing?"

"As part of my routine with new patients, I introduce myself and ask them what they'd like for me to read to them and all that. But when I stepped in, Billy was leaving, and the poor man was all agitated, groaning, and moaning—"

"Billy?" Sara asked.

They had reached the stairwell and were about to make their way down when Elisabeth stopped and turned to Sarah. "Billy Williams, he's the Sheriff." She continued down the stairs. "You met him yesterday, he said."

Sarah followed her. "I did."

"Anyway, I grabbed the patient's hands and started talking to him softly, like I used to do with my kids when they fell down or hurt themselves. He calmed down after a while, and we started talking. Or rather, I asked questions, and he nodded and moaned."

"Did he tell you what happened to him?"

"No, poor guy, nothing about himself or the incident. He kept repeating your name, so I told him the little I've been told about what happened to him, how you found him, and how they brought him here. As he calmed down, we connected. Somehow I could understand his grunts most of the time. When I didn't, well, I guessed. For whatever's worth, the things I guessed could be wrong," Elisabeth giggled as they entered the cafeteria.

Sarah poured herself a cup of coffee. "I'm glad he has you around. It must be quite frightening to find yourself in a hospital in such pain and not be able to remember anything at all. Not even who you are."

Elisabeth poured herself a cup of hot chocolate. "I've been thinking about that as well. I can't begin to imagine what that would be like." She shuddered and took a sip of her chocolate. "Ah…I love hot cocoa…always does the trick. Let's sit over there." She nodded toward a table by the window overlooking a small snowed-in garden. "This little garden is beautiful in late spring, summer, and early autumn. It's a great spot to read to my patients."

"I can well imagine. Have you heard if Sheriff Williams has figured out what happened?"

"No, he's looking into it. It's funny to hear you call him Sheriff Williams. Everyone around here calls him Billy. I'm sure he'd prefer Sheriff Williams, but that's what everyone called his daddy, and they can't bring themselves to call Billy that. His daddy was a wonderful man. Everyone loved him. He is really missed."

"What happened to him?"

"Killed in a freak hunting accident. They tell me Billy was really shaken up. After his daddy died he changed completely. He stopped being a happy-go-lucky kind of guy and became—well, a bit rough. There's lots of anger inside that man."

"He comes across as distrustful."

"You mean when he interrogated you?"

Sarah laughed. "I didn't see it as an interrogation."

"Sorry." Elisabeth giggled. "I read too many murder mysteries, and I've picked up the lingo. But you're right. Billy doesn't trust his own shadow. He spots evil around every corner. He's a good guy but somewhat lost."

"You have a clear picture of him."

"No, not really. Only what I hear and what I notice. Part of being a volunteer is to understand people and make them feel at ease. Well, as much as you can in a hospital."

"How did you come to volunteer here?"

She took a deep sigh, deciding where to begin. "I'm a widow, and my kids are all grown up and gone. One boy—well, he's a man now—single, living in Vancouver, though he travels all over the world for his company. My daughter is married, living in Montana with her husband. After Anthony—my husband—died, I had loads of time on my hands, and it was driving me crazy, so I volunteered at the Humane Society. I love animals, particularly dogs. I enjoy being around them. They have such varied personalities, and I got really good with them after my training. 'The dog sleuth,' they used to call me because I usually figured out what'd happened to them, and how to handle them, rehabilitate them, and even find them a good home. Then Walter talked me into coming here. I was reluctant at first, but now I love it."

"Walter?"

"Dr. Lawrence. He was a good friend of Anthony's."

"Your husband was a doctor?"

"Oh, no. Walter started as Anthony's doctor and over the years he became our friend. Anthony ran a resort near Winthrop. I live near there as well. That was one of the reasons I had a hard time deciding to volunteer this far north. It's a bit of a trek from home, particularly during winter. There are days I can't make it."

"I'm sure. I live near there as well, in the twin houses. You might've heard of them."

Elisabeth's eyes widened with disbelief. "Oh my God!" Realizing she'd yelled, she grimaced and lowered her voice. "You're *that* Sarah! Wow! I've heard of you!"

"Really? What have you heard?"

"About your Mademoiselle Tatin tart, for one thing. I should've put your name together. You're Conrad's new wife."

"I am."

"Hey," she said, as she leaned conspiratorially across the table, "I don't suppose you could teach me how to cook, could you?"

It was Sarah's turn to look surprised. "Teach you to cook? Me? I'm not—"

"C'mon. Rumor has it you'd never cooked before you moved here. But then you uncovered your family's recipe book and fixed some amazing dishes that impressed everyone, especially Conrad. Every time I go to his store, he can't stop raving about you and your cooking. Neither can Tom. You've bewitched both father and son."

"How come we haven't met?"

"I've been living in Montana for almost three years. My daughter Caroline insisted I move in with them after Anthony died. She worried about me all alone out here. She's very stubborn, like her dad used to be, and wouldn't stop pressing me. So I finally gave in and closed up my house and moved. Thank goodness, I refused to sell. In my heart I knew I'd be back. Washington state has been awfully good to me. I'm happy here. We had a marvelous time living in Seattle. My kids grew up there, and when Anthony got the job in Winthrop, I was in heaven—a dream come true."

"How's that?"

"Oh, I love it there. Every fall we would pack the kids into the car, leave Seattle behind, and immerse ourselves in the beauty of the North Cascades. The Cascades captivated me from the start. They have a stranglehold on me."

Sarah smiled. "Me too. I can't get enough of them. When I first came here—"

"Where from?"

"Pasadena, in California."

"Wow. All the way from down there to here? How come?"

Sarah shook her head, reluctant to tell her the real reason. "The pull of the Cascades, I suppose."

"I fell in love with their majestic beauty."

"That's a good way to describe them."

"It's exactly what I told Anthony during our first trip through the Cascades loop. Then I said, well, really I whispered, that he shouldn't be jealous. The best thing for him was to simply accept the fact that I'd fallen I love with them. They take your breath away, don't they? The clarity of the rivers and lakes, the emerald green of the trees, the blue skies spattered with pure white clouds."

"Exactly. And the colors are so vivid."

"Right. Every season has its unique color palette."

"Exactly. In the fall they lure you with gold, yellow, orange, and brown; then in the spring and summer, they shift to a deep green, and then they start all over again."

"Oh boy, oh boy! Sarah Thompson, you've been seduced by the Cascades."

"Without a doubt."

The two women laughed with the understanding of kindred spirits.

"That's why I knew I'd come back," Elisabeth said. "Montana was okay, but after a while I needed a Cascades fix, and quite frankly, my daughter and her husband needed their privacy. She didn't even put up a fight. She understood. I came home several months ago, and before I knew it Walter had talked me into volunteering. So here I am, and I love it."

"We have a spectacular view of the Cascades. You should come by our house."

"I'd love to. I've never been to either of the twin houses. I'm real curious about them, to be honest. Tom, Alyana, and their little ones live in the other house, right?"

"Yes. It's great to have them nearby, especially since the twins were born."

"Odd, those two houses, so unique, and so out of place for this part of the world. It's a mystery how they ever got built and why."

"It's not a mystery anymore."

Elisabeth reached across the table and grabbed Sarah's arm. "Really? I'm pretty sure no one had any idea, not even Conrad or his grandparents. What's the story?"

"Well, we've learned that they were built by one of Conrad's ancestors, Leonard Whitman, back in the 1820s. One house for him and his son, and the other for his twin sister, Louise and her daughters."

"Wow. That's why the houses are twins. Why did he choose the Queen Anne style of architecture? They're so unusual for that period and this area."

"Leonard was very wealthy and apparently liked that style. He sought to recreate a familiar environment for his sister and their children. They were the very best in these parts at the time, and they've been superbly restored. Though they aren't lavishly ornate like other Queen Anne–style homes I've visited, they are imposing, and visibly proud of their age."

Elisabeth burst out laughing. "What an odd thing to say. You talk as if the houses were alive."

Sarah smiled. "To me they are alive and part of my family."

"I believe you. Hey, gossip has it that your wedding was spectacular. Folks are still talking about how the house partied with all of you."

"She did."

Elisabeth laughed. "I'm sorry I missed it, particularly Conrad's song. They tell me he wrote your wedding song. And that he and Tom played their guitars in perfect harmony."

Sarah smiled, with tears in her eyes. "It was unforgettable. Best day of my life."

"How romantic. He must've gotten it from his grandmother."

"Did you meet Angela?"

"No, but she was well known for her guitar playing. Unfortunately, she'd already passed away when we moved here. She must've been a very special woman."

"That, she was."

"Well?" Elisabeth asked after a brief pause.

"Well, what?"

"Will you teach me how to cook?"

"I doubt there's anything I need to teach you. You're quite self-reliant."

Elisabeth grimaced. "Oh no, not in the kitchen. To be honest with you, I've never liked cooking. I fixed meals for Anthony and the kids, but I didn't like it at all. I adore food, as you can tell from the way I look, but I don't like to prepare it."

"You look fine." Sarah chuckled. "Attractively curvy."

"Thanks. Curvy...I sure like the sound of that. Much better than chubby, which is how I would describe me." She leaned toward Sarah in mock secrecy. "I love to eat."

"Why learn how to cook now?"

"Time to do it for fun, not because I have to. What do you say? Will you teach me?"

"Sure. Tell me when you'd like to come over and what you'd like to fix, and we'll do it."

"Great." She leaned across the table with a smile and said, "I'm sure we're going to be real good friends, Sarah Thompson."

Sarah nodded and smiled. "So am I, Elisabeth Ralston."

C H A P T E R 3

THE SCENE SHOWED a small, tidy kitchen typical of the 1970s, where the fifteen-year-old boy and his mother prepared dinner with the habitual comfort acquired over many years. The boy stood at the counter peeling vegetables while his mother, Shirley, an attractive middle-aged woman with ash-blond hair and gentle blue eyes, mashed potatoes and kept an eye on her fried chicken.

"Stephanie's almost ready to deliver her baby, so I'll be leaving in the morning. I've already made several meals so there's plenty of food for you and your dad in the freezer."

"How long will you be gone?"

"That depends on how the delivery goes. Hopefully, it'll be like when you were born—easy and quick. Right?"

The boy chuckled. "Sure, Mom. Whatever you say."

"Well, it was, and you've been a very easy child." Shirley reached around her son to pick up a pair of kitchen tongs, kissed him on the cheek, and returned to her chicken.

The boy tolerated the kiss with a smile.

The front door opened and then closed.

"There's your dad."

Moments later Hugo Michaels sauntered into the kitchen, a newspaper tucked under his arm, a frown etched on his face, in his mid-forties, tall, thin, and stern, with a receding hairline that he tried to conceal with limited success. He kissed his wife on the forehead and patted his son on the head. "What are you two gossiping about?"

Shirley shot him a disapproving glance. "We don't gossip."

23

"Stephanie's baby. Mom's leaving tomorrow," the boy answered as he dumped the chopped vegetables into a pot of boiling water.

"Is it time already?" Hugo asked with indifference.

"Any minute now," Shirley said.

In a choreography born of routine, Hugo removed his coat, folded it neatly, and draped it over the back of a chair by the door. He unclasped his minister's collar, placed it carefully over his coat, and undid the top button of his shirt. He then settled into a seat at the kitchen table and perused the newspaper.

"Hmm. Fertile one, your sister. That makes it six now, doesn't it?"

Shirley took the jibe in stride and forced herself to smile back. "It does. I liked your sermon today, by the way."

"Thanks."

"That bit about how those who are in the flesh cannot please God made the point," the boy said. "What was that from, Romans something or other?"

"Romans: eight and eight."

"It worked well with your message about our virtues becoming our children's virtues," Shirley added, patting oil off the fried chicken.

"What I really intended to impart," Hugo said with a self-righteous air as he peered over the newspaper, "was that *our* vices could become our *children's* vices. Things that cause people to sin are bound to happen, but woe unto that person through whom they come. God commands us to guide our children to Him, and lead them to the path of righteousness. We fail to do so at our peril."

"Well, the congregation certainly got the message, darling." His wife placed the platter of chicken on the table, kissed his cheek, and returned to the stove to put the final touches on the mashed potatoes.

They boy strained the vegetables over the sink, then placed them in a serving dish and added butter, salt, and pepper. As he tossed them together, he shot a mischievous glance toward his parents and bit his lip to avoid smiling. "I got some good news."

His mother stopped on the spot, but his father kept reading his newspaper.

"Well?" she said. "Speak up."

"I won the swim meet. Well, the elimination rounds, anyway. I'm in the finals, Friday."

Shirley dropped the spoon on the counter and ran to smother her son with hugs and kisses. The boy grimaced in mock resistance.

"Oh darling. I knew it. Dad, aren't you proud? He's done it again! What a way to end the school year. Our son will be the next Jim Montgomery."

"Don't exaggerate, Shirley."

"I'm not. I predict that Montgomery will win gold at this year's Olympics, and our son will be competing there four years from now."

"C'mon, Mom."

"Sweetheart, why didn't you tell me earlier?"

"Wanted to tell you both at the same time. How about it, Dad?"

The minister set down the newspaper, rose to join his son by the stove, and lovingly mussed his hair. "I'm proud of you, son. Real proud."

"I could've baked you a cake," his mother complained.

"When you get back, we'll bake one together. After I win the final."

"Boys don't bake cakes," his father said with contempt.

"This one does, he likes it." Shirley beamed with pride, then tossed her arms around the two men in her life and gathered them in an awkward group hug.

"Sarah…Sarah." Alyana reached over and gently touched Sarah's shoulder.

The two women sat in Sarah's living room while the twins frolicked in the playpen.

"Yes?" Sarah turned to her daughter-in-law with a blank expression.

"Did you find it?"

"Find what?"

"The recipe."

Sarah frowned down at the cookbook on her lap. "Oh dear."

"You left us? I didn't even notice. Another movie installment?"

"I'm afraid so. How long did I detach?"

"Not long. You kept flipping the pages, stopped, and then stared at one."

"I'm sorry. You must think I'm off my rocker," Sarah said with honest concern.

"Not at all, don't be silly." Alyana slid off the sofa to pick up a toy one of the toddlers had tossed out of the playpen. Back to her svelte silhouette after the birth of her twins, Tadan and Kaya, Alyana was a beautiful woman with a serenity that never faltered. Her silky black hair flowed about her shoulders with every move, as if happy to frame the seductive face and sea-green eyes. She mussed her eldest son's hair, and stroked her daughter's ponytail before sitting back on the sofa.

Sarah looked concerned.

"C'mon, tell me," Alyana said, putting an arm around her. "What was going through your mind right before the movie started playing?"

"Is that important?"

"I'm trying to find a connection."

"Okay. As soon as I opened my mother's old recipe book, I witnessed a scene in the kitchen of the young boy's family. He was helping his mom make dinner."

"Then the link could be food."

"Maybe, but why? These scenes pop up out of nowhere. It happens so fast, I'm not even aware of what's going on until it's over. I'm concerned that I may cause an accident when I drift off while driving. Aren't you worried that I might detach when I'm alone with your babies?"

Alyana chuckled. "No, not even a little. I'm sure that could never happen. Your grandmotherly instincts are way too strong to allow you to disconnect that much."

"I'm glad you believe that; nevertheless, it worries me."

"That's no surprise." Alyana laughed merrily as she patted Sarah's hand. "If you didn't worry, you wouldn't be the Sarah we all love."

"Am I really such a worrywart?"

"Not at all—that's not what I meant. You're a sensitive person, perhaps too sensitive given what your abilities force you to deal with. But it's natural to worry when you're faced with such unusual visions. I can't even imagine how disorienting it must be to have a movie playing in your head. But thanks to what you experienced with Angela, you learned that your conscious self is always in charge."

"Until Conrad mentioned it, I didn't realize that I glazed over and went elsewhere when I looked at the photos."

"You must've assumed you drifted off. Didn't you?"

"It didn't occur to me. I felt present with the stories, almost like I was there."

"So it's no different from being present while the movie plays in your head. Or is it?"

"The biggest difference is that in some of the old stories, I actually interacted with the ancestors. Even had conversations of sorts. In this movie I'm a bystander. A simple spectator."

"Well, maybe you'll play a part in the movie later on. Wow, wouldn't that be something? My kids' grandmother, a movie star."

"Only in my mind."

Both women laughed. The children glanced up and giggled, happy to participate in their joy.

"I may be wrong, but I have the impression that every time you drift off you're doing something that reminds you of the injured man," Alyana offered. "In this case you were looking for a recipe to make with Elisabeth, and you probably connected her with him."

Sarah sighed. "That's what Conrad thinks."

"And how about you?"

"I'm uneasy about this whole thing. Can't get used to this idea of a movie I have no control over. If this is how I'm expected to sense something about our mystery man, then who's communicating with me? Why a movie? Who is the boy? Could this be his family?"

"Hmm…maybe. The interesting bit is that it happens in the mid-1970s. Are any of the characters familiar to you?"

"No, not at all."

"How about the year, anything special about that year?"

Sarah shook her head. "Other than the bicentennial celebrations, nothing."

"What about their behaviors?" Alyana pressed on. "Anything someone's done that strikes you as odd or different? Anything that stands out?"

"Well, the man spying on the young couple is definitely odd. The rest are pretty ordinary. Almost too ordinary, in fact."

Alyana leaned forward and tapped Sarah's knee. "Maybe you should tell Elisabeth about this. She reads lots of mysteries, and this sure sounds like one—maybe she can help you piece it together. You've become good friends over the last few weeks."

Sarah rolled her head from side to side as she considered Alyana's suggestion. "We have, but I'm not comfortable enough with these visions to talk about them with someone other than you, Tom, and Conrad. For now, that's all I need."

"What do you need, Mama?" Elan asked as he snuggled next to Sarah.

"I've been watching a movie and was telling Mommy all about it," Sarah answered with a smile as she caressed her grandson's cheek.

"Tell it to me."

"It's a grown-up movie," his mother told him.

"Okay," he said. "Then can I go outside?"

"Cover up real good. Hat, mittens, boots," Alyana admonished.

"Yeah, yeah, Mommy, I will," he yelled as he ran, running toward the front door.

In no time Nina was at her mother's side. "Can I go, too?"

"No, you're getting over your cold. You can go out in a few days maybe. You don't want to start coughing again, do you?"

Nina shook her head and pouted.

"You have plenty of toys to play with here," Alyana said.

"Could we watch a movie?" she asked her grandmother.

"Sure. C'mon, let's go to your room and put a movie on. Which one is your favorite today?" They headed toward the foyer hand in hand.

"The mermaid one!"

When they were halfway up the stairs, the doorbell rang.

"I'll get it," Alyana yelled from the living room.

Sarah and Nina continued up the stairs while Alyana went to the foyer and opened the front door.

Sheriff Williams removed his hat and offered a nod of greeting. "Ma'am. Is this Mrs. Thompson's residence?"

"Yes, Sheriff. I'm Alyana Thompson, her daughter-in-law. Please come in."

As Williams walked past Alyana, Elan rushed up the porch steps to her. "Mommy, a sheriff's here!"

"He's visiting Mama, nothing to worry about."

"I'm coming in, too," Elan announced as he squeezed past.

She grabbed him by the arm. "Boots off, young man."

Elan dropped to the floor and yanked off his boots.

Alyana closed the door behind them. "May I take your hat and coat, Sheriff?"

"Thanks, ma'am." He handed them to her.

"Elan, please go up to the kids' room and tell Mama Sheriff Williams is here." She turned away to hang the sheriff's things on the rack by the door.

The boy dashed up two steps at a time, screaming, "Mama! Mama! A sheriff is here! He's got a gun!"

Sarah rushed out of one of the upstairs rooms toward her grandson, closely followed by Nina, looking ready to erupt into tears. In the living room the twins burst out crying.

"Elan, stop screaming. You're scaring the twins," Alyana yelled from the foyer. "Sarah, nothing to worry about, he's here to talk to you."

Sarah descended the stairs holding Elan and Nina's hands while Alyana hurried into the living room to calm the twins and stop their piercing cries.

"Sorry, I didn't mean to scare the kids," an embarrassed Williams said to Sarah when she reached the foyer.

"You didn't scare me," Elan clarified.

Williams smiled and nodded. "I can see that."

"Elan, darling," Sarah said. "You're the one that scared us all yelling about a gun."

"I'm sorry," he said shyly.

"It's a big gun," Nina said, letting go of Sarah's hand and coming closer to the Sheriff.

"It sure is," he replied, and to Sarah's surprise, he rewarded Nina with a warm smile. "But it's safely strapped in. See that?" He pointed to the holster's safety strap. "Nothing to worry about."

Both children approached him and stared at the gun.

Alyana returned to the foyer holding the whimpering twins. Sarah took Tadan and cuddled him in her arms, allowing Alyana to do the same with little Kaya. In moments, they'd both quieted down.

"Sheriff Williams," Sarah said, "you've met Alyana, and these are my grandkids. This is Elan and Nina, and the twins are Tadan and Kaya."

"Interesting names," Williams grinned.

"My name means full of grace." Nina announced.

"And yours?" Williams asked of Elan.

"Friendly one. Tadan means plentiful, and Kaya means composed. He eats a lot and she smiles all the time."

"You don't say," Williams chuckled.

"My daughter-in-law has kept the traditions of her Native American ancestors and—"

"Mommy's name means 'flowering,'" Nina interrupted.

"You always get it wrong," Elan told his sister. "It's 'forever flowering,' not 'flowering.'"

Ignoring her brother, Nina grabbed Sarah's hand and continued, "Mama's name means princess. What does yours mean?" she asked Williams who was clearly taken aback.

"Uh…I don't know."

The little girl shrugged and grimaced. "Mommy, tell him about his name."

"Maybe later, Nina. Sheriff Williams is here to talk to Mama."

"I like your uniform," Elan said.

"I like the shiny dots and the big gold spot," Nina added.

In another unexpected gesture, Sheriff Williams knelt to one knee to be eye level with the children. "Those are my buttons, and this is my badge."

"Can I touch it?" Nina whispered.

Sheriff Williams smiled and nodded.

Nina reached over and touched the badge with the tips of her fingers. "Wow."

"I'm going to be a sheriff when I grow up," Elan announced.

"Me, too," his sister chimed in.

"Will you teach us?" Elan asked him.

"Sure thing." Sheriff Williams rose and nodded, smiling as he mussed Elan's hair.

"Please come in, Sheriff," Sarah said as she nodded toward the living room.

"That's okay, Mrs. Thompson. You're busy with your family. I can come back another time."

"I'm going to the hospital tomorrow morning. We can meet there. At least you won't have to drive all the way back here."

"Sure thing. How about ten?"

"Ten is fine."

Williams nodded and grabbed his coat and hat.

"Until tomorrow, then." Sarah said.

"Bye," he said.

"Bye-bye," both children said in tandem.

To which Sarah added, "Have a good evening, Sheriff."

CHAPTER 4

SARAH AND CONRAD lay wrapped in each other's arms, their bedroom illuminated only by what moonlight seeped through the curtains.

"That's what I call perfect sex," Conrad whispered as he pulled the comforter up to cover his wife.

"I love your scent," Sarah said as she rested her head on his shoulder.

"And I love your response. It drives me crazy."

Their lovemaking had shifted to a higher plane, one that provided them with not only complete physical satisfaction but also the emotional reaffirmation of their bond.

"Will it ever change?" she asked.

"Not if we don't let it."

"Good. Then it never will."

They sighed and held each other in silence.

"That must have been quite a scene with Elan screaming and the twins crying," he said.

"Williams's face was priceless."

"I can't picture a smiling Williams."

"A softer Williams," Sarah added.

"Anything new on the movie front?"

"Nothing since the last installment when Alyana was here. What should I do?"

"Let the whole movie play out."

"You mean do nothing until it's finished?"

"Yeah."

"What happened? You started off pretty comfortable with this whole scenario. Now you're worried?"

"No, I'm okay. But it's one thing to understand what's happening, which we don't, and quite another to do something about it, which we can't. You should avoid doing something you'll regret later. That's why you should let it play out."

"Conrad, I'm only getting bits and pieces of this damned movie." Sarah broke their embrace and rolled over on her side of the bed away from him. "It's not like I can go into a trance and force the reels to play so I can get to the end."

"No need to get upset." Conrad turned toward her and placed his arm around her waist.

She held his hand and sighed. "It's so frustrating. I know I'm supposed to help this man, but after more than a month, I'm no closer to an answer than when I started. What if his family is searching for him? They must be terrified. We can't wait only because it's inconvenient for us."

"Okay, what about the possibility that he might not have any family?"

"So who's this family in the movie? Who is the boy?"

"He may be completely unrelated to the injured man."

"Okay, let's say that's so. We still have to help. What if his wife is searching for him? I can't imagine what I would do if you were lost somewhere."

"No, no, no. Don't go there. You'll make yourself crazy. You have enough on your plate dealing with these visions."

"He needs my help, and he deserves for me to be the best that I can be."

"Exactly. And for you to be that, you need to learn more. A lot more. Give yourself time."

"You're afraid I'm going to make a mistake."

Conrad was silent for a moment. "Maybe. Yes."

"So am I."

He snuggled closer to her. "Let's not talk about it anymore, okay? C'mon, try to relax. Close your eyes and try to sleep. Happy dreams, darling."

She heaved a deep sigh. "Let's hope so."

But no sooner had Sarah closed her eyes than the film reeled up again.

Under the perennial blue sky and radiant sun, the young boy and a friend pedaled their bikes along the two-lane road through Amaray. The friend—a freckled, pimply fifteen-year-old—sported a mischievous smile as the two headed out of town toward the lake.

"You know what your problem is?" the friend asked.

The boy rolled his eyes. "Here we go again. What's my problem, pray tell?"

"That! That's your problem right there. What the hell does 'pray tell' mean, anyway?"

"Cut it out, Robert."

"You read too much. You should get laid. That's what you need."

"Oh, come on! Not that again."

"You're dropping behind, man. You need to get with it."

"Not interested."

"Yeah, yeah…I get it. You're a 'romantic' or whatever stupid thing you call yourself from that silly book about rainbows you're always reading. You need to wake up. Get real. All you need to do is go on over to Tent City and get your cherry busted. Trust me, it'll make a man of you. Then you'll be at my level."

The boy chuckled and shook his head. "Why would I want to be at your level?"

"Because, man, if you haven't done it, we can't talk about it, and I need to talk. What kind of friend are you anyway?"

"Robert, I've told you time and time again. When I do it, it has to mean something. It's got to be forever, like my folks."

Robert cut his bike in front of his friend, forcing him to stop. "Man, listen to yourself. That's ancient history. Things are different now. The world has changed, and we gotta change with it. Don't you get it?"

The boy scooted past Robert and pedaled away. "Yeah, I get it."

Robert raced to catch up. "So get it over with."

"Not that way. It has to be for love."

"*Love*…who the hell even gets what that is? It's hard to love girls. You can't figure them out. Trust me, sex is a lot easier than love."

"I could love Ellie."

"You mean that girl who moved down the street from you?"

"Yeah."

Robert guffawed with fake laughter. "Are you kooky? She's sixteen. That means she's older, and older girls don't go for younger guys."

"A year's difference won't bother her."

"You're dreaming. Anyway she's super popular, and you're…not."

"So?"

"You're a nerd."

"No, I'm not."

"She'll never do it with you."

"Is that all you think about? Doing it?"

"Yes, know why? 'Cause I'm an okay dude. Dudes do it, nerds don't. And younger nerds like you, never."

"The only reason you even get what being a 'dude' means is because I told you all about that word. Otherwise you wouldn't have a clue. And you're neither a dude nor a dandy, and I'm not a nerd. Anyway, she doesn't have to find out how old I am."

"Dandy. I like that one. Is that the same as a dude or better?"

"Look it up, genius."

"Hey, man, don't take it out on me. It's a nature thing. Girls can tell when you're younger. They have a way of guessing. Anyway, girls like experienced guys, so go to Tent City and get yourself some."

"She and I could learn together."

Robert laughed as he pushed off and surged ahead.

A second later the boy caught up to him. "You can't beat me, dude."

"Oh yeah? You're in orbit. Try to catch me, nerd."

The boy sped up to keep pace. "I can pedal faster. Don't tempt me."

Frustrated, Robert slowed down. "Okay, wet rag, I wasn't even trying, anyway. But I'm serious; go down to Tent City and pay for it, like I did. You'll be a man, and then, maybe, you'll have a chance at sweet Ellie."

The boy surged ahead of Robert. "Forget it. Buzz off."

The two turned onto a dirt path and disappeared through the woods in a cloud of dust and laughter.

Minutes later they emerged from the trees and came to halt on the lake's public beach. They dropped their bikes side by side, threw off their shirts, kicked off their shoes, and raced toward the water.

Like everything else in Amaray, the beach was pristine—a ribbon of sand that stretched halfway around the lake, framed by the lush forest and an occasional outcropping of granite. Sunbathers of every age and description crowded the area, enjoying the warm weather and the lake's gentle waves. People were swimming, strolling on the beach, paddling canoes or rowing small boats. Children built sand castles, threw balls, or frolicked with their dogs. All in all, it was the epitome of a happy summer place.

As the boy was about to reach the water, he caught a glimpse of Ellie sitting on a beach towel reading a book. He stopped cold, leaving Robert to continue solo toward the water unaware that his friend was no longer with him.

After a brief hesitation, he took a deep breath and headed over to Ellie.

"Hi," he muttered, clearing a frog from his throat.

Ellie glanced up, squinting into the glaring sun and smiled. "Hi."

Despite his best efforts, the boy's eyes were drawn to her breasts. She wore a two-piece pink-and-white polka-dot swimsuit with a revealing décolleté. She had removed the straps from her shoulders to suntan them evenly, which, in the boy's eyes, made her even more alluring.

"Well?" she asked.

Worried that she might guess what he was eyeing and take offense, the boy looked down in search of something to say as he smoothed the sand with one foot. "What are you reading?"

"A book."

"What's it called?"

"Um…Evergreen."

"That's a strange title. I've never heard of it. Evergreen what?"

"It's translated from the French. The title is longer than what I said."

"Oh. What's it about?"

"A girl in love with an older man."

This apparent confirmation of his friend's theory stunned him into silence.

To escape the awkward pause, Ellie opened her book and pretended to read—her hands cleverly concealing the title of the book.

The boy, however, wasn't interested in the title. Instead, he studied her out of the corner of his eye, admiring her body and desperately hoping for inspiration as to what to say next. Finally he ventured a question. "Do you like to read that stuff?"

"Yeah. It's a great book. You should read it."

He nodded. "Okay. Would a guy like it?"

She mulled it over. "Um…not sure of that. Maybe not."

He nodded again. "It figures."

Back to silence, brushing the sand with his foot, searching for what to say next, then, a smile. "Are you going to the picnic Saturday night?" he mumbled.

"What?"

The boy cleared his throat. "I wondered if you'd be at the picnic Saturday night."

She considered his question for a moment before saying, "Maybe."

He nodded and she returned to her book.

Frustrated, the boy eyed her in silence for a moment.

"Okay, then," he said at last, "I guess I'll see you later."

The girl looked up. "See you."

Visibly disappointed, the boy turned away and strode off toward the water, grumbling to himself.

Ellie let her eyes follow him until he vanished in the sea of beachgoers and smiled.

"Have you come across a book called 'Evergreen'?" Sarah asked Elisabeth.

They were pacing up and down the hospital hallway while the nurses ran through their early morning routine in the injured man's room.

Elisabeth shook her head. "It doesn't sound familiar."

"It was written in French and translated into English."

"I can look it up if you like."

"I already checked the web and didn't get any hits in either English or French. Maybe I got the title wrong."

"Who told you about it?"

Sarah hesitated a moment. "Oh, uh… a friend mentioned it some time back. It might be a good book for you to read to our mystery guy."

"What's it about?"

"A girl in love with an older man, I believe."

"Hmm…maybe your friend made up the title." She leaned toward Sarah as if sharing a childish secret. "When I was in my teens, I loved to read Colette. Those books were considered very risqué back when they were written, but even in the '70s, they raised some eyebrows. So when anyone asked me what I was reading, I'd come up with something more tame."

Sarah chuckled. "That's amazing. I read Colette as well. I haven't met anyone that knew about Colette in years."

"Did you make up titles, too?"

"No, I didn't, but some of my girlfriends would do that when their parents asked what they were reading. They even covered the book jacket with newsprint or sleeves from other books."

"How come you didn't have to?"

"My parents didn't mind. They actually encouraged it."

"Wow. They must have been very modern."

Sarah shrugged. "Literary types."

"No wonder. But why would our guy like to listen to a story about a young girl in love with an older man?"

"A little spice never hurt anyone," Sarah winked.

"Why, Sarah!" Elisabeth elbowed her friend and giggled.

Their light demeanor turned sour as Sheriff Williams came down the hall toward them.

"I'll stay with you if you like," Elisabeth offered.

"Yes, thanks."

As the Sheriff approached them, he took off his hat and nodded. "Elisabeth. Mrs. Thompson."

They both nodded back and smiled politely.

"You have a nice family, Mrs. Thompson."

"Thank you. My grandkids were very taken with you."

A slight pink hue spread across Williams's face. He cleared his throat. "Okay to talk now?" he asked Sarah.

"Sure. What can I do for you?"

Williams eyed Elisabeth who looked right back at him, smiled, and didn't budge.

"Will you excuse us, Elisabeth?" Williams finally said.

"Billy, it's okay with Sarah if I stay. Hope you don't mind."

The furrows on Williams's forehead deepened in an expression of disapproval, but Elisabeth simply smiled, so he resigned himself to her presence.

"Very well; as you wish. Mrs. Thompson—"

"Please call me Sarah."

"This is an investigation, ma'am, so if it's all right with you, I'd prefer to keep it formal."

Sarah nodded.

"Anyway," Williams went on, "now that I've seen where you live, your family, and commitments, I'm even more puzzled that you experienced this 'feeling' and simply took off."

"What's so strange about that?" Elisabeth jumped in. "I have intuitions like that, too. Most people do. Why can't you believe her? Walter says you've been a pest on this point."

Sheriff Williams shot an angry glare at Elisabeth. "I'm sure you've got other patients to care for. This is official business. You better leave now, Elisabeth."

This time the message came across loud and clear—there would be no arguing with him. Elisabeth shrugged and placed her hand reassuringly on Sarah's arm. "Catch you later." She shot the sheriff a cold stare. "Billy, you and I are going to have a chat." And with that she turned away and marched down the corridor.

"Impossible woman," an irritated Williams sputtered.

"That's a matter of opinion."

The sheriff glanced up the corridor, placed the tips of his fingers on Sarah's elbow, and gently nudged her forward. "C'mon, Mrs. Thompson, let's find a bit of privacy."

The waiting room was empty, and they made their way to the nearest set of chairs. When Sarah sat down, he turned a chair around in front of her, straddled it, rested his arms on the back of the chair, and leaned forward. "Let's talk."

"I have no more information to give you, Sheriff. I've told you everything I know."

"We'll see," he said curtly. "You must admit that your actions are a bit suspicious."

Sarah's eyes widened. "Suspicious? In what way?"

Williams held up a finger for every item on his list, pausing each time for effect. "First, you have this 'feeling,' then you find this injured guy, and now you come visit him all the time."

"What's suspicious about that?" she said, unfazed.

Williams couldn't hide a sarcastic smirk as he raised his eyebrows. "Here you are, new to these parts…you've been here, what, about two years?"

Sarah nodded.

Williams went on. "Newlywed, surrounded by a loving family, and all of a sudden you're driving all this way on icy roads to visit a total stranger every day since you found him." He shook his head. "Your behavior goes way beyond that of a *Good Samaritan*, and that's suspicious to me." He leaned back and cocked his head.

"What are you implying?"

"C'mon, Mrs. Thompson, tell me the truth. Is this guy one of your old boyfriends and you're afraid to tell your new hubby?"

Sarah bolted up from her chair and glared at him. "Listen, *Sheriff Williams*," she stretched out his name with contempt. "You're grasping at straws. Launching unfounded accusations and insults at me will not help you solve this crime. I don't know him; he's not one of my old boyfriends, but I *do care* what happens to him. Whether you like it or not I *am* a *Good Samaritan*, and the sooner you accept that, the sooner you can find out what really happened, and help this man to put his life together again. I'll let you get back to work."

She spun on her heels and headed down the hall.

Williams shook his head as she walked out of the waiting room. "Feisty," he muttered.

Sarah marched to the injured man's room and sighed with relief when she found the door open and the nurses gone. Before she entered she peeked over her shoulder to make sure Williams wasn't following her.

"Good morning," the man said.

"Hi." She smiled as she approached his bedside. "You're looking a lot better; the swelling is really coming down."

"Yes, I'm better," he mumbled. "My head still throbs, though."

"Any memories?"

"No. It's maddening."

"Well, in time it'll all come back, I'm sure."

"Sarah," he whispered.

"Yes."

"I have a feeling you're the one."

"The one?"

"Yes."

"The one what?"

"The one who will help me."

"Typical reaction toward a rescuer," Dr. Lawrence whispered behind Sarah, making her jump.

"You startled me," she said.

"I'm sorry, my dear. Hello, there, Daniel."

"Good morning, Doc."

"Daniel?" Sarah asked, glancing from doctor to patient and back again.

"She hasn't been told?" Dr. Lawrence asked Daniel who shrugged. He turned to Sarah. "Elisabeth and the nurses have named him that. They needed to call him something other than *sir*, and since she's read him three or four books about Daniel Boone, they agreed on Daniel."

"Better than no name at all," the newly named Daniel added. "Doc, I heard what you whispered to Sarah."

"Well," Dr. Lawrence said, "it's typical."

"Nevertheless, that's my impression," Daniel said with conviction.

"Do you have any other impressions about her?" the doctor asked.

"She's going to help me find love," Daniel said as he reached for her hand.

Sarah held his hand in both of hers, a puzzled look in her eyes.

"You realize she's married," Dr. Lawrence admonished Daniel.

"Yes, Doc. I've met Conrad; I haven't forgotten that. I've lost everything that precedes my being here…except for one thing."

"What's that?" the doctor asked, raising his eyebrows.

"I know I've been in search of peace and love and that Sarah is the one who'll help me find them."

Relieved, Sarah patted Daniel's hand. "That's a good sign, isn't it, Doctor?"

"Well," Doctor Lawrence sighed, "yes and no. Time will tell."

"But it means there's something from his past that's egging him on."

"It's possible." Dr. Lawrence smiled at them. "But don't count on it."

"What else could it be?" Daniel asked. "It's got to be from my past. I'm certain."

"Well, if that's the case, there's no harm in hanging on to that belief, as long as you don't do something hurtful to yourself or someone else."

Daniel and Sarah gave the doctor puzzled looks.

"Listen, you two, caution is the operative word. If Elisabeth were here, I'd tell her as well. In cases of complete amnesia, as you're exhibiting, patients sometimes latch onto an idea or notion that somehow has been"—he paused, searching for the right word—"picked up or grabbed by the mind—something someone said or the patient overheard. Then, just like that, the notion becomes entrenched, and the mind gives it credence. It's like a lifeline; only it's not real, it's—"

"It *is* real for me, Doc."

"All right, Daniel, I understand. Don't go off on a fool's errand. Take your time. And you too, Sarah, don't rush things. The mind is a delicate instrument, and we need to tread carefully. In a week or so, Daniel will be discharged from the hospital, and we have to plan for his recovery as an outpatient. That should be our focus right now." The doctor glanced at his watch. "I'd appreciate it if one of you would ask Elisabeth to come by and have a chat with me when she gets a chance."

They nodded.

"Now, Sarah, I'd like some time with my patient."

"Of course, Doctor. I'll be back tomorrow."

"Don't forget, Sarah," Daniel called out as she made her way to the door.

"Forget?"

"You're the one."

Sarah smiled sheepishly and stepped out of the room, her stomach in knots.

C H A P T E R 5

THE FILM CONTINUED its uninvited play, focused on the young boy and his father leaving their house and heading down the street. Both wore black pants, short sleeve white shirts, and black ties.

The boy scampered excitedly about his father in an effort to get him to pick up the pace. "Wish Mom was with us. She loves dancing."

"Maybe next year."

"You're going to come next year, too?"

"Sure, why not?"

"You've never agreed to come before, even when Mom begged. So I—"

"Enough with the interrogation, son."

They continued down the next block in silence.

The boy dashed across the street, looking back at his father and signaling for him to hurry up.

His father crossed the street leisurely, reaching the curb right behind a car with its windows steamed up. He peeked in on a young couple necking in the back seat. Banging on the car door, he yelled, "Linda Marie! Tony! You should be ashamed. Get out of there before I tell your parents."

Embarrassed, the young lovers jumped out of the car and scurried down the street.

"Kids today have no morals," the minister said, admiring his reflection in a car window and adjusting his tie. "I should've worn my blue shirt."

"Mom said we had to wear white. You look fine, Dad, honest." The boy walked backward in front of his father. "You're going to like it. The whole town will be there, and they light up the park real nice, and the band is great, there's lots of food and games and—"

"Calm down, son. You're making me dizzy running around like that."

"Sorry. C'mon, it's around the corner."

"I'm well aware of where the park is," Hugo said impatiently.

They turned the corner and crossed toward the park, passing underneath a huge hand-painted banner that spanned the entire street. It read: *Amaray Annual Summer Picnic and Dance.*

The normally quiet park vibrated with music and laughter. The dance platform at the center of the park was strewn with white lights, as were the trees that lined the periphery of the picnic area. More strings of lights adorned with fake ivy hung over the picnic tables giving the entire area a magical glow.

"Look, Dad, I told you they have all kinds of booths and great food and—"

"Mrs. Foster is reserving seats for us at their table."

The boy stopped cold, while his father made his way into the park. After a few seconds, he raced after his father. "But you don't approve of Mr. Foster. You said that lawyers like him are the vermin of the earth and that—"

"That's enough, son." His eyes scanned the park searching for the Fosters. "There they are." With a huge smile, the minster shoved his bewildered son toward the Fosters' table.

They arrived to find the Fosters and two other couples already seated. Most of the group was in their mid-forties and early fifties, well dressed, bejeweled, and elegantly coiffed. The table boasted countless bottles of wine, whiskey, gin, vodka, and brandy, along with mostly empty glasses of all types and sizes.

As the minister and his son approached, Mrs. Foster rushed forward and snatched the boy's hand.

"You must be Danny. I'm so happy to finally meet you." She glanced at Hugo and smiled. "Good evening, Minister, nice of you to accept our invitation." She tilted her head and appraised the newcomers. "Aren't you both fine-looking, all dressed up the same."

A breathtaking woman of forty who could easily claim to be thirty, Mrs. Foster moved with an air of sensual abandon, her wavy auburn hair bouncing freely, her olive eyes filled with childlike malice. She wore a snug, low-cut, royal blue dress designed to accentuate her abundant cleavage, tied at the neck and waist leaving her back completely bare.

"Danny will sit by me," she decreed unceremoniously, holding the boy's hand tightly against her. "Minister, Andrew saved you the seat next to him."

Mrs. Foster clearly relished being envied by all women and coveted by all men. Her appeal was not lost on young Danny who blushed and attempted to retrieve his hand, which she seemed unwilling to relinquish.

"Fine," the minister answered with a forced smile. He made his way around the table shaking hands with the other guests. After the greetings he shuffled over to his place between Andrew Foster, a heavyset, balding man possessed with a booming voice and overwhelming laugh, and John Cleaves, a small, nervy man who reminded Hugo of a nervous rabbit.

"Decent of you to let us join you," the minister said with exaggerated joy.

"So, Hugo, how's the house of God these days?" Andrew Foster asked with a hint of sarcasm.

"Still looking for your salvation, Andrew. How's the lawyering?" Hugo ignored the jab.

"Very profitable. Better than begging for money for that church of yours."

"Begging? Is that what I do?" Hugo's jaw was so tight the words barely made it out.

"Don't let him rattle your chain," John Cleaves interjected. "He's a shyster. He's bent out of shape 'cause he bought a new boat for a pretty penny, and no one's paying attention to his bragging."

"So he insults me?" Hugo glared at Andrew Foster.

"It's not about you, Hugo, it's about your church always asking for my hard-earned bread. That's why I don't set foot in it. I prefer to pour my dollars into my favorite prizes—the wife there and now my big new boat."

"I still say it's too ostentatious, it's like a floating whorehouse," John said, sipping his drink.

"What do you care, John? You made a ton of money selling it to me."

"Yeah, but I do share my profits with the house of God. That's the difference between us. Besides, I did try to talk you into a more elegant boat, but you had to have it big and ostentatious."

Andrew elbowed Hugo who looked uncomfortable with the conversation.

"Yeah, more elegant for three times the money."

"You're paying for quality."

"I've told you I already got quality," Andrew said with a wink and a nod toward his wife.

With the exception of Hugo, all the men chuckled. Their wives eyed one another, then sipped their drinks and whispered among themselves.

Uninterested in adult banter, Danny scanned the picnic tables searching for Ellie.

"Looking for someone in particular?" Mrs. Foster whispered in Danny's ear.

Startled, he turned to find her close enough for her breath to caress his cheek and her breasts to press against his arm. He pulled away, but she quickly narrowed the gap again.

"The Millers. Are they here?" he asked, trying to change the direction of the encounter.

"The Millers? The folks who just moved here? Ah, you're after that cute little girl of theirs."

Danny blushed in spite of himself and tried to rise, but he was pinned between the table and Mrs. Foster. "I'll be right back. I'm going to look at the booths…Going to check them out."

She smiled seductively and gave the boy a small amount of room. He squirmed out of his seat, trying to cover his reaction to her proximity, but she caught his sleeve and pulled him back.

She leaned close enough to brush his ear with her lips as she whispered, "Maybe she's at the kissing booth."

He managed a timid smile, yanked his arm free, and rushed off, leaving her with a satisfied smile as he disappeared into the crowd.

Two rows of brightly colored booths faced each other along several hundred feet of the park, festooned with multicolored lights. The rides stood at one end of the walk created by the booths, while the food stands, kissing booth, and fortuneteller were clustered at the other.

Danny made his way through the crowd hoping to spot Ellie, but with no success. He was about to give up his quest when he spotted Robert standing in line at the kissing booth.

"That figures," he muttered.

As expected, a long line had already formed around the kissing booth, and Robert was close to the front. He spotted Danny and waved him over.

"Hey, c'mon man, get in line. Sue Ellen's doing the kissing."

Danny approached him. "Have you seen Ellie?"

"No. Did you catch what I said? Sue Ellen, man. C'mon."

"Be back in a while." His eyes continued to scan the park.

Robert threw up his arms in frustration. "You've got to be kidding!"

Danny strode away from Robert and the booths, and around to the periphery of the picnic area. He spotted a teenage couple making out, the same two that Hugo had evicted earlier from the car. The girl leaned against a tree, her hands gently fondling her lover's hair, while the young man pressed his body against hers, his hands stealing a touch of her breasts. Danny ogled at them for a moment until he noticed a man propped against another tree, cigarette in hand, sipping a beer, and eyeing him as he spied on the couple.

When the man's eyes met Danny's, he smiled and raised his beer in a toast to the boy. Several yards behind the man, a Jeep sat in the pool of light provided by a nearby streetlamp.

Danny smiled politely, turned away, and wandered back to the picnic area, waving hello to his friends and their families.

With an air of defeat he returned to his table and sat down.

Mrs. Foster snuck up, wrapped her arm over his shoulders, and nestled in next to him. "No luck?"

Danny stiffened as her breast rubbed against his arm. "Huh?"

"Didn't find her?"

He shook his head. "No."

"Is she aware you're waiting for her?"

"No. She doesn't give me the time of day. It's the age problem, I guess."

Mrs. Foster leaned closer. "Oh, I wouldn't be so sure about that," she said in a sultry voice. "The 'age problem' has a way of working itself out. Have you told her how you feel?"

"Hah! Are you kidding? I can't even talk to her. I can't find words." He turned toward Mrs. Foster, and his eyes darted down to her cleavage—her skin was smooth and shiny, her breasts full and luscious. He nervously cleared his throat and glanced around. Thankfully, his father was arguing with Andrew Foster and not looking in his direction at all.

"Tell her anything that comes to your mind. Be yourself. Growing up isn't any easier for girls. Make her relax."

"I'm the one who can't relax. Not when I'm with her. Besides she—"

Danny's eyes widened, and a small gasp escaped his lips as Mrs. Foster slid her hand under the table and placed it gently on his leg.

"She has a 'so what' attitude, right?"

Danny's heart pounded, and he struggled to keep his breath under control. "Sort of," he managed to say at last, his voice catching between words.

"That's her cover." She rubbed her hand along his thigh. "Trust yourself. Act like you always do, as you are right now. She'll love it. I certainly do."

Andrew Foster rose to his feet and hoisted his glass of wine. "Everybody. Could I have your attention, please? I have an announcement to make."

Everyone around the table quieted down.

"Thank you. I am proud to announce that I"—he paused and glanced around with a broad smile—"have been made"—he paused again and dragged the words out for emphasis—"senior partner in my law firm."

Everyone cheered, and most rose to their feet to toast the news, except for Hugo who offered a practiced smile.

Mrs. Foster squeezed Danny's leg and whispered in his ear. "Look who's arrived." She nodded across the park where Ellie strolled with her family. They were making their way to a table. "Go get her, tiger."

Before she finished, Danny had risen to his feet and headed off.

The driver of the Jeep, still leaning against the tree, finished another beer and tossed the bottle into a nearby trash can as he noticed Danny hurrying to Ellie's table. He turned his eyes toward Mrs. Foster for a moment, smiled to himself, and ambled a bit closer.

Danny slowed his pace in an attempt to appear casual when he drew near the Millers' picnic table. He took a deep breath and approached the family.

"Hi, Mr. and Mrs. Miller. How are you?"

"Hello there, uh…" Mr. Miller failed to conjure up Danny's name.

"It's Danny, Dad." Ellie stood up.

"Yes, of course, Danny. We're fine. How are your parents? Are they here?"

"My mom's at her sister's house helping her with the new baby. My dad's over there, with the Fosters." He stood in awkward silence, eyeing Ellie.

The girl smiled at him and waited patiently, but he remained frozen and silent, looking at her. After a few seconds she sat down and turned her gaze toward the band.

"Care to join us, Danny?" Mrs. Miller asked.

"No, thanks, Mrs. Miller. I was wondering if, uh…well, if Ellie would… like to dance."

"Of course she would. C'mon, darling, get on out there. Danny's waiting."

"Oh, Mom."

"Listen, sweetheart, it's my fault we're late getting here," her father added. "You need to make up for lost time, girl. Go on."

"Dad." Her cheeks turned bright pink.

Unsure as to what was happening, Danny rocked in place, becoming more nervous by the second. "That's okay," he ventured. "Maybe later."

"Nonsense." Mr. Miller patted Danny's back. "She's dying to dance with you. Been talking about it all afternoon. Girls, my boy, none can understand them." He walked over to his daughter, pulled her out of her seat, and gave her hand to a stunned Danny who reluctantly took it, but remained motionless.

Ellie yanked her hand away and walked off toward the dance platform. She climbed the steps and turned to wait for Danny. When he finally caught up, they stood face-to-face, motionless.

"Well?"

He swallowed hard. "Well, what?"

"You asked to dance, didn't you?"

"Oh, yeah," he said, sounding like he had woken from a dream. He offered Ellie his hand, gently pulled her closer, and they began to dance.

"Hope you don't believe my dad. I didn't talk about you all afternoon. He's like that."

"Like what?"

"He exaggerates and makes things up."

"Oh."

Her proximity was intoxicating, and his palms began to sweat, so he released her and wiped his hands on his pants. She smiled and wiped hers on her dress.

"Sorry, it's hot here, isn't it?"

"I hadn't noticed."

Unable to conjure anything to say, Danny slowly succumbed to his own nervousness. They swayed in silence.

"Congratulations on winning the swim meet," said Ellie with a disarming smile.

Relieved to have a topic, he smiled back. "Hey, thanks. You were there?"

"Yeah, I was there. Nice trophy. They say you have a whole bunch of them."

"A few," he responded, embarrassed.

Silence again. Danny desperately tried to come up with something clever to say, but the more he tried the more nervous he became, until he ended up treading on her toes.

She did her best not to complain.

"Sorry. Can we start again?"

"I imagined that being such a good swimmer you'd be a great dancer."

"Yeah, well…Hey, it's really hot. How about a soda?"

"No, thanks."

By now Danny was in agony. They danced in silence until the music ended, then stood in the middle of the dance floor facing each other in silence. Danny frantically dried his palms on his pants.

Lou Harrison, the school's star athlete, emerged from the crowd and turned Ellie away from Danny.

"C'mon, you beauty. Let's show this little sap how the big boys dance."

"Let go of me, Lou," Ellie protested. "Just 'cause you're a senior, it—"

"Hush up, my beauty. You'll love dancing with me, and you know it." He adroitly spun her around, and she giggled.

Standing awkwardly in the middle of the dance floor, visibly disappointed with himself and too embarrassed to move, Danny stared them down as they boogied away, laughing.

Mrs. Foster stepped close, took his hand, and led him into the dance. She held him gently and placed his hand on her bare back. Immediately, he retrieved it, unsure what to do, but she took his hand once more and placed it against her back softly pressing it in place. She winked and smiled reassuringly at the boy. Visibly calmer, Danny smiled back.

"How was it?" she whispered as she pulled him closer.

"Awful."

"She needs dance lessons."

"You mean I do."

"Nonsense. You're magnificent. Look at you now."

"It's different with you."

Mrs. Foster smiled. "How about the conversation?"

"What conversation?"

"I'll tell you what you should do. Next time, don't try to impress her with clever topics or interesting conversation. Ask about her. Believe me, we girls love talking about ourselves."

Danny danced to the beat of the music, not once stepping on Mrs. Foster's toes. As he finally relaxed, she pressed against him.

A look of terror came over Danny when he felt his body react to hers. He tried to pull away before she noticed, but she held him fast and rubbed against him. He swallowed hard as beads of sweat collected above his lip, and his breathing quickened. She looked into his eyes and smiled.

The song came to an end, and Danny turned to leave, but she held him back. The lights dimmed, and a slow ballad began to play. In no time the dance floor filled up, a mass of bodies swaying in unison to the music. Cuddled amid the crowd, Danny and Mrs. Foster danced in perfect unison. Suddenly the lights went out, and the park fell into darkness. The crowd protested loudly.

"Stay calm, everybody," announced the bandleader. "It's just the old generator acting up. Lights will be back in no time. We'll keep playing and you keep dancing."

Taking advantage of the dark and the concealment offered by the crowd, Mrs. Foster slid her hand behind his neck to force him toward her, and gently kissed his mouth. The boy's attempt to resist was short lived, and he surrendered to the moment and all the sensations that came with it. The kiss lingered, her lips shifting against his, her tongue in search of his. Then, satisfied, she pulled away and smiled.

The crowd cheered as the lights came back on.

"You're delicious, Danny Michaels." She abruptly turned and walked away, leaving him alone in the middle of the thinning crowd. He searched the floor for Ellie but failed to find her.

Instead, he spotted the Jeep driver, beer in hand, strolling conspicuously around the edge of the dance floor, his penetrating gaze fixed on Danny. Satisfied with having caught the boy's eye, he winked and nodded.

Danny looked away, confused, and made his way off the dance floor. As he emerged from the crowd, he turned back to find that the man's eyes remained locked upon him.

Disconcerted, the boy rushed away.

"Isn't it too much of a coincidence?" Sarah asked her husband as she poured wine into a couple of glasses. "All of a sudden everyone—well, except for the Jeep-driver character—has a name, and the boy's called Danny."

Conrad stoked the fire, joined his wife on the sofa, scooped up his glass of wine, and sipped it. "Yes, but it could also be your mind playing tricks on you."

"Tricks?"

"Well, maybe not tricks, more like a quirk. The hospital staff names our mystery man Daniel, and the very next installment of the movie tells you that the boy's name is Danny."

She scowled and shook her head.

"Like the doctor said, it could simply be your mind deciding to call him that because you heard the name earlier. You said Amaray wasn't real, so it's possible none of the names in the movie are real either."

"That could be…I suppose."

"It looks like it's turning into a racy flick. That woman is something else."

"I'll say. I'm glad the year is 1976; otherwise I'd worry that a young boy might be in danger."

"So, you're pretty sure this all occurred in the past."

"I can't imagine what else it could be. Why be so precise in all the sets, the clothing, and how they look?"

"I wonder if the year 1976 has special significance."

"What's the meaning of the whole story and all the characters? They're so real that at times it's as if I'm peeking into their actual lives."

"Well, that's what movies are supposed to do—tell us the story about an important moment. Books should do that, too, and photographs as well, for that matter."

"What if the boy is related to our mystery man? Or better yet, what if he's the mystery man at a younger age?"

Conrad shrugged. "I wouldn't make any assumptions. He could be either one, or he could be the boat salesman or the minister or the Jeep driver or none of them. It's impossible to say."

"The boy is definitely the main character. He's in every scene."

"Nothing is clear. I'm with Dr. Lawrence that you need to be careful regarding this business of Daniel telling you you're the one. It's asking too much of you. Don't take the bait."

"Bait?"

"Yeah, he believes, and wishes you to believe, that the feeling he has about you comes from somewhere in his past. But what if it turns out to be a false impression?"

"Maybe he senses that I'm psychic."

"If that's the case, time will tell. But for now, let's take it one step at a time."

They sipped their wine and enjoyed the fire crackling before them. Sarah cuddled next to her husband. He placed his arm around her shoulders and held her tight.

"It must be awful not to have any idea who you are," Sarah whispered at last.

"Yeah. Maybe as he gets settled away from the hospital, memories will start coming back to him. Doc mentioned that the trauma to his brain damaged the portion responsible for retrieving stored memories. Let's hope that as the swelling goes down he'll start remembering."

"The scary part is that they haven't ruled out that the amnesia may be the result of psychological trauma and not the head injury. If this movie is about him, maybe something horrible will happen. That Mrs. Foster is repulsive. And that man spying on the young boy—"

"There you go again. Don't assume anything. If it's psychological instead of physical, time will tell. Anyway, what Doc also said is that his loss of memory could be his way to protect himself from something that has already happened or from some impending threat. Hell, the man was beaten nearly to death. That's bad enough."

After a deep sigh, Sarah looked up at Conrad. "What if he never recovers his memory?"

"I hope that's not the case. I wouldn't like to have him dependent on us forever."

"That's not likely to happen. It took endless cajoling from Elisabeth, the nurses, and even Dr. Lawrence for Daniel to finally agree to move into the room above the store."

"What finally got him to say yes?"

"The fact that he'd be working. He absolutely refused to accept the room without giving something in return. He's determined not to be a burden. He'll do well by you."

"I like the fact that he had to be talked into it. Shows good character. Tom's already got a list of things for him to do, and truth be told, he's looking forward to having an assistant. Things have been hectic lately."

"I wonder how his list compares to Elisabeth's." Sarah chuckled. She sat forward on the sofa and turned toward her husband. "Did I tell you she's putting her volunteer work at the hospital on hold so she can care for Daniel?"

Conrad laughed. "No, but it doesn't surprise me. She's quite taken with him. I hope she doesn't get hurt. He could be married and have a family."

Sarah poured them both more wine then snuggled back into Conrad's arms. "Now you're the one making assumptions. I'm not sure if Elisabeth is attracted to him or simply likes a good mystery."

"I'd say a bit of both. Hey, that reminds me, Williams has been snooping around, and now he's started on me."

"You? How did you find out?"

"He's been asking questions around town, from what I'm told. And voicing suspicion about the fact that we've opened up our home and the store to a total stranger."

"That's nonsense. Everyone here respects you and—"

"That may be, but don't forget this is the Northwest. There's a natural mistrust of strangers."

"But how did they find out what we've decided? It was only a few days ago that Doc told us Daniel was ready to be released. Then it took another couple of days to talk Daniel into accepting our offer—he only agreed yesterday morning."

"This sort of news travels fast. Don't forget that what happened to him is far from common in these parts. Folks like to talk—especially with the Sheriff sniffing around and spreading innuendo."

Sarah sighed. "I suppose I can't blame them. Most people wouldn't do what we've done. We're only in the middle of this because this blasted sixth sense of mine insists that I have to sort this out and help him. Hard to explain that to people, and even harder to live in the middle of it." She kissed her husband. "Thanks for your patience, darling." She stood and picked up the wine glasses. "C'mon, let's have some dinner."

Conrad snagged the bottle of wine and followed her toward the dining room.

"Sarah," he said, "your sixth sense is nothing to sneer at. You've been given a precious gift that—I will admit—at times is scary and confusing, but always comes through in the end."

Sarah placed the glasses on the table and turned to her husband. "Are you worried about Daniel? I mean worried that he might do something violent or—"

"No." Conrad put down the wine bottle and stroked his wife's arm. "He doesn't strike me as the violent type. But I suspect folks around here probably are worried about that. I imagine that lots of what-ifs are floating around. There's so much speculation surrounding him. People wonder who attacked him, and why, and will they come back to finish the job. Things like this don't happen here. He's big news. And the fact that he appeared out of nowhere isn't very reassuring either."

"What makes you so sure he's not violent or that he won't invite violence into our lives?"

Conrad smiled and pulled the chair out for his wife. "Because you would've alerted us."

She didn't sit down but instead turned to him. "How can you be so sure? I'm not."

Conrad cocked his head and eyed his wife—his look implying the answer was obvious.

Sarah stared back, her eyebrows raised. "What?"

Conrad nudged her toward her chair. "C'mon, sit down."

"No, you sit down. I'll bring the casserole out. Answer my question."

"Darling, you sit. I'll serve." He gently pushed his wife down onto the chair and kissed the top of her head.

"You can't be that certain about my abilities."

"Oh, but I am."

"Why?"

"Because, if there were any danger to us, you would've sensed it by now, and you'd be scared. But you aren't. All these weeks you haven't even thought about it."

"And you have?"

He nodded. "Of course."

"Why didn't you tell me?"

"No need."

She pulled her husband toward her, and kissed his lips. "I do love you, even if you're so frustratingly sure of yourself...and me."

"Thank goodness for that. On both counts." Conrad disappeared into the kitchen.

Sarah smiled as she served the salad.

Moments later Conrad returned with the casserole, placed it on the hot-plate on the table and sat across from his wife. "I am worried about Williams, though. I don't like his attitude at all. He's nothing but trouble."

"He can't hurt us," Sarah said nonchalantly as she cut the casserole and served it.

"He can if he decides to turn folks against Daniel and us."

Sarah froze—holding the serving spoon in midair—paralyzed by a flood of memories.

Conrad took the spoon and gently held her hand. "What is it? What happened?"

Sarah turned to him as tears ran down her cheeks. "When I was six—"

"Damn. I shouldn't have told you. I didn't mean to remind you of—"

"All I did—"

"Yes, darling, you've told me."

But Sarah couldn't stop herself. "—was tell my friend Lindsay how sorry I was that her uncle had hurt her."

"I get it."

"It was her sixth birthday party. She was a month younger than me and…" Sarah's sobs came in fierce bursts.

"Calm down, darling."

Sarah shook her head and leaned forward. "Everyone heard me describe how he'd raped her. I didn't understand what I was saying. Lindsay screamed that she'd said nothing—"

"Please, Sarah, you've told me this before, it's—"

Sarah put her hand up as she gulped her tears down. "First they labeled me a liar and said I made it all up. Then when George went to jail and Lindsay's mom killed herself—"

"You were a little girl. You didn't mean to—"

"My family was shunned. Everyone said this business of 'seeing things' in my head was sinful, that I was possessed by the devil. Because of me we had to move away." She turned to Conrad, a look of despair imprinted across her face. "Because of me. Do you understand?"

"Yes, of course I do. It traumatized you. You should—"

"No, that's not it. Williams can—"

"He can't revive that. And even if he tries to, you didn't—"

"No, it's not about that. It's…" she paused.

"What?" Conrad came around the table.

"Because of me he can turn everyone against us."

"Hush." He wrapped his wife tightly in his arms. "Even back then, it wasn't your fault. And Williams won't—" he stopped and took a breath. "I will never let that happen."

Bolstered by her husband's determination, Sarah stared deep into his eyes. A look of utter resolve came over her. "Neither will I."

C H A P T E R   6

T HE MOON PAINTED streaks of white across the tranquil waters of Amaray Lake, pushing away the shadows in a secluded cove. Under the silvery hue, the nocturnal sounds of nature echoed and the sound of rustling leaves approached the shore.

A smiling Danny emerged from the nearby woods. In a flash he shed his shirt, shoes, and socks, dropped his pants and underwear and plunged naked into the lake. He broke through the surface of the cool water without a care, cavorting with abandon, enjoying the freedom of communion with nature. To catch his breath he floated belly up, scrutinizing the stars.

He allowed the gentle waves to carry him along, until an unexpected noise from behind the trees on shore startled him. He stopped and listened. When the noise came again he held his breath and stared intently into the dark forest.

To his dismay, the stranger from the Jeep emerged from the density of trees and sauntered down to the edge of the lake directly toward Daniel. He stood silently for a moment before lighting a cigarette. Only then did he address the boy.

"Hi. I'm Alexander."

The boy remained immobile, his freedom transformed into vulnerability.

"And you're Danny, right?"

Wondering what escape might be available to him Danny glanced at his pile of clothes and back to Alexander. With nowhere to go, he stared at the man.

Alexander ripped off his clothes and dove into the water, disappearing into the blackness. Moments later he popped up right in front of Danny, startling him and causing him to paddle fiercely away.

Alexander swam ahead, cutting off his retreat. "So you're a nature lover, Master Danny?"

The boy glanced toward the shore, sizing up his chances of escape.

Alexander laughed. "Not to mention that gorgeous creature that kissed you at the picnic, huh? Tasty morsel, that one."

Danny slowly eased toward the shore.

Alexander followed. "You're wondering, 'who the hell is this guy'? I'm wondering, 'should I tell him, or let him sweat it?'" Alexander disappeared abruptly under the water.

Danny turned in all directions searching for the unwelcome intruder, then started toward the shore. After a few strokes, he looked around for Alexander who had been under the water an alarming length of time, but only the moon's reflection stared back at him.

Alexander breached the water next to Danny, air bursting from his lungs in a great explosion. "Wow! Love the buzz you get when you hold your breath for a long time." Gasping, he swam around the boy like a shark circling its prey.

Danny moved away, keeping an eye on him, determined to maintain a safe distance between them.

"Hell, I haven't been skinny dipping in years." Alexander laughed. "And at midnight. It's great. What a blast. Thanks, Danny boy, what a gift." He dove once again only to emerge moments later directly in front of him.

He grabbed his shoulders and the boy's eyes widened.

"Right about now you're pretty worried wondering who the hell this crazy bastard is." Alexander smiled, released Danny and slid under the water.

Danny glanced about, certain that this lunatic was going to materialize and latch on to him. He made a fist in preparation for any needed self-defense. As the seconds ticked by he made his way toward shore using his legs and keeping his arms and fists at the ready.

Alexander reappeared a few feet from the boy and floated along belly up. Water droplets clung to the abundant hair that covered his body, made him sparkle in the moonlight like some mythological creature of the deep.

"Not to worry, my young friend. I mean you no harm. I'm a writer. Or so my agent tells me. A frustrated writer is more accurate. My publisher says I owe him for some advances and he demands that I write a fucking novel as my contract demands. I rented the log cabin up by the creek for the summer to fulfill my obligations. That, in a nutshell, is who I am, my young friend."

Danny stopped, but remained on his guard.

Alexander backstroked toward him. "And you are Danny, who spies on young lovers when they make out, steps on beautiful girls when he dances, and is passionately kissed by older women. Oh, and as of now, Alexander Pit—wait…no need for last names. They only get in the way and drag you to the bowels of hell."

Danny's eyes widened in astonishment as Alexander held out his hand.

"Wait. You can't be Alexander Pit—"

"No last names! You're forbidden!" Alexander chuckled and swam around Danny forcing him to turn in circles to keep up.

"So, Master Danny, you're a reader. A romantic. A dreamer. I should've guessed."

"I read your book. I've read *Rainbow of*—"

"Stop!" Alexander demanded. "Do not let me hear the title of that damn novel."

"But—"

"No buts. I refuse to hear it."

"Well, I've read…*it* five times. Honest I have. I saw the movie, too."

Abruptly, Alexander stopped swimming and glared at Danny. "I hated that stupid flick."

"It wasn't as good as the book, but I liked it…Boy! I can't believe this. You're Alexander Pi—sorry. I can't believe it."

"Shush! Only for you I am. Nobody else." He looked Danny squarely in the eyes. "You can't tell anyone I'm here. Not a soul. Promise me."

Danny held Alexander's gaze for several moments deciding if he meant what he'd said. Clearly, he did.

"No one would believe me, anyway. You're supposed to be dead. You died in Spain."

"That's right. I'm getting cold sitting here talking. Race you to shore."

Alexander slapped Danny on the shoulder and off they went. Danny swam past Alexander with ease then waited for him to catch up. As they emerged from the lake, Alexander bent down to catch his breathe, but broke into a coughing fit.

"Are you okay?"

When his cough ceased, he finally answered. "No. I'm never *okay*," Alexander sputtered. "*Okay* means death." He exploded with laughter. "C'mon."

They picked up their clothes and marched off into the darkness.

"No, Sarah, I have no recollection of living near a lake," Daniel answered. "Why do you ask?"

He stood behind the counter in Conrad's store, his face still colored by lingering bruises.

Sarah smiled nonchalantly. "Just throwing things out there hoping to jar your memory." She glanced around. "Where's Tom?"

"He's in the storage room. You need any more ingredients? I can get them for you."

"No, I only wanted to thank him for getting all this ready for me," she took the box from the counter. "You're healing nicely, by the way."

Now that the swelling had subsided, and the scars from the scratches on his face had almost vanished, Daniel's good looks were becoming apparent. Somewhere around his mid to late forties, he had a professorial air about him, most likely aided by the wool pants and corduroy jacket he liked to wear, although the rimless glasses and uncombed ash-blond hair also helped.

"Doc says I'm on the mend."

"Looks like you've settled in quite well."

"Conrad and Tom have made it easy for me. Besides, I enjoy working here. All I need now is to get my memory back. Need any help carrying that stuff?"

"No, I can manage, thank you. Anyway, I'm sure you'll start remembering soon enough. Well, I'm off. Please thank Tom for me. Until tonight."

"Bye."

She exited the store.

Daniel adjusted his glasses up and down, trying to focus on an inventory spreadsheet.

"We need to find you a different pair of glasses," Tom said as he emerged from the storeroom with a slew of boxes.

"Hey, let me help you with those." Daniel tossed his glasses onto the counter and limped toward Tom, the wound in his leg not yet fully mended.

"No need, I got it. Take it easy or you'll only hurt yourself again."

Daniel returned to the spreadsheet, put on his glasses, and frowned. "You're right; these glasses aren't quite doing the trick. Maybe something stronger will work. By the way, Sarah came by to pick up her groceries and asked me to thank you for getting it all together."

Tall and rugged like his father, Tom had wavy black hair, intense grey eyes, and an easy, unassuming charm. He sorted the boxes on the counter by size and product. "Check in the drawer behind the counter."

Daniel opened the drawer and pulled out a box with glasses of all shapes and sizes. "What are these for?"

Tom smiled at him as he placed items on their appropriate shelves. "Customers forget their glasses all the time, so we keep a bunch on hand to lend. Those you're wearing are the ones Doc picked for you from this drawer. Aren't they any good?"

"They're okay, but I'm having trouble focusing clearly." He sorted through the glasses trying each pair. "I'm getting dizzy with all these changes," he chuckled.

Tom came over to Daniel and grabbed a pair. "See this little number on the side here?"

Daniel shook his head.

"Put on the glasses Doc got for you. Now do you see the number?" Daniel nodded. "The ones you've been wearing are 2.5, so you probably need 2.75 or higher. Look for the number and then try the glasses."

"Thanks, Tom. Such a simple thing, and I didn't even know to look for that little number."

"Most folks don't have a clue it's there. Don't be so hard on yourself. You do great with keeping the book ledgers, and all that math stuff."

"Maybe," Daniel said with a self-deprecating smile. "I have no idea what I would've done without you guys looking after me."

The door chimes announced that someone had stepped into the store.

"Daniel, can you take care of that? I need to finish stacking the new merchandise."

"Sure." Daniel limped out from behind the counter, but didn't get far since Sheriff Williams had already made his way to the back of the store.

"Hello, Sheriff," Daniel said politely.

"Sir." Williams tapped the brim of his hat, spotted Tom and repeated the gesture. "Mr. Thompson."

"Good morning," Tom answered and continued to work on stocking the shelves.

Williams eyed Daniel with a mocking smile. "You're wearing too many glasses."

Daniel realized he wore one pair of glasses and had two pairs on top of his head. "I was trying them on, looking for the right ones." With a sheepish smile he shoved them in his pocket.

"Came to check if you'd remembered anything yet."

"I'm afraid not. Any luck with the fingerprints or the photos for the press? Have you found out who I am?"

"Not yet."

"Well, that's a relief." Tom interjected from behind the counter.

"Why would you say that?" Williams asked.

"I'd say," Tom went on, "you would've had a hit if he were in the FBI's files. The fact that he isn't tells us he's an innocent bystander who got attacked."

Williams's eyes narrowed and he cocked his head. "And how come you're so well versed about the FBI, Mr. Thompson?"

"Elisabeth told us," Daniel interjected. "She's up on all this investigative stuff."

"She reads too much." Williams stared at Daniel. "Folks around here say they're not really happy to have you around."

"Sheriff." Tom came up to Daniel and placed a hand on his shoulder. "We're okay with that. Daniel is doing well and slowly getting better. Our customers will be okay with him once they get better acquainted. They trust us."

"Maybe. I suspect your stepmother is hiding something." Williams shot a sharp look at Tom, touched his hat rim, turned on his heels, and departed as abruptly as he'd arrived.

"That man has serious issues," Tom said as he returned to his chores.

"I don't like that he doubts Sarah."

"He's trying to frost us. Don't fall for it."

Daniel sighed, took the glasses out of his pocket, placed them in the drawer, and chose a pair that remained on the counter. "I'll stick with the old pair. At least they look familiar."

Tom glanced at Daniel. "That's a different pair."

"You're kidding." Daniel stared at them, puzzled that he couldn't spot the difference. "I'm even disoriented in the present."

Tom laughed and patted him on the back. "Just yanking your chain. You got the right ones. C'mon, help me put this stuff away. We need to get this done so you can get to Sarah's French dinner on time."

"She's teaching Elisabeth how to cook. I'm curious how that's going to work."

Tom grinned. "Most likely Elisabeth is the one telling Sarah what to do and how to do it."

C H A P T E R   7

IN A SMALL clearing near Amaray Lake a rustic cabin was sheltered by trees. The Jeep sat parked to one side, partly concealed in the shadows of the forest. The lighting inside the cabin cast a golden aura upon its surroundings.

Alexander emerged from the woods, followed by Danny, their laughter echoing through the trees, their wet clothes clinging to their bodies.

Alexander leapt up the porch steps, swung open the front door, and ushered Danny in.

"Welcome to my humble abode."

Danny glanced around and smiled.

The rustic cabin was mainly one large room with a fireplace centered in the wall opposite the front door. There were a couple of worn-out sofas pushed to one side to make room for a large easel. Tucked in one corner were the kitchen area, and two doors leading to a small bedroom and a bathroom.

The easel held a large self-portrait that captured Alexander's intensity and zeal despite being far from finished. Paints, canvases, soiled rags, and sketching pads littered the room. A typewriter sat on the small dining table, the surface and floor swamped by crumpled sheets of paper. Beneath the table lay three unopened packages of typing paper.

Alexander went directly to a small record collection arranged against a corner wall next to a portable record player, fingered through the selection, and placed several records on the player. Seconds later, *Hernando's Hideaway* emanated from the two speakers. Alexander cranked up the volume before heading to a sideboard by the kitchen. He snagged a bottle, grabbed a couple of glasses, poured two whiskeys, and handed one to the boy.

Momentarily stunned by the whirlwind of activity, Danny considered his drink for a moment, took a sip, grimaced and stifled a cough.

"Let's build a fire outside. Follow me." Alexander shimmied out onto the porch.

Danny set his drink on the table by the typewriter and stepped outside.

Alexander pointed to a pile of firewood. "Bring as much as you can carry." Without missing a step, he pranced down the steps and over to a circle of rocks in a clearing in front of the cabin and uncluttered its center by kicking the burnt wood around to the beat of the music.

Danny arrived with an armful of firewood and piled it neatly next to the ring.

Dancing and singing to the music, Alexander signaled Danny to follow him back inside.

Danny finally broke down, dancing after him into the cabin. Alexander danced, drank, and sang as he gathered up as much of the crumpled paper as he could handle. He signaled for the boy to follow suit then snatched up the bottle of whiskey on his way out the door.

With his arms crammed full of crumpled paper, Danny joined Alexander outside and dropped his load into the circle of rocks.

Alexander piled wood on top of the paper and produced a cigarette lighter. In moments the fire took off sending scores of tiny sparks flying high into the night air. Delighted with the results, he turned to Danny, ready to toast to their creation, and stopped with his glass in midair.

"Where the hell is your drink?"

"I left it inside."

"Well, go get it."

"I'm not supposed to drink alcohol. I'm only fifteen."

"Bullfeathers! Go get your drink," Alexander commanded dismissively.

Danny rushed into the cabin, emerged with the glass of whiskey and joined his host by the fire. Alexander clinked glasses and downed his drink. Danny took a sip and grimaced.

"Gulp it down," he commanded with a nudge to the boy's elbow, forcing him to swallow his entire drink.

Eyes wide, Danny sputtered and gasped as the alcohol burned its way down.

Satisfied with the reaction, Alexander refilled their glasses and toasted. "C'mon, let's dance to friendship." With that, he took off prancing and singing around the fire.

They circled the fire for several minutes, and after a few turns, Alexander dropped to the ground, arms and legs stretched wide, and stared up into the night sky.

Moments later Danny joined him and the two lay side by side, catching their breath and contemplating the stars.

"The sky here is almost as beautiful as it is in Spain," Alexander said with a nostalgic sigh. "Toledo's the best. That's why El Greco painted it so often."

"I've never been outside Amaray, not even to Chicago."

"You've got to go out into the world to live life and find yourself. It's the only way you'll get to be everything you ever wished to be. I was a bullfighter."

"Yeah, one of those bulls killed you."

"Bastard got me right here." He pulled up his shirt to reveal a large scar below his ribs.

"Wow."

"Fucker. I had to spend the rest of that year painting portraits. And apparently, my friend, that is my true gift in life. Scattered all over Spain are Alexander's portraits of anonymous people." He snickered. "Hah! My gift."

Danny chuckled with him. "That's a good gift to have."

"No. I crave what you have."

"Me? What do I have?"

"You have the best gift of all—the gift of love. Everybody loves Danny."

Danny sat up and stared somberly into the fire, the effects of the whiskey apparent.

"Love is tough. I was in love with Ellie. But Mrs. Foster made me feel… well…I'd never felt what she made me feel. Her tongue and her…uh…I mean…she gave me…such a feeling."

Alexander rose up and squeezed the boy's shoulder. "My friend, this sky is not a feeling, this fire is not a feeling, and her tongue was not a feeling. *You* are the feeling, the only *real* feeling. Never forget that."

"Boy, you're right." Danny's eyes widened, impressed by such words of wisdom. "Wow, man…so what should I do? I'm after true love, like Wesley in your book."

"Then, go for it."

"With Ellie or Mrs. Foster?"

"With either one. Or better yet, with both of them." Alexander grabbed the whiskey bottle only to find it empty. Frustrated, he struggled to his feet and wobbled toward the cabin. "Need a refill." At the top of the steps he stopped and turned back to his new friend and pointed at him. "Keep one thing in mind. A man is remembered for what he seeks, not for what he finds."

Danny's eyes followed Alexander until he disappeared into the cabin, then they drifted back to the fire.

"Wow…that's really profound."

"Sarah, darling." Conrad reached for her hand.

Startled, Sarah shook her head. "Sorry, I got distracted. Did I miss anything?"

They sat in their living room, alongside Daniel and Elisabeth, enjoying a glass of wine and a handful of small appetizers.

"I told them the menu. A French meal all the way—isn't that decadent?"

"I'm not sure about decadent, but coq au vin certainly sounds *merveilleux*," Daniel exclaimed in a perfect French accent. "Thank you, ladies."

"Too bad you can't have any wine, Daniel," Elisabeth said as she sipped from her glass. "This one—" She tipped the bottle to read the label. "Saint Emilion is *s-u-a-v-e*. Good choice, Conrad."

"Glad you like it. I figured it was the least I could do for our wonderful chefs to complement our French meal. What are these by the way?"

"*Flotteurs*—means 'floats' in English." Elisabeth giggled. "Isn't that a funny name?"

"Elisabeth prepared the appetizers and the entire dinner," Sarah said with pride.

"I did the cooking, but Sarah stood by my side the whole time. We had great fun."

"Tell us all about it," Daniel said.

"Men don't like to talk about cooking," Elisabeth said.

"Yes, we do, don't we, Conrad?"

"Absolutely." Conrad winked at his wife then settled back on the sofa. "Go ahead. Tell us all about it."

Elisabeth shook her head. "I have a better idea. Let's play a game. You gentlemen have to taste a morsel and then guess what's in it. Whoever gets the most points, wins."

"What do we win?" asked Daniel.

"Fifty dollars," Elisabeth announced proudly.

Conrad leaned forward on the sofa, rubbing his palms together with mock greed. "That's definitely worth playing for."

"Now," said Elisabeth, "neither one of you has an advantage since Sarah and I worked with Tom to gather the ingredients. Unless"—she turned to Conrad—"you've peeked in the kitchen and the cupboards."

"I've been in Seattle all day."

Elisabeth turned to Sarah who nodded in confirmation. "Okay, you have to tell us what's in each dish. Understood?"

"You mean you expect us to name the actual ingredients?" Daniel asked.

"Yep, both for the appetizers and the dinner. After all, it's fifty dollars."

"How about it, Daniel—are you up to it?" Conrad was chomping at the bit to get started.

"Sure. How about we start with the tapenade?" Daniel asked, gesturing.

Conrad burst out laughing. "Whoa, you're already ahead of me... tapenade? I would've called it a spread."

"One point to Daniel," Elisabeth decreed. "What's in it?"

Each man spread some tapenade on a cracker, took a bite, and savored it.

"Well?" Elisabeth prompted. "You go first Conrad, since Daniel already has a point, and then we'll switch to him for the second ingredient, and so on. It'll be like ping pong with food."

"Olives," Conrad said.

"Kalamata," added Daniel.

"One point for Conrad, and one for Daniel." Elisabeth snickered and winked at Conrad. "He's beating you."

"Kalamata, eh?" said Conrad. "Okay, I'll be more specific. Do I go again?"

"No, second ingredient is Daniel's," Elisabeth ruled.

"Capers," Daniel said.

"There are too many brands of capers," Conrad interjected. "I have no clue which ones you used."

"Don't worry about brands, just the types, and only if it's applicable, like with the olives," Elisabeth clarified. "You're next, Conrad."

"Anchovies," he said, savoring another bite.

"And a bit of garlic," Daniel added.

"Wow," Sarah said with a chuckle. "You guys are good."

"Now to the floats," Elisabeth prompted.

"Sarah's delicious homemade baguette," Conrad said proudly as he reached over to caress her hand.

"And *Port-Salut* cheese. Is that right?" Daniel asked as he tasted the little float.

"Daniel, you know your French cheeses," Elisabeth exclaimed.

Daniel's eyes widened. "I do?" He pondered the question. "I guess I do."

"Your French accent is also very good. Parisian, I'd say," Sarah added.

"And you have a solid understanding of foods," Conrad said.

"A chef," exclaimed Elisabeth. "You could be a chef. Do you like cooking?"

"I have no idea, but I like good food."

"Well, why don't we test it out? Tomorrow morning instead of you going down to the diner for breakfast, I'll pick you up and you'll come to my house and make us some breakfast."

"Elisabeth," Conrad intervened. "It's not a good idea for Daniel to be seen going into your home, he—"

"C'mon, Conrad, he's perfectly safe with me, and I'm not worried about what people might or might not say."

"But—"

Elisabeth shook her head. "My mind's made up. I promise I'll have him back to the store by nine. Besides, it might help bring back some memories."

Conrad shook his head.

"Okay, how about this? If you bring Sarah down, she can chaperone us."

"I'm babysitting the little ones tomorrow. Sorry."

"There has to be a way." It was clear that Elisabeth did not intend to relent. "How about Daniel spends the night at my house tonight and that way no one will notice me picking him up. You can drive by the house in the morning and—"

"Elisabeth, no. That's not an option." Conrad was adamant.

"Conrad," Sarah ventured, "do you suppose Tom might be willing to pick him up and join them for breakfast?"

"There you have it. The perfect option," Elisabeth exclaimed.

Resigned but unconvinced, Conrad sighed and smiled. "Women...Well, Daniel, looks like you'll be fixing breakfast tomorrow if Tom's up to it."

"Don't go to all this trouble over me, please. I don't wish to impose on Tom and—"

"Let's call him and find out if he's available. C'mon." Conrad rose and headed toward the foyer. "Ladies, we'll join you in the dining room in a minute."

Daniel sheepishly followed Conrad to the foyer.

"I'm sorry, Conrad, for causing such a stir with your family."

Conrad shook his head. "Don't worry. Elisabeth is a bit headstrong and I'm concerned that—"

"It's not good for her reputation to be seen with me."

"There's that, yes, but also that she could get herself, and you, into... unexpected trouble."

"You don't imagine that I would take advantage of her?"

"No, of course not. But she's another story. She's taken a serious liking to you, and I—"

"A liking?"

Conrad chuckled. "Come on, Daniel. She's clearly smitten. Haven't you noticed?"

"No, not really. She's fun to be with, and I like her a lot."

"That's great. But for both your sakes, make sure it doesn't go any further than that."

"What do you mean?"

"What if you're married and have a family, or a girlfriend—or even a fiancé?"

A dark shadow descended upon Daniel. "Somehow, I don't believe that's the case," he muttered. "Wouldn't they have come after me by now? Wouldn't they be looking for me?"

"Maybe they are. In any case, until we're certain, promise me you'll play it safe. Okay?"

Daniel nodded, but Conrad remained unconvinced.

Illuminated only by moonlight that seeped through a small window, the attic welcomed Sarah as she stepped in later that evening. It enveloped her in a cocoon of comfort and security among cherished memories and furnishings from times past. She sat in Conrad's great-grandmother's armchair and chose not to flick on the old floor lamp, enjoying the moon's luminescence. Sarah leaned forward in the chair.

"C'mon attic, it's time for you to help me. I'm sure you're well aware of what's going on. Who's playing this movie in my head?"

The attic responded with its familiar cricks and cracks.

Sarah shook her head. "No. That's not enough. You have to give me more."

But the attic only repeated the same response.

"The last time you helped me unravel a mystery it had to do with the history of this house and its twin. We're friends, you and I. So please, I need your help. Who's playing the movie? Why? Is this boy Danny our mystery man Daniel? Why 1976? What am I supposed to do?"

Squeak. Pop.

"I need more than that, please."

In a flash, Sarah found herself looking through the ocular lens of the scope of a rifle. The scope slowly scanned the woods. Somehow she felt and heard the breath of the person holding the rifle—a man. Her eyes were his eyes, her view his view.

A deer appeared through the rifle's scope. The search stopped. The deer moved left and the scope followed. The hunter tightened his grip on the rifle and increased the pressure on the trigger. As the hunter fired, the deer's head moved revealing a man behind it. Through the lens of the rifle, Sarah followed the bullet headed toward the man.

The face of Sheriff Billy Williams flashed before her.

Sarah blinked and the view through the scope vanished.

She was back in the attic. Her breathing was rapid, her lips trembled, and her cold hands were clasped tightly onto the arms of the chair.

"What was that?" she whispered, her face white with fear.

Silence.

"Attic, what in the world did you show me? Did Sheriff Williams murder someone?"

Silence.

"That's not the answer I need," she said, exasperated. She leaned her head back and within seconds the screen in her mind took over.

C H A P T E R   8

The door to Danny's bedroom burst open and his father stood in the door-way tapping his foot. "You missed my sermon, boy."

Danny struggled to open his eyes, but they refused to cooperate. "What?"

"Don't tell me your mother is still getting you ready for church on Sundays. You're old enough to do it on your own. How can you be asleep at this hour?"

"What hour?"

"Don't get smart with me, boy. It's almost noon. You embarrassed me by not being there. Everyone asked me if you were all right and I looked like a fool trying to come up with an answer." He walked to the bed and peered down at Danny. "What's wrong with you?"

Danny rubbed his eyes and propped himself up on his elbows only to collapse back onto his pillow. "Oh…my head…I'm sick to my stomach…"

Concerned, his father placed a hand on his forehead. "You don't have a fever."

Danny grunted.

"What did you eat at the picnic last night?"

"It's not what I ate, it's what I drank." Immediately Danny caught his mistake, popped his eyes open and blurted out, "It was…uh…some chocolate milk Robert had."

Clearly satisfied with his son's explanation, the minister patted his shoulder and turned to go. "In this heat milk goes bad fast. Tell Robert to be more careful. Make sure you drink plenty of liquids and get some rest. You'll be better soon enough."

"Okay."

Hugo stopped halfway out the door. "Can you take care of yourself? I've got to attend to some business."

Danny nodded, grunted, and squeezed his head between his hands.

"You sure?"

He took a deep breath in an attempt to keep his stomach under control. "Yeah, I'll be fine."

"I won't be back till after dinner. Is that all right with you?"

Danny closed his eyes and leaned his head back on the pillow. "Sure. I'm going to stay in bed and sleep."

"At least change into your pajamas. Your mother would be horrified to find you sleeping in yesterday's clothing. I'll call you later, if I can."

"No, Dad, don't call. If I'm asleep you'll wake me up. Don't worry about me."

"Fine. By the way your mom called earlier. There were a few complications with the birth. All are fine, but she's staying an extra week to help her sister with the baby."

"How was your sermon?"

"Fell on deaf ears as usual. I'll be back tonight." Without waiting for a response he shut the door behind him.

Danny closed his eyes and groaned.

Moments later Robert crawled in through the open window. "You sick?"

Danny rolled over and covered his head with the pillow.

"You missed church."

He muttered through the pillow, "Go away."

"Man, you do look pretty bad. Geez, you slept in your clothes."

Danny removed the pillow from his face. "Go away."

Ignoring his friend, Robert sat on the foot of the bed, causing it to bounce several times. "Guess what. I'm going to let my hair grow. Chicks like guys with long hair."

Groaning, Danny rolled over and glared at Robert. "Don't be stupid, that has nothing to do with it."

"How would you know? Virgin."

"Oh, grow up for God's sake."

"Speaking of virgins, where does virgin wool come from?"

"Go away."

"From the sheep the shepherds couldn't catch." Robert exploded with laughter.

Danny groaned.

"Hey, could it be true what they say about going blind and stuff if you do it to yourself? Some guy said it uses up all your sperm and then you can't do it at all."

"Go away."

Robert scooted closer to Danny causing the bed to bounce again. "Boy, Sue Ellen sure kisses good. You should've been there, man. I spent four weeks allowance on her at that kissing booth. Sure would like to let her have a little of my—" he proudly clutched his groin.

Danny squinted at him through bloodshot eyes. "You're sick."

"Why, 'cause I'm into chicks and doing it with them? You should've caught my dance with her. I rubbed against her a little bit and she let me. How about you and Ellie?"

"She's different. I respect her."

"Hell, I respect Sue Ellen. Otherwise why talk to her? You can't just screw girls, Danny—you've got to talk to them. Tell them you respect them and that they're the one. That's how you score. It's simple, man. You should try it with Ellie. Bet you it'll work."

"What will?"

"Tell her you love her and she's the one. Girls only want you to respect them if you're going to try to screw them. That's how they know they're hot."

Danny crawled out of the bed and glared down at Robert. "You are so full of crap. Maybe all that jerking-off is melting your brain. I bet you'll go blind in about two weeks. Now go away. I got to shower."

"I'll wait. How about we go down to the lake? All the chicks will be there and—"

"I can't. I've got stuff to do for my dad. Go."

Robert leaped to his feet and headed for the door. "Candy ass."

The image faded out as a new one faded in.

Danny marched up the steps to Alexander's cabin and knocked on the door.

"Alexander."

He knocked again.

"Alexander?"

Slowly, Danny opened the door and peeked in. The lights were on, but the cabin appeared deserted. A blank canvas rested on the easel. He stepped cautiously into the cabin.

"Hello?" Danny called out as footsteps approached behind him. He turned to find Alexander coming in.

"I've missed you," Alexander strolled past, patting him on the back. "You need to come more often."

"But I was here last night."

In one blur of continuous motion, Alexander tramped across the room, poured a couple of drinks, handed one to Danny, and put on a jazz record.

"I can't drink this stuff. It took me all day to recover," Danny protested with disgust.

"Suit yourself, but it'll be easier if you drink. It's always easier if you drink." He strolled over to the easel. "I'm going to paint you. I'm all set. Sit on that stool, sip your drink, and let the jazz entertain you. How about some weed?"

"You're going to paint *me*?"

"Is anyone else here?"

Alexander laughed as he guided Danny to the stool and sat him on it. He gave him a cigarette, took one for himself, lit them both, and ambled over to the easel.

"I don't smoke. How should I sit?"

"Doesn't matter. You can move. Relax and look in my general direction. I'm not going to copy you. This is about getting your essence."

Danny walked over to the table, put out the cigarette in the ashtray, and returned to the stool leaving the drink behind. "How's your book coming along?"

"What book?"

"You said—"

"There you go again, 'you said, you said!' Don't believe what—"

"Okay, okay. I'm not supposed to believe what you say, only what you do. Okay then, I *feel*"—Danny emphasized the word *feel* enough to make sure Alexander caught his drift—"like reading your book, the new one you're writing."

"Touché," Alexander laughed with abandon without missing a single brushstroke. "There's hope for you my friend…there's hope."

"Well? Can I read it?"

"No."

Danny studied Alexander, who concentrated on the canvas.

"Shit!" Alexander threw the paintbrush across the room. "Books don't mix with painting. I've lost it." He glared at Danny. "You talk too much."

The long silence was cut short by Alexander's forced laugh. "Don't worry. It comes and goes. It'll come back. If not we'll go hunt for it. C'mon, let's go for a swim." In long strides he rushed from the cabin and dashed off toward the lake.

Danny chased him through the woods and caught up as he finished undressing and dove into the lake. The boy quickly shed his own clothes and followed suit.

Alexander howled like a wolf the moment his head broke through the surface of the lake. "Owoo…Owoo…I'd give anything to experience what animals feel, wouldn't you? They're genuine. No corruption with animals. Pure, unadulterated instinct."

Undulating his body, Alexander dove in and out in rapid succession. "Did I look like a giant dragon?"

Danny laughed. "No. You looked like a hairy snake. A giant hairy snake."

"Same thing."

"Not even close."

Alexander raced toward Danny, came to a halt right in front of him, and thrust his face menacingly forward staring into his eyes.

"Don't ever contradict me or hold me back," he said. "Promise."

"But—"

"Good. Fight for your beliefs. Even when you're scared shitless."

Alexander slithered beneath the water. A second later, he pulled Danny under. With that, the game was on. Laughing, they struggled back and forth, each trying to pull the other down. Younger, stronger, and by far the better swimmer, Danny resisted pressing his clear advantage. Before long, gasping for air and struggling to stay afloat, the older man signaled to stop. They shook hands, and floated belly up, catching their breath.

"Promise," Alexander insisted.

"I promise."

"What did you do today?"

"Recovered from last night and got rid of Robert."

"Robert?"

"He's my best friend…well, he was. You get me and he doesn't. You're my best friend now."

"And you're mine."

"Honest?"

"Honest."

Danny grinned and shook his fist in victory. "No one would ever believe that we're friends."

"You can't tell anyone about me."

"Okay, but why not?"

"I'm incognito. Tell me, how goes it in the love department?"

"Nowhere. I've been too sick with all that drinking we did last night. Anyway, Ellie would only turn me down again. I'm tired of it."

"Don't despair. Nothing worth having comes easily."

Danny glided toward Alexander who remained floating belly up. "Did you have as much trouble with women as I do?"

Alexander turned to Danny, a tender smile in his eyes. Floating belly up, he mussed the boy's hair.

"You and I are unusual—unique, one of a kind. We feel too much. We give ourselves completely to sensations and emotions. That means we have to work at life harder and longer."

As the words sank in, Danny beamed with pride and understanding.

"Keep that in mind, and force yourself to be brave with young Ellie. Don't let her intimidate you. Be her Prince Valiant."

"Wow…Prince Valiant…I like it."

"Any time Miss Ellie throws you a curve, picture yourself as Prince Valiant readying himself for battle and unwilling to step back. Forward, always forward. Simply dodge the sarcasm, the evasion, and all the uppity stuff. You're in control."

"Yeah, I can do that. It'll be easier to pretend to be a character instead of me."

"No, Danny boy, you *are* Prince Valiant."

"Yeah, but—"

"Sh. No buts. Never. Buts change direction and confuse the self. No buts."

Danny nodded. "No buts."

"Your Mrs. Foster on the other hand, she'd like to be *your* Prince Valiant."

They laughed.

"Tomorrow, my boy, you'll conquer your girl."

"I will."

Satisfied, they swam to shore.

The following morning Danny paced nervously up and down the street outside Ellie's home and mumbled to himself, "Prince Valiant. Always forward. Prince Valiant."

He took a deep breath, opened the gate, marched up the steps, and rang the bell. His heart pounded as he dried his sweaty palms on his pants and tried to calm himself.

Moments later Ellie opened the door, looking more beautiful than ever. "Hi, Danny. I saw you pacing up and down the street. Did you lose something?"

"Huh?" Taken aback, he quickly recovered. "No. Got lots on my mind, that's all. Came by to ask if you'd like to go to the fair they've set up by the pier. They have a Ferris wheel."

"Well, I—"

"Go check with your mom, I'll wait here."

Ellie smiled and nodded. "Okay, I'll be right back." She disappeared into the house.

Danny smiled with self-satisfaction and mumbled, "Prince Valiant… Prince Valiant."

Moments later Ellie returned. "She said it's okay. Let's go."

Stunned, Danny could only manage a weak, "That's great."

They strolled down the street in silence.

"Tell me about you," Danny finally said with aplomb.

"About me? Like what?"

"Stuff, I mean things about you. Where you were born, why you're here, what you like or don't like. Stuff like that, I guess."

"Why would you want to know that?"

Danny hesitated for a moment muttered, "Prince Valiant…"

"What? Did you say Prince Valiant?"

"Uh, yeah, I did…because I like reading about Prince Valiant. Do you?"

"Yeah, I guess."

"Well, there you go, that's something about me. I enjoy reading. I'd like to get to know you better. That's why I asked about you."

"Oh, I get it. That's nice."

Her smile melted Danny's heart, but he managed to keep his external demeanor in character—Prince Valiant was definitely in control. "Well?" he prompted after a long pause.

"Oh…uh, let's see, I was born in Chicago, then my folks inherited the Amaray house from an old aunt, and—"

"The lady that lived in your house was your aunt? How come I never saw you before?"

"We didn't visit her and she didn't visit us very often."

"Why move here then? You could've stayed in Chicago."

"My parents decided this was a better place for me to grow up."

"Tell me more."

"Not much more to tell, really. We moved here, and then my dad got a real good job at Whirlpool, quit his old job in Chicago, and here we are."

"You miss Chicago?"

"No. I like it here. I love the lake and the beach. It's easy to walk everywhere."

"There's the fair," Danny announced, pointing to a field outside town populated with tents, rides, and glittering signs. The breeze carried the din of music, laughter, and screams.

"Can we go on the Ferris wheel? Imagine how beautiful the view is up there."

"Let's do it then." Without hesitation, he took her hand and off they ran toward the fair and its tantalizing Ferris wheel.

Prince Valiant had won the day.

"Nothing. Not one single clue." Sarah protested. "Why spoon-feed me the information? Who is the puppeteer in this charade?"

"Hey, calm down. Seems to me the movie's picking up pace." Conrad's demeanor appeared relaxed, but Sarah could sense his apprehension.

They strolled hand in hand near their home, enjoying the early signs of spring. Their house sat at the end of a valley that may have been used for pasture or cropland at one time. It now offered a flowering meadow encircled by lush woodlands with panoramic views of the towering Cascades.

"Maybe the attic did answer your plea."

"Not likely. I haven't learned anything so far that would help me solve Daniel's mystery. And what about that glimpse through the scope of the hunting rifle? What's that all about? That entire episode wasn't part of the movie at all."

"Could it be that you're worried about Williams?"

"It's possible…my subconscious playing with my mind…a metaphor?"

"Metaphor…interesting. Okay, let's have it."

"Well, perhaps I'm the deer and you're the man who steps into view when Williams shoots us. I'm attracting his wrath toward our family and you end up injured."

"Did the man who comes into view behind the deer look anything like me?"

"No, not at all. He was burly and on the heavy side. Even though he wore a cap, it looked like he was balding. Completely different from you."

Conrad smiled. "Well, Madame Freud, then it's not a metaphor."

"How come?"

"It's a psychic vision, not a projection of your subconscious. You're quite clear about the looks of the injured man."

"But—"

"Listen to me. Stop thinking about Williams shooting us. First of all, it's not feasible, and furthermore it's not healthy. It'll drive you crazy. And that's not helpful," he said emphatically.

"Then what does it mean?"

"I have no idea and neither do you. Maybe it's a clue about Williams, or maybe it has nothing to do with him. Perhaps it'll become clear in the movie later on. The scenes are gaining momentum and you're learning more and more."

"But nothing helpful yet. Daniel—our Daniel, is in the dark as to who he is, and I can't do a thing to help him out."

Conrad put his arm around his wife. "We've made great progress. We've learned that Daniel can find his way around a kitchen, he speaks pretty good French, he's well read, and from the words he uses to express himself, I'd say he's well educated."

"Hmm…"

"Admit it, Sarah; that's significant."

"Maybe, but it's not enough."

"Stop being so hard on yourself. What's the rush, anyway? For crying out loud, the man's injuries have barely healed."

Sarah stopped walking and smiled at him. "Okay, no rush. You're right." She pulled him to her and kissed him.

He responded immediately, and as he kissed her, he opened her coat and slid his hands inside, encircling her waist, bringing her body closer to his. His hands slid up and caressed her breasts. "Let's go home," he said softly. "I need for us to be with one another, to enjoy ourselves, and forget everything else. Let's make love all day long and set this mystery aside for a while."

C H A P T E R   9

THE MARQUEE OF the Amaray Theater proclaimed the title *A RETROSPECTIVE - JAMES STEWART in ANATOMY OF A MURDER*.

Doing their best to be inconspicuous, Danny and Ellie emerged from the theater and glanced around before rushing down the street. A block later, breathless and excited, they crossed the street and slowed to a walk. After turning the corner, they stopped and glanced back toward the theater. Satisfied that no one had spotted them, they held hands and strolled cheerfully down the street.

"Now I get why my mom wouldn't let me watch it," Ellie said. "She'd be horrified if she knew."

"My dad would sit me down and give me an endless sermon on the evils of loose women and their lack of morals. Then he'd instruct me on how weak I am for coming to a movie like that, and probably close with a speech about how the gates of hell await me because I am responsible for corrupting your innocent mind."

"That's not fair, I'm the one that talked you into coming."

"You didn't need to do much. I wanted to see it too."

"The husband should've been convicted."

"What's interesting about it is that you really don't find out if he actually went crazy or if he knew exactly what he was doing when he killed the guy."

"I can't blame him for going nuts. She was awful, taunting her husband like that and flirting with all the other men."

"You can't be serious. I mean, she was bad, but he didn't have to go and kill the guy."

"I'm very serious. The whole thing was her fault. No matter how you look at it. She's a tart."

86

Attempting his best southern accent, Danny pretended to be shocked. "Miss Ellie, I do declare—what kind of language is that for a lady?"

"Well, sir…" she retorted in her own version of a southern accent, "it's nothing but the truth, sir."

Danny pulled her to him and kissed her, his arms locked around her waist. She closed her eyes, wrapped her arms around his neck, and surrendered to the kiss and the embrace.

"Your kisses are like honey," he whispered into her lips.

"Mm…yours are like chocolate ice cream."

He took her face in his hands and peered into her eyes. "I get how her husband could go crazy with jealousy. I couldn't bear it if you kissed another guy."

"No danger of that, is there?"

"I love you."

"And I love you," she answered softly.

They kissed again, then, hand in hand, resumed their way down the street.

"What a fool I was to be so afraid to talk to you."

"How could you be afraid of me?"

"It's that you're so perfect, and popular, and a year older, and you like books about girls in love with older men, and—"

"Stop, you're making my head spin. All that matters is that you got up the courage to ask me to the fair and then to kiss me…it was magical." She leaned her head against his shoulder.

He chuckled at the memory of the moment. "I can't believe I had the nerve."

"Luck helped. Being stuck at the top when the Ferris wheel broke down didn't hurt."

"It's the way you talk. You bewitched me."

She giggled. "And then you kissed me."

"I couldn't stop myself. The way your hair blew in the wind and glistened in the sun. The way your eyes sparkled and looked as blue as the sky, you were irresistible."

"For being a *whole year* younger than me, you have a flair for words." With a coquettish giggle she pulled him close and kissed him. "That reeled me in."

"It's all because you're *so* much older and experienced that you knew you shouldn't push me away. That was the key."

"The key is that you're a good kisser."

"You taught me."

"Nah…We learned together."

"What am I going to do without you for a week when you go visit your granny?"

"Oh, you'll manage. You'll go to that secret place you go to and be with your secret friend and forget all about me."

"Never," he whispered earnestly.

They kissed one more time.

The image faded to black.

Sarah kneaded the dough for some baguettes while a couple of pie shells cooled off on a rack. "Alright, puppeteer—whoever you are—we'll do it your way. I suppose that writing a movie is similar to baking; you patiently add one ingredient at a time until it all comes together in one stunning masterpiece. But I wish you'd hurry up so we can help Daniel."

"Talking to yourself?" Conrad kissed his wife on the neck and wrapped his hands around her waist. "Mrs. Thompson, this kitchen smells delicious."

Sarah turned and kissed her husband, gently nibbling on his lips. "But the taste of one of your kisses is much, much better."

"I'll buy that. Mm…I taste cherries."

"Cherry pie."

"Oho, I love it."

Sarah placed the dough in the fridge, covered it, and rinsed her hands.

Conrad handed her a towel. "How come you're baking all by yourself? Where's your sidekick?"

"She's taking Daniel to his appointment with Doc."

"Those two are up to no good."

"They'll be careful. I'm sure. What are you doing here at this time of the day?"

"I forgot the checkbook and was going to run in, grab it, and get back to the store. But now that I'm here, I've got a better idea." He took her hand and pulled her up the stairs to their bedroom.

"I don't like the idea of sneaking behind Conrad's back," Daniel told Elisabeth.

"We're not sneaking. He's okay with me taking you to your appointment with Doc." Elisabeth smiled at Daniel before returning her attention to the road. They were in her car headed north on a two-lane road.

"Yeah, but that's two hours from now," Daniel said pointedly.

"Listen, it's a beautiful early spring morning, the sun is shining, all the black ice is gone, the roads are safe, and it's a perfect time for the two of us to do a little exploring."

"I should've told him what we were planning to do."

"You were in the dark about what I planned to do."

"Then you should've told him."

"Okay, next time, I will. But imagine how surprised everyone will be if you do end up remembering something."

Daniel sighed and gazed out the window.

"Why so blue?" Elisabeth asked after a long pause.

Without turning to her, Daniel answered. "What if I never recover my past? It's been so long since the accident and I still have no idea who I am."

"You took a severe beating. You're lucky to be alive."

Daniel sighed, turned to her, and smiled. "You're such an optimist. What would I have done without you and the Thompsons?"

"I learned the hard way to look for the best in life. No point in doing otherwise. And that's what we all wish for you. So c'mon, cheer up." She peered intently up the road. "We're almost there. Anything look familiar?"

Daniel didn't react.

"Okay. We'll keep trying. Hey, what do you say we invite Doc to have dinner with us next weekend and you fix the meal?"

"That's a tall order. What do you propose?"

"He likes Italian. Can you make *osso buco*? He loves that. I made it for him once, but it didn't turn out that well. Maybe Sarah's mom's cookbook has a good recipe."

"I can give it a try if Doc would like to come all that way for dinner. Winthrop is more than an hour from Okanogan."

"I'm aware of that. I drove it every day."

"I forgot. Of course you did."

"Believe me, it's really not that bad, and the roads are good now. Besides, it's a beautiful drive in the spring with all the wildflowers in bloom. Anyway, he can stay at my house overnight. He used to do it all the time when Anthony got sick and we couldn't go to him."

"What was wrong with him?"

"MS."

Daniel looked puzzled.

"Multiple Sclerosis. His body gave up on him and his immune system slowly died. Ultimately his brain stopped communicating with his body. It was a long, mean illness that took away the person he'd once been."

"I'm sorry. It must've been so difficult for you."

"Difficult for everyone, really. Doc was wonderful, though. Always supportive, always encouraging, always there for us. When we could no longer drive north, he'd drive down to our house. He loved to visit Anthony and stuck by him till the end. We all became good friends."

"Tell me about Anthony. Were you happy?"

"Yes, a good man and a good marriage. No fireworks, but a nice, comfortable life."

"You wanted fireworks?"

A melancholic smile crossed her lips. "I had fireworks once with someone else."

"What happened?"

"He dumped me."

"How could anyone dump you?"

Elisabeth's eyes watered. "That's very sweet. Thanks, Daniel."

She stretched her hand out to him. Hesitantly, he reached over and took it. They both knew they shouldn't, but for that brief moment, they allowed the sensation of their mutual attraction to express itself. Then, with a shy smile, Elisabeth slid her hand away and returned her full attention to the road.

"I believe we're almost there. From what Sarah said it's right around the next curve—we can see if anything looks familiar."

"Okay. Let's give it a try."

"That's the spirit," she said cheerfully. She slowly pulled off the road and rolled to a stop.

They left the car and walked along the side of the road in silence. After half a mile, Elisabeth finally spoke.

"Anything?"

Dejected, Daniel shook his head. "Nothing. I'm sorry."

She slid her hand into his. "Don't worry, it'll come back. I'm sure of it."

He turned toward her, and without hesitation, drew her to him and kissed her. And then, just as abruptly, he pushed her away. "I'm sorry Elisabeth, I shouldn't have done that. I don't know what came over me. You looked so earnest, and you're so beautiful…"

Softly she placed her fingers on his lips. "It's all right. Please, don't worry."

He turned away and bowed his head in shame. "No, it's not all right. This is exactly what Conrad worries about, what he cautioned me about. I've let him down. I let myself down."

"What are you talking about?"

He turned to face her. "Elisabeth, what if I'm married? What if I have a family that's looking for me? What if I'm not free?"

"Yes, I've worried about that. Is that what has Conrad so worked up?"

"He's concerned we're going to do something we'll regret."

"Ah…I get it now."

"He's right, of course."

"Yes, he is."

They made their way back to the car in silence. When Daniel opened the door for Elisabeth, she looked at him and smiled, her eyes filled with affection. He nodded, closed the car door, made his way to the passenger side, and got in.

Elisabeth turned the car around and merged onto the two-lane road. They drove in silence for several minutes until she found the courage to speak.

"Do you have a sense of being in love with someone? Of having a wife and a family?"

"No, the opposite. I'm utterly alone. But—"

"What?"

"I do have the sense that I've been looking for someone…for someone I loved and lost."

"You haven't forgotten that? Doc said in time that notion would fade."

"Well, it hasn't."

"You still believe Sarah is the one?"

"I'm convinced she's the one who will help me. Yes."

"How's she doing so far?"

Daniel shook his head. "She's pulled away from me."

"She has been a bit distant lately, hasn't she?"

"It's like she's afraid."

"Yeah," Elisabeth sighed. "We're all afraid."

C H A P T E R   1 0

THE IMAGE FADED in to reveal a pastel-colored living room right out of a 1970s issue of *Better Homes and Gardens*. The plush white carpet was covered in tiny divots left behind by Mrs. Foster's high heels as she paced up and down.

She sported a very tight yellow dress with a zipper down the entire front. She nervously zipped it up and down, revealing glimpses of her shapely bosom each time.

The doorbell rang and she stopped pacing. With a wide smile she walked to the foyer, glanced at her reflection in the mirror, fluffed her hair, and opened the door.

Danny's smile greeted her. "I made it. Got wet, though. Started to pour down as I left."

She grabbed his hand and pulled him in, slamming the door. "I'm so glad you could come on this rainy morning. But look at you. You're drenched."

"I'm okay, don't worry."

"Take off your shoes and socks."

"Oh, yeah they're soaked. Shouldn't mess up your house."

Danny plopped down on the floor and removed his shoes and socks, pushing them to one side of the door. When he stood, his wet clothes clung to his body and water puddled on the tiles.

"Come on, let's get you out of those wet clothes."

"I'm okay, really."

"Nonsense." She took his hand and dragged him up the stairs.

"I'm sorry about my dad."

"What do you mean?"

"Well, that he wasn't there to take your call and come help. He'll be back this afternoon, unless Mrs. West is too distraught. Sometimes widows, or their kids, need his company till they sort things out."

"Oh. That's nice. But I'm glad you could come."

Once upstairs, she ushered him into her bedroom—also decorated in pastels, with the same luxuriant white carpet. The king-size bed was wrapped in a quilted silk bedspread and covered with sumptuous cushions. A huge armoire nearly covered one wall.

"Do you like it?"

Confused by her question, he glanced about. "You mean your bedroom?"

She nodded with pride.

"Uh…it's nice. So what can I do for you, Mrs. Foster?"

"The first thing you can do is get out of those wet clothes. I'll bring you some towels."

"No really, I'm okay."

"But I'm not. I won't have wet clothes in my house. Do as I say." She pushed him in the direction of the bathroom.

Danny remained motionless, unsure whether he should obey or not.

"Okay," she said, "have it your way."

She trotted off to the bathroom and returned with several plush rose-colored towels. "Take off those clothes this instant, young man."

Danny hesitated for a moment before he finally grabbed a towel with one hand, and struggled to remove his wet pants and shirt with the other. He wrapped the towel around his waist over his underwear.

Mrs. Foster eyed him, amused.

Once his wet clothes were off, he carefully placed them on the back of a nearby chair.

Mrs. Foster reached for another towel and placed it over Danny's head and shoulders. Without hesitation she dried his hair, then brought the towel down rubbing his back and chest. When she reached his waist, she unceremoniously pulled his underwear down to his ankles.

"Oh, no." He stepped back in alarm.

"Oh, yes." She yanked him forward. "Step out."

He wriggled his feet out of his underpants.

Without missing a beat she continued patting him dry. "You're delicious," she said softly.

Alarmed by this unexpected turn of events, Danny froze and held his breath.

She dropped the towel used to dry his hair and chest, and then slid her left arm around his waist. With her right hand, she caressed his cheek.

Danny attempted to step back but she held fast.

"What's the matter?"

"I—"

"Don't worry, you're not to do a thing. I'll do everything. Let me teach you."

"Teach me? What?"

"Hush."

Wrapping both arms around his waist she tightened her embrace and kissed him. As her lips shifted, her tongue searched deep for his.

Danny remained petrified, eyes wide with apprehension. "Mrs. Foster, I…I'm only fifteen…you're married…and I…this is…a sin and—"

She placed a finger upon his lips. "Shush."

The image went black. A moment later it revealed Alexander's cabin.

With only a small lamp to illuminate the cabin, Alexander stood at the easel and painted Danny's portrait while he listened to Ella Fitzgerald sing *Someone to Watch Over Me* and hummed along.

The door to the cabin burst open and Danny stormed through it, startling Alexander.

"I did it! I did it!" the boy yelled, attempting to catch his breath.

"What? What?"

"Mrs. Foster," he said, beaming with satisfaction.

Alexander dropped his brush and palate and grabbed Danny by the shoulders. He started to jump up and down holding Danny at arm's length.

"Good old Mrs. Foster. Was I right or was I right?"

"She's incredible. We did it three times this afternoon!"

"Three times! Man…what a first. This calls for a celebration. Hell, it *screams* for a celebration." He rushed to the table, grabbed his keys and tossed them to Danny. "Drive us to the store. This deserves champagne."

"I can't drive."

"Why not?"

"I'm only fifteen."

"That didn't stop you from banging a married woman. C'mon."

Alexander threw his arm around Danny's neck and wrestled him out the door and toward the Jeep. He pushed Danny into the driver's seat, raced around the car and jumped in.

"Let's haul ass."

"But—"

"Put the key in the ignition, start the damn car, turn on the headlights, and push on the accelerator. How hard can that be? Do it."

Danny did as he was told, and the Jeep lurched forward as he released the clutch. He clenched the steering wheel for dear life as he hesitantly pressed on the accelerator with his right foot and the brake with his left.

A few feet later, the vehicle stalled.

Alexander sighed and shook his head. "Did I tell you to step on the brake?"

"No," Danny managed to say through his embarrassment.

"Then stop doing it. If you need to stop, take your right foot off the accelerator and then press on the brake with that same right foot. Use your left foot only to operate the clutch. Got it? There's nothing to it."

Danny swallowed hard and nodded. "Okay, I'll try again."

"Put the gear shift in neutral."

Danny obeyed. "Now what?"

"Pump the accelerator a couple of times, and then start the ignition."

Danni followed orders and the engine revved up.

"Okay, press the clutch, and then shift into first."

The gears began to grind savagely as Danny wrestled with the shift. Amused, Alexander smiled to himself and shook his head. The grinding stopped as the gears engaged.

"Ease off the clutch and press the gas pedal slowly."

The car lurched forward several times until it finally rolled smoothly onto the dirt road.

"I've never driven before. This is fun."

Alexander howled with delight. "You never screwed before either, and that's even more fun."

The two laughed in unison. Moments later the Jeep chugged to an abrupt stop as the engine died again.

Alexander's laugh echoed through the forest as the scene faded out.

The image returned to reveal the Jeep, no longer lurching, as it cautiously advanced down a dirt road through the woods surrounding the lake.

It meandered into a clearing, then pulled onto a small beach facing a formidable waterfall that plunged into the lake.

Overcome with enthusiasm at the sight of the place, Alexander leaped from the car before it came to a full stop and raced to the edge of the water. "This is awesome."

Danny shut off the headlights and the engine, climbed out of the Jeep, grabbed a grocery bag, and joined Alexander at the water's edge.

"Exhilarating. There's a special…smell and taste in raw nature." Alexander spoke softly as he ripped off his clothes. "Isn't it grand how much light the moon and the stars produce when unencumbered by civilization? It's divine." He plunged in, and swam toward the waterfall.

Danny set down the grocery bag and quickly followed suit. They dove repeatedly under the waterfall and laughed as the powerful currents tossed them about.

After a while, Alexander swam to shore to catch his breath while Danny, the expert swimmer, put on a dazzling display of his abilities.

Having finally recovered, Alexander removed the champagne from the grocery bag, popped it open, grabbed a couple of cigars and lit them. With bottle and cigars held high above the water, he waded, not without some difficulty, to a large rock that protruded from the lake. He placed the bottle in a secure spot and hopped onto the water-worn surface.

As soon as the boy joined him on the rock, Alexander proffered a cigar to Danny, who, after a single puff, began to cough ferociously.

Alexander laughed and patted him on the back as he struggled to recover. "To you, my friend." He took a swig of champagne and handed the bottle to Danny. "You've been blessed. Not everyone loses his virginity to such a loving woman. Cherish her memory."

"You bet I will. Forever." Danny toasted to the heavens and took a sip.

Under the moonlight, the two naked men sat on the rock smoking, drinking, and taking in the beauty of their surroundings. Two kindred spirits separated only by experience and time.

Danny glanced at Alexander and caught him wiping a tear from his cheek. "What's wrong? Why are you crying?"

"For love. You should try it sometime." Alexander forced a smile. "This place has me all shook up. Raw nature like this gets into your soul, permeates your senses and grabs a hold of what really matters within you."

"Wow."

"Sorry, chap."

"Sorry? For what?"

"I don't like to get so emotional, it breaks open too many scars. But now you've witnessed that I'm a sentimental fool."

"You're a romantic. That's why you could write it so well in your book. That's why Wesley—"

"Stop." Alexander shook his head. "Let's not go there. Let's stay in the here and now with you and your awakening to love and manhood."

Danny smiled. "Okay. But how about you? How did you lose your virginity? I bet it was something special, like me."

After a sarcastic grunt, Alexander glared into the foaming water beneath the waterfall and remained silent. At length he sighed heavily and turned to Danny with a grimace of disgust chiseled across his face. "A whore stole it from me." His eyes wandered up the waterfall. After another long sigh he looked at Danny and smiled. "And I can never get it back."

"How could you get it back? Once it's gone, it's gone forever." Danny sipped more champagne and puffed on his cigar. It was clear that he disliked the taste, but understanding that it was a rite of passage, he forced himself to puff on it nonetheless.

"Not if you don't let it. It's all about the purity of love."

"Have you ever been in love?"

A sad grin formed on his lips. "Once."

"What happened?"

"Nothing."

"What do you mean?"

"I let it go. I let it slip through my fingers. Gone, vanished, nothing to talk about."

"I don't get it."

"You will. Someday."

Danny sighed and stared into the waterfall. "How come she chose me?"

"For the same reason I chose you. You have what we covet."

Danny stared at him inquisitively.

Alexander gently placed his hand on Danny's head. "Innocence."

"I don't get it, Alexander. You've gotten all philosophical on me and I don't understand what you're saying."

Alexander smiled and mussed Danny's hair. "Fair enough. It's quite simple. We're all corrupt. We're like vultures, every one of us. Your Mrs. Foster, your father, your mom, the grocer, the mailman…me."

Danny shook his head. "That's not true."

"Oh, but it is. Why do you suppose it's so easy with Mrs. Foster and so hard with Ellie?"

"Well, because…Ellie is…she's…well, she's—"

"She's like you, the proud owner of her irrepressible innocence."

"Wait a minute, I'm no longer like her. I lost my innocence this afternoon."

Alexander guffawed and slapped Danny on the back.

"Not quite, my friend, you've lent it out. Put it momentarily aside."

"No, no, no. It's completely gone. Believe me, it's gone. Zip…history. Disappeared for good. It's—" He stopped as an unpleasant thought crept into his mind. "Oh, God, what will I do about Ellie now? What will she think of me? Oh, God!"

Danny put his face in his hands and shook his head.

Alexander placed a hand on his shoulder.

"Listen, my friend, as long as you believe that what you're doing is honest, as long as you love your Mrs. Foster for what she is, as long as you accept life as it is, without question, without premeditation, without malice…your innocence is still yours…very much yours, and Ellie will never notice the difference. So enjoy the moment."

In one fluid motion, Alexander jumped to his feet and threw himself into the churning waters and disappeared. He emerged on the backside of the waterfall and moved beneath the plunging water and let it pour down his face.

Danny jumped in and swam toward him, but stayed away from the fall.

Moments later, Alexander joined him. "Don't let yourself worry about this, Danny. All is well. It's a part of life. And yours has barely left the starting gate. So let yourself go and just be."

The boy nodded and said, "You inspire me to think. I like that. I wish you could stay here forever."

"I will, in a manner of speaking. Memories never die…unless you let them."

"How did you guess Mrs. Foster was going to…well…"

"Seduce you? Possess you? Have you? Fuck you?"

"Yeah."

"Say it."

"What for? You've already said it."

"Because you have to own it."

Exasperated, he yelled, "Okay, love me. How did you know she was going to love me?"

Alexander smiled. "Your Mrs. Foster and I are very much alike, my friend."

"Bull."

Alexander stared at Danny for a moment, then swam back to the rock and climbed out. Danny followed, but stayed in the water.

Alexander picked up the bottle and downed several gulps, smacked his lips and stared out at his young friend. "Why do you suppose I'm here, in this godforsaken little town?"

"To finish your novel. And for your information God has not forsaken my *little* town. Look at how much this place has affected you."

"Touché, Master Danny, you got me there. Okay, the fact is that I'm here looking for…well…I'm in search of…" Alexander ran his fingers through his hair as if trying to shake loose some long-lost memory. "The whore that stole my—" he looked at Danny and shook his head. "Never mind that." After a deep sigh, he went on. "For me, life has become…premeditated, fake, a series of repetitive clichés always leading back to the same place. But you, you take life as it comes. To you the colors are real, the people are good, and you have no clichés." He looked up at the sky shaking his fist and bellowed. "Damn you! Give me back my innocence! Give me the world that Danny sees!"

Alexander waited silently for an answer from the heavens, but none was offered. Shaking his head sadly, he leaned back on the rock and gulped down more champagne.

"There you have it, Danny boy—innocence is not to be mine. But damn, do I yearn for it. So does she. That's why she chose you. That's why I chose you. We thirst for what you have. Although, after today colors and people will change for you. I'm afraid you may have started the long journey toward corruption, my friend."

Danny clambered onto the rock and sat next to Alexander.

"C'mon, be cool. I've had the best experience of my life. First you tell me how great I am, and now you tell me I messed up? Which is it?"

Alexander roared with laughter and lovingly squeezed Danny's neck shaking him vigorously. "I'll shut up."

"No, tell me the truth."

"The truth. Ah, that's hard to do…impossible, I'd say. Who can even tell what truth is?"

"What do you mean? The truth is simple and clear, uncomplicated. My dad says it's the lies that complicate life, make a mess of it."

"Your dad. Well, he'd be all over that, wouldn't he? After all, he's in direct contact with God, right?"

"Not sure about direct contact, but he reads the bible and interprets it."

"Aha. There you have it, my boy, *interpret*. How do we know that he's interpreting the truth of what it means? Isn't it his—by that I mean your father's—opinion? His view? His truth? What if he messes up the truth to serve his own corruption? What if—"

"Oh no, my dad could never do that."

"Well, then you should talk to him about your Mrs. Foster and ask him for the truth you seek."

"Are you kidding? I can't do that. He'd be horrified if he knew what's happened."

Alexander looked him in the eye and nodded. "There you have it. No room for truth."

Sarah jerked back as if slapped. Blinking repeatedly, she glanced around. She sat in a corner of the public library in front of a computer monitor. A large atlas rested on her lap and several maps were strewn about the desk.

"This is not right," she muttered.

"What did you say?" The question came from an older gentleman sitting across the desk.

"I'm sorry. I was talking to myself," she said, embarrassed.

"Not to worry. I do that often, honey."

Sarah smiled. "Did you happen to notice how long I've been here? I got so immersed in my research I lost track of time."

"I'd say half an hour or so. The librarian"—he nodded toward a woman behind the counter—"came to ask you something a few minutes ago and you didn't even notice her. She's a bit worried about you. She's called someone to come by and check on you."

"Oh dear. Thanks. I'll go talk to her." Sarah closed the atlas and placed it on the table. She logged off the computer, collected her belongings, and went to the counter.

"Hi, I'm sorry to have worried you. I'm okay. I was focused on my research."

"Glad to hear, Mrs. Thompson. Since you were asking about Sheriff Williams, I took the liberty of calling Billy to ask if he could come by and check on you."

Shit.

"Thanks. But I'm perfectly okay. If you don't mind, please call him back and tell him that there's nothing to worry about. Bye."

"Good-bye. I'll give him a jingle, but he may already be on his way."

Crap.

Sarah hurried out of the library and rushed to her car. As she approached it, she spotted Williams. He'd parked near her car and was making his way toward her.

Damn, damn, damn.

"Hello, Mrs. Thompson. Rushing off to rescue someone?" He asked with a sarcastic lilt.

"Sheriff, what brings you here?"

"Checking on you. They tell me you had an *episode* in there."

"Oh, no, no, no. No episode. I was very focused on what I was doing and didn't hear the librarian. That's all. Sorry you were bothered. Thanks for coming, though. Good-bye."

"Leaving already?"

"Yes."

"Where are you going in such a rush?"

"I don't mean to be disrespectful, but where I'm headed is certainly none of your concern." She walked around him and made her way to her car.

Williams followed. "What's with the attitude? And why the big hurry?" he asked.

"I have something to do."

"It is said that your husband comes from a long line of women who were into some weird hocus-pocus. Are you a witch, too?"

Sarah froze and all color drained from her face.

Williams remained slightly behind her—a satisfied smirk on his face.

"I'm not sure what you mean, Sheriff," she finally managed to say.

"Sure you are. Bet that's what led you to our crazy mystery guy to begin with."

Sarah turned to face Williams, eyes narrowed. "First of all, Daniel's not crazy, and second of all, I'm not a witch. What's the matter with you, anyway? Why are you so—"

"Whoa there missy, this isn't about me. This is about you. And let me tell you something else," he said, pointing his finger at her. "I don't like you asking questions about me, and certainly not about my father. Do I make myself clear?"

Despite the man's menacing stance, Sarah stood her ground and stared into his eyes. "Then stop harassing me, or I'll get to the bottom of what actually happened the day your father died. Do I make *myself* clear?

Williams's face turned ashen. "I don't like threats, especially coming from witches."

"Okay by me since I'm not a witch, but if I come across any, I'll be sure to warn them." Sarah stomped off to her car.

"I'm not finished," he called after her.

She spun back toward Williams with an icy glare. "But I am. Good day to you, sir."

She got into her car, slammed the door, started the ignition, and sped off.

Williams frowned as she drove away, his jaw clenched in anger.

CHAPTER 11

SUN BLAZED THROUGH the window when a startled Danny woke to find his mother sitting at the edge of his bed, with a look of deep concern.

"Good afternoon sleepyhead. Are you feeling all right?" She placed her hand on Danny's forehead. "No fever."

"Mom!" Danny yanked the blankets up to his chin. "What are you doing here?"

"What's the matter with you? I live here."

"I mean you're not supposed to be back yet. Are you?"

"Danny, what on earth's going on? It's past one o'clock and you're still in bed."

Avoiding her gaze, he muttered, "I've been staying up late…reading."

Shirley scooted closer to him with a smile and gently combed his hair with her fingers. "You and your books."

Visibly uncomfortable, the boy slid out of the bed completely forgetting he was naked.

"Danny, where are your pajamas?" his mother said.

Danny jumped back into bed and slid under the covers, muttering, "Oh God. I'm sorry."

His mother stared at him in bewilderment. "What is going on?"

"I…well…I was hot…that's it…I was hot so I took them off, and…well… I fell asleep, and, uh…I forgot I didn't have them on…so—"

"Something is going on here. What is it?"

Danny feigned a scolded puppy look. "Nothing, Mom. Honest. You caught me by surprise, that's all. I was hot. I was alone. No harm done." He reached over and took her hand. "Dad would say it's indecent to sleep without pajamas and all of that, but with the heat I plain forgot and fell asleep. Please…don't worry about me. I'm fine."

Satisfied, she smiled. "I guess you're right. I'm a little on edge. I got here real early, and your father had already made his bed and left."

"Really? I didn't hear him at all."

"The strange thing is that I can't find him. He's not at his office or the church, so I've been waiting for you to wake up and tell me where he is."

"I have no idea. But Dad's been real busy. I haven't had dinner with him since you left, or breakfast, or lunch either. Come to think of it, I haven't seen him at all except for the evening of the picnic and the next morning. Hey, would you believe that he went to the picnic with me? After all the years you've been asking him to go with us."

"Yes, he told me when I called to tell him I'd be staying longer. He said you both had a grand time."

"Really? He said I had a good time?"

"Yes, of course. Didn't you?"

"Did he tell you I danced?"

"No, he didn't mention that. Did you?"

"Well, I did. I liked it."

"With Ellie?"

"Yeah, we've been going out."

"Ah, so that's what's going on."

Danny blushed and nodded shyly.

"So, you were with Ellie last night?"

"No. She's out of town visiting her grandmother. I was reading, like I told you."

"So when did your father come in?"

"I didn't hear him at all. He's been gone by the time I wake up and… well…at night he's real quiet I guess. They should tell you where he is at the church office."

"He didn't tell them. I've left a dozen messages for him to call all this past week and he never called back. Now no one can tell me where he is today."

"Yesterday he had to go over to console the Wests."

"Andrew finally passed away?"

Danny nodded. "Dad left a little note telling me he'd be gone and if anyone called to tell them that he had to attend to the widow and her kids. It rained all morning, and then it got real muggy. Mrs. Foster called..." he stopped in the middle of the sentence, his face turning beet red. "So...well...I told her Dad was gone."

"Allyson Foster? What did she want?"

"No clue. She called for Dad...didn't say what about."

"That's odd."

"Is it? Why?"

"She's not in the congregation."

"Maybe she'd like to be."

"That's possible. Anyway, don't worry darling." She leaned down, kissed Danny on the forehead and headed for the door. "How about if you get showered and dressed and go to the store for me? I'd like to wait here in case your father calls or comes home." She left, closing the door behind her.

"Sarah, how could you?" Conrad's eyes burned with anger and with something even more alarming—betrayal.

Her heart ached from being the cause of his pain. "I'm sorry," she said.

Conrad paced up and down the living room. "Sorry is not enough. How am I supposed to protect you if you go off and act so irresponsibly?"

"Conrad, I couldn't stay put and do nothing."

"Then do research on your own, but don't go around town asking folks about Williams and his father. How could you? You must have known he'd hear about it. For crying out loud, Sarah, he's a cop."

"Right, he's a cop who's more worried about badmouthing me than solving the attack on Daniel. I find that troublesome."

"So your answer is to investigate him?"

"I went to the library to search for the lake in an old atlas. I was trying to help."

"I'm not asking about what you did today."

"I also searched for a photo of Sheriff Williams's father."

"Whatever for?"

"I had a hunch—I needed to find out if he's the man I saw through the rifle scope."

"And?"

"He is…well, he was."

"And?"

"And that means the image the attic showed me is not related to the movie in my head."

"And?"

"That's all. The movie and all its troubles are separate from the hunting incident."

Exasperated, Conrad threw up his arms.

"Do you realize you've probably angered him even more? Didn't you consider the risk of *him* going after you?"

"No, the opposite. I thought if I had something on him, he'd leave us alone."

Conrad dropped onto the sofa shaking his head. Sarah joined him, but didn't reach out.

"I can't bear the look in your eyes," she murmured. "I was sure you'd be proud of me. Don't you realize I confirmed that the hunting incident is about Williams?"

"I do, but you put yourself in harm's way when I specifically asked you not to."

"I never imagined you'd feel betrayed. I overcame my fear and confirmed a psychic vision. That's what you've always encouraged me to do. How's that a betrayal?"

"If you don't understand, I can't explain it."

"I'm sorry I upset you," she said softly. "I'm frustrated doing nothing. Plus the seduction of the boy by this woman…I had to do something."

"I can accept you being tied up in knots with the story, but to threaten Williams is simply not acceptable. You know better, Sarah." He rose, crossed the room and climbed the stairs.

Sarah remained behind, tears streaking her cheeks.

Conrad's concern was understandable, but Sheriff Williams was nothing more than a bully, and she had come too far to let a bully force her back into submission.

She leaned back on the sofa, closed her eyes, and wept.

Without regard, the movie played on.

Danny pushed a small cart through the aisles of the grocery store, stopping to consult his shopping list. He reached for a box of Trix cereal from the top shelf and when he turned back he came face to face with Andrew Foster.

The boy froze.

"What's the matter, boy?"

Danny tried to speak, but only managed a doleful peep.

"You act like you've seen a ghost. They say I'm ugly, but I hope I'm not that bad."

"Mr. Foster," Danny managed to say. "I was—distracted. I wasn't expecting you…I mean, well you don't do the shopping real often, do you?

Mr. Foster laughed with his customary intensity and slapped the boy on the back. "Hell no! I'm looking for you."

Danny lost his grip and dropped the box of cereal into his shopping cart. He held on to the cart handle for dear life, his hands trembling. "I can explain. Well, I hope I can."

"Explain what boy? You sure you're all right? You look ashen."

Danny managed a smile. "I'm fine, sir."

"Anyhow, your mom told me you were here, so I stopped on my way—"

Danny closed his eyes and prayed.

"What are you mumbling about, boy?"

"A prayer. I pray a lot. Please, do go on." Danny broke into a cold sweat.

"A prayer? Is that what the kid of a minster does, pray in the middle of the grocery store? You're odd. Don't understand what my wife sees in you, but she's told me all about you and—"

"She's a wonderful lady, she really is. You shouldn't blame her, it was—"

"Blame her? Hell, I'm the one to blame. I'm always so darn busy. Take this last week for instance. I've been in Chicago the entire time. Just got back and I'm off again tomorrow."

Danny reached over and patted his arm. "Don't blame yourself. Really. Things happen."

"Nah. It's me. It's obvious. Anyhow, that's where you come in."

Danny's nervous tremor returned and drops of perspiration formed on his forehead. He wiped the sweat off his upper lip. "Now, Mr. Foster, I'm a kid, so please don't do anything rash."

"Rash? Nonsense. At your age you can do about anything Mrs. Foster needs."

"Well…I guess you're right. I guess I already have, haven't I?"

"That's what she tells me." Andrew glanced at his wristwatch. "Listen, I've got to go prepare for my trip. I'm going to be gone most of next week, and when I get back it'll be hell for a while until I catch up. So, come to the house tomorrow at about one, and I'll show you exactly how you should do it, before I leave."

"Show me how to do it. Are you sure about that?"

"Hell, yeah. You're dense aren't you? My wife said you were a smart kid."

"No, I get it. You're going to show me how to—"

"Listen boy, I can't stay here and spell it all out. Be there at one tomorrow."

Danny leaned against the cart and nodded.

"I hope you do what she wants better than you talk. If not, there'll be trouble." He headed toward the door of the store, turned, and pointed his finger at Danny. "One o'clock sharp."

"Yeah, okay. One o'clock."

"Sorry, Sarah, Conrad's not here," Daniel said while he stacked cans of fruit on a shelf to one side of the store. "Didn't he tell you?"

"He left before I woke up. I fell asleep on the sofa last night and…he didn't wake me."

"He should be back any minute now. He went to deliver some groceries to Mrs. Albers. She's been laid up since she slipped and broke her hip."

"Where's Tom?"

"Alyana and the little ones came by to whisk him away for a quick bite. They're down at the diner if you'd like to join them."

"No, thanks. They should have him to themselves. Was Conrad in a good mood?"

"Same as always. Why?"

"He's been a bit worried lately. Anyway, it's nice to get to chat with you. How are you doing? Any recollections?"

Daniel finished his chore and joined Sarah. "No, although Doc insists that I'm on the verge. He says this cooking business is going to be the door that opens my past."

"I don't doubt it. Your *osso buco* was out of this world."

"Thanks, but let's not forget that you and Elisabeth were right there the entire time. It's your mother's recipe, anyway."

"Daniel, c'mon admit it. Elisabeth may have helped by reading the recipe, but you were always a step ahead. Not to mention your Italian."

"Yeah, how about that? I can speak French and Italian."

"*¿Y que tal el Español?*" Sarah slid in a quick question to test his Spanish.

"*En efecto hablo español,*" Daniel answered without hesitation.

"You're a veritable United Nations. You must've lived in Europe."

"You keep saying that, but it's not likely."

"Why not?"

"I'm not the adventurous type."

"Speaking of adventure, does the name Amaray ring a bell?"

"Amaray…no, it doesn't. Is it a town in Europe?"

The door to the store swung open, and Sheriff Williams stepped in. He caught sight of Sarah and Daniel and shot them a sarcastic smile. "Well, well, if it isn't the witch and the gimp."

"Sheriff," Daniel said with an unmistakable chill in his voice, "you're out of line."

"Yes, I am," Williams answered, a smirk across his lips.

"Please apologize to Mrs. Thompson."

"I'll do no such thing," he said with a caustic chuckle.

"It's all right, Daniel, if he wants to call me a witch, he can go right ahead. I don't care."

"I bet you'll care if folks around here start turning their backs on you and your family."

"And I suppose you'll see to that," Sarah said with a coldness that surprised even her.

"I could."

"And I would imagine your reason for making such a threat is so that I don't keep looking into how your father died. Am I right?" she asked, raising an eyebrow.

"That's none of your business," Williams snapped.

"But it could be…Do you remember how you followed that deer through the scope of your rifle and how your father came into view behind the deer?"

All color drained from Williams's face. "How…" he tried to speak but his throat had closed.

Sarah smiled triumphantly. "Let's make a deal, Sheriff. You put an earnest effort into finding out what happened to Daniel and drop this ridiculous suspicion that the two of us are up to something, and I'll keep what I know to myself. However, if you insist on calling me a witch or threatening me and my family, I'll dig into your past so deeply you'll be begging me to stop." She allowed her words to percolate for a moment before going on. "Do we have a deal?"

The sheriff's face turned crimson with anger. "I don't *deal* with witches."

Sarah stood her ground and stared him down. "Your choice, but I suspect you'd rather I not uncover what you fear the most."

Williams's eyes narrowed and his mouth thinned to a small slit, but he remained silent.

"Sheriff, I have no interest in hurting you or anyone else. And people around these parts are proud of your father. I'm sure you'd like them to be as proud of you. If I do find what you fear the most, what's to stop me from sharing it with folks?"

"You wouldn't dare."

"Why not? Isn't that what you threatened me with?" Sarah asked.

"Listen—"

"No, you listen. All I ask is that you leave me be and that you focus your investigation on finding out who attacked Daniel. I propose a truce. We could actually work together, instead of against one another." She allowed him to digest her words. "How about it? Do we have a deal?"

"Work together?" Williams said with a sneer. "You expect me to trust you, to give you information, to—"

"Yes. Believe it or not, Sheriff, I might be able to help. What do you say?"

Williams glared at her, then at Daniel, and then back at Sarah. "I'll get back to you." He spun on his heels and stormed out of the store.

Sarah's knees buckled. Daniel rushed to her side and caught her, then eased her onto a small chair by the shoe rack.

"Are you okay, Sarah?"

She nodded, then shook her head. "I can't believe I did that. Conrad will be livid."

"Livid? He'll be proud."

"I doubt it."

"Why would Sheriff Williams call you a witch?"

Sarah looked up at Daniel and sighed. "I've got a bit of an intuitive gift."

Daniel plopped down on a nearby chair. "You're a psychic?"

The store door opened and Daniel stood up. "Hey, Conrad."

Conrad made his way toward him. "Daniel, how are things?"

Sarah stood up. "Hi, darling. I've been visiting with Daniel."

Conrad smiled as he came closer to her, took her hands in his, and kissed her. "You're ice cold, and you're shaking. What happened?"

"Man, you should've seen her with Williams. She was fierce." Daniel beamed with pride.

Conrad stared at his wife, his forehead furrowed. "Williams was here again?"

"He just left, didn't you see him?" Daniel asked.

"No. What was he after?"

Sarah started to answer, but Daniel's excitement couldn't be contained and he blurted out, "He threatened Sarah with telling folks she's a witch, and she came right back at him threatening to find out how his dad died and tell everyone. A good old fashioned standoff, and she won."

"How did she win?" Conrad was visibly troubled.

"She made a deal with him to stay out of his private life if he'd leave her alone and focus on finding out who attacked me."

Conrad turned to his wife in amazement. "And he went for it?"

"Well, not exactly." Daniel glanced at Sarah. "But he didn't say no."

"One more thing," Sarah said shyly. "I told him I'd like to help him in the investigation."

Conrad looked at his wife, sighed, and pulled her to him, wrapping his arms around her. "What am I going to do about you, woman?"

"I told her you'd be proud of her."

"Are you angry?" she asked softly.

Conrad kissed her forehead. "Since I can't fight you, I might as well join you."

Beaming, Sarah kissed her husband.

"C'mon, you two, you're making me jealous. Besides, I need to ask Sarah about her psychic abilities."

Conrad stared into Sarah's eyes in disbelief. "Psychic abilities?"

She nodded.

"I'm gone less than an hour, and my whole world is turned upside down. What else have you done?"

"That's it," she said with a smile.

"Tell me all about it, Sarah," Daniel insisted.

"Daniel, this isn't the time or place." Conrad interrupted. "How about you come over for dinner tonight and she can tell you then, okay?"

"I'd rather not impose again."

"Nonsense, we'd love to have you over." Sarah offered. "Don't expect too much. I'll whip up a simple beef stew. Is that okay?"

"I'd be pleased to come," Daniel said.

"Okay, then. Time to go home, darling, you've created enough excitement for one day." Conrad took Sarah by the arm and escorted her toward the door. "Daniel and I have work to do. Can you get home without getting into any more trouble?"

"I should tell Tom and Alyana what happened. They're down at the diner and—"

"Tell you what, ask them to join us for dinner. It's better if we're all safely at home before we talk about this…although, with Williams all riled up, I'm not sure home is even safe."

"You don't mean—"

Conrad raised a hand. "Let's not talk about it anymore now." He smiled and eased her out of the store.

Sarah climbed into her car and pulled out of the parking lot.

CHAPTER 12

Alexander sat before his typewriter staring at a blank page. Smoke curled up around his eyes from the cigarette attached precariously to his lip. The floor and table were covered with the customary clutter of crumpled papers and bottles. Exasperated, he threw his chair back, strode to the open window, and gazed out into the darkness.

The front door burst open and an agitated Danny stormed in. "Mr. Foster discovered all about me. He's going to kill me tomorrow. What do I do? Alexander, you got to help me."

"Whoa. Calm down, calm down. How did you find out he's going to kill you?"

"He told me."

"He told you he's going to kill you tomorrow? That's decent of him." Alexander pulled his chair back up and sat down in front of the blank page in the typewriter.

"What do I do?"

"Go for it. 'In for a penny, in for a pound.' You got to face him. Confront him. Defend her. Fight for your love. For your dream."

Danny shook his head. "But I'm too young to die."

"To love life you can't stand on the outside looking in. You crash through, enter it, be all the way inside it, and endure it." He paused. "Hey, that's pretty good, I should write that down." He then proceeded to do exactly that.

Danny stood in the middle of the room, head bowed, trying not to cry.

"How come you didn't come by earlier?"

"My mom is back, I had to stay for dinner. I couldn't sneak out."

"Coward."

"She catches every single noise in that house, so I couldn't."

"Chicken shit."

Alexander's repeated chastisements brought Danny out of his stupor. "Listen, I did it for you. If they found out I've been coming to visit you, your secret would be out."

Alexander read what he'd typed, yanked the page out, crumpled it, and tossed it across the room. "Piece of crap."

"What should I do?"

Alexander turned to Danny. "About what? Oh…right, your imminent demise. Well, what can you do? Either you run away from home and leave town, or you face Mr. Foster. Do you need seconds? I can't be your second, sorry. My lack of commitment forbids it. Maybe Robert?"

"What do you mean seconds? What are you talking about?"

"Didn't you say that he told you he'd kill you tomorrow?"

"I'm pretty sure that's what's going to happen."

"In a duel, right?"

The color in Danny's face drained. "What? He didn't say anything about a duel."

"Then how is he going to kill you?"

Alexander stood up and walked toward the easel. Danny's painting had progressed nicely and the resemblance had become far more evident. Alexander studied the painting, tilting his head first to the right and then to the left. Danny's spirit was clearly evident, the eyes displayed a hint of innocent mischief, and the smile offered an open invitation to imagine his innermost secrets. Alexander smiled, proud at last of his work.

"Well, the good news is that if you die, it'll be okay. I've got everything I need to finish your portrait. I'll send it to your parents posthumously. And anonymously, of course."

"You're not taking this seriously."

Back at the desk Alexander cranked a blank page into the typewriter and began to type.

Danny paced back and forth becoming more frantic with each passing moment.

"Stop pacing, you're distracting me."

"What's wrong with you? I'm going to die and you don't care. What kind of friend are you?"

Alexander turned to him. "Okay, here it is. I'll keep it simple. You have dipped your pen into the inkwell of passion and now you must pay the piper for the pages inscribed with your elation and your folly. In other words, either you show up at the appointed time and face the consequences, whatever they may be, or you run away as far and as fast as your fleet little feet will carry you. Only you can decide what price you're willing to pay. Okay?"

Danny stared at Alexander with a faint smile. "I get it, you mean like Wesley in *Rainbow*?"

"Exactly."

"But Wesley, was a man—a young man, but a man. I'm only a kid."

Alexander returned to his typewriter. "Kids don't screw married women. I've given you Wesley, use him."

"Wesley wasn't afraid."

Alexander stopped typing and turned toward Danny in silent disbelief.

"Okay, he *was* afraid, but not as much as I am. Besides he fights for his dream at the end of the book. I've barely even started. I'm only on page twenty…thirty tops."

Alexander exploded with laughter, but Danny failed to find the humor in it. When his amusement finally subsided, Alexander returned to his typing. Danny resumed pacing.

"What happens when the entire town finds out what I did?"

Alexander typed with mock concentration.

"What will Ms. Eldrige say?"

Alexander stopped. "Who?"

"My English teacher—she's very good to me. Will she call me a victim or a villain? What about Ellie? What will she say? Oh God. Ellie." He sped up his pace and clutched his head as if trying to contain an inevitable internal explosion. "What about my parents? Oh God! It'll kill them. Shame them forever and ever—especially my dad. Can you imagine what people will say about the minister's son and how he failed as a father? Oh God." He turned to Alexander and pulled on his arm. "Alexander, help me. Please, you've got to help me."

Alexander slammed his fists on the table. "Danny, I've given you Wesley, I've given you my opinion. The rest is up to you." He rose and headed into his bedroom. Seconds later he emerged with a shabby looking book and handed it to Danny. "Here, I was going to give it to you when I left, but since you might leave me first, you should have it now."

Danny took the tattered book and stared at the cover. He opened it to find the corners frayed and the pages stained from countless rereading. Beaming, Danny closed it and caressed the cover. He turned to Alexander and smiled. "*Rainbow*...Your book."

"My very own copy. You deserve to have it now."

Danny's eyes began to tear as he tenderly thumbed through it.

"Read the title page."

"You've dedicated it to me?"

"Read it."

"'Danny, you have no potential...you are complete. My love to you, my best and only true friend. Alexander Pitman.'" He looked with awe into Alexander's eyes. "You've signed it. You actually signed it even though you told me you never do that."

"Remember why I don't sign books?"

"You said it traps your soul."

"There you have it."

"I don't know what to say."

"Good." Alexander returned to his typewriter.

Danny rushed over and hugged him. "Thanks."

Alexander smiled to himself. "Yeah, yeah. You've got to go now. I need to write."

"But—"

"Go."

Alexander began to type again. Stunned, Danny backed away and, book in hand, silently left the cabin and walked off into the night.

"Sarah, this stew is delicious," Elisabeth managed between bites.

Sarah blinked, her surroundings wrenching her back to the present. "Oh. Thanks."

"You created a unique flavor blend. I'd love to see the recipe," Daniel chimed in.

"Well, not my doing at all. It's probably my mother's secret ingredient—chicken stock—coupled with the long cooking time."

"It sure worked great," a cheerful Elisabeth added. "I can't thank you enough Sarah, for asking me over and teaching me how to make it. I had a ball, and the little ones learning all those words in Spanish and French while we cooked their dinner turned out to be a treat."

"They had a great time, even the twins," Sarah told Alyana. "They kept us plenty busy."

"They're a handful, and I appreciate having an afternoon for housework. It's hard to keep up with four kids. I never have enough time, even with the European tradition that Sarah started."

"What tradition?" Elisabeth asked.

"To have the children eat before the adults. Listen to the silence. Now that they're asleep upstairs, we can all enjoy a nice evening of adult conversation."

"Well, for my part, I'm looking forward to sleeping in tomorrow morning with my wife at my side," Tom said as he winked at Alyana.

"We'll all have a nice sleep"—Elisabeth giggled—"after the pineapple compote dessert with tequila and Tuaca we've prepared for you. Wait till you taste that."

"That's a first, even for me," Conrad said as he patted his wife's hand.

"Darling, is this is a good time to talk about what to do about Sheriff Williams?"

After a brief hesitation, Conrad nodded. "It's as good a time as any."

"Daniel's told you what happened at the store this afternoon," Sarah went on, "so now that we're all aware of what transpired, we should—"

"Pretty gutsy, Sarah," Tom interjected.

"Gutsy? That wasn't my intention, but I refuse to live in fear again."

"Fear?" Daniel asked with surprise.

Sarah glanced at her husband who smiled and nodded.

She took a deep breath and looked straight at Daniel. "I grew up denying that I had a sixth sense because as a little girl my ability caused horrible trauma to my best friend's family."

"Why? Did you misinterpret one of your visions?" Daniel tilted his head.

"No, I spoke the truth. But it was a truth no one wished to hear—or accept."

"Oh." Daniel lowered his eyes. "Now I get it." He swirled his fork on his plate, and then looked up at Conrad. "You're worried Sarah might cause me similar trauma, aren't you?"

Everyone's eyes turned to Conrad. "What worries me is that, at this point in time, she doesn't have enough information to make an informed decision. And I'm worried Williams might try to do her harm."

"Dad, you're not serious." Tom stiffened. "He's a cop, he wouldn't hurt Sarah."

"I don't mean physically, but he's definitely capable of causing public distrust, and you're well aware of the harm prejudice can do."

"C'mon Dad, no one could possibly think ill of Sarah," Tom insisted. "Everyone in these parts is well aware of Grandma and her gift. It wouldn't be any different with Sarah."

"Tom, Grandma was born here. Sarah's a newcomer and you understand as well as anyone how mistrustful folks here are about outsiders."

"Yes, but not Sarah. She's part of our family—part of you, part of me, and Alyana. For that matter, Sarah was summoned by Grandma to come here and to join our family."

"You realize how odd that sounds—your dead grandmother calling from beyond and beckoning Sarah to come here? Williams can wreak havoc with talk like that."

"He could certainly try, but he wouldn't succeed," Tom said, but he spoke hesitantly.

Conrad glanced around the table. "What do you all think?"

"I agree with Tom and Sarah," Alyana answered first. "Papa, there's no question that prejudice can cause a great deal of pain, but we can't live in fear.

Some folks might behave badly—people who don't know us well. But we shouldn't allow their actions to affect us."

"But," Daniel interjected, "I'm well aware that public opinion carries a heavy load."

"What do you mean? You're on to something?" Elisabeth asked excitedly.

Daniel shook his head. "I'm not sure what it is, a feeling, I guess. Somehow I'm aware of the price one pays when we challenge those whose approval we seek." He looked at Sarah. "As much as I admire your guts and how you stood your ground against Williams, I have to agree with Conrad about the harm public opinion might bring to you and your family. It's hard enough for most people to understand the generosity you've extended to me, let alone—"

"That's no reason," Sarah said emphatically. "To begin with, you were attacked, and everyone understands how difficult it must be for you to have lost everything."

"And yet it's my presence that has caused all this trouble."

"You're the victim," Elisabeth interjected. "The attack on you may be what brought Sarah to everyone's attention, but let's not lose sight of the fact that you *are* the victim."

"Okay," Conrad cut in, in an attempt to regain control of the discussion, "I think I get where we all stand, and it's true that there's no point in living in fear, particularly of things that are beyond our control. However, the cat—as they say—is out of the bag. Williams knows that Sarah is psychic and he'll do whatever he'll do. We must do our best not to provoke him, to tread lightly and exercise caution. Are we all together on this?" He tilted his head and eyed Sarah pointedly.

After a few seconds, she nodded.

With a collective sigh of relief, everyone smiled, and returned to their dinner.

"I think I can help him uncover who attacked Daniel," Sarah said as she sipped her wine.

"Now, Sarah—"

"Conrad," she interrupted, "I have to do the best that I can with the gift I've been given."

"But not until you have all the facts." Conrad insisted with controlled impatience.

"You mean until the movie that's playing in my head makes sense." Sarah shook her head. "It doesn't make any more sense now than when it began. I suspect it's waiting for someone other than me to interpret it."

"You have a movie in your head?" Elisabeth asked excitedly. "Is it about Williams?"

"She doesn't know," Conrad snapped. "She shouldn't even be talking about it until she's certain of its meaning." He reached for Sarah's hand. "I'm sorry. I don't wish you to live in fear, and I'm proud you're no longer hiding your gift. But you must keep your visions to yourself until you understand them. If you jump to conclusions the wrong people might get hurt. Including us."

Sarah lowered her eyes and nodded. "You're right. I need to be more careful." She looked up at Elisabeth. "I don't wish to keep this movie from you, but I truly don't understand it. All I can say is that it isn't about Williams, but about Daniel, or someone close to Daniel."

"Sarah, please, you have to tell us about it," Elisabeth insisted.

"No, Conrad's right. I'll wait a bit longer. Maybe things will become clearer."

"What's the harm in telling us?" Elisabeth pushed.

"If it isn't about Daniel, it could confuse him, or influence him," Alyana replied calmly.

Elisabeth pouted and then shrugged. "Okay, so you can't tell us about this movie, but what about Williams? How could you help him with the investigation of Daniel's attack?"

"I have this feeling—" Sarah started to answer, then glanced at her husband who squeezed her hand and smiled. "I sense that Williams is on the verge of figuring out where Daniel came from, but he's so worried about me that he keeps getting derailed."

"Why is he worried about you?" asked Tom.

"He fears my psychic abilities."

"Why? What does that have to do with Williams?" Tom insisted.

Elisabeth gasped. "Oh my God, Sarah. He's afraid you'll find out how his dad really died, isn't he?"

Sarah nodded. "I believe so."

"What? It was a hunting accident." Tom's forehead furrowed as he shook his head. "This doesn't make any sense."

Sarah glanced at Conrad and then back at Tom. "I'm certain that Williams believes he's the one that killed him."

Elisabeth brought her hands to her mouth. Alyana reached for her husband's hand. For a moment everyone stared at Sarah in silence.

"Did he?" Tom asked at last.

"I'm not sure yet. But I've seen what Williams sees in his dreams."

"How he killed his father?" Elisabeth whispered.

"Yes."

"Oh, Sarah." Alyana reached over and embraced her. "How awful it must be for you to sense these things—to experience such horror."

"And all this because you felt the urge to help me. That's what I mean when I say that everything bad that's happened is because of me." Daniel's words were barely audible.

"Daniel," Sarah said gently, "I'm glad I helped you, I'm glad we're all here tonight—together—trying to make sense of it all. I'm glad to call you my friend. I'm not thrilled with the visions about Williams and his fears, nor am I certain about the meaning of the movie playing in my head, but if you trust me and give me time, I hope I'll be able to help you."

Daniel smiled. "I trust you, and if there's one thing I can give you, it's time."

CHAPTER 13

DANNY AND HIS parents sat around the kitchen table finishing breakfast.

"I do notice you." The minister sighed with exasperation. "I'm busy."

"You come home late at night and leave right after breakfast, you don't come for lunch or dinner as is…as *was* your habit. I can't figure out what to make of it."

"I'm *very* busy, Shirley. If anyone in the world should understand that, it would be you."

"I understand that your congregation needs attention, but this is too much. We are your family."

"I have my work, Shirley. You have Danny, doesn't he keep you company?"

"He's having fun. It's summer."

"He should get a job. Look at him, he's half asleep."

"I'm not half asleep," Danny protested.

"Then what's the matter with you, boy? You're acting like you're at a funeral."

"You're arguing and…this could be the last meal I have with both of you."

Hugo Michaels rose, pushing his chair back. "Don't be so melodramatic, son. We're sparring like any old married couple. It doesn't mean we're splitting up. Pull yourself together." He folded his newspaper, placed it on the counter, and headed out of the kitchen.

"That's not what I—"

"Get a summer job. Start looking today."

"But Hugo, he should at least have a few weeks of fun with his friends."

"Shirley, you baby this boy too much. I have to go. I'm off to the ministers' meeting, which means I'll be wasting my whole day with a bunch of useless preachers. Oh, and I won't be home for dinner, so don't wait up for me." With that, he turned, and left.

Dejected, Shirley collected the breakfast dishes from the table and carried them to the sink. "He didn't even give us a kiss good-bye. I don't like it. Something's going on with your father. He's hiding something."

"I guess." Danny, head down, made circles in his cereal.

"I hope he hasn't got some awful disease he doesn't want us to know about. Or maybe something's gone wrong with the congregation. You're familiar with how some of those people on the Board of Directors are."

"Uh-huh." Danny continued swirling with his spoon, resting his head on his free hand.

Shirley stared out the window as she rinsed the dishes. "He doesn't look ill. Does he?"

"I suppose."

Shirley turned and took a good long look at her son. She shut off the water, dried her hands on her apron and approached him, caressing his hair. "I'm sorry, please don't worry, he'll be fine. It's my fretting. I get a bit lonely sometimes—I'm not used to him being gone so much. You don't need to find a job today. Take your time and enjoy another week of summer. Go on," she said, removing his cereal bowl, "get your swimming trunks and go join your friends at the beach. They'll be waiting for you."

"But, Mom—"

"No buts, do as I say." She kissed him on the forehead and ushered him from the kitchen.

Danny turned back and embraced her. "I love you, Mom. Don't forget that, whatever happens. I love Dad, too. Make sure you tell him." Without waiting for a response he rushed out.

Bewildered, Shirley stared after her son as the scene faded to black.

Robert and several teenage boys ran out of the lake to join Danny who had parked himself on the sand in a distant corner of the beach away from the crowd.

They dropped down next to him, lit up a couple of cigarettes, and passed them around. Danny refused their offer to partake and instead sat staring pensively into the horizon.

"Anyway," Robert addressed the group, clearly finishing a story he'd started earlier, "I told her to sneak out of her house with me, and we could come here and count the stars."

"So what did she say?" demanded Chris, a chubby, freckle-faced redhead who showed signs of having exceeded his allotment of sunshine for the day.

"Thursday at midnight," Robert boasted, looking about with feigned indifference. "I'm going all the way. The Milky Way and the Big Dipper."

"How'd you do it? Sue Ellen, man, she's a fox," an amazed Paul exclaimed.

"No big deal." Robert dragged deeply and then released the smoke as slowly as he could.

They spotted a group of young girls walking down the beach, Ellie among them.

"Hey, Danny. Ellie's here." Robert poked his friend.

Danny turned to catch a glimpse of Ellie and her girlfriends as they set their towels carefully on the sand, then dashed toward the water. Ellie wore a bright yellow bikini that accentuated her lithe body.

As she frolicked with her friends at the edge of the water, she caught a glimpse of Danny and his friends eyeing them from afar.

"C'mon, let's go get them." Chris sprung to his feet followed by Paul and Robert.

After a few steps, Robert stopped and turned back to Danny who remained motionless. "Coming, Danny boy?"

"Go ahead, I'll catch up."

"What's wrong, man? You're so gloomy."

"When you're close to death, everything is meaningless."

"Death? What the hell are you talking about?"

"You wouldn't understand."

"You're turning into a real bore." Robert ran off to join his friends who had already started teasing the girls. They, in turn, pretended to ignore them.

Danny rose slowly to his feet and sauntered toward Ellie who had broken away from the group and headed over to meet him halfway.

"Hi Danny," she said with her typical bright smile.

"Hi. Glad you're back." He turned toward the horizon unable to look at her directly.

"We got home yesterday. What have you been up to?"

Danny drew in the sand with his foot, unwilling to make eye contact. "Not much. You?"

"I got really bored. Kept thinking of you."

He nodded. "That's nice."

Clearly taken aback by his demeanor, she furrowed her brow ever so slightly. "Are you okay? You're acting—"

"I'm not acting," he snapped.

"Sorry, I didn't mean to—"

"Well you did."

"Suit yourself, then." With that, she ran back to her friends, plunged into the lake, and swam away from the beach.

Danny's eyes followed her, tears trickling down his cheeks.

"Ellie, I don't deserve you. I'm going to die for lust, not for a noble cause. Since it's my first big sin I hope I'll be forgiven. I promise to watch over you from heaven." He placed his hand over his heart. "I love you, and I'm sorry."

The camera tilted toward the sky and faded to white.

Mrs. Foster's clothes lay scattered all over the white carpet intermingled with Danny's. The comforter and blankets also lay on the floor.

Naked on the bed, Danny rested next to Mrs. Foster, both their faces shiny with perspiration, and their breathing heavy with lingering passion.

"You learn fast, young man. I like it." She kissed him softly. "Better now?"

"How did you talk Mr. Foster into hiring me to take care of your roses and garden?"

She gazed into his eyes. "Let's not talk about him. Tell me about Ellie."

"She's angry with me."

"Whatever for?"

"I sort of ignored her this morning."

"Why?"

"I felt really uncomfortable around her. I shouldn't be with her while I'm with you."

"Why not?"

"It isn't proper."

Mrs. Foster laughed and rolled toward him, playfully kissing his nose. "You're so pure."

"Pure what?"

"Pure, as in untainted. Wholesome."

"I don't get what that has to do with Ellie."

"You and I," she explained deliberately, "are lovers. You and Ellie, on the other hand, are boyfriend and girlfriend. Would you ever go beyond merely kissing her?"

"No, of course not. She's not that kind of girl. Sorry, I didn't mean to imply—"

"It's okay, don't worry. I understand. That's actually my point—two completely different relationships that shouldn't interfere with one another."

He closed his eyes. "It's so easy to be with you and talk to you."

"Always remember how it was with me."

"As if I could forget."

"Promise."

"I promise, I promise. I'll love you forever."

"No, not that. You won't do that. But promise you won't forget me...ever. My touch, my smell, my skin, my lips, my—"

"Tongue, your—"

Her lustful kiss drowned out his words.

"She's corrupting him through and through," a visibly irritated Sarah told Conrad.

They were strolling along the Methow River on a warm Sunday morning. The twins slept in the hiking wrap-slings that each of them wore, while Elan and Nina scampered about them.

"Don't get upset, you'll wake Kaya," Conrad urged Sarah, squeezing her hand.

"She's fast asleep."

"If you get angry Kaya will feel it."

Sarah nodded and took a deep breath. "Mrs. Foster is a monster. What's with all the immorality?"

"I'm with you. It's not like you can save him, so why show you the corruption of this teenage boy? What's the point? Where is this heading?"

"Trouble, nowhere but trouble."

"But why?"

Sarah shrugged. "What if the Danny in the movie is our Daniel?"

"Where are you going with this?"

"Nothing specific, but the more I learn about this boy and how this woman is twisting him around, the more I fear that our Daniel somehow may have been running away from these painful memories. The boy in the movie is certainly heading toward disaster with this relationship. Who wouldn't prefer to forget something like that?"

"But if all of this happened years ago, somewhere in the Midwest, what is Daniel doing here in the Northwest?"

"Maybe he came looking for someone connected with whatever happened back then. What if this someone is his attacker?"

"Well, that's a possibility, but there's no way to be certain until you have more clues."

Sarah sighed in frustration.

"Look at it this way, you're getting more and more information as the movie plays out. It's speeding up, too."

She nodded in spite of herself. "I would certainly like to be of more help to Daniel, though. The attraction between him and Ellie may get—"

"Ellie?"

"What?"

"You said 'the attraction between him and Ellie.'"

"I did? I meant to say Elisabeth."

"I know you did."

"Oh dear. What if this slip of the tongue is more than a mistake? Could the movie be about our Daniel and our Elisabeth when they were teenagers? Do you realize what that means?" Sarah stopped and faced her husband. "I should ask them."

Sarah's burst of enthusiasm caused Kaya to stir for a moment.

Conrad shook his head. "I knew you'd wake her."

"She didn't quite wake up. Anyway, I should—"

"Stop. You should do nothing. We're speculating. For now keep it in the back of your mind. Don't do something that you might regret later."

"You're right." She stared into his eyes. "Thank you," she whispered.

"Whatever for?"

"For loving me. I've been tough to cope with lately."

Conrad laughed, and little Tadan stirred in his wrap-sling. "Oh-oh." Conrad gently coaxed his grandson back to sleep. "You may have pushed me to my limits a couple of times, but don't forget that I'm also learning to deal with this gift of yours."

"Learning? You?" Sarah asked as they closed the distance between them and their frolicking grandkids. "You had years of experience with your grand-mother and your aunties."

"That was different. I grew up with it. They knew when and how to listen to their visions, but most importantly, when and how to act on them. You on the other hand, are just learning. And so am I, but where you and I differ is on how to act."

"But we shouldn't be at odds over that."

"Nevertheless we are. My instinct is to protect you, and when you run off and do things that make that more difficult, it unnerves me."

"My parents were after protection when they forced me to bury my abili-ties. I'm wary of that."

"You have to understand that it's tough to be on the outside. You shouldn't deny your gift, but I simply can't let any harm come to you."

Sarah took her husband's hand. "We'll have to learn how to keep this teeter-totter balanced, won't we?"

"As long as we take it slow, we'll be okay."

Sarah sighed and nodded. Hand in hand, the two strolled back to their little valley bookended by the twin houses, with their grandchildren trotting playfully about them.

C H A P T E R   1 4

"Sarah and Conrad would disapprove of us being alone. But here we are, two disobedient children," Daniel told Elisabeth with a wink.

She blushed and giggled. Having finished their Sunday picnic, they relaxed on a blanket in the middle of a flower-filled meadow with a spectacular view of the Cascades.

"How did you ever find this place?" he asked her.

"When I decided to bring flowers to my patients I took short hikes around the area in search of wildflowers so I wouldn't go broke. One day I stumbled upon this meadow. It's stunning, isn't it?"

"It is. It reminds me of something but I can't put my finger on it."

"You're remembering something?" Elisabeth reached for Daniel's arm, but aware of her forwardness, she immediately retracted it.

"Don't be embarrassed," he chuckled. "It's alright. I don't mind you touching me."

"I'm well aware that it's not right. Anyway, what is it that you felt?"

"A sensation that I've been in a place of natural beauty like this one. It gives me a sense of belonging, as if within it I'm safe. Makes me feel like a kid again, with no worries, no problems, nothing but joy."

"That's wonderful, Daniel. With a little luck maybe something will shake loose and more will come out."

After a long pause, Daniel replied, "Maybe."

"C'mon, don't get down again. Let's take a stroll before the sun sets."

Daniel folded the blanket and took in a deep breath. "This should be allergy heaven with all this pollen floating about, yet it doesn't affect me, or you."

"I'm immune, somehow. Are you allergic?"

"No, not really. No idea why I said that. Common sense, I guess."

They walked in silence to Elisabeth's car, put the basket and blanket away, and turned back toward the meadow, making their way toward the mountains.

"What's on the other side of that boulder?" Daniel asked.

"Good question, I never walked that far. Should we take a look?"

"Sure."

They walked in awkward silence for a few minutes until Daniel asked timidly, "Elisabeth, why do you have so much interest in me?"

She smiled and almost patted his shoulder, but decided to place her hands in her jeans pockets instead. "You're my patient."

"It's okay to touch me, it won't lead to anything more. And I'm not your patient."

"Of course you're my patient. I may not be a doctor, but I'm someone who cares for those in need and you're one of them."

"I agree that I'm in need of help, but you stopped volunteering at the hospital and are devoting yourself entirely to my care. Why?"

"To begin with, I'm actually back to work at the hospital. I only stopped during the last part of winter. It was too much to handle with the roads so icy, plus I needed to make sure that your injuries were healing properly. Anyway, Doc was happy for me to keep an eye on you."

"Elisabeth, you're avoiding my question."

They reached the boulder and walked around it. Beyond was a ravine leading down to the sparkling waters of a rushing river. They stood staring, intoxicated by the vista's beauty.

"Oh, wow," Elisabeth uttered.

"Gorgeous."

"It's the Methow River." She pointed to the Cascades. "It originates up there. It's a tributary of the Columbia River, the largest river in the Northwest."

"Spectacular." He reached for Elisabeth's hand. "C'mon, answer my question."

She took a deep breath. "I've connected with you," she said softly, entwining her fingers with his. "There's something about you that I can't...well...I can't resist."

"Exactly the answer I'd hoped for," he tightened his grip on her hand. "I feel the same."

They stood in silence, absorbing the raw power of the wilderness around them as the sun disappeared behind the peaks, their hands speaking to one another, their hearts heavy with the knowledge that their emotions were forbidden.

Sarah reached to turn on the attic light, then stopped. She let her eyes take in every corner of the room. The soft moonlight poured through the window so she left the light off, smiled, eased into the armchair with a sigh, and closed her eyes.

Danny snuck out his bedroom window late at night, and made his way to the cabin.

The light of the lone lamp Alexander used when he wrote shone through the window. Danny snuck up quietly to surprise his friend, but when he peered through the dusty pane he saw Alexander slumped over his typewriter. He appeared to sleep soundly. An empty bottle of whiskey, a dirty glass, and an ashtray filled with cigarette butts sat beside him. The quantity of crumpled papers covering the floor and table had grown.

Danny stepped through the door and tiptoed to the easel. His portrait was almost completed and captured the boy's blend of youth and maturity. He sneaked toward Alexander and, as quietly as he could, gathered up the wadded paper from the floor.

The subtle noise was enough to wake Alexander, who straightened up and placed his elbows on the table and held his head with both hands. "Oh shit."

"Sorry to wake you. I need your advice. I'll clean up and make you some coffee first."

"Don't touch anything."

Danny stopped. Alexander arched his head back, stretched and rubbed his eyes. "Pour me a whiskey with ice."

"But—"

"Do it."

Danny hesitated a moment before taking the glass. He disappeared into the kitchen and reemerged with ice, and reluctantly poured the drink.

Alexander snatched the drink and ambled over to the easel to contemplate his work. He sipped the whiskey and frowned with disgust.

"Why do you drink that stuff if you don't like it?"

"Because I have to write."

"What's that got to do with it?"

Alexander walked to the door, and slammed it. "Don't leave the front door open, my soul can run away."

"But it can't."

"Ever ponder if when your soul gets sick of you it might try to escape?"

"No. Why would my soul be sick of me? My soul *is* me."

Alexander attempted to laugh, but the throbbing in his head stopped him instantly. He raised the glass to his temple and ran it across his forehead and back. "You're right, Master Danny, *your* soul is you. But for me it's different. I've trapped my soul for years in a cavern of mediocrity, and now—thanks to you—it demands to get out."

Danny considered the concept for a few seconds and then shrugged. "I don't get it."

"Good. Don't even try. It might infect you." He turned back to the painting, running the cold glass across his forehead. "What did you ask me?"

"I asked why you drink if you don't like it."

"Ah, yes. Do you understand what a book really is for me? It's the result of becoming completely and utterly fed up. I need to get angry enough, fucked enough, guilty enough, scared enough and, most importantly, drunk enough, before I can surrender to the need to write and spill my guts all over the page. Then, just like that"—he snapped his fingers—"as if by some ghastly magic, a book is born. Plain and simple, it's the spawn of gluttony, overindulgence, and satiation." He gulped his drink with a grimace and extended his arm toward Danny for a refill. The boy obliged.

"Glad you didn't die," Alexander called out as Danny stepped into the kitchen again. "But you shouldn't come out here this late at night. My soul needs to recharge with meaningless sleep once in a while."

"Oh, yeah. Sorry for coming so late," Danny said returning from the kitchen. "Turns out the whole thing was about having her husband give me a job so we could be together." He poured the whiskey. "We made it four or five times. I lost count."

"You did her husband too? Man, talk about gluttony."

Danny laughed. "No. Don't be ridiculous. I did it with Mrs. Foster. Her husband hired me to work on his rose garden. He's gone a lot so he can't tend to the roses."

"So, you're getting paid to prune his roses and prod his wife. Nice twist."

Danny frowned and handed him the drink.

Alexander took a sip and walked up to him and patted his cheek. "Is that what brings you to Hell City this late at night? Your conscience is clamoring for forgiveness?"

Danny backed away. "No. What's happened to you? You're acting really weird."

"I don't act. I am. Cough it up. Why are you here?"

"I need your advice. I was going to ask my dad, but after tonight, I never could ask him."

"What happened tonight?"

"He told me I have no morals."

"He knows you're fucking a married woman?"

"No! Oh God, no! He hated the women in a movie *Family Plot,* but I didn't mind them. He kept telling me how sinful they were and stuff like that. He's too…well too—"

"Preachy, uptight, religious, moral, and a fucking fake."

"He's not fake. He's the real thing. That's the problem. Anyway, you're the only one I can ask. But you're in a strange mood, so—"

"I'm not *in* a mood, young man. I *am* a mood. Don't analyze me, or you'll get lost in my cavern, and my soul will crawl deeper and deeper never to be found. On the other hand, it might jump into your pocket, join with yours, and run away. I'm sure she'd like that." He slumped onto a chair and closed his eyes, holding the ice-cold glass up to his forehead. "Never mind all this shit I'm spewing, spit out your problem and leave me be."

Danny stared at the floor. "I have…well, maybe I have…but I don't have the symptoms in the book. It's red and sore, but no discharge or burning or itching or anything like that."

Alexander peeked at Danny through one eye. "What book?"

"The Medical Guide."

Alexander opened both eyes wide and exploded with laughter, winced, and squeezed them shut. "Oh, that's rich. Medical Guide, eh?" He chuckled a bit more then squinted at Danny and said, "You're probably irritated. Hell, four times in one afternoon! I'd be sore too. Happy, but sore."

Danny rushed over and grabbed his arm, spilling some of the drink over Alexander's face. "Are you sure? That's all? Are you absolutely certain?"

Alexander laughed as he dried his forehead with his hand and licked his fingers. "There's nothing certain in life, my friend. Only what we choose to believe. Rub some ointment on and keep it zipped for a day or two. If you can," he added, with another chuckle.

Danny gripped Alexander firmly. "Tell me the truth. Please. Has this ever happened to you? Is it normal? Are you sure it's not a—"

"A what? Don't stop. A what?" Alexander came to his feet, a serious look upon him.

The boy managed to whisper, "A venereal disease?"

Alexander stared solemnly into the boy's eyes and nodded. "You guessed, huh?" He glanced away, seeming reluctant to go on. He turned back. "You sure you can handle the truth?"

Danny nodded almost imperceptibly.

"Well then, no lies. I'll tell you the truth. But I warn you—you're not going like it."

Danny swallowed hard. "I can handle it. I knew it was bad."

Alexander placed his drink down and grabbed Danny by the shoulders, squaring him off. "I had the same thing years ago, when I was in Spain. Almost killed me. It's a very rare parasite. It's called *Granulona Inguinalis* over there. No idea what they call it here. Now, I don't mean to scare you, but you need to face the truth. It's dangerous…or it can be. There's only one possible cure, and it's not going to be fun. Are you man enough to do it?"

"I am," he muttered with a look of terror etched on his face.

Alexander placed his hands on Danny's shoulders and looked him sternly in the eyes. "Are you absolutely sure?"

"Yeah, yeah."

"Okay, you asked for it. This is what you have to do: first, shave off all the hair around your groin and up here, like this." He ran his hand from his groin up to his belly.

Wide-eyed, Danny stared.

"Then, you pour some…" He shook his head. "No. I shouldn't tell you." He turned away.

"I can handle it. Please, go on."

"Okay." He faced the boy. "Well, you pour gasoline on it."

Danny scowled with disgust. "Gasoline?"

"There you have it!" He threw his arms up in desperation. "You're not ready. Never mind, forget it. It won't kill you for several years anyway." Alexander stormed off toward the dining room leaving Danny to ponder his possible fate.

"No, no. Go on. It's only that…I don't think I have parasites. But if you say so…"

Alexander turned to Danny. "Okay, there's only one way to find out. Come here. You need a table. The next step is the hardest but also the most important. Once you've shaved and poured on the gasoline, you get a really sharp knife and put your dick on the table. Then you light a match and set the whole damn thing on fire."

"What?"

"And when the little bastards come running out, you stab them one by one like this." He demonstrated, stabbing the table in desperate random thrusts. He exploded into laughter, laughing so hard tears streamed from his eyes.

Insulted and thoroughly embarrassed, the boy glowered at Alexander who continued to laugh uncontrollably. Unable to bear the humiliation, Danny turned and fled from the cabin.

"Told you you couldn't handle it!" Alexander yelled after him between laughs.

"Alexander, are you the one showing me this movie?" asked Sarah.

The attic offered only silence.

"It's been months now, and all you've shown me is corruption and lies. I need you to confirm if these incidents are in Daniel's past. What happened to him? What am I supposed to do with this piecemeal information? Is all this even real? Whoever you are, tell me that at least."

Silence.

"Either tell me or leave me alone."

Abruptly, the image of a much older Alexander flashed before her as he made his way down a wooden staircase, his face contorted in pain and shock. His left hand gripped the bannister, his right hand clutched at his chest as he felt his life slip away. His eyes focused ahead of him, searching, inquiring, fear and curiosity entangled as one. He slumped to the floor.

That scene vanished only to be replaced by an image of Daniel, staring in disbelief up the same staircase. He had none of the facial blemishes and scars caused by the beating.

Without warning, a tornado of shadows came crashing down the staircase while flashes of blood and violence exploded incoherently. There were hints of a knife, splatters of blood, and flashes of fists, all intermingled chaotically in the dark chasm that swallowed Daniel. The images vanished as abruptly as they had appeared.

A stunned Sarah clutched the arms of the chair, catching her breath.

"Good God, what was that? Please."

Silence.

"You can't do this to me. It's imperative that you tell me. Did Daniel perpetrate this violence? No. He couldn't. But...*what* then? Is Alexander dead? Did Daniel see him die? Did he kill him? No, that can't be what I saw. But he was in the same house, on the same stairwell. Those shadows...are they the attackers? Did they kill Alexander and try to kill Daniel?"

Silence.

"Alexander, are you the one talking with me?" With a heartfelt sigh she leaned back and released her grip on the arms of the chair. She glanced around, closed her eyes, and listened.

Silence.

"It's okay," she whispered. "I won't judge." She waited. "What do you fear, Alexander? Why not speak to me openly, clearly?"

Silence.

She inhaled again. Then, she exhaled and smiled. "You're here to help Daniel. I get that now. You're searching for your soul, aren't you? He has it and you need it back."

A creak. At long last, the attic had allowed the exchange.

"Okay, then, I'll help you find it, but you'll need to give me more. I don't understand what you showed me."

Silence.

"All right. Small steps until we're more at ease with one another."

Illuminated by the moonlight, she stood and moved toward the door.

"Thank you, attic. Keep him safe, Alexander."

A soft creak whispered good night.

She stroked the wood of the doorway and closed the door gently behind her.

CHAPTER 15

A CRYSTAL-CLEAR DAY on Amaray Lake flickered into focus.

At one end of the lake, Danny and Hugo, fishing rods in hand, sat in a small boat that rocked to the rhythm of the waves.

"Robert is getting on my nerves," Danny said.

"How come?" Hugo reeled in his line to check the bait. Satisfied that it was fine, he slung it out over the water.

"All he talks about is girls, girls, and girls."

"That's what all boys your age talk about, isn't it?"

"But he's so vulgar about it."

Hugo laughed. "So last night you were defending the behavior of those disgusting women in the movie, and today you're an authority on decency?"

"No, it's not that. It's that there's more to girls than being sex objects."

Hugo stopped laughing and looked away. "You're too young to be talking about sex."

"I'm not too young."

"Yes, you are. When I was your age, I didn't even know what the word meant."

"That was then. Now we know exactly what it means."

Hugo gave his son a condescending glance. "You don't either. How could you? We haven't even had our talk yet."

"That's old fashioned. Nowadays we learn about it from magazines and books, and school and from those who—well, who've done it. Really Dad, you need to be more in tune with my generation."

Hugo shot an angry look in Danny's direction. "Don't get smart with me. Is this what you had in mind asking me to fish with you? To talk to me about sex?"

"I know all I need to know about sex."

"Danny, for Pete's sake, how could you say that? You're a kid."

"I'm a lot more experienced than you give me credit for."

Hugo was visibly taken aback. "Don't tell me that you and that neighbor girl are—"

"No! Of course not, I'm in love with Ellie. I wouldn't have sex with her. I mean…not until we're married. That's the point."

Relieved, Hugo smiled and shook his head. "Well, that's a good way to look at it, but you're losing me, son. I don't understand what you expect from me."

"Well, there are women you love from afar, and then there are women you don't."

"Is that so?"

"You're not taking me seriously, are you?"

"I am. I'm simply not sure what you are asking." He pulled in his empty line and frowned. "First let me row farther out, we're not catching anything here."

Danny reeled in his line while Hugo grabbed the oars and rowed further into the lake.

"It's about figuring out who is who," Danny explained.

"I still don't get you."

"Dad, was Mom your first…love?"

Hugo stared inquisitively at Danny. "What's this all about? What are you getting at?"

"I can't figure out how to handle Ellie, and I—"

"Handle? You mean you wonder if Ellie cares for you?"

"She does, that's the trouble."

Hugo spread his arms in dismay. "Now you really have lost me."

"Okay, so I love Ellie, but I also love…well, this other…well—"

"You love two girls?"

"You can say that."

"Well either you do or don't. Which is it?"

He nodded emphatically. "I do."

"And they both care for you?"

"Yes, in their own way they do."

Hugo smiled. "Some would say that's a nice problem to have, but not at your age. Put a stop to it all and stay away from girls until you grow up. You're way too young to be talking about love and getting involved with girls."

"How can you say that? I'm fifteen. And learning about girls and love is a part of growing up. It must've happened to you too."

Hugo frowned. "No, it didn't. I would never have permitted it."

"But you told me you fell for Mom in your teens."

"Yes, but that was different. I knew we'd be married. You're far from that."

"But I do have these feelings and I need your advice."

Hugo allowed his son a fatherly smile. "Listen, I understand your dilemma. I don't like it, but I do understand it."

"So what do I do?"

"I take it you can't make up your mind as to which one of these two girls you prefer?"

"Well, not exactly…I…well—"

"What is it?"

"One of them is innocent and pure, and the other is a bit on the wild side."

"Wild?"

"Fun. Like crazy, like *wow*. I'd like to be with both of them, but I can't bring myself to do that."

"That's good, son. I'm glad to hear that."

"I somehow can't be with the innocent one because I'm…well, I'm more mature than she is and I can't cross the line with her."

"That's good."

"But I can't leave the wild one because she's lots of fun."

"Fun as in 'having fun,' right? Let me make sure I understand. When you say wild, she's not one to get you and her into trouble, is she?"

Danny blushed and looked at his feet shaking his head. "No."

"You care for both the same?"

"No, not really."

"Then what's the problem? Choose the nice and pure girl. She should be the one you care for the most. It's holier and safer."

"I love them both the most, it's a different 'most.'"

"Son, you're not making sense. You're completely confused. Like I said before, forget about love altogether. You're too young to take things so seriously. Enjoy life for as long as you can without the complications that women bring into the picture."

"You love Mom."

"I do."

Danny gazed out at the horizon. "I want to have what you have with her. The same as what Wesley had in *Rainbow*. I told you about that book."

Hugo squeezed his son's shoulder. "You and your books. Life is different from books."

"Dad, books *are* life. They're written to show us how—"

"Those books are fantasy, like that movie the other night. They're made-up stories. You can't live your life according to a book."

"You do."

"I most certainly don't."

"You do, Dad."

Hugo turned crimson with anger. "Now you're being ornery to make your point."

"Dad, you follow the Bible. That's a book."

"I follow God's teachings, that's different."

"God's teachings were written in the Bible. You follow the Bible's written words."

"Son, you can't compare the Bible with a novel, a made-up story, a book of fiction. The Bible is not pretend. I'm offended that you'd make such a comparison." Hugo's brow furrowed. "This discussion is over. I forbid you to compare The Bible to a book of fiction. Understand?"

"I do, Dad, but I'm not comparing. Honest. I'm telling you that sometimes a book—well the story in a book—inspires me, the way the stories in the Bible inspire you. I'm after what Wesley found in *Rainbow*."

"And what is that?" Hugo said forcing himself to regain composure.

"Love, pure love. The kind of love that you told me you and Mom have."

"And what do you think that is?"

"I don't think, you told me all about it."

"I did?"

"You once told me that the love you and Mom have ties you forever to one another and doesn't let anything come between you. The love of *soul mates*, you called it."

Hugo looked stunned. "How could you quote me so well? That was a long time ago."

"Because they were true and sincere, like the words in *Rainbow*. C'mon, Dad, don't get sad about it. Look at me. I'm a bit confused, but happy to be in search of that. Isn't that good?"

Hugo turned back to his son, his eyes conveying a blend of sadness and tenderness. "It is good, son. I'm certain you'll find your soul mate when the time comes, but for now, be a kid."

"Too late for that, Dad," Danny muttered under his breath.

Hugo shot the boy a look of concern. "I hope what you said doesn't mean you've crossed the line with this wild girl you speak of."

"What exactly do you mean by that?"

"Do not play word games with me, son. This is not a conversation where your bookworm know-how will impress me. Have you—"

Danny interrupted his father. "The wild girl is a doll, she's nice and cares for me, she gets me, understands me. She's easy to be with. The other girl is… well…a bit more…reserved, and I'm nervous with her, it isn't so easy, yet she's a doll too."

Hugo shook his head. "I don't like this business. Not one bit. Care for my advice?"

Danny nodded.

"Will you abide by it?"

With a hint of reluctance, Danny nodded again.

Hugo smiled thinly. "Good. Stay away from this wild girl you're so fond of before you're tempted to do something you'll regret forever. Something that could ruin both your lives."

"I won't—"

"Oh, you will. Believe me, you will be tempted," Hugo said sadly. "That's our lot in life, to be enticed and tested. God keeps an eye on us to make sure we stay away from temptations."

"No sermon, Dad—"

"This is not a sermon." Hugo glared at his son. "Pay attention. I'm speaking the truth." He turned away, staring into the waters of the lake. "You're too young to understand what temptation is and what it does to a man's soul. You don't know what it means to realize you've been lured into sin, and can't help yourself. You can't stop. You're enticed over and over again, and each time you give in you slip deeper and deeper toward hell. You're aware that it's wrong, and nevertheless you crave more." A tear appeared on his cheek, and Hugo wiped it away.

Danny stared at the anguished face of his father. "I'm sorry Dad. I didn't mean to remind you of the lost souls you've had to help."

A pathetic smile appeared on Hugo's face. "I'm the one who's sorry. That was uncalled for." He paused. "My point is, stay away from girls as long as you can. Enjoy your youth."

"Okay, Dad, no sweat. I dig your meaning. Don't get upset."

Hugo laughed, and at that moment a fish tugged on his line, and he proudly reeled it in.

In the Fosters' garden, a shirtless Danny pruned the rose bushes. He removed the dead leaves and patted down the newly dug soil around each rose bush, sweating heavily in the hot summer sun.

From her window, Mrs. Foster studied him as she ran a fingertip sensually along her lips.

Danny reached for the hose to water the roses, but first brought the stream to his lips, bent forward, and held the nozzle over his head to cool himself. He straightened up, shook the water from his hair and sprayed the roses.

He glanced up at the window and spotted Mrs. Foster.

She slipped her hand under her blouse and caressed her breast.

The boy dropped the hose, shut off the water, and raced toward the back door.

"He chose Mrs. Foster over young Ellie," Sarah told her husband with raised eyebrows. She'd stopped by the store hoping to ask Daniel a few questions, but had found Conrad alone.

"He's very young, and he's struggling with tough decisions. He clearly distinguishes right from wrong, but Mrs. Foster's seduction is too powerful a temptation for a teenage boy."

"He's on his own. Alexander's been no help at all. He's the one who enticed him into living the life of a libertine in the first place."

"But he told the boy that he and Mrs. Foster were after the same thing, his innocence."

"But Danny didn't catch his meaning. Why would they do that to an adolescent boy?"

"Power, I would imagine."

Sarah considered it for a moment. "She definitely enjoys the power to have him satisfy her lust. But Alexander's different. He seeks inspiration and is smitten by the kid's youth and innocence. He envies him."

"Same difference. They're both selfish and immoral. Poor kid. Anyway, what brings you here?" Conrad said. "You could've told me this last installment tonight at dinner."

"I came to chat with Daniel. Where are they?"

"Tom is making deliveries. Daniel is with Elisabeth fixing dinner for Doc. This will be his last visit with Daniel. He's all healed."

"Physically maybe, but what about his memory?"

"It'll come back in time. Don't tell me you came to tell him about your visions in the attic?"

"How about hint here and there to jar his memory?"

"Sarah—"

"I get it, I get it. I shouldn't rush. But the movie showed that Danny's made his choice—he dumped Ellie for Mrs. Foster and—"

"We're not sure of that."

"Oh, c'mon Conrad, if not that, then what?"

"That's the point."

Sarah rolled her eyes. "Okay, I'll wait one more day. After that, I'm going to Williams."

Conrad shook his head in exasperation. "You are maddeningly obstinate."

"It's not that. We agreed to wait three days for Alexander to clarify the images before I acted on them. He hasn't. We also agreed that I'd go and try to make peace with Williams. If I'm extra nice to him he might agree to work with me."

Conrad hesitated. "I should go with you."

"You'll make him nervous. He's a bit afraid of you and all the support your family has around these parts. Folks love you."

"Buttering me up won't work."

"Anyway, I'm a frail woman and if he feels superior to me, maybe he'll open up a bit."

"A frail woman? Really, Sarah."

"I don't mind being perceived that way if we make progress." Sarah leaned over the counter and kissed Conrad. "I'm off to bake him a chocolate-strawberry tart to soften his heart."

"What about me? I have a heart, too."

"Of course, I'll fix one for us as well."

"Please don't get into any trouble."

"I'll try."

CHAPTER 16

"Daniel, you've got so many neat tricks up your sleeve." Elisabeth beamed as she cut the tips of the asparagus diagonally like he'd instructed. "These look so much better."

"The look and taste of food go hand in hand. I hope it's not too much asparagus. Doc may not be too keen on eating both asparagus soup and asparagus with beef."

"But they looked so wonderful I couldn't resist. Better to cook them than to waste them. Doc will understand. Besides, the flavors are so different it won't matter. Here," she handed him a bowl filled to the rim with freshly cut asparagus.

Daniel took the bowl and touched her hand. Their eyes met and they blushed. Gently, their hands separated, leaving behind only the memory of the moment.

"You're making great progress as a cook," he said.

"I do enjoy it now that I'm not obligated to do it," she said, and smiled.

"C'mon then, let's roll out the dough. It's been a good ten minutes since you got it out of the fridge."

Elisabeth grabbed the dough and handed it to Daniel.

"No," he said. "You do it. Roll the dough into a nice ball first."

"I've never made a tart crust. Isn't it awfully hard?"

"There's nothing to it if you have the correct recipe. Some pastry chefs make it look difficult and add lots of unnecessary steps to get you to pay good money for their desserts, but it's quite easy. Now, before you roll the dough sprinkle a bit of flour on the counter and the ball. Rub a bit of flour on the rolling pin, and then roll it in one direction to flatten it."

Clumsily, Elisabeth attempted to do as he said. Daniel nestled behind her and placed his hands over hers, gently pushing the rolling pin. He stood so close that his breath stirred the loose hairs behind her right ear, causing them to flutter in rhythm with his voice.

"The key to good baking is to love the dough and work it with delicacy," Daniel whispered. "Tender strokes up down, then diagonally, then horizontally as we shape it into a nice disc." Again and again they rolled the pin until they'd flattened the ball into a large circle.

Elisabeth felt her knees weaken, her heart pound and her breath catch. "This is nice," she managed to utter, hoping the moment would last forever.

"It is," he whispered back as he pressed closer, his body aching with need.

Once finished, he took a step back. "Be careful not to overwork the dough or it'll lose its essence," he said in a raspy voice.

Before Elisabeth could turn to engage him, the doorbell rang.

"Doc's here," Daniel said as he left the kitchen. "We may be ready with dinner, but I'm not sure I'm ready for this physical exam," he muttered to himself as he headed for the front door. "If I pass, it means the end of our visits. I'm not ready for that."

Having finished his examination, Dr. Lawrence sat at the desk in Elisabeth's study. He wrote a few notes in his medical chart while Daniel finished buttoning his shirt.

"You're on the road to a full recovery," the doctor said. "Your injuries, both internal and external, have healed very nicely. All that remains now is to retrieve that memory of yours."

"How do we do that? I have a few familiar feelings, Doc, but no specific recollections."

"Well, that's really not my department. I could recommend you to a good psychiatrist or psychologist if you wish."

"And what could they do that you can't?" Daniel said as he sat in the chair across the desk.

"The mind and emotions are tied to our well-being and those fall within their field of expertise, not mine. They could guide you better than I can."

"I don't like psychiatrists or psychologists. I don't trust them."

"Oh?" He lowered his glasses, raised his eyebrows, and stared at Daniel.

"What? Why are you looking at me like that?"

"You're very firm in your opinion about psychology. Where does that come from?"

Daniel shook his head. "I can't tell where it comes from but I'm not even comfortable talking about it. It's as if I'm repulsed by the mere suggestion of being probed by such a doctor."

"Are the sensations you mentioned earlier as strong and definite as this one?"

"Pretty much, as if I've experienced that same situation before."

"So you've been 'probed' by a psychiatrist or psychologist before, and you didn't like it."

Daniel remained silent for a moment before answering. "Yes, I'm almost sure."

"Okay, we can leave it at that."

"But I don't want our sessions to end. You're the only one I can really open up to."

"You've made good friends here, I'm sure you can speak freely to them."

"Doc…There's something I'd like to talk to you about, if you don't mind."

"Not at all. What's up?"

"I've fallen in love with Elisabeth."

"Daniel, you need to tread carefully. What if you're not free?"

"Yes, I understand, Doc. I realize what the dangers are, but it…it's happened to us."

"You mean you and Elisabeth have—"

"No, no. We've acknowledged that there is some chemistry between us, that's all. We both understand we shouldn't give into it. Nevertheless, it's happened. Sarah and Conrad have cautioned us, too, but we have this strong attraction to one another and it's hard to resist."

Dr. Lawrence sighed and leaned back in his chair. "Well, that certainly complicates things."

"I'm convinced that I'm not attached to anyone, that I came here, to this part of the world to finally be happy. I've been searching for love, and as it turns out, I found it. Sarah saved my life, and thanks to her I found Elisabeth. My gut tells me it's alright."

"Your gut, as you say, might also be telling you what you hope to hear, not necessarily the truth. How about that?"

"Yes, I'm aware that could be the case, and it's the reason I need to keep meeting with you, so I can speak of it, discuss it with someone other than my own muddled head."

The doctor crossed his arms and frowned. "It's okay with me, but if you agree, I'd like to consult with Dr. Baylor, a psychiatrist friend. I'm a good listener, but the affairs of the mind are honestly not my specialty. If he can guide me, I'll be a lot more comfortable. Okay?"

"I can't stop you, but frankly I'm leery he might guide you into doing or saying something that could make things worse."

"My goodness, Daniel, that's a very strong fear."

"It is, isn't it? Could I possibly have been in a mental institution?"

"That didn't pop into my mind, but clearly it popped into yours. Do you have a sense of having spent time in such a place? Any images or sensations?"

Daniel remained silent for a minute, probing the recesses of his mind. "It's not like I was in a place. I do have a sense of being locked up. But it's more like I locked myself up."

"Hmm. Describe that feeling to me."

His eyes darted about nervously. "It's as if I'd erected a sort of medieval tower, brick by brick, to keep me safe, so no one and nothing could hurt me." He finished with a deep sigh.

Dr. Lawrence allowed him a moment to recover before intruding in his thoughts. "That's a very clear image. How does the tower feel?"

"Familiar. Comforting."

"In what way?"

"As long as I'm inside this fortress, nothing can harm me."

"Can you leave at any time or are you held against your will?"

Daniel remained silent, combing through the emotions that tied him to the fortress he'd discovered. At length, he looked up. "It's not a jail or a mental institution. It's more like home—a place where I can be myself without interference. A place of solace."

"Solace. Interesting. Why choose that word?"

Daniel shook his head. "It's appropriate for what I sense. This tower, these feelings, and this sense of confinement are all new to me. I'm surprised myself."

Dr. Lawrence scribbled a few quick notes before rising from the desk.

"Okay, let's stop here for tonight. I'll come back next week, and we'll try to move on. In the meantime start keeping a diary of all these sensations you're experiencing. Writing them down could trigger a memory, or perhaps as we look at them, the pieces will fall into place."

"I'll do that, Doc. But I need to start paying you. I'm making some money now."

Dr. Lawrence shook his head and smiled. "Put your money aside. Let's not get bogged down by that. When the time comes, we'll deal with the financial aspects of your recovery."

"But, Doc—"

"Don't 'but Doc' me. For an old widower like me, coming over to Elisabeth's for a nice home-cooked meal is a treat. You are a great cook, and I'm the beneficiary of your skills. That sounds like a good exchange in my book."

"It's not enough."

"Of course it is." He patted Daniel's shoulder. "No more arguing. Let's join Elisabeth. By the way, it's a good idea to not give into your feelings for her for the time being."

"We're trying."

"It's not enough to try. You must decide not to do it. It's in your control."

Daniel sighed and nodded. "I will, Doc."

But Dr. Lawrence could spot Daniel's reluctance. He opened the door and the two made their way to the living room. "I'll drive you home and we'll plan the menu for next week…that is if Elisabeth is willing to keep hosting these dinners every week."

"What are you two up to?" Elisabeth asked as she emerged from the kitchen.

"If it's okay with you, I'd like to keep coming once a week for these dinners and spend time with Daniel."

Elisabeth frowned. "He isn't well yet? What's wrong?"

"He's fine, Elisabeth," Dr. Lawrence said, patting her cheek. "But we need to do more work on his memory, so I selfishly insisted on being treated to more of these wonderful gourmet meals."

"He won't take any money, so we agreed on an 'exchange of skills,' as he called it," Daniel said. "Though I'm on the winning end of that deal."

"Well," Elisabeth said, "I'm delighted to have you both here. No need to drive him home either. He could stay in the guest room."

"Elisabeth, I'll have to insist that you and Daniel proceed with restraint. He's at a crucial point in his recovery and it's best if he's in his own room at night. You must promise me that, both of you"—and he looked them squarely in the eye before continuing—"that you will not give in to your attraction for one another. You and possibly others could get hurt if you do."

They nodded, but both lowered their eyes—a sign of indecision, Dr. Lawrence knew only too well.

C H A P T E R   1 7

SARAH DEPOSITED THE tart on the passenger-side floor of her car then climbed into the driver's seat. She turned on the ignition just as the movie started playing.

Unshaved and disheveled, Alexander sat on the porch steps to his cabin, a cigarette in one hand and a half-empty bottle of whiskey in the other, humming. With the cabin in total darkness only the moonlight illuminated the surroundings.

Danny approached him with noticeable reluctance. "Hi."

Alexander raised the bottle in salute. "Well, hello there. Where has my best friend been?"

"Busy."

"Busy. To hell with busy. Come here and give me a hug, I've missed you."

Danny perched nearby, but at a safe distance. Refusing to be denied, Alexander scooted across the step and swung his arm around Danny spilling some of the whiskey on the boy's shirt.

Danny pushed him away. "You're drunk."

"Nah. If I were, I'd be writing or doing something *creative*. Listen, friend, you shouldn't abandon me like that. I need you around. I need you so I can measure up." He hugged the boy again, and this time Danny managed a smile as Alexander thrust the bottle at him.

"I've missed you too. It's not the same without you. But you were so mean to me—"

"Don't hold on to the past. It stinks. It's putrid. The past sits there, un-touched, unmovable, rotting. Let bygones be bygones. Go get us some ice and glasses."

Danny rose and disappeared into the cabin.

"How's your pecker? Still in demand?" Alexander yelled over his shoulder.

Moments later, Danny returned with a couple of glasses filled with ice. He sat by Alexander and poured the whiskey, and then set the bottle down between them.

"You bet. I've got to tell you all about it," he replied, unable to conceal his manly pride.

"No, don't."

Danny turned to him, perplexed. "But you——"

Alexander got to his feet and stumbled toward the woods. "I hate this goddamn silence. Let's get the fuck out of here. Let's go to Tent City." He staggered back to Danny, grabbed his hand, and dragged him toward the car.

"Let's not. You——"

"Shut up and get in. I'll drive." He pushed Danny into the front seat, floundered to the other side while extricating his keys from a pocket, and got in.

"You're in no condition to drive."

"You're not my keeper, so shut up."

The engine started and the headlights illuminated the forest ahead as the car lurched away in a cloud of dust.

As the dust cleared, Tent City came into view, a barren clearing in the middle of the woods, where tents and huge awnings were set up haphazardly, giving it the appearance of a massive, rundown, disorganized circus.

The Jeep skidded to a stop on the periphery. Alexander stumbled out of the vehicle almost before the headlights had a chance to go dark. Danny emerged apprehensively on the opposite side and frowned as his eyes scoured the surroundings. Alexander threw his arm around Danny's shoulders and dragged him past the makeshift perimeter.

The entire place was lit by strings of glaring white light bulbs of different sizes connected by electrical wires that hung precariously from improvised light poles. A couple of incongruent neon signs advertising gaudy adult entertainment added a touch of strident color to the otherwise stark camp-like atmosphere. Different styles of music, all too loud, escaped from tents into the night air to mix with the smoke from countless impromptu stoves and cooking fires. Several men and a handful of women sat at lopsided tables, or stood about, laughing or eating what had issued from the improvised kitchens. Others walked dirt paths that led to various establishments.

Women outfitted in tattered see-through negligees and racy underwear milled about most of the tents flashing artificial smiles at prospective clients as they strolled past. When Danny and Alexander staggered by, they blew kisses, wagged their tongues, or licked their lips suggestively.

"C'mon, boys. I'll do you both," a woman in green lace underwear cried.

"Hey, Bella, don't take 'em both. Let me have the little one. Hey boy, I've got what you're looking for," yelled a large woman in a red negligee.

Alexander trudged on without as much as a hesitation, dragging Danny with him as they lurched past the women toward a large tent with a neon sign that advertised *The Blues Bonnet*.

"Best jazz ever, right there in this shithole," Alexander yelled over the din.

They slipped through a flap into the large tent where a giant of a man stood in a cloud of cigarette smoke.

"That'll be five bucks."

Clearly prepared, Alexander pulled a bill from his shirt pocket and handed it to the man, who gave Danny a cursory glance and then pointed them in the direction of the bar.

Alexander yanked the boy deep into the establishment. The stench from years of dirty, drunken humanity invaded Danny's nostrils, causing him to hold his nose.

To one side of the tent stood a large, improvised bar backed with posters of jazz musicians and naked women pinned to the canvass of the tent. The bar hosted a small crowd of customers. Next to it, a tiny platform held a band—an albino and four African American men. The loud jazz drowned out any possibility of conversation, so those spectators who remained sober enough tapped their feet and drummed on tables, or nodded their heads to the beat.

Dragging Danny by the arm, Alexander pushed through the crowd to the bar and sat his young companion next to him. He yelled to the bartender, "Two double whiskeys on the rocks."

The bartender nodded.

As they waited, Alexander tapped Danny on the shoulder to the beat of the music. The boy turned toward him and smiled.

When the drinks arrived, Alexander handed the bartender a fifty. "Get us a table, pal."

The bartender's broad smile revealed a gap where his four front teeth used to be. He nodded, ducked out from behind the counter, and headed toward one of the tables in front of the stage. He argued briefly with the two men sitting there, snatched up their drinks, and returned to the bar with the men close behind, protesting and waving their arms in the air. The barkeep signaled toward the door, and the huge bouncer headed his way. As the bouncer approached, the two men made conciliatory gestures and settled onto two empty barstools.

When the bartender nodded toward the table, Alexander steered Danny over and slammed his drink down on the now-empty table. He shoved the boy onto a rickety chair and then spun his own chair around and straddled it, resting his chest against the back. He toasted with Danny and after a big gulp clamped a hand onto Danny's shirt and pulled him closer.

"Did you notice the bartender?" he yelled.

Danny nodded.

"That's a man who lives life and doesn't settle for an imitation. I love the bastard." Smiling, he released Danny and glanced at the bartender who gave him a thumbs-up.

A waitress in a faded-pink baby-doll negligee, bent very close to them with the clear intention of using her breasts to encourage a better order. Alexander examined her with glee.

"I'm Lola. What'll it be, gents?"

"Oh momma. You're all right. How about a couple of double whiskeys and a little suck?"

Lola smiled at Alexander. "That's extra, sweetie, and you can get it right through that door there when you're ready."

She licked her lips lasciviously and nodded toward a curtain off to one side of the stage. Alexander reached over and squeezed her breasts.

Lola pulled away, slapping his hand. "Hey. No free samples."

Alexander handed her a folded bill. She examined it and smiled at him with great satisfaction. "I'll make an exception for you, honey."

The dancer on stage paraded about in a half-hearted attempt to follow the music while Lola headed to the bar for their drinks.

Alexander yelled, "Yeah, momma. Shake it, baby, shake it."

Embarrassed, but unable to avert his eyes, Danny slumped into his chair and turned toward the dancer as she sauntered up to a man waving a dollar bill. She leaned toward him as he placed the bill between her breasts. She squeezed them tightly together to capture his hand.

Lola set the drinks on the table, and Alexander slipped her another bill.

"Two more, darling," he ordered as he slapped her bottom and gulped down his drink.

"You're going to be sick, drinking like this. Why don't we go home?" Danny implored.

Alexander gulped down Danny's drink and said, "C'mon, don't tell me you're not having fun, boys your age dream of this shit. Oh, I'm sorry. I forgot you're past this small-time stuff. After all, you're banging your hot Mrs. Fo—"

"Shut up."

Alexander clamped his hand over his mouth in mock horror, holding his breath until his face turned crimson, and expelled all the air in his lung with one explosive puff. "Whoa, what a buzz." He turned toward the dancer and yelled, "Hey! Baby! Come over and shake it right here."

He pulled a few bills from his pocket and slammed them on the stage.

Danny retrieved the money and stuffed it back in Alexander's pocket. "Don't be stupid, you're going to get robbed."

"Fuck you." He put two fingers in his mouth and whistled.

The dancer glided over to Alexander and squatted with her legs spread before him. Laughing with exaggerated enthusiasm, Alexander handed her a bill. She smiled at him, sat back and spread her legs, shaking them up in the air. Alexander grabbed Danny by the scruff of the neck and pulled him up close to her.

"Whose is better? Hers or Mrs. Foster's?

Danny shook himself loose and glared angrily at Alexander, who guffawed at the boy's reaction and shoved him back onto his chair.

"Fuck. Relax man. We're having fun."

Alexander stood up, jumped on stage, and pounced on the dancer.

Immediately, a couple of bouncers went after him, pulled him off the dancer, and knocked him out cold. When Danny tried to intervene, one of them simply pushed him unceremoniously back onto his chair.

The bouncers hoisted Alexander up effortlessly and carried him out of the tent where they dumped him face down in the dirt next to an overflowing trashcan.

Danny stood there for a few seconds, stunned. His idol, the writer he had most admired, lay unconscious and covered in filth.

Danny knelt beside him and shook him back to consciousness. He helped him to his feet and together they stumbled off down the dirt path.

"Can we go home now?" Danny insisted.

"I just wanted a little taste. They didn't have to get so upset." Alexander pushed away from him. "You're not very good at promises." He staggered down the path.

Danny hurried to catch up with him. "Where are we going now?" he asked, exasperated.

"To get fucked." And with that, he shoved Danny into a tent to his right.

The boy pulled up just shy of an older woman wearing something that resembled an old curtain more than a dress. "Careful, boy," she warned in a husky voice.

Alexander stumbled in behind and chuckled. "You can do better than that."

"How can I help you gentlemen?" Husky Voice inquired.

"Show us the best you got," Alexander replied.

The woman yelled toward the back of the tent, "Get out here. We got business."

Seconds later, three girls emerged through a curtain with big smiles on their faces. They varied in age between their late teens and late twenties as far as Danny could guess. He tried to flee but Alexander blocked his way and pushed him toward them.

Alexander chuckled as he seized one of the girls by the wrist, handed her to Danny and then pushed the two of them through the curtain. "Show her what you got, boy."

Parked in her idling car on a roadside lookout point, Sarah yelled, "My God, Alexander, you're a piece of work!" By now she had grown to expect the silence and took it as a sign that more would come.

She glanced around and realized where she was. "At least I had the good sense to pull off the road."

"What are you after?" She took a deep breath and screamed, "Answer me!"

As usual there was only silence. The movie had played and she knew nothing more would be disclosed until the next installment.

"Listen to me, you revolting bastard, I'm on my way to Williams's office, so now would be a very good time to show me if there's anything I need to be aware of before I get there?"

Silence.

"Have it your way. But it'll take that much longer to work it all out, and that's on you." She tightened her grip on the steering wheel. "You broke his heart. For what?"

Silence.

"Whatever your reasons, you've achieved your goal. I'm repulsed. No wonder you were afraid to reach out to me."

She put the car in gear and merged onto the highway.

"I realize horrible memories like these would need to be forgotten, but it all happened so long ago, why do this now?"

The hum of the road was the only response.

"You're one cruel and exasperating man."

C H A P T E R   1 8

SARAH REACHED THE outskirts of town and proceeded toward the Sheriff's Office, trying all the time to steady her nerves.

She parked the car, grabbed the tart, and shut the car door. She was about to lock it when Williams tapped her on the shoulder. She spun around in alarm.

"You startled me!"

"Really. If you're psychic how come you didn't see me coming?"

Sarah took a deep breath and forced herself to remain calm. "That's not how it works."

A sardonic smile crossed his lips. "Why are you here, Mrs. Thompson?"

"Well, I came by to speak with you, and brought you a pie I made. I hoped to find out if you've made any progress in figuring out who attacked Daniel, and ask if I could be of any help."

"No, to all of that. You can go back home. I don't eat pie."

"Technically, it isn't a pie. It's a strawberry chocolate tart." She shoved it at him, leaving him no option but to take it.

She smiled at him. "Has a famous writer ever lived around these parts?"

The unexpected question obviously intrigued Williams who cocked his head. "Writer?"

"Yes, writer."

"What kind of writer?"

"As in books. He also painted portraits."

"What does that have to do with you or Daniel?"

"I have a feeling that he might be connected. That's how this 'psychic thing'—as you call it—happens with me. So I propose that we work together in case I get more such *feelings*."

Williams stared at Sarah.

She pressed on. "I don't wish to make any trouble for you, believe me, but whether you accept it or not, God gave me a gift and I mean to use it to help others."

Williams remained silent.

Spotting her chance, Sarah pushed forward. "I believe this writer may have written a book called *Rainbow*, or at least that word is in the title, and may have lived in the area. Do you know of any such person?"

Williams mulled it over. "If I do, what's it to you?"

Sarah knew she'd hit the jackpot. "Maybe we could visit him and find out if he—"

"He's dead."

"I suspected as much, but I'd hoped his heirs would've—"

"No heirs. The place is locked up."

"Can we drive by?"

Williams glared at her but Sarah remained firm, her eyes locked onto his.

"You sure are one stubborn lady."

"I don't see myself that way. I have a duty to be of help, that's all."

"How the hell did you come up with this guy?"

"Same way I saw your father die."

Williams tightened his jaw and glowered at Sarah.

"Sheriff, for all we—"

"Be quiet!" He glanced around to make sure no one had heard her. "Don't go bringing that up. You get me?"

"I do. But it's important that you understand how I sense and perceive things. That's all. I didn't mean to upset you. I'm sorry."

He squinted as he considered her. After a few seconds he said. "Lock your car and follow me."

After Sarah did as instructed Williams opened the passenger door of his car and nodded for her to get in. He placed the tart on the floor behind his seat and got into the driver's side. Without a word, he gunned the engine and sped out of the parking lot.

"Where are we going?"

"Somewhere we can't be overheard."

The silence hung over them like a shadow as the car sped down the two-lane highway. A few minutes later he steered the vehicle onto a dirt road that snaked through the woods.

A quarter mile later, he stopped the car in the middle of nowhere and got out. He walked around the car glaring at Sarah until he reached the passenger side and opened the door for her.

"We're here," he announced.

Sarah looked around apprehensively. They were in the middle of the forest. Alone.

"Well?" Williams asked.

"Well, what?"

"Where did it happen?"

"What?"

"If you're a psychic, you ought to be able to find it."

Sarah got out of the car, took a deep breath, and looked around her. "This is the forest where your father was killed, isn't it?"

"You tell me, Psychic Lady."

She looked at him and nodded. "It is. Your father was killed right over there." She pointed to a small clearing behind a massive boulder.

All color drained from Williams's face.

"I can tell you in detail what I saw. Sometimes the images are not very clear at first, but with time they come into focus and I grasp the entire picture."

"How?"

"How does it happen you mean? How do the images come to me?"

He nodded.

Sarah shrugged. "Sometimes it's a flash, like a photograph. Sometimes it's a series of flashes, and others are clear stories, as if I were reading a chapter from a book or listening to the thoughts of someone who lived through the event. Other times it's as if I'm witnessing past moments from someone's life. It varies. When I was a child I could actually feel something that was going to happen in the future."

"When you were a child? How long have you been doing this?"

"I was born with the gift, but didn't accept it until recently, so I don't have much experience in 'doing this.' You're already familiar with Angela Thompson, my husband's grandmother and her daughters."

"Angela was a special lady, so were her girls. I'm sure you caught on that I made up that stuff about folks calling them witches."

Sarah nodded.

"I never bought the story that they were psychics, though. Angela was real smart, that's all—the rest is a bunch of bull."

"Needless to say, I disagree with you. I'm a bit like she was, in my own way."

Williams turned away shaking his head and staring at the ground. At long last, he looked up. "Okay. So tell me what you saw of my father's death."

She stepped around him and walked slowly toward the clearing. "It felt as if I were seeing what happened through the ocular lens of a rifle scope. Through it I slowly scanned the woods. Only, I wasn't the one holding the rifle. I could hear the breath of whoever was actually holding the weapon— a hunter. The search stopped as a deer came into focus. Through the rifle's scope he followed the deer as it moved left. I felt the hunter tighten the grip on the rifle as well as the increased pressure on the trigger. As the deer moved, it revealed an older man at the precise moment the hunter pulled the trigger. I could see the bullet heading toward the man who stood behind the deer." She turned back to him. "Then your face flashed before me, and it all faded away."

Williams stared at Sarah, his face pale with shock, his lower lip trembling. Sarah held his gaze.

"I was the hunter you felt," he said at last. "You described what I saw and what I did." He turned away. His shoulders convulsed as the pain and weight of his regret overwhelmed him.

Sarah didn't move, didn't speak, and didn't interrupt.

After a few moments, he wiped his face, stood erect again, and turned to face her. "I'm sorry I lost my—"

"Please, don't. No need. I can tell you're in pain."

"Not a soul knows it was my bullet that killed him."

"Are you sure it was your bullet?"

He turned and pointed. "He was right there, and I was over there." He pointed again. "You saw what happened."

"Did you have the bullet tested?"

"What are you talking about? There was no need, we were hunting, and he got shot. It was an accidental death. Only no one realized it was my bullet that killed him. There were lots of hunters out here that day. End of story."

"Maybe it wasn't your bullet."

"Why would you say that? You described what happened, what I did."

Sarah walked up to him and gazed deep into his eyes. "Because I didn't see him die from the shot you fired."

CHAPTER 19

A FAR MORE courteous Sheriff Williams escorted Sarah to her car. "Thank you, this was an eye opener. I'll see what I can find out about that writer and get back to you."

"I'll look forward to hearing from you." She unlocked her car door and he opened it.

He held out his hand.

Sarah smiled, and shook it. "Good-bye, Sheriff." She climbed into her car and headed out.

The Jeep's headlights momentarily illuminated the forest around the cabin until it came to a halt and the lights were switched off. Danny jumped out of the driver's seat and ran around the car to the passenger door.

Alexander, dirty, drunk, and soaked in the stench of sweat, slithered out and latched onto Danny.

"Fucking body. Why won't you obey?" Alexander pushed Danny away. "I don't need to lean on you, boy."

"This way, the cabin's over there."

"You go. Get the hell out of my sight. You're a fucking fag."

Danny reached for Alexander's arm, but he yanked it away and stumbled into the vehicle.

"C'mon, Alex—"

"Why didn't you fuck her? 'Cause you're a fag. That's why. You keep telling me all these stories about your precious Mrs. Foster. But you're a liar. A good-for-nothing fake."

Danny stared at his idol in disbelief. Unable to control his tears, he raised his hands to wipe his eyes, and turned away.

Alexander stopped, suddenly aware of the boy's pain. His face contorted as he howled and dropped to the ground, sobbing. "I'm sorry…I'm sorry…I always fuck it up. Danny, I love you…please, forgive me."

Danny knelt next to Alexander and put an arm around his shoulders.

"You shouldn't help me!" he said. "You shouldn't forgive me. I'm a good-for-nothing piece of shit. I'm the fake, Danny, not you, that's why I love you. I aspire to be you, goddammit. I hanker to be Danny."

"No, you're not a fake, you're drunk."

"Oh yeah? If I'm drunk, how come I can't write?" Alexander crawled on all fours and sniffed the ground like a dog. "There's a revolting stench around here. Can you guess what it is?"

Danny sniffed the air. "Well, there's—"

"Failure…that's what it is, the stench of failure." He sat down, holding his head between his hands, and resting his elbows on his knees. "How can one repeat oneself? I can't be what I was twenty years ago. Honest, I can't." He began to convulse in sobs of despair.

"Now what? What's wrong?"

Alexander glared up at him. "I'm a loser. A fucking con. My life is a sham."

"C'mon, don't be so melodramatic, you're not a loser. You're unique like me. We're one of a kind."

"Unique? Ha! I lied. *My* lie to you and to me. I lied to both of us."

"No."

"Oh yes, my friend. Friend? Hell, I don't have a friend. I don't need a friend. I wouldn't know what to do with a friend." He struggled to get to his feet, but stumbled back to the ground.

"C'mon, let me help you."

Alexander yanked his arm away from Danny's grip, fell flat on his face, and went on, his face in the dirt. "*Rainbow* was a fluke. A fucking accident. I've spent the rest of my useless life trying to repeat a fucking accident."

"Your new novel is as goo—"

"It's trash. It's fucking shit." In a fury he managed to get up only to stumble again and collide with a nearby tree. He threw his arms around it to steady himself.

Danny moved closer. "No, it isn't. It's good. I've read some of it. I like it. Hey, you're bleeding."

Alexander's tears mingled with the blood dripping from his forehead. "Don't you get it? I tricked you. I fucking deceived you. Conned you. I'm nothing. You're everything. You're doing the magic. I'm a fraud. A fucking wizard with an audience of one."

Alexander jerked forward and began to heave violently.

Fighting back his own tears, Danny looked away. He wiped his tears, took a deep breath, and turned back to find that Alexander had passed out.

Danny rolled him over and shook him back to consciousness, got him to his feet and helped him toward the cabin.

Ten minutes later, Alexander lay peacefully tucked into his bed. The gash on his forehead was neatly patched and Danny sat beside him.

Alexander opened his eyes, recognized his surroundings and smiled. "What a clever boy. You saved me all on your own."

"How do you feel?"

"Like I smashed my head against a wall."

"Actually, you hit the ground first, and then a tree. No wall."

Danny started to get up when Alexander grabbed his arm. "Don't leave… please."

He smiled. "Okay, but it's late, I'm—"

Alexander patted the bed next to him. "C'mon. Sleep by me."

After a moment's hesitation, Danny slipped off his shoes and crawled on top of the bed. "I'll stay until you fall asleep. But I've got to get home. It's real late."

Alexander closed his eyes and sighed. "It's been twenty four years since I wrote that damned book."

"So?"

"I've written nothing since. Nothing."

"So what? A wise man once told me, 'Don't hold on to the past,' and I quote: *It stinks.*"

Alexander took the boy's hand, sighed again, and closed his eyes. "Why do you have to bring up all the shit I dish out?"

"'Cause I like it. Most of it, anyway."

"Promise you'll always be here when I need you."

"Sure."

"It won't happen, but it's nice to hear you say it."

"I mean it."

"Even after what I put you through tonight?"

"Even after."

"Why?"

"You were drunk. You're in pain."

"It doesn't excuse what I've done, what I've become."

"No, but that's what artists do, first they suffer, and then they create. Something good will come out of all this."

Alexander smiled. "You really believe that, don't you?"

"I do. Give it some time."

"How long?"

"As long as it takes."

"What if I don't?"

"Then you'll go on suffering till you do."

"Will you forgive me then?"

"Yeah."

"Okay, I'll hold you to that."

Danny watched him drift off to sleep, gently pulled his hand away and silently put on his shoes. He turned off the light and sneaked out into the night.

"Where on God's earth have you been?" Conrad stood on the porch as Sarah made her way up the stairs. "Why didn't you answer your cell?" Without waiting for a response he stormed into the house.

Sarah dug into her purse. "I had to stop on the side of the road and—" she found her phone. "Oops, I'm sorry. I turned off the ringer to talk with Williams and forgot to turn it on."

She entered the house, shut the door, and followed her angry husband into the living room. "I'm sorry to have worried you."

Conrad stalked about the living room like a caged animal. "Sarah, I've been more than worried. I thought something had happened to you. Tom's out looking for you, Alyana is calling everyone, and I went as far as to call the Sheriff's office and demand that Williams explain himself."

"What? Why?"

"You were nowhere to be found, and look at the time. It's the middle of the night for crying out loud!"

"Sorry, I had to pull over. Alexander played an awful part of his movie as I was driving back home. I had no choice but to stop."

Conrad continued pacing and growling trying to defuse his anger.

Sarah stepped toward him, but he raised his hand as a clear signal not to come close. She stopped and offered another apology. "I'm so sorry, I forgot about the ringer on the cell, and—"

There was a knock at the door. Conrad strode past his wife and found Williams standing outside.

"Hello, Mr. Thompson. I see that Sarah—Mrs. Thompson—found her way safely home. I'm glad she's all right."

"Yes, thank you. Please come in. Sarah, here's Sheriff Williams. Excuse me, I need to tell my kids she's home. I'm sorry to have bothered you." Conrad grabbed his cell phone and stepped outside, leaving Williams and Sarah standing by the front door.

"Please come in, Billy. Can I get you something to drink?"

"Don't bother, Sarah; I'm relieved you're okay. Where've you been? Don't tell me you went off in search of that writer's property."

"No. Come in, please."

"I really need to be on my way." He turned to leave and then stopped. "Oh. You recall I told you we found some keys near Daniel that night you found him?"

"Yes."

"Well, the keychain had a metal tag with the word *Rainbow* inscribed on it. That writer's ranch is called *Rainbow*."

Sarah gasped. "Oh my God."

"I have to admit that you may have tapped into something."

"Are you going out there?"

"Where?" Conrad asked.

"Billy says Alexander did live in these parts. He's dead now, but his ranch is called *Rainbow,* and the keychain found next to Daniel has the word *Rainbow* inscribed on it."

"You knew the man's name?" an astonished Williams asked Sarah.

"Is that his real name? Alexander?" she asked in disbelief.

"Yeah, his name was Alexander—"

"Pitman?" Sarah interrupted.

Williams nodded, and shot a bemused look at Conrad.

"Sheriff, please come in. Let's not stand out here," he said.

"No, I have to go. Sarah, I'll call you with an update. Mr. Thompson." He gave a quick nod, put on his hat, and stepped off the porch.

Conrad escorted his wife into the house, shut the door and locked it.

"Is Tom okay? Is he on his way home?"

"He is, and he's glad that you're all right." He raised his eyebrows and tilted his head inquisitively. "Billy? Sarah? You've made some serious progress."

"Yes, all is well. He's no longer fighting me. On the contrary," she added with pride, "I suspect that he's quite impressed with me."

"What on earth did you do to bring him around like that?"

"I told him about the images of him and his father."

"Why?"

"Billy has wondered for years whether it was his bullet that killed his father."

Conrad froze and stared at his wife. "He actually told you that?"

"Yeah. Turns out that what I saw through the rifle's scope is exactly what Williams saw through his weapon the day his father died. I'd say I've tapped into his subconscious."

"Williams's subconscious?"

"Yes, but I got the impression that his bullet may not be the one that killed his dad."

"An impression?"

"A very strong one. I'm not sure if it's correct or not, but I told him about it."

"And?"

"Well, needless to say, he was intrigued."

"I imagine so."

"My description of the event was so accurate that he couldn't deny my abilities. It overwhelmed him enough to accept all of it."

She stepped close to her husband, looking up at him. "I'm so sorry I worried you."

Without hesitation, Conrad pulled Sarah to him and kissed her. It wasn't a tender, gentle kiss. This kiss demanded submission and acknowledgment, and conveyed desperate need.

Sarah surrendered without resistance.

His hands frantically unbuttoned her blouse, seeking the comfort of her breasts. Kicking off her shoes, she opened his shirt and undid his belt, yet their lips never parted and their tongues remained intertwined.

Her skirt reached the floor before his pants did, and he slipped off her underwear as his hands pressed into her skin wishing to absorb her very essence. She tried to reciprocate, reaching for his underwear, but in one fluid motion he yanked them off, and threw his socks and shoes to one side.

He pressed her to him, his lips devouring hers, and without letting go, carried her into the living room, easing her down onto the carpet.

He entered her with a desire she'd never experienced with him before. His need for her exploded in forceful shoves as he placed his hand behind her lower back, lifting her to him each time he thrust into her. His desperate passion, his need to fully possess her, aroused every fiber in her body until she shivered beneath him. His lips never left hers, their mouths exchanging the words they couldn't utter but needed to convey, their love for one another confirmed by a passion impossible to contain.

She took him in without reservation or hesitation, giving her soul to him as he gave his to her through the intimacy of physical connection, the union of one body entwined with the other.

They climaxed together, their cries of pleasure intermingled as their hearts raced, and the joy of their fulfillment exploded. Then, in tandem, the convulsions of their bodies subsided, and their breathing slowed, until only their union remained. In perfect stillness, they savored the warmth of being one.

They remained in their embrace for a long time, enjoying the tranquility between them, understanding the fear that had brought them together in this desperate act of love.

After a while, Conrad rolled onto the floor next to his wife, his hand grasping hers. "I'm sorry I was so forceful," he whispered. "I was so scared I'd lost you."

She rolled onto her side, kissed her husband, and laid her head on his chest. "Don't apologize; I'm the one to blame. But on the other hand, this was pretty damn spectacular."

Conrad slipped his arm under her and embraced her. "You're something else, Sarah."

"Wait till I tell you what Alexander did."

"*No.* Not now. Tonight it's you and me, and no one else. Tonight you're all mine."

CHAPTER 20

Sarah rolled the sheet of pasta dough in preparation for dinner. As she labored cautiously to create the perfect linguine noodles, the image of another sun-drenched Amaray day slipped in.

Danny relaxed on his porch reading a book, a small baby blue blanket on his lap and a frosty glass of lemonade on the table nearby.

Mrs. Foster strutted up to the porch holding a bakery box in both hands. She wore a tight pink summer dress that accentuated her womanly figure, matching high-heeled pink shoes, and a pink-and-white hat. Her hair bounced luxuriously with every step.

"Hello, there, darling boy," she exclaimed as she stopped next to him.

Danny blushed and glanced around nervously. "Mrs. Foster, what are you doing here?"

Shirley appeared at the front door. "Danny, what a thing to say to a visitor. Hello Allyson, how nice of you to come by."

Shirley stepped forward and extended her hand after wiping it on her apron. She wore a plain, loose, white linen summer dress with a blue apron and white sandals. Her hair was in a ponytail adorned with a simple blue ribbon.

"Hi Shirley, came to bring some pastries for our sick boy."

"You didn't have to bake for me, Mrs. Foster," he said.

"Oh darling boy, no, no, no, I don't bake. I bought them at that quaint little store down the street. That nice lady who lives in that horrid imitation French cottage makes them and sells them to Mr. O'Connor. They're quite good."

"Let me get you a chair," Shirley offered. "I'll be right back."

"I'll get it Mom," Danny attempted to stand but Mrs. Foster caught his arm and pulled him down.

"You stay here. You're ill."

"But—"

"She's right, Danny, I'll be right back." Shirley disappeared inside the house.

"What are you doing here?" the boy whispered.

"I miss you. You do look a bit pale. What's wrong with you?"

"Nothing."

"Then why didn't you come to work?" she asked with a suggestive wink.

Shirley returned with a chair and placed it next to Danny. "I'll bring another for me, and we can visit. Will you have some of the pastries and lemonade, Allyson?"

"I'll take the lemonade. The pastries are for our sick boy."

"I'm not *sick*. I'm…not well, and I don't want any pastries."

"Danny," his mother scolded, "watch your tone." She turned toward Mrs. Foster. "On top of everything else he's got an angry bug, he's been grouchy, and completely out of sorts."

"Oh?" Mrs. Foster smiled. "He probably needs love, loads of love."

Shirley chuckled and disappeared into the house.

"You've got to go, Mrs. Foster. You're making me nervous."

"Danny, darling, how could I?" She reached over and grabbed his hand.

He yanked it away and looked around apprehensively. "You're going to get both of us into trouble. Go home. I'll come tomorrow."

Mrs. Foster waved toward the sidewalk. "Oh, look who's here."

At that moment Ellie, beaming with joy, dashed up to Danny's porch.

"What are you doing here?" Danny asked, irritated by the discomfort of the situation.

"Gee, what a welcome. I only came by because I was told you were sick. But," she said with a shrug toward Mrs. Foster, "he doesn't look ill at all, only grumpy."

Shirley came out with a chair. "Ellie, how nice to see you. Here's a chair, sit down."

"I don't think I'm welcome, Mrs. Michaels."

Shirley glared at her son. "Nonsense. Care for some lemonade?"

Ellie nodded, but remained standing as she addressed Mrs. Foster. "You told me he was sick, but he looks fine to me."

"You told *her*?"

"What's wrong with that?" Ellie retorted.

"I'm not sick, that's what's wrong."

"Then what are you doing on the porch in the middle of summer, covered with your baby blanket reading a book, instead of at the beach?"

"Who said it's my baby blanket? And what does it matter what I do with my own time?"

"Now, now, young lovers," Mrs. Foster cut in, "you mustn't quarrel. C'mon Ellie, sit right here by me." She patted the chair next to her as Shirley returned with a third chair.

Ellie sat down, arms tightly folded across her chest.

"I'll be right back with some lemonade," Shirley said and left again.

"How long has it been since you two were last together?"

Danny shrugged.

"Two weeks. Ever since I came back from my trip he's been giving me the cold shoulder," Ellie said.

"So now the two of you are going to compare notes on me?"

Ellie jumped to her feet. "Listen, buster, I don't compare notes about you with anyone because there's nothing to compare."

Mrs. Foster winked at Danny and took Ellie's hand, coaxing her to sit down again. "Now, Danny, play nice. Unlike boys, we girls like to help each other. Listen to me, young man, Ellie here is a beauty, and unless you act smarter, you're going to lose her to someone else."

Danny shrugged and looked away.

Mrs. Foster went on. "Why on earth would you break up with her? You two were a much talked-about lovely couple until…when was it? Oh, around the time you started working on my garden, right?"

Danny frowned, and Ellie nodded.

"So what could possibly have come between you?"

"Nothing!" Danny bellowed, jumping to his feet. He rushed into the house, almost colliding with his mother who held a tray of glasses. "Sorry, Mom. I'm going to lie down."

"Danny, come back this instant. You have guests."

His bedroom door slammed shut.

Sarah sipped her wine and looked at Conrad. "That floozy is using him to amuse herself."

They'd enjoyed a quiet dinner at home with only a couple of candles lighting the table, while soft music played in the background.

"I wish we didn't have to spend our dinners talking about this darn movie?" Conrad protested.

"I'm sorry—"

He sighed. "Don't be. You need to share it and I need to help you. But after a full day's work, I look forward to a restful evening with my wife."

"I don't have to go on and on about it. Anyway, tell me about your day."

"Nothing to tell, really. Anyway, finish your assessment of the last movie installment."

"That's it, really. That sick woman stole Danny's youth."

"A tough lesson at an early age."

The phone rang and Conrad went to take the call. Sarah could only make out fragments of the conversation. Moments later he returned to the table.

"Williams found Alexander's estate, *Rainbow*. He asked that we meet there tomorrow."

"Did he say if they found something helpful?"

"No. He asked that both of us be there. He insisted I come, too."

"Oh?"

"Says you'll need me at your side."

"*Stehekin*—The Way Through," Daniel said pensively.

"Interesting name, isn't it?" Elisabeth whispered as she admired their surroundings.

She had picked up Daniel early Sunday morning and taken him to the dock of the *Lady of the Lake* ship in Lake Chelan. They were now cruising on their way back from *Stehekin*.

"Can you imagine what the Native American tribes must've endured when they traveled by foot or canoe through the Cascades? No wonder they named it The Way Through once they got there. They were relieved to survive it," Elisabeth said.

"It's hard to imagine, considering that even now the only way to reach this remote community is by water, floatplane, or hiking over those same mountain trails. Makes their achievement that much more remarkable."

"And makes the place even more special."

"I couldn't live there, though. They need boats and barges to bring them everything from groceries and supplies, to cars, equipment, building materials, and even us tourists."

"That's probably why there are less than a hundred year-round residents."

"A smaller than small community where no secrets would be safe."

"Secrets?" Elisabeth asked with a puzzled look.

"Did you notice the houses?" Daniel asked her. "They stand there, side by side, unapproachable, concealing their inhabitants, screening them from outside curiosity…and from each other. This idyllic landscape with its spattering of cute hillside homes is a façade. The worst secrets are always hidden away in ordinary, ideal-looking houses."

"My goodness Daniel, that's quite chilling."

"Maybe it's me. Maybe my feelings have nothing to do with the scenery but more to do with whatever darkness populates my lost memories."

Elisabeth turned to him. "Could you be trying to forget people in your life?" Despite the wind blowing her hair over her face, the concerned look in her eyes was clear.

"Don't you start analyzing me. I have enough with Doc scratching away inside my head."

"It was an odd thing to say, that's all." She turned away to face the wind, her hair now flowing nicely behind her.

Daniel remained silent for a while and then gently placed his hand on her shoulder. "I'm sorry. For some reason this place unsettled me. Nevertheless, as much as I complained about you whisking me away at dawn, I do appreciate that we're here together now."

"It's about time. I don't understand why you're making such a big deal about us being alone. We're surrounded by people, look around you."

"It's not the people. It's us and what we might do." Daniel removed his hand from her shoulder causing her to turn toward him again.

She pushed her hair away and took Daniel's hand. "We don't have to hold back. I'm willing to take the risk."

Daniel gently freed his hand. "I'm not sure I am." He turned and headed toward the stern.

Elisabeth watched him walk away. She turned to face the wind and little by little it whisked away her tears.

They remained separate from each other until Daniel forced himself to return and face her. This time the wind swirled around his hair, but the effect was entirely different—it endowed him with an aura of splendor.

"Please don't be angry with me," he said. "I can't—"

"We're not children, Daniel. We understand what we're getting into. If we're willing to live with the consequences, whose business is it what we do or don't do?"

"The business of the people we might hurt."

"What if there's no one?"

"Once we find out, we'll decide what to do."

"In the meantime—"

"We wait."

She tilted her head. "You're acting as if something has happened. Did you remember something...or someone?"

"No."

"Then, what is it?"

"I need to be certain of my feelings for you."

She paled. Her eyes erupted with tears, betraying her efforts to appear calm and collected.

"Please, Elisabeth, don't—"

This time, she walked away from him.

CHAPTER 21

AFTER DINNER, DR. Lawrence sat with Daniel in Elisabeth's study. "Well," he leaned back in the desk chair, "I'm so full I'm not sure I'll be of much use to you tonight. That was some meal. Where do you suppose you learned to cook so well? The lamb was delicious, the roasted potatoes were perfect, and those tartelettes...the third one did me in."

"I'm glad you enjoyed yourself," Daniel said. "We had a good time preparing it."

He nodded. "Too much I'd say. That, coupled with your escapade to Stehekin—"

"I get it, Doc," Daniel interrupted. "Next week, dinner will be at the Thompson's—no doubt your idea to make sure we aren't alone in the kitchen. Just like you showing up early tonight to keep an eye on us. I've got your number, Doc."

Dr. Lawrence blushed a bit and smiled. "Well, it's easier that way, wouldn't you say?"

Daniel remained motionless.

"So," the doctor forged on, "where could your culinary expertise come from?"

"I have no idea where or how I learned. And yet, as we were fixing dinner, I got the impression that I may indeed have lived in Europe, perhaps even in Latin America and Asia."

"What makes you say that?"

"The familiarity of the foods, the recipes that pop in into my head, my ability to communicate in French, Spanish, and Italian, and a smattering of Mandarin, Thai, and even Japanese. It all indicates that I lived in those places, spent some time there."

"Elisabeth said she'd been showing you photos of faraway lands. What do you experience when you look at them?"

"An old, comfortable feeling. The kind I experience going into my little room above Conrad's store. A safe haven."

"Elisabeth might be right. You may have been a chef in many parts of the world."

Daniel shrugged. "Perhaps."

"Something's going on. What is it? What's bothering you?"

"I'm so tired of this uncertainty. I'm like a ship lost at sea, going nowhere, accomplishing nothing. I trudge along, day in and day out, without purpose or direction."

"We all understand your frustration. But time is your best ally. Considering your injuries, you're lucky to even be alive."

"I'm a grown man, Doc, and here I am working at a job that a teenager would do during the summer, mooching off the kindness of folks. I'm tired of it all."

"Maybe that's a good sign. Perhaps this uneasiness will push your mind."

"What if I don't wish to remember?"

Dr. Lawrence leaned forward and peered at Daniel over his glasses. "What are you saying?"

"What if I'm running away from something, or someone and I don't wish to remember? What if I broke a promise, or let someone down, or did something awful and can't deal with it?"

"Daniel, have you uncovered something?"

"No." Daniel rose and turned his back to him. His voice dropped to a whisper. "But I'd rather not find out what I did if it means that I can't be with Elisabeth for the rest of my life."

Dr. Lawrence leaned back on the chair. "Ah. Elisabeth—she's what's bothering you."

Daniel turned back and glared at Dr. Lawrence. "Yes, Elisabeth. I'm afraid I won't be able to stop myself, and that makes me sick."

"Whatever do you mean?"

"I hate it when people lose control. I hate the idea that I might lose control, and yet I'm this close to doing exactly that with her."

The doctor rose slowly. He came around the desk to Daniel, placing his hand on his shoulder. "Come back and sit down. Please. Let's talk about this." He nudged him toward the chair in front of the desk. He dragged the other chair close and rested his hands on Daniel's knees. "Now, listen to me very carefully, Daniel. You're making tremendous progress in retrieving emotions, if not specific memories. You sensed your dislike for psychiatrists, you're pretty sure that you don't like people who lose control, you've guessed that you've traveled the world, you speak several languages, and you're certainly at ease in a kitchen. That's a hell of a lot of progress by any measure."

"But other than the languages, the rest are mere impressions, nothing concrete. The only solid thing right now is my love for Elisabeth, and that's the one thing I can't act on for fear of the unknown. I can't take it, Doc." He slammed his fist on the desk.

"I get that, but each time we chat you discover more about who you are and what you like or dislike. Your true personality is emerging little by little."

"But without any tangibles, what good will that do?"

"Have you been writing like I asked you?"

"I tried, but I couldn't."

"Why?"

"I felt as if I shouldn't."

Dr. Lawrence sat back. "That's odd. Why shouldn't you?"

Daniel shook his head. "I wish I had an answer, but the truth is that I simply can't."

"Have you ever written in a diary before?"

Daniel looked up, seemingly searching for the answer. "I doubt it. The concept of writing feels uncomfortable. It feels like suffering. It feels like it might steal my soul." He sighed. "On the other hand, maybe that means that I have written and couldn't handle the outcome."

The doctor moved back behind the desk to jot down a few notes in Daniel's chart.

"What did your friend the psychiatrist have to say?" Daniel asked, his tone disdainful.

Dr. Lawrence stopped writing and looked up at his patient. "Ah, I wondered when you'd ask me that. Well, I'm not going to tell you. Given that you chose not to go to him, I've decided to apply his suggestions without letting on if what I am doing is my idea or his."

"I don't care as long as you keep meeting with me and tolerating all my crap. Although I would prefer that you didn't write in that chart of yours."

"Is that so? Why?"

"I detest the idea that there is a chart about me, over which I have no control that reflects the terrible things I've been through for anyone to read."

"Interesting," he said as he wrote a few more notes.

"Now you're sounding like a psychiatrist."

"I am, aren't I? Forgive me. But I promise you no one will have access to this chart but me. Now, let's go back to why *you* won't write."

"Fine with me, but I can't come up with anything else to tell you."

"Have you ever been criticized for something you wrote?"

"I have no idea."

"Was someone you knew criticized in a way that hurt him or her?"

Daniel scowled. "Mm, maybe. That notion struck a chord."

"Good. What can you tell me about that?"

Daniel remained silent for a long time, once more seeming to search for something, but then shook his head. "Nothing."

"Well, mull it over until we meet next time. All I ask is for you to be as patient as you are with Elisabeth when you're teaching her. She's a handful in that kitchen, by the way."

A heartfelt smile traced across Daniel's lips. "Yes, she's a bit of a challenge, always has to do it her way. But the fact is that her way has turned out to be pretty good at times. Better than what I could come up with. She takes good care of me, keeps me busy so that I don't get depressed about all the bad stuff."

"That's good, but you must keep your physical distance from one another."

"Alright, alright," Daniel said impatiently.

"That's why we insist on being around you. It makes it easier."

"Easier?"

"For you to keep your hands off each other when I or the Thompsons are around."

"I suppose so."

"Not that it stopped you from holding her hand to help her cut the onion, or caressing her bare shoulder when you congratulated her on how she made the little tart shells all by herself."

Daniel couldn't hide a smile. "Nothing escapes you, does it?"

"You're playing with fire."

"You and the Thompsons keep beating that into me. But I find comfort in my feelings."

"Are you referring to the feeling of doing what you shouldn't, or your love for Elisabeth?"

"Both."

"Then here's something else for you to ponder. Is your love for Elisabeth real or simply a desire for forbidden fruit?"

Daniel frowned. "You're good, Doc. To be honest, at this moment I don't have a clue how to answer that question."

"Then you better give it some serious consideration so you don't succumb to what you desire, rather than true love."

"Boy, that's a challenge I don't look forward to."

"Will you do it?"

Daniel stared across the desk at the doctor. "We'll find out next time we meet, won't we?"

C H A P T E R   2 2

"I'M INTRIGUED AS to what we are going to find in Alexander's place," Conrad said as he drove through the mountain pass, "and why Sheriff Williams insisted that I come. He must've found something that might affect you. What do you think?"

Sarah stared out the window.

"Sarah?" He glanced at this wife. "Alexander's whisked you away. It better be good."

As Danny approached Alexander's cabin, the clicking sound of the typewriter reached his ears. He stopped, fearful that Alexander may have sought inspiration in bourbon once again. The moonlight lit his face as he circled the cabin a couple of times.

He peeked through the open window to find Alexander typing away, no sign of a bottle or a glass on the table.

Alexander spotted Danny, stopped typing, and smiled. "Danny boy! Come in."

"Are you sober?"

"What are you, my nanny?"

"I don't care much for you when you're drunk, that's all."

"Hey, we've been drunk together before, you didn't mind then."

"Not that kind of drunk. The other kind."

"Ah, you mean the satiation for inspiration kind."

"Yeah."

"Well, for your information, I haven't had a sip for days."

"I don't believe you."

Alexander shot to his feet causing his chair to flip over onto the floor, and stomped to the window. Nose to nose with the boy, he blew right onto his face. "Now you believe me?"

Danny recoiled. "Ugh, you have bad breath."

"Yeah, but no alcohol."

Danny smiled. "So what are you up to?"

"Isn't it obvious? I'm writing. And painting. Look." He pointed across the room. "I finished your portrait. What do you think?"

Danny leaned through the window to get a good view. What he saw stunned him. The portrait, though far from being a realistic rendering, was unmistakably him. Alexander had completely redone the style so it conformed to his perception of the boy, with broad strokes that gave him an air of soulful mischief and inner strength.

"Wow! That's amazing!"

"Yeah, I do portraits okay. It's the writing that's shit."

"It's not. Look at *Rainbow*."

"Forget that one. I'm writing a new one."

"Great! What's it about?"

Alexander leaned against the windowsill. "It's quite simple, really. It used to be a father-and-son story, but now it's a story about two friends, which is what it was meant to be all along. Only I didn't figure it out, until the other night." He placed a hand gently on the boy's shoulder. "Listen, Danny, I'm sorry I put you through hell. Is that why you haven't come by to visit me, or have you been busy with the Mrs. or Ellie?"

He shook his head. "Neither. I'm sick of women."

"Nonsense. You're too young for that."

"Listen, I won't disturb you if you're inspired. I'll come back in the morning."

"Don't put me off. C'mon, let's go skinny dipping and you tell me what's worrying you."

"But—"

Alexander burst out of the cabin and pranced toward the lake, shedding his clothes along the way.

Danny rushed after him through the woods picking up the discarded clothes. By the time he reached the shore, Alexander stood waist deep in the water splashing about.

"C'mon on, buddy."

Danny undressed and swam toward his friend. "This reminds me of the night we met."

"Indeed. The best thing that's ever happened to me."

"Yeah, sure."

"I mean it. You've become my inspiration, my muse."

"What's gotten into you? Are you going to start acting weird again?"

Alexander approached Danny and grabbed him by the back of the neck, looking him sternly in the eye. "You need to listen. And you must believe me, because I don't do serious often, and I have to be serious for a moment. Got it?"

Danny nodded and tried to break the hold, but Alexander held fast.

"You have a purity that I crave and an honesty I envy. In my stupidity I almost spoiled that the other night, but you protected it. However, I managed to get a taste of it, enough to cleanse my soul—well, maybe not totally, but as much cleansing as it could tolerate. Thank you for that." With a smile he released the boy's neck, and ruffled his hair.

"Does that mean your soul doesn't need to run away any more?"

Alexander laughed. "You do listen to my shit, God help you. Yes, my friend, for now my soul is quite content. It won't last long, though. Inevitably, I'll find a way to screw it up. I always do. There, I'm done being serious. Your turn—what's bothering you?"

"Mrs. Foster is toying with me and Ellie."

"Whoa, a ménage à trois. Boy, she really plans to devour your purity. Whereas I am happy having a little taste."

"C'mon, I'm being serious."

"So am I. Okay, I'll be quiet and listen."

"They came to visit me when I was sick a couple of days ago."

"You were sick? Is that why you haven't visited me?"

"To be honest, I wasn't really sick. I was pretty shook up about Tent City and—"

"Say no more. I get it. Tell me about your women."

"Mrs. Foster came over to visit me and invited Ellie to come as well. Then she began to taunt us about why we aren't a couple and stuff like that. I told her why I couldn't be with Ellie. She played with us as if we were her toys."

"Then what happened?"

"I got angry and left them with my mom."

"Well done, my boy. Well done."

Danny faced Alexander. "What should I do?"

"What do you want to do?"

"Nothing, I guess."

"Nothing is also a way of doing. Do nothing, then."

"Nothing?"

"That's what you said."

"But—"

"Well, what is it, then?"

"I'm all confused."

"Good."

Danny splashed water on Alexander. "Stop it. You're toying with me, like Mrs. Foster."

"Hey, I'm being supportive."

"You don't know how to. It's not who you are."

"Then you need to teach me if I'm going to write a book about friendship."

"That's all I am to you, isn't it, research for your book. Forget it."

With that, Danny swam back to the shore, dried himself with his shirt and got dressed.

Alexander remained in the water. "Danny," he called out at last. "You're more than research, believe me. You're my teacher. My friend. I've forgotten how to treat a friend."

Danny turned to him and smiled. "Okay, but it's better if you're you. Don't pretend."

Alexander joined Danny on shore. He picked up his clothes and patted his hairy chest dry, threw his wet shirt on the ground and sat on it. "I've lost track of how not to pretend. I lost myself to pretense years ago."

"Read *Rainbow* again, you're there on every page, in the heart and soul of Wesley."

Alexander reached over and placed his hand on Danny's back. "What a dreamer you are. Didn't I tell you that book was a fluke?"

Danny shook his head. "You wrote it. That's who you really are."

"Touché. Anyway, let's get back to you and your ladies. What are your plans? Who do you choose to be with? Or should I say who do you want to fuck?"

Danny shivered and Alexander pulled back his hand.

"Don't tell me I've ruined the joy of sex for you. I must've been quite a sight."

Danny remained silent, his head down.

Alexander nodded and sighed. "Then by all means do nothing until the urge returns. Believe me, it'll come back." He got to his feet, slipped on his pants, and offered his hand to help Danny. "It'll never be the same for you, though. Please forgive me, if you can."

Danny stood on his own avoiding Alexander's gaze. "You were drunk."

"Yeah, that's it," he said sadly.

"So give me some friendly advice."

"I did."

"What? Do nothing?"

"Sometimes it's good to distance oneself from the heart of things."

"You mean, run away?"

"No. No, no, no. I've done that and it doesn't help. I mean, detach for a while."

Alexander threw his arm over Danny's shoulder and guided him back to the cabin.

The Amaray sunshine was in full splendor as Danny trudged up the steps and knocked on Ellie's door. He wiped his hands on his pants and took a deep breath as she opened the door.

"Hi," he blurted out.

"Hi," she responded with a forced smile. "This is unexpected. You feeling better?"

"Yeah. A lot better." He shuffled about as he searched for words. I…uh… need to say that you and I…that maybe we shouldn't—"

"Just say it. You came to break up with me." Her eyes filled with tears.

He avoided her gaze. "Yeah…for a while. Maybe later on we—"

Ellie slammed the door in his face.

Danny heard her sob through the door. He dropped his head in shame and shut his eyes.

"What a shit I am," he mumbled, and then shuffled off the porch and down the street.

Danny made his way to Mrs. Foster's house where he stood several feet away from the front door. After a deep breath, he straightened up and resolutely knocked.

Moments later, Mrs. Foster appeared wearing a baby-blue summer dress which, like most of her clothing, accentuated her considerable cleavage. She smiled with genuine surprise.

"Danny, darling. Welcome." She stepped to one side to allow her lover entrance.

"I'm not coming in. I'll never come in again. I'm going to keep working on the roses because that's what Mr. Foster hired me for, but that's it."

Mrs. Foster's eyes widened, a look of disbelief across her face. "Why? What's happened?"

"I don't want to sin."

"Oh, you've talked to your father. He's forcing you to do this."

"No! I could never tell him. It would kill him. I can't do it anymore. That's all."

"But—"

"Mrs. Foster, please, let me be." He turned and walked away.

"You promised."

He stopped to glance back at her. "I promised not to forget you, and I never will."

"You said you loved me," she said.

Danny walked away from her, and without turning back, waved good-bye.

Conrad's truck had come to a stop in the midst of several police vehicles, a coroner's van, and other official cars parked before a secluded, somber-looking house in the middle of a wooded area. A small army of men traveled to and from the house.

"That's it?" Conrad asked. "I expected Alexander to give you something a bit more helpful on our way to his house."

Sarah's eyes scanned the house and its surroundings before settling on her husband. "Nope. That's it. Alexander's very stingy with his help."

"Why is he making it so difficult?"

"That's his style." She leaned back on the headrest. "How long did I detach this time? Were you talking to me when I drifted off?"

"No more than a minute."

"I wish you could have seen the finished portrait of Danny. It's truly magnificent."

"He should've given you a heads up."

"He orchestrated this entire scenario so that I would react in a given way."

"What do you mean?"

"He's pushing me to feel fear, or shock, so that I'll connect with something deeper, something he doesn't dare share with me. He has a flair for the dramatic."

"That he does. Well, c'mon, let's find out what he has in store for us."

Sarah jumped down from the truck and stared at the three-story house. Built in the gothic style with grey and black tones, it had a steeply pitched, gabled roof, carved asymmetrical side panels, and pointed-arch windows. A stained glass door served as the focal point of a one-story porch adorned with gothic arches. An obvious and purposeful statement of individuality, the design of the home didn't resemble anything else in the area, yet it somehow looked perfectly comfortable in its surroundings.

Sarah stood transfixed, her hand resting on the open door of the truck.

Conrad waited a few seconds before asking, "Are you okay?"

As if awakened from a dream Sarah focused on him. "Yes. Can you believe this house?"

"Eccentric, isn't it?" Conrad said as he shut the door.

"Looks like its owner."

"In what way?" Conrad took Sarah's arm and they walked to the front porch.

"Its boldness—a uniqueness that borders on arrogance."

Sheriff Williams emerged from the house and clambered down to meet them.

"Thanks for coming," he said as he tilted his hat. "Be prepared, folks. There's lots of blood in there. No bodies, but lots of blood. I need you to put these disposable booties on over your shoes, and make sure you don't touch a thing."

They slipped on the booties and followed Williams up the stairs to the front porch. Sarah hesitated for a moment, and then clenching her husband's arm cautiously, she entered the house.

As advertised, spatters of dry blood covered the foyer and stairs. Police officers and crime scene investigators milled about the elegant vestibule, collecting evidence.

Sarah froze and released her husband's arm as she stared up the stairs.

A flash of mixed images flooded her mind—Alexander descending the stairs gripping his chest, the tornado of violence around Daniel, the blood, the knife, and the pain.

"Sorry, Sarah," Williams called, "we can't stop here now. We're going to the library."

Sarah blinked and realized that Williams stood right in front of her. Conrad stood behind her, a hand gently resting on her shoulder. Cautiously, she followed Williams into the library.

Sarah gasped as she caught sight of the magnificent room. It featured a wall-to-wall window that gave a spectacular view of the surrounding forest, and overflowing floor-to-ceiling bookcases, one of which framed the door to the library. Every available surface in the room was piled high with magazines, books, notes, manuscripts, and papers. The fourth wall framed an enormous antique mahogany desk and three paintings.

"This room has been processed already, so you can touch things or sit if you need to," Williams said as he closed the door behind them.

Sarah's eyes rested on the painting in the middle and momentarily lost her balance. She reached for something to steady herself as both Conrad and Williams rushed to her side.

"What happened?" Conrad asked.

"I'm okay. A bit startled is all."

"May I get you something?" Williams asked.

"Yes, I could do with a bit of water, if you don't mind."

"Be right back." Williams rushed off.

Sarah whispered to her husband, "That's Danny. That's the painting Alexander did."

"That means that—"

"Danny is our Daniel."

And without warning the movie took hold of Sarah's mind.

It was the middle of the night when Danny burst through the door to Alexander's cabin, breathless and pale.

Irritated by the interruption, Alexander glared at the boy from his typewriter, but before he could complain, Danny hissed with unusual urgency.

"My dad is here! He went to hide under the bridge!"

"Calm down, calm down. What bridge?"

"The one over the creek. He's going to sneak up on us and try to catch us."

"Okay." Alexander sounded perplexed.

Dumbfounded, Danny looked at him. "Okay? What the hell is wrong with you? This is bad, really bad. He'll find out that I've been sneaking away. He'll discover you're here."

"And?"

"Are you serious? I'll be in real trouble and you can forget about the town not finding out who you are."

Alexander laughed. "Why in the world would he hide under the bridge?"

"Isn't it obvious? He's waiting to spy on us and catch us."

"Catch us at what? Talking?"

"Drinking, skinny dipping, smoking, Tent City, and…everything."

"We're not doing any of those things right now, are we?"

"No, but—"

"*You* know we've done those things, but he doesn't, and now we're simply talking. So why is he hiding under the bridge?"

"To give us time to get into trouble."

"That's pretty damn decent of him. But I don't buy it. It doesn't sound *ministery*."

"*Ministery*? What the hell does that mean?"

"Ministers don't hide under bridges they attack head on. Maybe he isn't after you. Maybe he's looking for someone and went under the bridge instead of over it. C'mon, let's go find out."

Alexander ran out the door snatching Danny on his way.

Only the moonlight that filtered down through the trees lit their way as they neared the bridge. The two slowed down and cautiously approached it. They could hear voices somewhere below. Alexander turned to Danny and beamed with superiority at having solved the puzzle.

"Told you so," he whispered. "You stay here. Hide under those bushes so he won't see you. I'll take a look and find out what's going on."

Alexander stealthily climbed down the side of the bridge and peeked under it. The minister and Mrs. Foster were on a blanket by the stream making love. He slammed his back against the bridge and climbed back up, shock etched on his face.

Danny noticed Alexander's reaction and rushed to join him. "What is it?" he whispered.

Alexander pushed him away. "Let's go."

"What's the matter?"

"Nothing. Let's go."

"I want to see."

Alexander stared into his friend's gentle eyes and smiled ruefully. "Truth sometimes kills, but it also liberates. What the hell, you're entitled. Go ahead."

Danny sneaked down to find his father copulating with Allyson Foster. Horrified, he leaned against the bridge, breathing heavily.

Alexander placed his hand over Danny's mouth and signaled him to be silent. He then dragged the disheartened boy away from the bridge and back to the cabin.

In shock, Danny dropped to the floor in front of the fireplace, sobbing.

Alexander placed a blanket over the boy's shoulders and poured him a glass of whiskey.

"Gulp it down."

Danny obeyed. Alexander took the glass from him, poured a couple more drinks, joined him on the floor, and then draped his arm around his shoulders in a gesture of consolation.

"I shouldn't have looked under the bridge," Danny whispered at last.

"You insisted."

"You shouldn't have let me."

"I tried to stop you, but you can't hide from the truth."

"Why not? You do."

"Yes, *I* do, but you shouldn't. You needed to face it."

"Why?"

Alexander remained silent for a moment and handed him the drink. "Because you don't want to become me. Because you needed to find out who your father really is."

"Why is he with her like that?"

"Same reason you are."

"But I'm not married. I don't have a kid and I'm not a minister. Hell, I couldn't even bring myself to be with Ellie after I was with her."

"That's what sets you apart from him."

"How could he? What about my mom? What do I tell her?"

"That's his mess to deal with, not yours."

Danny turned teary eyed toward Alexander. "I shouldn't tell my mother what they're doing?"

"That truth lies between them. It's not your duty to deal with; it's your father's."

"Are you saying I shouldn't do anything?"

"No, you must tell them that you know."

"Them?"

"Your father and his lover."

A couple of tears trickled from Danny's eyes. "What for? You're saying I can't do anything, anyway."

"You can rid yourself of their corruption and force them to confront themselves."

The boy gulped down his drink, then collapsed in tears. He cried in Alexander's arms.

"It's up to you to decide how any of us are going to affect your life, but one thing is clear, you are not your father. Remember that. You're far superior to him and her, and certainly to me."

Daniel looked up at Alexander. "I wish I was five again, and I could shout across the street for Robert to come out and play. I wish all of this had never happened."

Alexander embraced him with fatherly tenderness, kissed his forehead, and wiped away his tears.

"Sarah, what's the matter?" Conrad held his wife in his arms, her eyes focused on the painting of young Danny, tears running down her cheeks.

She dropped her head on her husband's shoulder and quickly recounted the scenes she had witnessed. Just then, Sheriff Williams entered.

"Here," Williams said as he handed Sarah a glass of water. "My God, Sarah, you're shaking. What in the world has happened to you?"

Sarah took the glass with both hands, and after a few sips, placed it on top of a pile of papers that lay on a small table, and slumped onto a nearby chair.

"She's shaken up by all that blood we had to walk through," Conrad said quickly. "You were right in asking me to accompany her." He placed a reassuring hand on her shoulder.

"This library doesn't fit in," Sarah muttered as she reached for her husband's hand.

"You're right," Williams said as he looked around the room. "Not only because the violence didn't carry into this room, but we also found no evidence of anything missing."

"Missing?" Conrad asked.

"It doesn't appear as if anything of value was stolen. Other than our search for evidence and moving things about, this library is exactly as he left it."

"Alexander died of a heart attack, where did all that blood in the foyer come from?" Sarah asked as she rose from the chair with Conrad's help and walked over to Alexander's desk.

"How did you know he died of a heart attack?" Williams asked.

"I got an image of him dying as he came down the stairs in the foyer."

"I'll be damned," Williams said with a shake of his head. "I still can't get used to her coming up with stuff like this. Anyway, you're right. His house-keeper found him at the bottom of the stairs. His death certificate indicates a heart attack."

"So, where did all that blood from?" Sarah asked again.

"I was hoping you'd be able to tell me."

Sarah shook her head. "All I get are shadows and lots of violence. Nothing helpful. May I look around this room? Have you learned anything new since you called us?"

"Yes on both counts. Guess who's his heir?"

"Daniel," Sarah answered without hesitation.

"How did—"

Conrad nodded toward the painting on the wall. "That's him when he was fifteen."

"Now that you mention it, I do see the resemblance," Williams said. "I'll be damned. That means he knew Alexander since he was a kid."

Sarah spotted a letter-size envelope addressed to *Daniel Michaels* next to a loosely bound manuscript. "Conrad, look."

Conrad opened the first page of the manuscript and read aloud, "*Secrets of Innocence, Screenplay by Alexander Pitman. Amaray, 1976.*" His eyes met his wife's with the mutual recognition of the source of the images that had been playing in her mind.

"Quite a coincidence isn't it," Williams noted, "that our mystery man is given the name Daniel, and his real name is the same? Too much of one if you ask me."

"The nurses and Elisabeth chose the name for him," Conrad said.

"So we've been told."

"You don't suspect Daniel?" Sarah asked in disbelief.

"At this time I'm not sure what to believe. Something serious happened here, and we need to get to the bottom of it before we reach any conclusions. You must agree that it's suspicious that this entire estate and its contents now belong to Daniel."

"Why?" Sarah questioned him.

"Mr. Pitman's attorneys say that he contacted them to finalize his will only a couple of weeks before his death. They knew nothing about him other than the information Pitman gave them to process the will. Same story with Pitman's manager, all he knew was what the will outlined. No clue as to who this Daniel Michaels was or where he came from. His housekeeper said that he told her around the same time, that if something ever happened to him, she should inform the attorneys and they'd tell her what to do. I find these events highly disturbing."

"Maybe he realized he was dying and made all the arrangements," Conrad offered.

"Possibly." Williams nodded. "But we can't confirm that. What if Pitman was coerced?"

"Coerced? You mean by Daniel?" Sarah's tone carried restrained irritation.

"Yes. It's possible."

"Billy, that doesn't make any sense," Sarah protested. "Why would he? Has he been in here before? Did the housekeeper meet him or witness him forcing Alexander?"

"No," Williams said, "but coercion takes many forms, and the perpetrator doesn't need to be present."

"That's too—"

"Read the note in your hand, Sarah."

She opened the envelope and removed the note. It had two handwritten words: *Forgive, Alexander.* She sighed as she handed it to her husband.

"Something heavy transpired between these two men," Williams said. "And until we find out more, we shouldn't jump to any conclusions, one way or another."

"We should tell Daniel we've learned who he is and bring him here," Sarah suggested. "Maybe it'll jar his memory and he'll be able to tell us what happened."

"No, not yet," Williams was quick to respond. "We're processing the blood and need more time for the lab results."

A bewildered look came across Sarah's face. "I don't understand. Why not tell him?"

"Sarah, it's clear that you have complete faith in Daniel. But what if he's faking his amnesia? Have you considered that? A crime has been committed here and—"

"But he's the victim," Sarah protested. "He's the one who was beaten to a pulp and left for dead on the side of the road."

"That may be so, but with all this new evidence I need to tread slowly in case there's more to this. Maybe there were other heirs who came to claim their inheritance and he—"

"You can't be serious," Sarah objected.

"I am. Sarah, please understand. We have a crime scene here with no clear explanations, and we need time to find out exactly what took place. Maybe you'll even get a flash—or whatever it is that happens—that will help us all, including Daniel. I must ask you to be patient and not tell anyone, particularly Daniel. Or Elisabeth, she's not capable of keeping a secret."

"Darling," Conrad cut in, "I have to agree with Sheriff Williams, we need to wait. If Daniel isn't faking his amnesia and we hit him with a ton of information about Alexander and this place, his inheritance, this screenplay, the blood in the foyer, it might do more harm than good. Obviously something is preventing him from remembering. We should probably discuss this situation with Doc." He turned to Williams. "I assume you don't mind if we do?"

Williams nodded in agreement. "As long as he keeps it to himself."

"You're right." Sarah said with a sigh. "I've been so frustrated with my inability to help Daniel that I didn't think it through. Sorry."

"No need for apologies, Sarah." Williams smiled. "You've helped a lot. We wouldn't even be here if not for you, and I need you to do your thing and come up with what could have happened here."

"Can we see the rest of the house?" she asked.

"Only the downstairs. The upstairs is being processed. Don't linger or touch anything in the foyer as we cross over. As a matter of fact, don't touch anything anywhere. Follow me."

They stepped into the foyer and made their way into the simple, yet warm living room. There were two ceiling-to-floor bookcases filled to capacity, and the furniture was elegant, but unpretentious. Several of Alexander's self-portraits, all as enigmatic as the man himself, adorned the walls. Ornaments that appeared to be from all over the world were scattered atop all available surfaces or hung on the walls in any available space between the paintings. As in the library, a masculine tone permeated the entire room.

"Those paintings are of Alexander himself," Sarah told Conrad. "That, I would imagine was when he was in his early twenties, that one next to it is as he was when he met Danny, and the others appear to be from later years. It's as if he never stopped searching for his true self."

"Interesting notion," Conrad said. "Each portrait shows a different facet, but his appeal is constant in all of them. If his paintings were true to life, one can see how easy it must've been for him to influence others. Did you ever meet Pitman?" he asked Williams.

"Nope. He kept to himself. I saw him in town a couple of times, but nothing more."

"How long had he lived here?"

"Records show he bought the land back in the mid-seventies. He built the house and barn, but didn't show up till the mid-eighties or thereabouts."

"Barn?"

"Well." Williams raised his eyebrows. "Pitman called it 'the barn' in his will, but it's where his studio is. Just outside the back door. Anyway, he traveled a lot. He hired Walter and Dottie Ferguson who, along with their kids, looked after the house and property from early on. They must've done right by him given the pretty sum of money he left them in his will."

"Do they have any idea as to what could've happened here?" Conrad asked.

"None. They haven't been in the house since they locked it up after his death and gave the keys to the attorneys."

"That's too bad," Sarah muttered.

"Any ideas?" Williams asked Sarah.

She smiled. "No, if I get anything, I'll tell you. It doesn't always happen instantly. It may take a day or two."

They stepped into the dining room. It was well appointed and functional, with exquisite wooden masks from faraway lands dressing the walls, and similar knick-knacks spread on the table, sideboard, and buffet. A small bar occupied a corner of the room with an antique cabinet filled with expensive crystal.

"No sign of any feminine influence in this room or the others. I guess he never married," Sarah said more to herself than to the others.

"Lifelong bachelor," Williams offered. "No children or anyone else to leave all this expensive stuff to. Only Daniel who's obviously not his kin."

"He left nothing for anyone else other than the Ferguson family?" Conrad asked.

"Nope. All his millions go to Daniel," Williams said with a smirk.

"Millions?" Sarah's eyes widened in disbelief.

"Pitman's attorneys say around two million in liquid assets, plus this property and its contents, estimated at another two or more."

"I didn't realize the extent of his attachment to Danny," she whispered, shaking her head.

"Did Daniel ever find out that Alexander had made him rich?" Conrad asked Williams.

"He must've. He picked up the paperwork and the keys to the estate from Pitman's attorneys in Seattle last November. He flew in from Paris and—"

"Paris, France?"

"Yeah, he lives there."

"How did they find him?" Conrad asked.

"Apparently Pitman gave them his address and phone number. They said he flew in, met with them, signed all the paperwork, and headed this way to check it out."

"Billy," Sarah turned to him, "have you found Daniel's wallet or anything of his here?"

"Nothing so far, but we're not done with the upstairs. Not even the paperwork he picked up from the lawyers has surfaced yet. His rental car is gone too."

"I can only imagine the shock Daniel must've felt when he found out Alexander left him his entire property...his entire life's work," Sarah muttered.

Conrad placed his hand on her shoulder, and she turned to him and managed a smile.

They entered the small yet practical kitchen, devoid of any of the amenities befitting Alexander's personality that characterized the other rooms. The cupboards contained everyday dishware, glasses, and cooking utensils, but nothing more. To one side of the kitchen stood a fully equipped laundry room. All of the appliances dated back to the eighties, and other than a microwave, there was no evidence of the comforts modern kitchens offer.

"This is more like it," she said with a sigh of relief, "the only room so far that has offered a glimpse of the Alexander I've come to know."

"What do you mean?" Williams asked.

"The Alexander in the...my visions did not appear to be someone who cared for the finer things in life, or so I presumed. Except for this kitchen, the house and all its contents make me wonder who he really was or how truthful my impressions have been."

"You mean you can be wrong?" a bewildered Williams asked.

She smiled. "Yes."

Williams frowned. "I had the impression you couldn't be wrong once you got the vision. You've been right on the money so far."

"Sometimes the images are very clear, other times they aren't, so I'm forced to draw conclusions. It's not a perfect science."

"I guess not," he said, clearly unsettled. "All the more reason not to say a thing to him. You get me?"

"Not exactly."

"Your assertion that he's innocent might be wrong. What if he has a co-conspirator? Have you thought of that?" Williams's smirk had returned.

"No, I haven't." Sarah's tone carried a hint of irritation.

"If Pitman was coerced and Daniel hasn't been here, he might've had a coconspirator who did have access to the rich man."

"That's a bit farfetched," Sarah protested.

"Is it? You didn't even know that Pitman was wealthy and had left it all to your Daniel. That's a really big gap."

"Now, wait a minute—" Conrad stepped in, clearly annoyed.

"No offense, Mr. Thompson, but Sarah has said she can't really be sure how accurate these visions of hers really are."

"You're right, Billy, I'm not sure about some of the visions, but it's highly unlikely that Daniel conspired against Alexander."

"What makes you so sure?"

"I have a gut feeling about it."

"Well, my gut feeling is that it's possible Daniel had some differences with his coconspirator once the property had been turned over to him and that's when he got beaten all to hell."

Both Conrad and Sarah glanced at each other and then back at Billy. The three remained silent for a few moments.

"You're right, Sherriff," Conrad said. "That is a viable possibility."

C H A P T E R   2 3

SARAH MADE HER way up the stairs to open the windows to allow the afternoon breeze to flow through her house, when she was overcome by an uncontrollable sadness.

Engulfed by the solitude of the forest, Danny ran as if he might never stop. After several minutes he slowed to a walk again, gasping for breath and fighting back tears until, at last, exhausted, he sank to the ground and screamed in agony.

Concealed among the trees, Alexander resisted the temptation to console his friend. "Be strong, Danny. Be strong," he whispered.

Gradually, the boy's screams dwindled into wracking sobs.

When at last his breathing and tears subsided, he rose to find himself next to a fallen tree branch. He picked it up and beat it frenetically against a nearby tree as his face—bathed in sweat and tears—turned crimson with anger. Finally, exhausted, he slumped to the foot of the tree, knees to his chest, head on his arms, crying the pain away.

After several minutes he dragged himself up and headed off into the forest.

Unaware of time passing, he found himself standing alongside the creek, the bridge silhouetted against the trees mere yards to his right.

His father and Mrs. Foster emerged from under the bridge with their arms around each other, laughing without a care in the world.

With steely determination, he marched up to them and blocked their path. The two froze at the sight of him, Hugo horrified, Mrs. Foster pleased. With stone-cold eyes, Danny glowered at the two people he'd once loved and now despised.

No one uttered a word.

After a few moments, the minister's son simply walked away and disappeared into the darkened forest.

Sarah sat on the bottom rung of the staircase in her home, eyes bathed in tears, her head on her husband's shoulder.

"Not one single adult is there to help that kid pull through this mess," Conrad whispered.

"His poor mother…it'll break her heart."

"Why didn't you ask Williams to let you take the screenplay so you can read what Alexander wrote? You've been dying to find out how the story ends."

"I've waited this long, a little more won't hurt. Alexander isn't done telling it to me his own way. There's more to come. "

"I don't like you to be so distraught."

"I'll be all right." She patted his arm.

"If I hadn't showed up to pick up the invoices I'd left behind, you would've sat here at the bottom of the stairs crying all on your own."

Sarah smiled. "Now it's both of us at the bottom of the stairs. What a pair."

"C'mon, let's take a walk." He stood up and reached for her hand. "The fresh air will do you good."

Sarah rose and wrapped her husband in her arms. "I'm okay, only saddened by what Danny had to confront at such an early age."

He tightened his embrace and kissed his wife. "C'mon."

"There's no need. Anyway, you have to get back to the store so Tom can go to school for that parent-teacher conference. Elisabeth is coming to help me with the twins and learn how to make corn tortillas. She's looking forward to that."

"Speak of the devil, looks like she's here," Conrad said as a car drove up. He kissed his wife once again and gazed into her eyes.

"I'm fine. Don't worry. Doc will get here early so that we can bring him up to date."

"Who'll keep an eye over Daniel and Elisabeth while we're with Doc?"

"The kids are spending the night here. The little ones will keep our older charges busy."

"We've turned into a veritable nursery. When is Alyana getting here with them?"

"Any minute now."

The doorbell rang and he kissed her once more before opening the door.

"Hi." Elisabeth's eyes were as puffy as Sarah's. "Conrad, I didn't expect to find you here."

"Hi to you, too. I'm off. Daniel and I'll be working another couple of hours while you two battle with the homemade tortillas." Conrad winked as he passed Elisabeth. "No more crying." He nodded at his wife. "Either of you." He stepped off the porch and headed to his truck.

"He's such a nice man." Elisabeth sighed.

"That he is. Come on in." Sarah reached out for Elisabeth's arm, gently coaxed her into the house, and closed the front door. "What's the matter? You've been crying."

"So have you. Why were you crying?"

"A very sad scene played in my head, that's all."

"Tell me about it."

"I can't, not yet, maybe soon. Tell me why you've been crying." Sarah led Elisabeth toward the living room.

"It's Daniel. I've lost him."

Alarmed, Sarah stopped and turned. "What happened? Has he left? Where has he gone?"

Elisabeth's eyes filled and she shook her head. "No, he's here, but he's left *me*."

Sarah took her friend's hands in hers. "Settle down on the sofa, I'll make us a cup of tea."

Elisabeth wiped her eyes. "I'd rather come with you. I don't care to be by myself."

In the kitchen, Sarah put the teakettle on. "Let's sit here together while the water boils," she said as she pulled two chairs away from the kitchen table.

"I should be helping you with dinner instead—"

"Not to worry. We have plenty of time to get ready before Daniel and Conrad join us."

"What's on the menu?"

"One of my father's favorite meals, tortilla soup followed by *puntas de filete en salsa colorada con arroz blanco y chícharos.*" Sarah smiled.

Elisabeth had to chuckle. "It's probably a Mexican meal since we're making corn tortillas from scratch. I think *filete* means steak—like filet mignon—*colorado* may mean color, *blanco* is white, and *arroz* could be…rice. No idea what the last part means at all. Is it steak in some colored sauce with white rice?"

"Yes, tips of steak in tomato sauce with white rice and peas. Daniel and I will be comparing recipes as we make the meal. It'll be lots of fun. For dessert we're making *torta de cielo con compota*—heavenly tart."

"Sounds delicious. What's the tart made of?"

"Almonds. By the way, we're also babysitting the twins this afternoon. Okay with you?"

Elisabeth nodded.

"That'll keep us busy, so before they get here, you need to tell me what happened."

"It was horrible, Sarah. I made a complete fool of myself. I offered myself to him and he rejected me. He doesn't love me."

"Elisabeth, he needs to be careful."

"No, it's not that. He said he wouldn't do anything until he was sure of his feelings for me. Up until that moment I hoped we knew exactly how we felt about one another."

The kettle whistled and Sarah turned it off and poured the hot water into a teapot. "In my opinion he's simply trying to be honorable. He recognizes that there's a possibility he may be attached to someone else." Sarah put teabags in the pot before placing it on the kitchen table along with a couple of mugs. "Do you take milk and sugar?"

"Yes, a cloud of milk, as you like to say, and three teaspoons of sugar. I love my sweets. Maybe that's the problem, I'm too fat."

"Elisabeth, stop. That has nothing to do with his feelings for you. It's obvious how much he cares for you and you for him. Look at us, why are we here tonight cooking together in my house instead of yours? To keep you two under our watchful eyes."

A hopeful smile crept onto Elisabeth's lips, and her eyes regained a little of their usual sparkle. "You really believe that's all it is?"

"Without a doubt. Now, let's be practical. Take a look at this from his point of view. What if he had taken you up on your offer? You would've been intimate with one another and your love would've flourished. But if he later found out that he was attached, that would force him to end it, and you'd both be hurt. Isn't that much worse than restraining yourselves a little longer?"

Elisabeth responded with a reluctant nod.

"C'mon, Elisabeth."

"I didn't expect him to reject me."

"The truth is that you shouldn't have offered yourself to him. It was not a smart move on your part to put him in that position."

Elisabeth sighed. "You're right about that, but somehow I don't believe that's what held him back. I suspect he's not entirely sure of his love for me."

"Like I said before, I seriously doubt that."

"Sarah, I—" Elisabeth's eyes filled. "I can't lose him. I love him so much, it hurts."

Sarah reached for her friend's hand. "Please, Elisabeth, you need to give him time."

"The last time someone asked me to give a man time, I ended up losing him."

"Hopefully this time will be different."

They looked into each other's eyes, fully aware of their own uncertainties.

"Let's get the tortillas going. It'll make us both feel better." Sarah stood and placed her teacup near the sink. "Doc's going to arrive a bit early," she went on, "to chat with Conrad and me. So you and Daniel will be helping with the children's baths and bedtime ritual. You'll enjoy it."

Concern clouded Elisabeth's expression. "Why do you have to talk with Doc?"

Sarah hesitated for a moment. "Nothing to worry about. It's that a couple of scenes from this movie have got me a bit confused. I'd like to run them by him."

"When are you going to tell me about this film? If I knew more, maybe I could help."

"Not until I have a better grasp of its meaning. Soon, I hope."

"I've got to hand it you, Sarah. I can't even begin to imagine what it must be like to be a psychic and have these bizarre visions floating through your mind. Yet you're so calm about it, and so together. Then, to top it all off, you're worried about Daniel and me. How do you manage it?" Elisabeth rose to her feet and hugged her friend.

"Oh, c'mon, it's really not that big a deal." Sarah lied as she kissed her friend on the cheek. "I treasure your friendship and Daniel's. You're both very important to me. So please, don't despair, and do your best to be patient. Okay?"

Elisabeth sighed and moved to clear the kitchen table. "I'll try. It'll be difficult being near Daniel tonight. Awkward, anyway."

"Nonsense. Be our usual warm and loving Elisabeth, and the rest will take care of itself, trust me. Here." She handed Elisabeth a wet towel. "Wipe the table clean and then dry it. We'll use it to work the dough."

"Won't it stick?"

"Ah, we have a secret weapon. We'll put some parchment paper on top before we make the cornballs. You'll knead the dough and then—"

"You'll help me, right? I can't afford to fail again."

Sarah smiled. "No failures tonight, I promise. You'll love flattening and shaping the tortillas. It's fun, and besides, the scent and taste of a fresh corn tortilla is to die for."

"Hey, if Daniel likes my tortillas, maybe they'll soften his heart toward me again."

"Don't push him."

"If only I could see the glimmer in his eyes when he looks at me one more time, it'll give me the strength to wait. I can hope for that, can't I?"

Sarah smiled and nodded. "As long as you don't hope for more."

"So this is the moment of truth. Whose recipe did we eat?" Conrad asked.

They sat around the dining room table enjoying the heavenly tart.

"Team effort. A combination of my mother's and grandmother's recipes plus Daniel's unique touch," Sarah said.

"What do you mean?" Alyana asked.

"He's got good instincts," Sarah said. "He suggested we marinate the meat in a paste of crushed garlic, jalapeños, cilantro, salt and pepper with a dash of olive oil to enhance the flavor. He also added brandy to the tart, which, we can all agree, made it even better."

"It was delicious, whatever you did," Dr. Lawrence offered. "I've never had Mexican food that tasted so fresh. Those homemade tortillas were the best I have ever had."

"Not my doing. Elisabeth made those." Sarah winked at her friend.

"Daniel doesn't believe I can do anything right." Elisabeth had cleared the dessert plates, and she vanished into the kitchen. Daniel glanced around, perplexed.

"What did I do?"

"I'll go chat with her." Sarah followed Elisabeth.

Daniel sighed and shook his head. "Nothing I did in that kitchen today met with her approval—I swam against the current all the way."

"She's out of sorts." Conrad smiled. "A woman's prerogative."

"Not just women, Papa," Alyana offered. "Tom gets moody too, particularly when it's time to bathe the kids."

"Aw, c'mon, that's not fair," Tom protested. "I'm all thumbs with two babies."

"A nice excuse. Maybe you should take lessons from Daniel. He did very well today."

"C'mon, Alyana," Daniel interjected, "all I did was pat them dry and tickle them. Boy, did I laugh, their giggles were contagious."

"Yeah, thanks for that, buddy," Tom laughed. "It took ages to calm them down and sing them to sleep."

"I would've liked to have gotten that much love as a kid." Daniel sipped the last of his wine, a distant look in his eyes.

"You connected with your childhood?" Dr. Lawrence asked.

Startled, Daniel focused back. "No. Being with these two and their brood made me a bit melancholic, I guess."

"Speaking of which," Conrad said as he rose to his feet, "Doc, you and Daniel can use the attic for your session. It's on the top floor and completely private. Plus, Sarah keeps it neater than any other room in the house. You'll be comfortable there. I'll bring in another chair."

Everyone rose from the table on cue.

"Dad, I'll take the chair."

"No, thanks, Tom. I need to show them the light. Besides, I'd like to share with them a bit of what the attic means to Sarah." He grabbed a chair and made his way toward the staircase.

"I'll get my chart and glasses and be right there," Dr. Lawrence said on his way to the foyer.

When the three men reached the third floor, Conrad switched on the hallway light and then opened the door to the attic. He stepped in and switched on the floor lamp.

The room came to life with a soft warm glow—like a smile of welcome for new visitors.

Conrad placed the chair near the armchair and turned to his guests. "Sarah spends a lot of time here conversing with those the rest of us don't connect with quite so easily. She learned all about my ancestors from my grandmother, thanks to this attic. It's a special room. A gate into other worlds, I would say. Sarah hopes it'll help."

Daniel stepped in and immediately began to pace. Dr. Lawrence glanced at Conrad and nodded that he should leave, which he did without a word, closing the door behind him.

Dr. Lawrence settled into the armchair, put on his glasses, and placed the medical chart on his lap.

"I have the impression that I'm unhappily married, Doc," Daniel blurted out.

The doctor peered over his reading glasses. "So you're on to something."

"Maybe. Glimpses…images of a woman—a beautiful woman—and a teenage girl."

"And you assume they're your wife and child?"

"They must be. Why else would I conjure them?"

"What makes you say you're unhappy in the marriage?"

Daniel stopped pacing and faced the doctor. "I experience resentment toward her."

"The woman or the girl?"

"The woman. The girl is different. I enjoy her."

"Why don't you describe these women to me?"

Daniel resumed pacing. "Interesting room, this attic."

"Yes, comfortable."

"It's easy to imagine how Sarah could connect in here. I like it."

"Are you avoiding my question?"

Daniel stopped pacing and glanced at Dr. Lawrence. "No, I'm not. I have a sense of peace in here. It's a nice feeling."

"Then, why are you pacing?"

"I don't like the pictures that are popping into my head. I don't like this woman." He paused for a moment, then forced himself to continue. "Anyway, she has wavy auburn hair, she's sensual as hell, and has olive green eyes that mock me."

"Mock you?"

"Yeah, there's something about the way she looks at me that makes me shudder."

"How about the girl?"

Daniel smiled. "The girl is blond, beautiful, and innocent. I feel love for her."

"How old are they in these images?"

"The woman is mid-thirties, I'd say, and the girl's in her teens."

"Why do these images represent your wife and child?"

"Because I can't imagine who else they might be?"

"Is the woman the mother of the young girl?"

Daniel dragged the chair in front of Dr. Lawrence, straddled it, and placed his arms across the back. "Now that you mention it, I doubt it."

"What's their relationship then?"

Daniel furrowed his forehead. "I really have no idea."

"Then let's not jump to conclusions about your marital status yet."

"But they must be important to me if they're the first memories I can come up with."

"Maybe, maybe not. But this is a very good sign. You're starting to recall your past, and little by little you'll put the pieces together. Or, with a little luck, maybe it'll all come back to you in a flash."

"Is that what your psychiatrist friend tells you?"

"It is."

"And is that what all the secrecy with Sarah and Conrad was about?"

"No."

Daniel stared at Dr. Lawrence for several seconds. "Sarah knows who I am, doesn't she? I could feel it tonight by the way she looked at me."

"She does."

"Do you?"

"Daniel, we all are after what's best for you. That means we need to tread with caution. There are probably good reasons why your mind has chosen to block out your past. I believe it's healing itself along with your spirit. You gave your body time to heal from the cuts and bruises, now your mind needs time to heal itself so it can regain the will to recall."

"Are you saying that can't happen if you tell me who I am, where I came from, or who's waiting for me?"

"That information is evolving just as your memory is."

Dejected, Daniel sighed and dropped his head. "Can't you at least tell me my name?"

"Daniel."

"My real name is Daniel?"

"Yes."

"Wow. What's my last name?"

"If you knew that, I'm sure you'd go off and research yourself, and I wouldn't blame you if you did. Rest assured that we all are watching over you."

"Does Elisabeth know?"

"Not yet. She hasn't been told your real name is Daniel, either. Only Sarah, Conrad, and I—and, of course, Sheriff Williams—have that information."

"Williams?"

"Yes."

"Has he found out who attacked me?"

"Not yet."

Daniel picked up the chair and replaced it. Leaning on the back of the chair he shook his head. "This is extremely unsettling." He clenched his teeth. "I'm angry...Actually, I'm furious at your unwillingness to tell me. It isn't fair."

Dr. Lawrence nodded. "I understand that. All I ask is that you give us a little more time. And I'd like to see you every day from now on. The Thompsons have agreed to bring you to my office. I'm convinced we'll make a lot of progress in the next few days."

"You can't decide what to tell me until you consult your doctor friend. Am I right?"

"In part."

Daniel lowered his eyes and whispered, "What you've learned about me must be shocking, otherwise—"

"Daniel, listen to me. Don't jump to such conclusions. As you trusted me with healing your body, trust me with this now. Please. The mind is not to be toyed with, and as I would consult with my colleagues on how to help heal a critical wound to someone's body, I need to consult how best to help heal your mind and guide you through its recovery. That's all."

"I understand, but it's irritating as hell that all of you know who I am and I don't."

"I can only imagine, but please give us a little more time. It won't be long, I promise."

Daniel glared at him. "What choice do I have? None of you will tell me."

"Not at the moment."

"Then why taunt me? Wouldn't it have been better to keep me in the dark?"

Dr. Lawrence sighed. "Perhaps, but you asked, and I won't lie to you."

Daniel resumed pacing, his hands absentmindedly rubbing his head. "I appreciate that Doc, but I'm having a lot of trouble keeping my temper in check right now."

Dr. Lawrence stood up, went to his patient, and placed his hand on his shoulder. Daniel shrugged him off.

"Look at it this way, the good news is that we've discovered who you are, so that mystery has been solved. All that remains is to learn where you came from while allowing your mind the time it needs to bring the memories back on its own terms."

Daniel turned to face the older man, his eyes glistening with angry tears. "I refuse to wait anymore, it's making me crazy."

"If you'd pulled a muscle, it would hurt, and you would have to rest and not use it until it got strong again. What we're doing is for your own good."

Daniel backed away, reached the wall, and leaned his head against it. "I'll do as you say, but please understand I'm furious." After a few moments he turned with a worried look upon his face. "What about Elisabeth? Won't it help her if she's told? She's upset with me as you probably noticed tonight. Maybe that'll make her feel better."

"I did notice that she's not herself. What brought on that change?"

"I told her I needed to come to terms with my feelings for her. She didn't like it. I can't blame her."

"And what exactly are your feelings for her? Have you figured it out?"

"I love her so much," he said as his jaw tightened, "that I ache every second that I'm not at her side. But now I'm terrified that I'm attached to someone I hate."

"Let's not go down that path for now. There's much left to uncover."

"Why not tell Elisabeth what you've discovered?"

It was the doctor's turn to avoid Daniel's gaze, so he returned to the armchair, took his glasses off, and distractedly cleaned them with his sweater. "Because she wouldn't be able to resist telling you all about it. For now, a certain distance between you is what's best."

"You mean well, Doc, but it's infuriating. It stings to be a prisoner of kindness."

"You're not a prisoner."

Enraged, Daniel approached the doctor. "Then what would you call it? I have no identity, no driver's license, no possessions, no freedom, and no name. I'm completely in your hands to control as you wish. That makes me your prisoner."

"Daniel—"

"We're done here. I'm done with this whole charade. If I could, I'd take off this minute and drive as far as possible from here—from all this—I'd escape." He took a deep breath. "As it is, all I can do when I leave this attic is wait until you're all damn well ready to release me. Tell me that's not captivity." He turned on his heels and stormed out of the attic.

Dr. Lawrence whispered, "I hope to God we're doing the right thing."

EMBRACED BY THE armchair in the attic, Sarah stared directly ahead unaware of her surroundings, viewing the movie in her mind's eye.

A simple, varnished coffin lay at the bottom of an open grave. A shower of roses tumbled onto the lid followed moments later by two handfuls of dirt. Six feet above, Danny and his tearful mother, both dressed in black, stared down into the grave, enveloped in uncomfortable solemnity. All around them the citizens of Amaray departed in silence, heads bowed, shoulders slumped, faces somber. Once they had walked a safe distance they began whispering among themselves and shaking their heads as they trudged away from the cemetery and the church.

Concealed by a weeping willow, Alexander observed the funeral scene from afar, his eyes as grey as the fog around him.

A preacher approached Shirley and the boy. "Shirley, Danny, I understand how tragic and confusing this is for you, but I'm sure that God will provide an answer for what has happened."

"God has nothing to do with it," Danny retorted. "My father killed himself in a selfish act of shame."

"Daniel," Shirley interjected, wiping away her tears, "watch your tone. I'm sorry, Adam. He's distraught. We both are."

He turned toward the boy. "Danny, you of all people must try to understand. There can never be a simple explanation for suicide. It is never the answer to our problems, but for some, when the circumstances surrounding their lives become too overwhelming, they decide that it's their only option. I'm sure your father—"

"You know nothing about my father. No one did." Danny spat on his father's grave and walked away.

"Daniel!" Shirley called out. "Please!"

"I need to be alone," he yelled back without turning.

"The reception—"

"Let him be, Shirley," Adam said as he took her arm. "It's always difficult for a boy his age to handle the death of his father, especially when that death is self-inflicted. He needs answers."

"How can I help him to understand when I don't even understand it myself?"

Adam eased Clara away from the graveyard and toward a nearby car. "Maybe you'll come across a letter or something he left behind that will make his actions clear to you."

"No, I've done that and didn't find a thing. All he left was that little note on the kitchen table asking us not to judge him too harshly. Whatever it is he did, he kept it to himself. Was he in trouble with the congregation or with the church?"

They walked past Alexander who had been eavesdropping on their conversation.

"No, not at all. I'd received a couple of complaints that lately he'd been a bit remiss in his duties, but you're familiar with how that is. There are always malcontents who must complain about this or that. Nothing out of the ordinary."

"He'd been very busy this summer. He was gone a lot."

"Well, I can assure you that his death had nothing to do with his duties or the church."

When they reached the car, Adam opened the door for Clara. "I pray that in time you and Danny will be able to make your peace with what's happened, and hopefully find an explanation for his death. I am available if either of you should need me."

Clara dropped her head and silently slid into the car and shut the door.

The car drove away as Alexander hurried off to find Danny.

He spotted him heading through the forest to the lake.

Within the safety of the lonely woods, Alexander called out to the boy, "Danny, wait up."

Danny stopped and turned toward him, the moisture in the air mixing with the tears that streamed down his cheeks. "What are you doing here?"

"I was at the funeral. I followed you here. I'm sorry about your dad."

"You should be." He stormed away from Alexander.

"It's a good thing to mourn, but make sure you don't let this anger eat you up."

"I'm done with you and your sick advice."

Alexander caught up to the boy and placed a hand on his shoulder.

Danny slapped it off. "I need to be alone. Go away. I don't need you or your stupid advice."

"You need to let out your rage. So if being angry at me helps, go right ahead."

Danny spun around, his face a mask of fury. "*Angry* at you? No, you stupid man, I hate you! I despise you! I listened to you, and it ruined my life!" He turned and ran away.

Alexander hurried after him. "Listen, anger is good. But you have to direct it where it belongs. It's okay to be angry with your father. He deserves it. Don't turn away from it."

The boy came at him again with his hands clenched into fists. "Enough with your stupid opinions! My father's dead because of me, because you told me—"

"You can't be serious."

"I've never been more serious." He kept coming at Alexander forcing him to step back. "My father is dead because I did as you told me. I confronted him. I shamed him. Don't you get that? Because of you, I...killed my father."

Alexander stepped toward the boy, who raised his fists in defiance. He stopped and raised his hands in a gesture of appeasement, and cleared his throat. "Danny, you didn't kill him. This isn't your fault. He made that choice. He's responsible for his own death and no one else."

"No! I made him do it. Me confronting him made him do it. I killed him!"

"Please, you can't think that. It isn't true."

Overcome with anguish, the boy closed his eyes. After a long pause, he whispered, "I wish I could erase the summer months. I wish it could start all over again. Most of all, I wish I'd never met you." He opened his eyes and glared at Alexander with utter disdain. "Look at me, same hands, same legs, same feet, even these woods are the same, and so is the lake. And yet, everything is different. Everything has changed. *I* have changed."

Alexander stepped forward and reached for the boy's shoulder. "In time you'll—"

Danny smacked Alexander's hand away. "Don't touch me! All of this has happened because of you. So stay away from me. I don't want to see you ever again."

"Danny, please, you—"

"Shut up! It's my turn to dish it out. I've been nothing more than a source of amusement to you. You brainwashed me into having sex with a married woman, and then you made me kill my father. I bet you were after something to use in your damn book. So stay the hell away from me!"

Danny ran off into the woods, leaving Alexander behind, stunned, and heartbroken.

Sarah gasped, her hands clutching the armchair in her attic. She bolted up and scurried down the stairs to the phone. Her hands shook as she dialed.

"Dr. Lawrence, please. This is Sarah Thompson. Please tell him this is a very important call. He must take my call…Thank you."

She waited for a moment.

"What is it, Sarah?" the doctor asked with obvious concern.

"Thank God, Doc. I found out that Daniel's father committed suicide right after the boy confronted him with his mistress. Daniel blames himself for his father's death. He's convinced that by facing his father he pushed him to kill himself."

Dr. Lawrence remained silent for a moment. "That's certainly a serious burden to carry around all these years," he finally said. "Fifteen, you say his age was?"

"Yes. Conrad should get there with Daniel any moment now, so I needed to tell you before your session. As a boy he blamed Alexander for it all, including Mrs. Foster's seduction."

"Thank you, Sarah. I appreciate your call. You're certain about these images, right?"

"The movie playing in my head is definitely from Alexander's point of view, so it could be distorted or it could be the real thing. Until the police find more evidence, it's hard to say. All I can do is tell you what's been presented to me."

"Hold on a second, please, Conrad's here."

Sarah could hear agitated voices in the background.

"Sarah," Conrad said on the phone, "Daniel's gone."

"What do you mean, gone?"

"He wasn't in his room this morning. Tom and I opened the store as usual, but Daniel wasn't there. We assumed that he might have taken a walk after breakfast. When he didn't show up we went upstairs. No sign of him. My second assumption was that he'd decided to make his way to the hospital on his own. He hates being dependent on us, so I drove up here. No sign of him."

"Oh my God, Conrad, where could he be? What if he remembered who he is and he's on his way to Alexander's?"

"Doc's calling Williams on the other line to find out."

"I'm on my way. I'll meet you at the estate."

"No. I'll come get you. We need an okay from Williams to go to the estate. Hold on, Doc is telling me something."

Sarah heard their muffled voices at the end of the line.

"Sarah, Doc asks that you please call Elisabeth, and without telling her that Daniel is missing, find out if he's with her. Call us right back."

"Okay," she said and hung up.

She dialed Elisabeth's number. The phone rang and moments later the answering machine came on. She waited for the welcome message to end. "Hi Elisabeth, sorry I missed you. This is Sarah and I'd hoped we could bake some bread together. You've been waiting to 'master the art,' as you call it. Give me a buzz if you can. I'll try you on your cell."

She looked for the cell number and dialed again, but it also went into voicemail.

"Hi Elisabeth, this is Sarah. I just left a message on your answering machine. I'd hoped you could come by to bake some bread. Anyway, give me a buzz as soon as you can so that I don't wait in vain."

Quickly she dialed again. "Hello, this is Sarah Thompson, my—"

"Your husband is right here, hold on a moment please," the doctor's receptionist clicked off and Conrad came on the line.

"Well?" he asked.

"Voicemail both at home and cell. They probably ran off together."

"I seriously doubt it. Where would they go? What would they gain by it?"

"They're distraught at not being able to be together. They may not be acting rationally."

"I guess you're right. Anyway, Williams is checking if it's all right for us to go to the estate. I'll mention to him that Elisabeth is not reachable either. Maybe he'll have some idea where to look for them. I'm on my way to get you. Call Tom and Alyana and bring them up to speed." He paused.

Sarah felt his hesitation. "What is it?"

"Do you have any sense of what's happened? Have you felt—"

"With the exception of the last scene that played in my head about—"

"Doc's told me all about it. What I mean is, have you had any images or sensed something that might help us."

"Nothing. Not a very helpful psychic, am I?"

"That's not what I mean."

"Nonetheless, I have no clue."

"I'm on my way. In the meantime, why don't you go to your attic in case it has anything to offer?"

Sarah sighed. "I don't expect it will, but I'll give it a shot."

She hung up the phone and climbed the stairs to the attic. She huddled into the armchair, but immediately got to her feet and roamed the room, running her fingers across the furniture.

"Well attic, here we are again, together in an unusual mystery. What's real in this movie?"

Silence.

"I figured as much. We're pawns in a game we don't know how to play."

A creak followed by a crack.

"Don't suppose you can tell me where they are?"

Silence.

"Of course not. We can sense these things, you and I, but only when the time is right...or when we're supposed to."

Crick crack.

She stopped. "So you have something to show me. What is it? Why would—"

The enraged shadows swirling around Daniel as he looked up the staircase in Alexander's foyer exploded into her mind. The violence played out before her, only this time she could see through the shadows, the blood, the pain, and then...a man, tall, dirty, unshaven, with greasy long hair, furiously punching Daniel with his fists. A ring...no, two rings...one on each hand, a skull and a cross, each with protruding purple stones...or were they green stones covered in blood?

The images vanished. Sarah steadied herself against the wall and caught her breath.

"Has Daniel gone after his attacker? Is that what he's doing? Who is that man?"

Silence.

"Elisabeth, please stop crying," Daniel begged, "you're going to kill us."

Elisabeth swerved off the road, stopped the car, and shut off the engine. She turned to Daniel. "How can I? First you dump me. Now you tell me you *think* you're unhappily married and that you have a teenage daughter. How do you imagine that makes me feel?"

"I didn't dump you."

"You didn't tell me you weren't sure how you felt about me when I threw myself at you?"

"I did say that, but—"

"But nothing. You dumped me, you walked away," she managed to say between sobs.

Daniel reached for her hands, but she yanked them back.

"Elisabeth, please listen to me. I did say that I needed to be sure of my feelings and didn't accept your offer, but I didn't dump you. I needed to sort out whether I truly loved you or was merely attracted to the…'forbidden fruit,' to coin a phrase."

She looked up at him, her pink swollen face bathed in tears. "What forbidden fruit?"

He caressed the tears off her cheek. "You."

"Me? What do you mean?"

He continued caressing her tears away as he answered in a soft voice. "I enjoyed the excitement I felt stealing a kiss from you, a touch. It drove me crazy. It was in my mind constantly. I dreamed of ways I could come close enough to catch the scent of your hair."

Her face softened, but her eyes continued to shed tears. "You thought of me like that?"

"All the time." He smiled. "But Doc told me I needed to sort out—"

"You told Doc how you felt about me?"

"I did. I needed to tell someone. I needed to let it out. It was killing me not to be able to be with you."

"Really?" she asked with an attempt at a smile.

His hand caressed another tear away and then made its way to her lips. Softly, he ran his fingers over them. "I can't begin to tell you how much I desire you—what I'd give to kiss those lips."

She whimpered.

He pulled his hand away and looked down. "I needed to find out if what I felt for you was more than the desire to have what I couldn't."

"And…" She hesitated, looked away, and whispered, "What did you find out?"

He gazed into her eyes as his own filled with tears. "That I love you more than I can bear. There's something about you that tugs at my soul. I desire you something awful, but it's more than that. It's as if I've loved you all my life. When I'm with you, something deep inside me feels a sense of comfort, of belonging, and a peace that transcends all other emotions. I feel we are one.

I can't explain it because it makes no sense. But no matter what happens next, I need you to believe that I love you and will always love you. Have no doubt of that."

Blind with tears, she reached for him, and somehow found his mouth. They kissed with the passion of unfettered desire.

"Thank you," she whispered.

He pulled her to him and kissed her again and again, then whispered into her mouth, "I love you, I adore you, and I long for you."

She inhaled his love, allowing its power to penetrate every single cell in her body. "I'm head over heels in love with you, and nothing will ever take that away from me." She rested her head on his shoulder and kissed his neck.

They remained locked in the safety of their embrace for a while, allowing the anguish and fear of loss to slowly dissipate. They both understood that this moment might have to last them an eternity, so they savored it as long as they could.

At length he kissed her one more time and let her go. "Now, shall we find out what awaits us?" he said in a raspy voice.

Elisabeth nodded, wiped her face, and smiled at the man she so desperately loved. "Let's do it."

She started the engine and merged onto the highway.

Daniel sighed, wiped his own cheeks, and looked out the window. "I'm not entirely sure this is the road to the house I remembered. It's like finding a needle in a haystack."

"Well, this is pretty far from where Sarah found you, so we may indeed be on the wrong road. On the other hand, folks do talk about a gothic ranch somewhere near Conconully."

"A gothic ranch, sounds like a horror movie."

"But that's the look, isn't it?"

"Gothic yes, but not a ranch, a house. The image of that house keeps popping up. Strange for a house like that to exist around these parts."

"There's lots of open land up here, so folks can build anything they choose. It's a coincidence that I've heard mention of such a ranch. I'm glad you told me."

"So am I," he said as he reached for her hand on the steering wheel and softly caressed it.

"It's awful," she added, "that Doc and the Thompsons refuse to tell you the truth about you. They should be helping you like I am."

Daniel turned to her. "I understand their reasoning. They're afraid I'll snap. Something in my past must be bad enough to make them scared of how I'll react. I don't like it, but I understand it. You're different."

"They knew I'd help you."

"That's why they asked me not to tell you. But I'm sure we'll put together whatever this horrible past of mine is, one piece at a time."

"I love that your real name is Daniel. It would've been hard getting used to calling you Tom or Larry, or Gordon. You look like a Daniel."

He laughed. "Oh? How do *Daniels* look?"

She giggled. "Like you. What a coincidence we named you that."

"That was all your doing."

She smiled and nodded. "I wonder why I picked that name? It wasn't merely the book on Daniel Boone that we were reading. Somehow, you looked like a Daniel to me."

"Whatever the reason, thanks." He reached over and caressed her shoulder.

She smiled and rested her cheek on his hand. "I'm glad we're doing this—although you shouldn't have walked all the way to my house at dawn. I could've picked you up."

"I needed to piece together the puzzle in my head, the house, the woman, the girl. Besides, the walk was invigorating. Now here we are in the early morning and—wait. Stop!"

Elisabeth swerved off the road and stopped the car. "What is it?"

"That dirt road, that's the road. Go back."

She turned the car around and drove onto an almost imperceptible dirt road. "You were on this road?"

"It definitely looks familiar. I hope we're not trespassing."

"If we are, we'll apologize. No harm done."

They drove in silence to a clearing, where Alexander's house appeared before them.

"Oh my God, look at that, a gothic house," Elisabeth whispered with disbelief.

They approached the estate and noticed yellow tape along the front of the house.

"There's police tape all around it," Daniel mumbled.

"That means it's a crime scene."

Daniel stared at her. "What crime?"

She shrugged. "No idea, but that's what I've read and watched on TV about crime scenes. The police are investigating something in this house, and they don't allow anyone to go in."

"What should we do?"

They remained in the car, silently staring at the house.

"We could look through the windows," Elisabeth suggested.

They glanced at each other and smiled. Quietly, as if not to awaken the absent inhabitants of the house, they emerged from the car, and made their way toward it.

They tiptoed up the porch steps and approached the first window. They peeked in and caught a glimpse of the room, but without any interior lights, they couldn't make out the details. They made their way around the porch, but all the windows had shutters or curtains that prevented them from peering inside the house.

As they returned to the front, Elisabeth turned to Daniel, a mischievous look upon her. "How about the doors in the back? They didn't have any police tape."

"But it's clear the cops don't want anyone in the house."

"It's clear they don't allow anyone to enter the front of the house, but nothing says that if the back is open we couldn't go in."

"It's private property. We can't barge in."

"We won't disturb a thing."

"No, Elisabeth. We can't. I won't put you in harm's way. Let's go come up with a plan."

She smiled and took his hand. "Okay. But I'm willing to go in and help."

They stepped down and were making their way to the car when Daniel noticed another building. "Elisabeth, look there, a barn."

Elisabeth turned toward it. "That's odd, I don't smell animals. Do you?"

"No. Maybe the police took them away."

"Maybe, but their scent should've remained. Shall we take a look?"

"What if someone comes, Sherlock? We're trespassing onto private property and a crime scene."

"You're right. Let's hide the car behind—"

"Let's not. Instead, let's go somewhere safe and develop a plan on what to do next. By now everyone'll be looking for us and I'm sure they'll be upset. We should at least call them."

"All right, Watson, let's go back to the car."

When they got there, Daniel turned toward the house for one last look and froze.

Elisabeth had already sat in the car when she noticed that Daniel remained standing by the passenger door. She called out, but when he didn't respond, she went to him. He stared at the house, transfixed, his face devoid of all color.

"What is it? What happened?" her voice quivered with concern.

"The foyer of that house…I fought a man in there."

"Fought? What man?"

Daniel shook his head. "Some guy. I caught a glimpse of what happened."

"What's his name?"

"No idea."

"Describe him to me."

"Tall, handsome, with a penetrating gaze. He's powerful as well as gentle, yet something about him makes me recoil."

"How old is he?"

"Mid to late twenties or so."

"Why did you fight him?"

"I'm not sure. It's strange. As if on the one hand I need to hug him, like an older brother or long-lost uncle, and on the other, I need to push him away."

"Is he the one who beat you up?"

Daniel nodded. "I suppose so, but I'm not certain."

"C'mon, let's go do some digging about who lives here."

Daniel obeyed and climbed into the car, still staring at the house. Elisabeth shut the passenger door and ran to the driver's side. "You're shaking. Are you afraid?"

"I'm not sure. I'm ice cold."

"I'll turn on the heater." She reached over and switched it on. "You'll be warm in no time. It looks like we can drive up to the barn. It won't be trespassing if I jump out and take a peek inside, will it?"

Daniel shook his head and managed a faint smile.

She drove toward the barn mere moments before a sheriff's car pulled into the dirt road leading up to the estate.

Daniel caught a glimpse of the car and reached for Elisabeth's arm. She turned in time to spot the sheriff's car as it drove toward the house and slowly made its way around the property.

"What do we do?" she asked.

"Drive into the woods over there the minute his vehicle is concealed by the house," Daniel whispered. "Whatever you do, don't speed up. Drive slowly. A cloud of dust will alert him that we're here."

She did as instructed, and stopped once the car was concealed by the foliage. From their new location, they couldn't see the sheriff's car at all. Daniel rolled down his window and listened for it.

"I think he's leaving," he whispered.

He turned to find that Elisabeth had turned white as s sheet. She sat tilted forward, clutching the steering wheel for dear life, eyes wide open, and lips trembling.

"Stay here," he whispered. "I'll take a look and make sure he's gone." He quietly opened the car door and stepped out, leaving it ajar.

He slinked toward the edge of the woods and peeked around a large rhododendron in time to notice a cloud of dust settling along the dirt road near the barn. He listened for the patrol car, but heard only the wind rustling through the trees. He returned to Elisabeth. Glancing all about and whispering, he said, "I think he's gone, but I'm not sure. I can't see him or the car."

CHAPTER 25

Sarah and Conrad stared nervously out the window in Williams's office. When the sheriff walked in, they turned to him, anxious to hear his news.

"Nothing so far. The estate's exactly the way we left it, no sign of them there."

"What about the rings?" Sarah asked.

"There was a group of young men, maybe twenty years ago or so, who wore similar type of rings, but nothing recent." Williams pulled out his chair and settled behind his desk.

"What happened with those men? Where did they go?" she asked.

Williams nodded for the Thompsons to take the chairs across from him. "Probably all middle aged by now and living elsewhere. Nothing ever came of those youths, although my dad did have a hell of a time with them now and again. I remember him telling their folks that he had to keep them locked up for a couple of days for causing trouble. Nothing serious, though."

"You went with your dad on official business?" Sarah's curiosity had been aroused.

Williams leaned back in his chair and smiled. "He knew I wanted to be sheriff like him so he'd take me on some of his cases 'to get a taste of the real thing,' as he used to say, especially if it had to do with kids my age. Two lessons in one you might say."

"How old were you?"

"A kid when it started but I continued through high school. When I came back from college and the academy, I got hired by the county and worked side by side with him until—" He lowered his eyes as the smile slipped away.

"Please," Sarah said, "tell me about these youths. The ones with the rings."

He looked up and smiled. "Well, Miss Sarah the Detective, not much to tell, they were a rambunctious bunch prone to getting into trouble more than others, but nothing major. Caused some big headaches not only for my dad, but for businesses and homeowners."

"What sort of trouble?"

"Disorderly conduct mostly, breaking and entering, petty theft, smashing windows, vandalizing private property, bashing mailboxes, things like that."

"It seems like it would be worthwhile to check into them," she said.

"We are. If any of them still live around here, we'll pay them a visit. Now, I've asked our sketch guy to come in and draw the man you saw. If we show the sketch around, maybe someone will recognize him."

"Won't he ask where she's seen this man?" Conrad asked.

"I already told them all about Sarah. Don't worry, they're pretty impressed with how much she's told us about the Pitman estate and the other clues she's come up with. Your wife's a bit of a celebrity in this office now."

Sarah frowned. "I'd rather not be."

"Too late for that. Some are skeptical, others are fascinated, and I'm the wait-n-see type. But overall, we're going along with you."

Conrad placed a comforting hand on his wife's arm before turning to Williams. "Any news from the lab on who the blood belongs to?"

"So far it's all Daniel's, although we found some bloody fingerprints other than Daniel's on the banister and on the door. We haven't found out who they belong to as of now."

"Why not?" Sarah wondered.

"They're badly smudged, which makes matching them more difficult. But if we find the guy you saw in your"—Williams hesitated—"visions, we can fingerprint him and compare."

"What about the housekeeper and her family?" Conrad asked. "Their fingerprints would be all over the house. Won't that make it difficult?"

"We're in the process of checking all of that. In the meantime, let's try to figure out where Elisabeth went with Daniel. What could be driving them to take off like this?"

Sarah shrugged. "No idea."

"He doesn't like being dependent on us," Conrad said, "and when Doc told him we knew who he was he got pretty upset. He might be searching for clues—maybe looking for Alexander's place."

"With no memory of Pitman, where the hell would he go?" Williams asked.

"Maybe Elisabeth—"

"You told her about Pitman's place?"

"No! But she's been driving him around to jar his memory. Maybe they got lucky."

Williams smiled at Sarah. "Could that be? Any visions on that?"

Sarah shook her head. "I told you, it doesn't work like that. He could've remembered Alexander and—" She stopped, the image of the rings crashing into Daniel's face flashed before her with such violence that she snapped her head back to avoid the impact to her own face.

She blinked and found Williams standing in front of her. "Are you all right, Sarah?"

Conrad was kneeling at her side, his hands on hers, eyes filled with concern. "What happened?" he asked.

She inhaled shakily, in search of her voice. Again her head jerked back, her hand coming up to shield her face as she screamed, "Don't hit me!"

Still trembling, Elisabeth pulled her car into a small lot next to a roadside coffee shop. Daniel rushed to open the door for Elisabeth, helped her out, and escorted her into the diner.

A waitress behind the counter nodded toward the empty booths. "Anywhere you like," she said.

As they passed by, Daniel said, "A couple of coffees, please."

He helped Elisabeth into the second booth and then scooted into the seat across from her, stretching his hands out to hold hers. "Are you okay?" he asked softly.

She nodded and smiled. "I panicked when that patrol car showed up. Not sure why, it's not as if we were doing something illegal."

"We were about to, though, weren't we?" Daniel smiled.

The waitress slid the coffees onto the table along with a small jug with cream. "Anything to eat?"

Elisabeth shook her head, and Daniel answered, "No, thanks. Coffee will do for now."

The waitress turned to leave as a man spun away from the counter and bumped into her on his way out of the diner.

"Watch where you're going!" she snapped, almost falling onto their table.

The man waved her off with an obscene hand gesture.

Daniel caught a brief glimpse of the ring on his hand, and all color drained from his face.

"What is it?" Elisabeth asked. "What's wrong?"

"The ring! Did you see his ring?" Daniel whispered, watching the man exit the diner.

"What ring?"

"The ring that man was wearing."

"No, I didn't. Why?"

The man slammed the door behind him.

"Elisabeth, that's the man who attacked me. I'm—"

"This guy doesn't look anything like you described."

Daniel stood up.

"Where are you going?"

"To get his license plate. Stay here. I'll be right back." He rushed out to the parking lot.

Elisabeth leaned back with a sigh and sipped her coffee. She grimaced and poured some cream and several spoonfuls of sugar into her coffee, took a sip, and smiled. She leaned back again and took another sip. No sign of Daniel. Through the window a corner of the parking lot was visible, along with the road, and the woods beyond. She drummed her fingers impatiently on the table, and when Daniel failed to return she got up and went to the door.

"Hey, you need to pay," the waitress called out.

Elisabeth turned and said, "I'm not leaving. I'll be right back." And she rushed out the door.

"Hang on, Sarah," Conrad said in his most comforting tone as he reached over to his wife and held her hand, "I'm entering the hospital parking lot. How are you doing? Any changes?"

"No, only blackness—I can't *see*." She yanked her head back and covered her eyes with both arms. "Agh!"

Alarmed, Conrad stopped the car in the middle of the hospital driveway. "What is it?"

"A blinding light, and I—" She grabbed her throat.

"What is it?"

"I can't...breathe."

Conrad sped toward the emergency entrance of the hospital and past Williams who had pulled over when he noticed they'd stopped.

As Conrad pulled up, a couple of doctors and nurses rushed out with a gurney.

"Doc's on his way—the sheriff's office called to alert us," one of the nurses told Conrad.

"She's lost her sight, and now she can't breathe," Conrad told her.

In no time they had Sarah on the gurney with an oxygen mask over her face.

"It's oxygen," said the nurse. "Breathe in."

Sarah attempted to breathe in, but convulsed and coughed violently. She yanked away the mask and screamed, "Take the gag off!" Her voice sounded as if her mouth were obstructed.

The doctors and nurses looked at Conrad, but all he could do was shake his head. Williams caught up with them as Dr. Lawrence rushed up to meet them.

"She thinks she's gagged," Conrad said. "And she can't see."

Sarah struggled to free herself from the restraining hands, screaming out, "No!"

"Sarah." The doctor placed his hand on her forehead and leaned toward her. "I'm Dr. Lawrence. I'm here to help you—calm down, please, calm down. Don't fight the gag, let it sit there and you'll be able to breathe." He placed the oxygen mask back on her, holding it firmly.

Sarah continued fighting, shaking her head, and struggling to free herself.

Dr. Lawrence remained calm and focused, holding the mask in place and stroking her forehead as he repeated his instructions. "Sarah, calm down, calm down. Breathe through the gag, c'mon. Breathe through the gag. You can do it. Take some air in slowly through your nose. You can do it. Take air in through your nose. If you can, open your mouth and breathe in."

Sarah opened her mouth widely and attempted to inhale.

"That's good. Take in more air. Slowly, don't rush it."

In time her body relaxed, and her agitation subsided.

"Sarah, we're taking you to an examination room. Everything's going to be okay. Keep breathing slowly. I'll be at your side, and so will Conrad. Stay calm. Don't try to speak, simply keep breathing through the gag and try to relax. Do you hear me?"

She nodded.

They wheeled her into one of the examination rooms and closed the door behind them.

Sheriff Williams stood in the middle of the emergency room entry hall, a look of complete bewilderment upon his face. His cell phone rang. He took the call and rushed out.

Elisabeth scanned the parking lot—no sign of Daniel or the man he had followed. Her car, and two others, along with a couple of motorcycles were all that remained. She ran to one side of the diner and then the other, but found only trash bins, old crates, and bits and pieces of rusty abandoned equipment. She rushed back into the diner.

"Where did my friend go?" she yelled at the waitress.

The handful of patrons looked up at her.

"He went out the door," the confused waitress replied.

"But which way did he go?"

She shook her head. "Did he dump you with the bill, honey?"

"That's not the *point*. Did you notice which way he went outside?"

"Don't you worry, hon, coffee's on me. Lousy bastard, running off. You deserve better."

Elisabeth inhaled deeply, shook her head, lowered her eyes, and tried to calm down. She dug into her pocket and smiled at the waitress. "Thank you, I do appreciate your generosity, but it's not about the coffee. Do you know that man who bumped into you after you served us?"

"You mean that good for nothing Hank?"

"Is that his name, Hank? Hank what?"

"What do you want with him?"

"My friend recognized him. Does he wear some sort of special ring?"

"Yeah, so what?"

"What's his last name? Where does he live?"

The waitress looked around uncomfortably as a couple of men stood up from their table and approached Elisabeth.

"Why are you so interested?" asked a short, bald, obese biker with tattoos on his arms, neck, and head, easing uncomfortably close to her.

She stepped back to find that the other man, just as intimidating, but slightly taller and with long, greasy black hair, stood directly behind her. She looked over at the waitress who simply shrugged and smiled.

"Look, my friend recognized him, and I guess they left together, for old times' sake," she said in a small voice.

The fat man grinned, exposing greenish teeth. "What's your interest in the ring?"

Recoiling from the sight and smell of his teeth, Elisabeth leaned back. She forced a feeble smile and answered, "Nothing. My friend said he recognized the ring, that's all."

"Your friend a biker?" the longhaired man grumbled behind her.

Elisabeth turned toward him and bumped into the protruding belly of the tattooed bald man. "I just met him. He might be," she said faintly.

"C'mon you guys, give the girl some breathing room," the waitress commanded. "Don't pay attention to these assholes, hon, they're only messing with you."

Elisabeth turned to the waitress and managed a weak smile as she said, "Thank you."

The two men, however, didn't budge, trapping Elisabeth between them.

The longhaired man leaned toward her, sniffing at her hair, and whispered, "You sure smell nice. Why don't you dump that jerk and come with us? We'll help you forget him."

Disgusted, Elisabeth pushed him away. The tall man lost his balance and bumped into his fat companion, who shoved him back.

Elisabeth glanced around the coffee shop. None of the other patrons were bikers, and several were eyeing the goings on with curiosity, but no fear—locals, entertaining themselves at the expense of an outsider.

With renewed courage she faced the bikers and the waitress. "Will you please tell me where I can find this Hank?"

"He's a loner, that one," the waitress replied. "He's got his—"

"None o' your business where he lives," the fat man interrupted.

"It is, if my friend is with him," Elisabeth said resolutely.

"What if your friend dumped you?"

"He wouldn't," she said with conviction.

"A man takes off like that, hon," the waitress said, "you're better off without him."

Elisabeth turned and glared at her. "Maybe, but I'm determined to find out if he's man enough to tell me to my face."

Two of the women in one of the booths applauded. "Way to go, girl," said the younger one.

"Hank's got a place up there off Fish Lake Road, way up in the hills," said the older woman sitting with her.

"Now, Mary Jo, what'd you have to go and do that for?" asked the longhaired man.

"She's got the right. Leave her be. She's got bigger balls than you two put together," the older woman said. "Now sit down and finish your coffee 'fore I come teach you some manners."

The two men mumbled under their breath and slouched back to their table.

"Thanks," Elisabeth said as she rushed out of the coffee shop.

She jumped in her car, started the engine, and entered *Fish Lake Road* in her GPS, but the only option it gave her was in Leavenworth. Frustrated she took off in a storm of gravel and merged back onto the two-lane road.

A few hundred feet ahead she pulled into a gas station. She stepped into the small old-fashioned roadside convenience store and paid for a full tank.

"Can you tell me where Fish Lake Road is?"

The attendant, a man as old as the store, looked puzzled for a moment and then smiled. "You mean South Fish Lake Road, it's up north of here. You can either go past Conconully and through the National Wild Life refuge on unpaved roads, or back down to Okanogan, catch the 97 and head north till you get to Pine Creek Road, and then get off on South Fish Lake Road or Pine Creek Road. I don't recall how the signs are labeled from 97. You can't miss it, drive up the highway and you'll find it veering off to the left." The old man looked quizzically at Elisabeth. "You look real familiar."

She smiled. "I'm a volunteer at the hospital up in Okanogan. Maybe you met me there."

He smiled, showing a wide gap left by his missing front teeth. "That's it. You read to my Lilly when she had her operation. She's been reading ever since."

"Lilly, yes, I do remember your daughter. I'm glad she enjoyed it. I love reading to my patients. How is she now?"

"Oh, she's doing well. Her and Alex and the kids live down in Leavenworth now. Got a little curiosity shop in the middle of town. They're doing fine. She reads to her kids every night."

Elisabeth smiled with satisfaction. "That's wonderful. She was lovely."

"What's up on South Fish Lake? It's a lonely road up in those hills."

"I'm looking for a guy named Hank. Does he live there?"

"Sure does. Nasty business, that one. The Ferguson farm's up there—his folks died, and Hank took it over on account as he's the eldest. Only it's on North Pine Creek Road."

"And where is North Pine Creek Road?"

"Right off of South Fish Lake Road or Pine Creek road."

Elisabeth frowned.

"Sounds complicated on account of all these roads having double names from one side to the other, but you can't miss it," the storekeeper chuckled. "Keep an eye out for the street signs, there aren't many, but they're there.

Tonasket folks got no imagination when they named their roads. When you come to the sign for North Pine Creek Road, take a right. The Ferguson place is up in the hills. You'll probably spot an old mailbox with their name on it. But more than likely you won't find Hank there, and I'm not sure you should go up there on your own anyhow. If you need to talk to him I'd check the jail first."

Elisabeth's eyes widened as she asked, "The jail? Why?"

"He's a troublemaker, always in an' out of jail for one thing or another, a big disappointment to his folks. Nothing like his younger brother, Walter, who makes a good and honest living."

"Does Walter live nearby?"

"He used to live down in Okanogan, but maybe he's taken off."

"Why?"

"Him and his wife came into some big inheritance. They may have packed up and left."

"You said his name is Walter?"

"Yep, that's it. His wife's called Dottie."

"Where do they live?"

"Wait a minute, maybe they're in the book." He reached under the counter and produced a beat-up phone book. He searched through it, grabbed a piece of paper, and wrote down the address. "Here," he said, handing it to Elisabeth. "If they haven't moved, they should be there. I wrote their phone number, too. You should call before you go to make sure they're still there."

Elisabeth held out her hand. "Thank you, Mr.—?"

"Brown, Elmer Brown, Ms. Elisabeth," he said with a broad smile as he wrapped her hand in both of his.

"You remembered my name. That's very nice of you."

"You made my girl—well, my grown girl—real happy while she ailed. We'll never forget you and your kindness. Wait till I tell her you came by."

"Give her my best, please."

"You're welcome to use the phone."

"Thank you, Mr. Brown, but I've got to rush. I'll use my cell. You've been very helpful."

"Take care and come by again," he called out as she reached the door. "By the way, if you go to Leavenworth, look up my Lilly, their shop is right in front of the big tree in the square. It's called the Magic Box."

"I'll do that. Thanks again."

She returned to her car and dug her cell phone out of the compartment under the armrest. The screen showed several voice-mail messages, all from Sarah.

Before returning Sarah's calls, she decided to call Walter Ferguson. There was no answer.

She dialed Sarah's number, but the call went straight to voice mail. Elisabeth sighed impatiently while Sarah's greeting played, and then spoke. "Sarah, sorry I haven't called you back; I've been with Daniel. He remembered some kind of gothic house in Conconully, and we came by to check it out, but we found it to be a crime scene so we took off. We were at a coffee shop, and Daniel recognized a man with a ring and went after him. Now he's disappeared. The man he went after is a criminal called Hank Ferguson. Please call Williams and tell him about this Hank person. I'm sure he's familiar with him. He lives in a farmhouse somewhere off of Fish Lake Road or North Pine Creek Road. I'm on my way there to find Daniel."

C H A P T E R   2 6

EYES CLOSED AND breathing with difficulty, a much calmer Sarah lay in a hospital bed. Conrad stood nearby holding her hand.

Dr. Lawrence gently removed the oxygen mask. "Sarah," he said, "there's nothing physically wrong with your eyes, or your lungs, and by now I'm sure you're aware that you aren't actually gagged. You're experiencing these symptoms through your mind only."

Without opening her eyes, Sarah nodded.

"Is it possible you're having some sort of psychic connection with someone who is blindfolded and gagged?" Dr. Lawrence asked tentatively, glancing at Conrad.

Sarah nodded.

Conrad looked at Dr. Lawrence and said, "This all started when we were at the Sheriff's office trying to figure out where the hell Daniel and Elisabeth were. Sarah felt, or sensed a couple of fists coming right at her."

"Fists?"

"Yeah, she's had this vision before of a man with a couple of odd-looking rings beating Daniel. Only this time the fists must've come right at her."

"These rings," Dr. Lawrence said, "could one be in the shape of a cross?"

Sarah grabbed his arm. "Yes, yes," she muttered between coughs.

"Easy Sarah, don't overexcite yourself."

"How—" she tried to speak, but he stopped her, placing his free hand over hers.

"Breathe in slowly. Try to stay calm and I'll tell you."

She inhaled and attempted to relax, her hand clasping the doctor's arm.

"Several of the wounds on Daniel's face had the shape of a cross. I imagined that he'd been hit by someone with either a weapon in the shape of a cross or a ring with that shape."

Sarah nodded.

"The other ring she mentioned," Conrad went on, "is shaped like a skull with a protruding gem."

"I've come across those rings, but not for a long time."

"Williams told us about a gang of teenagers who wore those years ago." Conrad said.

Dr. Lawrence remained silent for a moment and then looked at his patient. "Sarah, could you somehow be experiencing what Daniel is currently going through?"

Sarah opened her eyes, sat up, and gulped air.

Both men held on to her.

"I can see, I can breathe." She looked at the two men by her bedside as tears rolled down her cheeks.

Conrad embraced her as tightly as she could tolerate.

"Glad to have you back," Dr. Lawrence said, smiling.

"It's Alexander," Sarah said. "He made me experience what Daniel's going through. He's been kidnapped. His assailant hit him, blindfolded him, and gagged him."

"What about Elisabeth?" Conrad asked.

"No idea. I don't sense anything about her."

"How could Alexander make you experience those things?" Dr. Lawrence asked.

Sarah rolled her head. "I've never felt anything like it before. When I was little, I could sense things that were about to happen or were happening to others, but I've never actually felt these things before. The moment you told me that my symptoms might be what Daniel was feeling, I knew you were right. Alexander sensed that I understood his actions, so he let me go."

"You said he's been kidnapped?" The doctor asked.

"It looks that way," Sarah answered. "He's definitely in danger."

"Williams should be brought up to speed," Dr. Lawrence said.

Sarah looked at her husband and then back at Dr. Lawrence before saying, "He would only suspect that Daniel's run away. He's convinced that Daniel's guilty of something evil and distrusts my visions, as he calls them. This'll freak him out. He won't buy it."

"We can't keep Williams out of it," Conrad said. "He might be hard to convince, but he should be told you've sensed that Daniel's been taken."

"I agree," the doctor said.

"How do we explain what happened to me? What will my medical chart say about my episode? Psychotic blindness? Extreme anxiety? Crazy woman imagining things?"

Dr. Lawrence held her hand and smiled. "Don't worry about that."

"Don't worry? I made a fool of myself. I can only imagine what the deputies in the sheriff's office think of me. Let alone the doctors and nurses who saw me go nuts."

Dr. Lawrence smiled. "Yes, that's true, but we deal with people in distress all the time. Your chart will simply say that you're healthy and your symptoms subsided upon examination."

"You're not going to label me psychotic?"

He chuckled. "No need for that."

Sarah sighed and smiled.

"I'll speak with Williams," Conrad said.

Sarah squeezed her husband's hand and smiled. "Thank you, darling. He'll take it better coming from you than me. I'm almost certain that the man who attacked Daniel has taken him. Alexander made that very clear."

Conrad kissed his wife's forehead. He reached inside his pants pocket and found it empty. "I must've left my cell in the car. Doc, is she ready to go?"

Dr. Lawrence tilted his head before answering, "She's okay physically, but I'd recommend she stay put a while. This has been a serious shock, and a bit of quiet and isolation would do her good."

"But—" Sarah started to protest.

"Hush," Conrad said, "stay a while. I'll deal with Williams. You do as the Doc says and rest a bit. I'll be right back." He kissed her, smiled at Dr. Lawrence, and left the room.

"Okay, Sarah," he said, "lean back, take a few deep breaths and try your best to relax. I'll be back in an hour, and we can chat about this episode. I'm very interested in how it happened, and really curious to learn all about this Alexander fellow."

"I'm not tired, and I don't care to rest. We need to go after Daniel. There's no time to waste. He's in danger."

"I understand your anxiety, but let's give Billy a bit of time to process this information. Besides, what could you do now? Where would you go?"

Sarah considered this for a few seconds, then eased back onto the bed, and nodded. "You're right. I can't even guess where to go."

"If you lie quietly here for a while, maybe something more will come to you."

Resigned, Sarah sighed. "I'll do as you say. But please don't keep me here too long."

"Get some rest," he said with a smile.

Sarah closed her eyes until Dr. Lawrence stepped out of the room. A second later she opened her eyes and sat up on the bed and stared straight ahead. "Okay, Alexander, where is he?"

The room grew unnaturally dark.

Alexander stood before her at the foot of the bed. He appeared much older, in his seventies, exactly as he'd looked the day Sarah saw him die. "Not even now, after what Danny's gone through, does he remember." His voice sounded tired and rough.

She gasped. "Alexander."

"You felt the horror?"

She nodded. "But why put me through that? Why not just tell me?"

"Writers don't tell, we show."

"To hell with your games! You shouldn't have done that to me!"

"Not games. That's who I am."

"But why not show me instead of having me go through all that? I was terrified."

"Like I said, that's all I could do."

"Okay, then, where is he? Can you at least tell me that?"

"I'm not sure what will happen next. Like this conversation—all of a sudden I'm here, talking to you. I have no idea why or how it happens any more than you do."

"Maybe it's because you have something important to tell me?"

Alexander considered her question. "I need you to understand why he refuses to connect with his past, and why he hates me."

"I understand perfectly," she answered in a soft voice. "You should've realized you were forcing him to grow up too quickly and make decisions he wasn't ready for."

Alexander gazed upon her with deep sadness. "I should have, but I didn't."

"Why haven't you come before?"

"Because you needed to experience the whole story. Now we're near the final scene and I have nothing to show you. I never finished the story. I didn't finish the book or the screenplay."

"You wrote a book as well?"

"I did, it's in the house. But it lacks the finale. The book ends in the same place, after his father's funeral, with Danny telling me how much he hates me."

"So what does that have to do with me?"

"I need you to make sure it's finished."

"Alexander, that's crazy, I'm not the writer of this tale, and that's not the point. He's in danger and you need to—"

"Danny is the writer."

"You're asking Daniel to write the ending?"

"I need him to finish the story. I want him to find relief."

"What makes you think he will?"

"You're going to help him."

Alexander stared at her. She could sense his plea, his sorrow, and his remorse.

"He's never forgiven you?"

"No."

"Did you try to reach him when you were alive?"

"Many times, but he wouldn't have it. In the end I followed him and made sure no harm ever came to him."

"Followed him?"

"At a distance. He never knew."

"You spied on him?"

Alexander moved closer to Sarah. "No. I needed to make sure he was safe."

Sarah could sense the anguish in his soul, his desperate need to repair the damage he had inflicted on the young boy so long ago. "I sympathize with your plea Alexander, but how can I help him find relief if I don't save him now."

"You will. In time, you'll do both."

"Will you guide me?"

Alexander smiled and walked toward the door. He turned to her. "You know I will." He vanished. The room went dark as night, a pinpoint of light seeping through a tiny hole.

The road that led up to Hank's farm wound through the isolated hills away from everything. As Elisabeth drove, she felt a growing sense of dread. She should've waited for Williams. But she hadn't heard from Sarah and wasn't sure if she'd received the message to call him. Maybe she should've called Williams herself earlier, now it was too late.

"But what if Daniel went of his own accord? What if he remembered his past and didn't want me to find out how despicable it was?"

Her insecurity grew with every turn of the road, her imagination taking her places she'd rather not go, but couldn't avoid. No matter how frightened she was she needed to prepare herself for what might lie ahead.

"What if Daniel is one of those bikers who fought one of his buddies for something or someone? His wife and daughter could be at Hank's. And I might be driving into a bikers' compound. They might attack me. But why would they? I've done nothing to them…I just want to find Daniel. On the other hand, what if Daniel was taken against his will? I have to help him. Regardless of the outcome, I must find him."

As her mind reeled, her body tensed, the clamminess in her palms intensified, and a slight tremor overtook her body. "Take a deep breath and calm down, Elisabeth," she scolded herself. "Don't get too worked up or you'll be no good to anyone."

She dialed once more and it went directly to voice mail. "Sarah, I'm on South Fish Lake Road off of 97, north of Riverside looking for North Pine Creek road in an isolated area around Tonasket. I'm searching for Hank Ferguson's farm and all these horrible scenarios keep playing in my head. I have no idea what I'm going to find, but I can't stop myself. Call me. Please, call."

She then dialed 911. "This is Elisabeth Ralston, and I need to be transferred to Sheriff Williams right away."

"Is this an emergency?"

"It sort of is."

"You can tell me and I can pass it on."

"Darn, it's too hard to tell."

"You've called the emergency line, ma'am."

"Oh, what the hell. Tell him that there's been a kidnapping and that I'm at Hank Ferguson's farm on North Pine Creek road off of South Fish Lake road." She hung up and sighed. "I hope I don't go to jail for this."

When Conrad returned to Sarah's hospital room, he found her dressed and ready to go.

"Finally. Let's get out of here."

"What are you doing? You heard what Doc said."

"Yeah, but I'm okay, and we need to find Daniel. He's locked up somewhere. Oh, and Alexander paid me a visit. He'll help. We've got to go." She rushed to the door.

Flabbergasted by the suddenness of it all, Conrad could only muster a weak, "Go where?"

Sarah stopped and turned back to her husband with a shrug. "No idea, but I'm sure Alexander will show me soon enough. Can you believe that he refused to tell me where Daniel is because 'writers don't tell, they show'?'"

"He said that? You've got to be kidding."

"Oh no, he was serious. In any case, I can't stay here. What did Williams say?"

"He's on his way to the farm of a Hank Ferguson, the older brother of Walter Ferguson who was the caretaker of Alexander's estate. The bloody fingerprints could be Hank's."

He stepped close to her. "Where's the farm?"

"He didn't tell me."

"We have to go and hope Alexander will help me pinpoint where Daniel is."

Conrad took her in his arms. "Sarah, this is police business. It's not safe."

"You'll be there with me." She tightened the embrace and then broke it off. "C'mon, I'll call Williams…where's my cell? Where's my purse?"

"We left it in Williams's office when you…when we came here."

Sarah stepped into the hall. "We'll use your phone. Let's go, please hurry."

"Wait," Conrad called out. "We need to tell Doc you've left." He walked up to the emergency room receptionist while Sarah rushed out of the hospital.

Hank Ferguson opened the trunk of the car and yanked Daniel out of it, blindfolded, gagged, and with his hands tied behind his back. His face was crusty with blood and he struggled to stay upright as Hank dragged him by his hair away from the car.

Unable to reach Williams on his cell phone, the Thompsons opted to go to his office to get the farm's address and retrieve Sarah's purse.

"Mrs. Thompson." The receptionist's smile welcomed them. "I'm so glad you're well."

"Thanks, Cathy," Sarah said with a smile. "So am I. Nothing serious, a very bad migraine that took my breath away."

"Those are awful. My aunt Gladys gets those, and she's got to lie down in a dark room for a day or two before she can be herself again. I'm happy you recovered so fast. I've got your purse right here." She handed it to Sarah.

"Can you contact Sheriff Williams? I can't get him on his cell, and I need to give him some extremely important information. He's headed to Hank Ferguson's farm, but can you tell us where that it is?"

Cathy appeared uncomfortable.

"Sheriff Williams told me where he was going," Conrad added, "but at the time I didn't realize that Sarah had vital information for him, so I didn't ask him for the address. I'm sure he won't mind you telling us."

Cathy nodded. "It's up north off 97, then off Pine Creek road, that becomes South Fish Lake Road, and veers off onto North Pine Creek Road."

"Hold on," Conrad interrupted, "I have to write all this down."

"Sorry," Cathy said, "I forget how confusing those double names can be. Anyway, the Ferguson farmhouse is on North Pine Creek Road. Reception for cell phones is pretty spotty in those hills and that's why you haven't been able to reach the sheriff. The dispatcher can tell him you're on your way."

"Thanks," Sarah said, "we'd appreciate that."

"By the way, Mrs. Thompson, your cell's been ringing. You should have several messages."

Hank tied Daniel to a vertical wooden beam in the middle of a darkened underground chamber, lit only by a kerosene lamp. He removed the blindfold and gag, and then stood ominously above him.

"I'll ask you one last time, who've you told about me?" Hank glared menacingly at Daniel, his demeanor made even more frightening by the faint light illuminating his face.

"No one."

"You think I buy that shit? I ain't no fool?"

"I told you, I've had amnesia. I don't have any memories."

Hank paced before Daniel, his face contorted in anger. "Whatever this *nesia* is, I don't buy it. What the hell were you doing at Pitman's place anyway?"

"I have no idea who that is…what you're talking about."

Hank squatted in front of Daniel, his face menacingly close as he growled, "Listen, I left you for dead once, this time I'm making damn sure. So don't you mess with me."

"I'm not, believe me. I can't even remember who the hell I am."

"Bullshit. Then why did you come after me at the diner?"

"I spotted your ring and it brought back memories of you hitting me. That's all."

Hank stood up and spat on Daniel. "You must think I'm stupid." He paced again, rubbing his head in frustration. "Did you call the cops? Did you tell them about me? Are they coming after me?"

"I didn't tell anyone. Believe me."

Hank slapped Daniel with the back of his hand. "Fuck you." He grabbed the lamp and stomped out, leaving Daniel in the dark with only a faint ray of light seeping through a small hole in the rocks above him.

CHAPTER 27

Elisabeth turned on to North Pine Creek Road and, after a series of bends and twists, spotted an old mailbox marked *Ferguson* in faded paint. Next to the mailbox, a gravel driveway meandered onto the property. Elisabeth drove past the driveway and pulled off the road.

She turned off the car, got out, and quietly closed the door. She headed toward the farmhouse, walking to one side of the gravel driveway on the overgrown dry grass.

The only sounds were her rapid breathing and pounding heartbeat. The silence of the place coupled with her signs of panic brought a tremor to her body.

Suddenly, three large dogs rushed toward her, barking and growling viciously.

She stopped and turned sideways, keeping an eye on the dogs in the periphery of her vision, but making sure they couldn't catch her eyes. She dropped to one knee, lowered her head and straightened her arms, made tight fists, and in a low commanding voice, making sure not to show her teeth, she ordered, "Stop. Down. Stop." The dogs stopped charging, but continued barking and growling. After a few tense moments, they approached slowly, still growling but clearly having understood her stance.

Once more she commanded, "Down. Stop."

The growling subsided and two of the dogs sat while the leader of the pack approached warily, sniffed her, and then circled around. She remained immobile, not showing her teeth, and avoiding direct eye contact with the animal, waiting for the dog to feel at ease with her.

Satisfied, he sniffed her hand and licked it. Now that his scent was on her, she slowly sat down and offered her other hand to the other dogs. They approached with caution and sniffed her a few times before licking her hands in a tentative welcome.

She sat for a while to allow the dogs to become comfortable with her presence. She petted them when they approached to sniff or lick her. After a few minutes she cautiously got to her feet and slowly resumed her walk up toward the farm with the dogs alongside. "I'll be damned, that darned Humane Society training works," she whispered. "C'mon, you beasts," she said, "let's go find out if that son-of-a-bitch master of yours has my Daniel."

She approached with caution, though the house looked empty. She peeked through the windows to see if anyone was inside. Two of the dogs lost interest and wandered off. One remained at her side, nuzzling up to her for a pat on the head from time to time.

She made her way to the barn and peered through a crack. With no one in sight, she dared to open the door and step in. The barn was devoid of animals, but littered with old equipment, two rusty motorcycles, broken-down furniture, tires, a wrecked truck, and engine parts.

She had just closed the door behind her, when she heard the roar of a car speeding up the driveway. The dogs took off barking, and she took cover behind the overgrowth to one side of the barn.

Hank stopped the car, and without turning off the engine, rushed into the house. Moments later, he returned with a rifle, threw it onto the passenger seat, got in, and sped down the driveway, leaving in his wake a cloud of dust and three dogs barking for attention.

Elisabeth bolted out of her hiding place and raced down the driveway, the three dogs barking behind her. But as she reached her car, Hank stood up from behind it, cocked the rifle, and aimed it at her head.

"Looking for your boyfriend?"

Elisabeth paled.

At gunpoint, he led her to his car, which was concealed several feet away. "Get in the car, bitch." He shoved her into the back seat and hit her on the temple with the butt of the rifle. She collapsed, unconscious. Hank pushed her in, shut the door, ran to the driver's side, and drove away onto a dirt road that split off a short distance from his own driveway.

Moments later, the sheriff's car and two patrol cars approached the Ferguson farm. As soon as they spotted Elisabeth's car parked near the property, they stopped.

A couple of officers approached Elisabeth's car, weapons drawn. They peeked through the windows. The officer on the driver's side opened the door and popped the trunk lid open. The other officer searched it and found nothing. He gave the all-clear sign to the cars parked below.

Williams got out and made his way toward the car.

Robinson handed him Elisabeth's wallet, saying, "Belongs to Elisabeth Ralston. She left her wallet and cell phone in the compartment under the armrest."

"Damned woman," Williams spat out. "What's she gotten herself into?"

"No sign of force or violence around the car, sir."

Officer Collins approached Williams. "Sir, a woman's shoeprints go up to the driveway."

He followed Elisabeth's footsteps. "They stop here," he yelled, "then nothing. The grass to the right appears to have been walked on, but it could've been anyone. There are tire marks in and out of the driveway and a couple of the woman's footprints facing forward. It looks as if a car sped off across them."

"Okay," Williams said. "Let's pay a visit to dear old Hank. Be ready, but let's try not to scare him. Robinson, you got that ultrasonic dog repellant?"

"Yes, sir."

"Collins, make sure you're ready to spray those dogs with the mace. I'm not sure this ultrasound business will keep them away from us."

"Yes, sir."

As expected, the moment they went up the drive, the dogs charged. Robinson utilized the repellant and the growling and barking quickly turned to yelping as the pack stopped cold. Collins used the spray, and the dogs fled, squealing and howling.

"Shit." Williams chuckled. "That stuff really works."

The officers cautiously made their way to the front of the house. Williams knocked.

"Hank, this is Sheriff Williams, I need to talk with you."

There was no response. Williams signaled for the officers to go around the house and look for any sign of Hank while he continued knocking.

"Hank Ferguson, this is Sheriff Williams. Open up. We'd like to have a word with you."

Silence.

The officers returned, indicating that there was no sign of Hank.

"Check the barn, look for him in the shack, or any other hiding place. Spread out."

Williams knocked again. "Hank, open up! Where's Mrs. Ralston? Her car is outside your property. We need to talk to her."

Silence.

Sarah tossed her cell phone into her purse. "I finally get a signal and she's not answering," she told her husband. "Why not pick up? I hope she's not in any trouble."

"Williams should be almost there. He'll take care of her."

"If he can find her." Sarah looked out the window as they drove alongside Fish Lake Road. "How much farther is Hank's farm?"

"Well, we're way behind both Elisabeth and Williams so we—"

"Conrad, stop!" Sarah called out.

Conrad pulled over and skidded to the side of that road. "What is it?"

"That's the road, the one we just passed."

"No, that's not it. It's a dirt road that—"

"It's not the farmhouse, but I sense that's where Daniel is."

Conrad looked at his wife, a hint of disbelief betraying him.

"Don't look at me that way. I felt a strong pull when we passed that road. Then I caught a quick flash of a ray of light coming from a crack in a rocky ceiling, like a cave. We need to go through there. I bet you that Alexander's showing me."

"I don't like this 'showing' business of Alexander's. He's put you and me through hell. And let me tell you, making you feel what Daniel experienced was too much."

"Believe me, I understand. We'll be cautious. Please, let's turn back."

Conrad recognized that he had no choice. With a reluctant nod he turned the car around and headed onto the small dirt road. "It doesn't even have a name, Sarah. How can we tell Williams where we are?"

Daniel heard Hank panting and puffing as he approached the underground chamber. He could see a faint glow from the kerosene lamp approaching. As the light grew brighter, the groaning and puffing grew louder. Finally, Hank emerged into the underground chamber with Elisabeth's unconscious body slung over his shoulder. He dropped her to the ground, and she partially rolled toward Daniel, her face and head covered in blood.

"Elisabeth! What have you done to her, you son of a bitch?" Daniel cried out, his face flushed with fury as he tugged at the rope that anchored him to the pole.

"Not as much as I will if you don't start talking," Hank spat out between gasping breaths. He put down the kerosene lamp and cocked the rifle as he pointed it to her left foot. "I'm gonna shoot one foot first, then the other, then one knee, then—"

"Stop!" Daniel shouted. "She's done you no harm, let her go!"

"You can't tell me what to do, so start talking, you son of a bitch!"

"Okay, okay. I'll tell you anything—only don't harm her."

"Talk."

"I told Sheriff Williams. Have you heard of him?"

"You're doing the talking, not me. What did you tell good ol' Billy Boy?"

"I told him…well…let me think…first I described you…only I didn't remember exactly how you looked…so give me a second…with this amnesia…I told you I have this illness, and it makes it difficult to recall things. But I can…let me see…I told him you were blond…and with short hair…but I was confused as you can well understand, so I don't believe he's looking for you, because, it's clear that you're not blond, and you don't have short—"

"You're shitting me!"

"No, it's true, please…I'm ill. My memory is…give me a second…I'll remember more, I'm sure."

Conrad's truck emerged into a small clearing leading up to what appeared to be the entrance to an abandoned mine. They spotted a car parked by the entrance.

Sarah jerked back and grabbed Conrad's arm. "Stop. They're here."

Conrad stopped the car. "Who?"

"Elisabeth's here. She's been hurt. Her head is bleeding," Sarah said as she held the right side of her head. "He hit her on the head with the butt of the rifle."

"How—"

"Alexander showed me. Hank's got them both in there. He's pointing the rifle at Daniel."

Conrad pulled out his cell phone. "I'll call Williams." He dialed, but quickly realized he had no reception. "Stay here Sarah. I'm going to try to get a signal."

Without waiting for a reply, he quietly got out and walked a few feet away from the car and the entrance to the mine, moving right, then left, until he found a spot with reception. The call went through.

"Sheriff Williams's office," Cathy answered.

"This is Conrad Thompson, we have an emergency—" he heard crackling, and realized he'd stepped out of the area where the phone had reception. He took a couple of steps back.

"Mr. Thompson, are you there?" Cathy asked.

"I am, sorry, we have bad reception. We believe that Hank Ferguson has Daniel Michaels and Elisabeth Ralston inside an abandoned mine."

"Where are you?" she asked.

"We're at the entrance to the mine. We veered off of 97 on to Fish Lake Road or Pine Creek Road—I'm no longer sure which is which—and then we took a dirt road with no name. I couldn't tell you where this is."

"I'll transfer you to dispatch, they'll tell you what to do. Hold a moment."

Conrad waited for a second, not daring to move and lose the connection.

"Dispatch here. Mr. Thompson, does your phone have a GPS?"

"Yeah."

"Then I'll patch you through to 911 and inform them you're on the line. Leave your phone on. Do not lose the connection. We'll track you down."

Conrad heard the 911 operator come on the line. "We got you sir, leave the phone on and we'll track you down. Are you all right?"

"Yes, but others are injured."

"Okay, stay calm; we're checking your location right now."

"Hurry, please." He turned around to signal Sarah that all was well, only to realize that she was no longer in the car. "Damn!" he yelled.

"What is it?" the operator asked.

"My wife's gone into the mine."

"Mine?"

"Yes, we're outside some old abandoned mine."

"She's gone inside the mine?"

"I didn't see her go in, but she's not in the car. Damn, damn, damn!"

"Remain calm, sir."

"Listen, I'm going to leave the phone on the ground so I can go look for my wife. Tell Sheriff Williams we're both inside the mine and to approach with caution."

Without waiting for a response, he carefully placed the phone on the ground, making sure the reception bars were not affected. The voice of the operator called to him to stay put. He rushed toward the entrance to the mine.

Sarah made her way into the abandoned mine following the light and the sound of voices. As she drew nearer, she could hear the anger in Hank's voice and the anguish in Daniel's.

"Please, give me a second," Daniel, pleaded.

"You're out of time. I'm shooting her foot off."

"Your father wouldn't approve," Sarah said as she stepped into the chamber.

Hank spun around pointing the rifle at her. "Who the fuck are you?"

"My name is Sarah, and your father, Henry, whom you used to call Pa Ree, on account you couldn't say Henry when you were little, has sent me here to stop you."

"My dad's dead, you bitch."

"Yes he is. Nonetheless, he told me to tell to you that no matter what you've done in the past, you've never hurt a woman. He begs you not to start now."

"What the—"

"He tells me how proud and happy you felt when you were seven and you went fishing with him and you caught a trout on your own. You had it for dinner."

"How do you know that?"

"He says when you brought Rex home and nursed the beat-up old dog back to health you were happy and proud of what you'd done. He asks you to bring back those feelings instead of the anger you feel now."

Hank's eyes widened as he glared at Sarah. "What the hell?"

Conrad had made his way into the tunnel. He heard the calm voice of his wife and decided to remain hidden, yet near enough to step in to help if need be.

"Pa Ree says you were a good son," Sarah went on.

"Bullshit. He hated me. I turned out bad. My little brother is the one he liked. That dipshit got all the breaks and I got all the crap."

"You took care of Walter and your mom after the rotary tiller cut off your dad's fingers. You found him in the field, and all on your own wrapped his hand, picked up his fingers. He says you carried him to the farm and then drove him to the hospital. You saved his life. He says—"

"Stop this shit!" Hank cried out, his eyes flooding with tears.

"It's the truth, isn't it Hank?"

"You must've heard all this stuff around town, and now you're here to mess me up."

She cocked her head again. "He says no one but you and him were there the time you killed your first deer, and you felt so bad you dropped to the ground crying because you felt so guilty for taking its life. Pa Ree held you in his arms until you stopped crying."

"You can't know that. It's impossible," he whispered. "Who the hell are you?"

"Pa Ree loves you and he begs you not to harm Elisabeth or Daniel."

"You're some kind of witch. Damn it! This shit's scary! Whatever you are, this ain't right."

"Okay, I'll stop if you wish. But we both know I'm telling the truth. And that's what scares you."

Conrad heard footsteps behind him and quietly moved back. He found Sheriff Williams and his men entering the tunnel and signaled for them to be silent. He approached Williams and whispered, "Sarah is in there trying to talk Hank down. She's connected with Hank's dead father, Henry, and he's helping her talk to him."

Williams's eyes widened in disbelief.

"Sounds strange," Conrad whispered, "even to me, but it's true. Come and listen."

Without a sound, they made their way close enough to the entrance of the underground chamber to overhear the conversation.

"Shut up, shut up, shut up! Don't say another word, bitch!" Hank paced the chamber like a caged animal, both arms out, the rifle clasped tightly. "How could you…how do you…this is all wrong." He spun and leveled the rifle at Sarah. "Who the hell are you?"

"My name's Sarah, and I have received a gift from God. I can talk with those who are in need like Alexander Pitman, who sent me here to stop you from harming Daniel and—"

"Pitman's dead, witch!"

"That's not what I am. I can simply see and hear things you can't."

"Alexander Pitman?" Daniel whispered.

Hank turned and aimed the rifle at him. "You remember him now, you son of a bitch?"

"Alexander Pitman?" Daniel asked again, more to himself than to Hank or Sarah.

"Yes, Danny, Alexander sent me to you," Sarah said.

"Alexander Pitman," Daniel muttered one more time.

Hank turned to Sarah with a puzzled look. "What the hell's wrong with this bastard? Is he crazy? Did you turn him into this *nesia* he keeps yapping about? You here to put a spell on me?"

Sarah smiled. "No, I'm not a witch. I'm here to help you so that you don't do something you'll regret forever."

"Too late for that."

"Hank, listen to me. It's not too late. Pa Ree says he forgives you."

"My pa is dead!"

"Yes, and I can speak with the dead. That's the gift God gave me."

"You can really talk to dead people?"

"Yes, at times. I can speak with souls who remain behind because they need to finish some business before they can move on. Your pa asks that you listen to me. He says you were a good kid until you started hanging out with the Sander boys. They turned you, but you didn't let them do the same to your little brother."

"That's only 'cause they were my band, not his."

"Pa Ree says you can't fool him now that he's on the other side. He knows the truth."

In spite of himself Hank chuckled. "That old goat."

"He's real sad you went and killed Billy Williams's dad." No sooner had Sarah uttered these words than her eyes widened with astonishment.

Hank was clearly shocked. "My pa was long dead when—"

"You're the one who killed Sheriff Williams's father," Sarah said, staring into Hank's eyes. "You were following the deer through the scope of your rifle." She glanced at the rifle. "The same rifle you're holding now," she went on, "but you didn't set out to kill him. He'd locked you up, for five days. My God, Hank, you killed him because you were angry with him."

Hank turned to her, his eyes filled with tears and rage. "The son of a bitch had it coming. He kept putting me in jail for no reason. He had it coming."

"That's not true. He locked you up for your own good, to sober you up. You didn't plan to kill him. But after you got out of jail you went on a binge. You were drunk and had no business hunting. You lost your head."

"Pa Ree told you this?"

"I saw how it happened, Hank. I saw the sheriff's death the same way you did, through your rifle's scope."

Hank looked at the rifle. "How could you? You weren't there. I was on my own."

"Alexander Pitman was trying to show me how you've—"

"Alexander's dead?" Daniel interjected.

Hank pointed the rifle at Sarah. "Make this bastard stop!"

"Hank," Sarah went on, "put the rifle down. Pa Ree says you're not going to harm me. And you're not going to harm Daniel or Elisabeth, either."

Hank turned the rifle on Daniel. "That house was supposed to be empty. This shit ass had no business going into Pitman's place."

"He did have business. He's Pitman's heir."

"Fuck," Hank said and shook his head. "You're shitting me."

"It's true. Pa Ree asks you to give yourself up. It's time for you to do the right thing as you did when you were younger, before the drinking. He doesn't want you to die."

Hank looked at her, his eyes full of tears. "Tell him I didn't mean to kill the sheriff. He really liked that old bastard."

"He knows."

"I didn't mean to beat up this guy so bad either. He surprised me. He had no business being there. Pitman was dead, so I went after some of his stuff. My brother got a shit load of inheritance money 'cause he took care of the guy's property. So why shouldn't I get some of his shit? I was on my way out when all of a sudden this son of a bitch was standing there by the stairs, staring at me. Freaked me out. Before I knew it I'd beat him so bad I thought I'd killed him. So I dumped him in the trunk, took off up the mountains, and tossed his body on the side of the road. Go figure—the son of a bitch wasn't dead. How was I supposed to figure I hadn't killed him?"

"Put the rifle down, Hank," Sheriff Williams said as he entered the chamber with his weapon leveled at Hank's chest.

Hank dropped to his knees.

Williams yanked him by his shirt and pulled him up, his nose almost touching Hank's. "You son of a bitch, you killed my father and all these years…"

"I'm sorry," Hank muttered.

Williams spun him to the ground, placed a foot on his back, snatched up his arms, and handcuffed him. "Get this piece of shit out of my sight," he commanded.

A couple of officers grabbed Hank and dragged him out of the mine, passing by the two officers who were holding Conrad back until the scene was secure. The moment they released him he rushed to Sarah and wrapped her tightly in his arms.

Williams knelt next to Elisabeth and examined her. "She's alive, unconscious, but alive."

"Thank God," Daniel said. As soon as they untied him, he rushed to her.

An officer held him back. "It's best if you don't touch her. We'll take care of her. You need some medical attention yourself. C'mon, let's get you out of here."

"No, wait. I'm okay. Give me a second." He approached Sarah and Conrad. "I remember," he said. "I remember Alexander."

Sarah and Conrad embraced him, tears of relief overtaking them all.

"C'mon, you three," Williams said. "Let's get out of here and make room for my officers to tend to Elisabeth until the paramedics get here."

"But—" Daniel protested.

"No arguing, Mr. Michaels. Please, let's get out into the fresh air. We'll take care of her."

"Michaels," muttered Daniel, "that *is* my last name."

CHAPTER 28

Daniel lay impatiently on a hospital bed—head bandaged, face bruised, and lips swollen.

Dr. Lawrence stepped in, a broad smile across his lips. "Good news, Daniel. No damage to your brain. There's some swelling, so we'll keep you here a couple of days for observation—"

"Elisabeth, Doc, how is she?"

"She's asleep. We've given her something to help her rest and relieve the pain from that nasty blow to her head. Her skull isn't broken, and we've sewn the wound, but she's got a severe concussion. We're keeping her here a few days to make sure she heals properly. Don't worry she's well taken care of. Nurses and doctors are doting over her."

"Can I see her?"

"In due time. We're going to keep her sedated so that she can rest."

"Did she say anything when she came to? Did he…rape her?"

"No, no, nothing like that. He knocked her out."

"Did she tell you that?"

"Yes. Rest assured; he didn't molest her at all. She's happy you're okay. But when we told her Hank's been put in jail, she started fussing over some dogs she found over at his farm."

"She went to his place?"

"That's where Hank found her. She was looking for you."

"And you're sure he didn't—"

"Yes, yes, I'm sure. Put that out of your mind. She's recovering from a mean blow to the head, and that's all. She's very relieved you're okay and that you've reconnected with your past. So let's focus on you for the moment. Tell me how much memory you've recovered."

"It's hard to tell since I have no idea what I'm missing."

"That's true. Tell me how it happened?"

Daniel smiled. "I imagine that after all that you've gone through with me, the least I can do is explain how my memory came back."

"Well, I'd like to hear it, first as a physician, but also to make sure that your memories match what we've learned about you."

"I get it, a bit of a test, huh?"

"Something like that." Dr. Lawrence chuckled.

"Fair enough." Daniel's eyes wandered as he began to recall. "It started in the mine. I heard the name Alexander Pitman, and it sounded familiar. Then, all of a sudden, it popped into my head that I had met Alexander when I was in my teens."

"Then what happened?"

"I heard Sarah talking to Hank about his father, Henry, but all I could think about was how sad it was that Alexander had died."

"And then?"

"My mind went back to when I met him."

"What else do you recall from that time period?"

Daniel looked puzzled. "Should there be something special?"

"Something that affected you profoundly."

Daniel's eyes narrowed. "You mean my father's death?"

"How did he die?"

"You can't possibly know about my father."

"Why not?"

"How could you? My last name wouldn't be enough."

"Answer me."

A sudden understanding came over Daniel. "Sarah. She's talked to my father, just as she talked to Hank's dad."

"No, she hasn't, at least not in the same way. Why won't you answer my question?"

"He killed himself," he said with evident annoyance. "Are you satisfied now?"

"You still blame yourself?"

"How the hell did you find that out?"

"Why are you here in the Northwest?"

Daniel frowned and then nodded. "Sarah said that Alexander made me his heir. Now tell me, how did you discover those details about my childhood?"

"Daniel, you didn't remember the fact that you're Alexander's heir on your own. Why?"

"It's as if I did, and I didn't. I'm aware of it, but I'm not sure how. But that's not important. Tell me, please, how did you find out about my father?"

"Sarah mentioned a movie playing in her head, right?"

Daniel nodded.

"Alexander's been showing her your story."

"Showing?"

"Apparently it's a screenplay that Alexander wrote about what happened in 1976."

"How much information do you all have about what happened then?"

"Pretty much all of it. Well, from Alexander's point of view, of course. Williams, Conrad, and I have all read his screenplay, but—"

"And Elisabeth?"

"No. We've told her nothing about it. They discovered the screenplay only two days ago, before I told you we knew some things about you."

"Has Sarah read the screenplay? How detailed is it?"

"Detailed enough."

Daniel closed his eyes, took a deep breath, and shook his head.

"You were a kid, Daniel."

He opened his eyes and smiled. "Sarah read the details as well?"

"No. Sarah hasn't read the story. She lived through the events that are described in the screenplay. All played out in her head, mind you, exactly as Alexander wrote them."

"Doc." Daniel reached for his arm. "How can that happen? How can Sarah connect to Alexander or to Hank's dad for that matter? How—"

"She's both a psychic and a medium, which, as I understand it, is quite unique and precious. She's had these abilities since she was little, so did Conrad's grandmother. It's a talent that very few people are born with, like being a prodigy in the arts or sciences."

"Psychic and medium? Aren't they the same?"

"From what I've gathered, not all psychics are mediums. A psychic can connect with the present and the future; a medium serves as a vessel between this life and the afterlife. Sarah can do both."

"And Alexander showed her the screenplay instead of talking with her? Why so elaborate? Why not tell her and get it over with?"

"He said that's what writers do—show and not tell."

"That sounds like him."

"Apparently, Alexander also wrote a book, unpublished. He left them both for you to finish."

"Me? Why would he do that? I'm not a writer."

"Well, Sarah should be the one to address that with you since she's been the one communicating with him. Let me bring her in, if that's okay."

"Sure."

Dr. Lawrence opened the door. "Come in, Sarah. He's doing well, his memory's back, and he's full of questions."

"Daniel," she said, holding her hands out to him, "you look good in spite of that second beating Hank gave you."

Daniel reached for her hands and pulled her to him, embracing her tightly. "Thank you, thank you, thank you, Sarah."

Sarah blushed and giggled as he released her from the embrace.

"I'm glad you're so happy," she said. "This ordeal has been quite a roller coaster for you."

"Where's Conrad? I'd like to thank him, too."

"He's with Billy. By the way, he also asked to see you. Doc doesn't want too many of us in here at the same time."

"But I'm fine, Doc."

"Just the same," Dr. Lawrence said. "I'll leave you two alone for a moment, and then I'll bring Billy in. He's got something to tell you."

He smiled and left the room.

Daniel slid to one side and tapped the bed for Sarah to sit down.

"Okay, what questions do you have for me?"

"Can you really speak with Hank's father?"

"Yes, but it was Alexander who facilitated the exchange."

"How can that happen? How do you do it? How come Alexander is talking with you? Why would he do that?"

"Whoa," Sarah smiled and tapped Daniel's hand. "One question at a time, okay?"

Daniel nodded.

"The most important thing for you to know is that Alexander's been trying to help you."

"But he's dead."

"Yes, but not gone."

Daniel shook his head in disbelief. "It's so—" he paused, searching for the right word.

"Paranormal?" Sarah offered.

"I'd be terrified if I were you."

"Tell me about it," she joked. "It's taken me a lifetime to overcome my fear and not run away from it. I've come to accept it as a gift that allows me to help others—even myself."

"So Alexander told you all about me and what happened in the summer of 1976?"

"Well, he actually showed me. He refused to tell. The writer in him had to show me the story scene by scene. To be honest, it nearly drove me crazy. I couldn't make heads or tails of it for the longest time."

"It's embarrassing…my story," Daniel said, almost in a whisper.

"Nonsense, Daniel. There's nothing embarrassing about it. You were an honest, caring boy who got tangled up in an adult web of deceit."

"My father—"

"Your father's decision to end his life had nothing to do with you. Yes, you confronted him, but he could've chosen to face his demons and atone for his conduct. The decision to take his life was his and his alone. I would hope that you've reached that same conclusion."

Daniel nodded. "Intellectually, maybe, but not emotionally. The scar ran so deep that I couldn't shake it. I haven't allowed myself to love—I mean, truly love—a woman, or anyone else. I've always feared it—dreaded the possible betrayal. But now I'm different."

"What's changed?"

"Being free of my past allowed me to fall head over heels in love with Elisabeth."

"Then I take it you're not married? The woman and teenager you recalled are not your wife and child?"

"No, those were the images of Mrs. Foster and my very first love, Ellie, my beautiful blond neighbor back home."

Sarah smiled. "Which means you're free to be with Elisabeth. That should be wonderful news for you both."

Daniel beamed. "Oh yeah."

"And your fear of love?"

He shrugged. "It'll have to take a back seat."

"Good."

The door opened, and Dr. Lawrence entered with both Williams and Conrad.

"Conrad," Daniel cried out. "Thank you for all you've done, and for letting Sarah do her thing." He reached out for Conrad's hand and gave it a heartfelt shake.

"You're welcome, Daniel. Good to find you so chipper."

"Mr. Michaels," Williams said, "I owe you an apology. I treated you—"

"No apology necessary, Sheriff. And since I'm no longer a suspect, I hope you'll call me Daniel."

"For sure," Williams said with a nod, "and please call me Billy. Everyone does."

"Hard to believe," Daniel said, "that Hank turned out to be responsible for your father's death. And all these years you had no idea?"

Williams shot a quick glance at Sarah before answering, "No. We concluded it had been a hunting accident, but we…" He hesitated. "We weren't certain who'd pulled the trigger."

"In a way it did turn out to be an accident," Sarah added. "Hank didn't set out to kill him, but alcohol and anger got the better of him, and in the end he couldn't stop himself."

"A tragic loss of a good man," Dr. Lawrence said.

"Daniel," Williams said, "I need your approval for a crime-scene cleaning crew to come into your home and remove all the blood and mess left behind in the foyer."

"My home…sounds odd."

Williams glanced at Dr. Lawrence, concerned that Daniel hadn't recovered all his memory. The doctor nodded reassuringly.

"Is it okay, then?" Williams asked again. "Blood has many contaminants, and I suggest we get you a specialized crew with experience in cleaning up crime scenes. You'll have to pay for it; the state doesn't do it for you, but we can have it done while you're laid up here."

"Yeah, for sure. Thanks," Daniel said. "Have you found my wallet and the rental car?"

"We're still looking," Williams said. "I'm sure we'll find it all hidden somewhere in the Ferguson farm. Hank's been real cooperative since he decided to atone."

A couple of days later, Daniel was released from the hospital. However, Elisabeth remained behind. The concussion had affected her sense of balance and temporarily caused a problem with certain words.

This time around, it was Daniel who visited every day, reading to her and keeping her spirits up.

"They found my rental car," Daniel said as they strolled through the small hospital garden. "Hank had stripped the license plates and given it to his buddies as payment for some gambling debts."

"That's good," Elisabeth said with a smile. "Your wallet—you got it back? Did you already tell me?"

"Yes, I did, and yes I got it back." He gently caressed her hand that rested on his arm.

"Will they let me go home soon? I'm a lot better now. I'm no longer having trouble with words, although I do have some short memory lapses here and there, but Doc says it's nothing serious. I have a deeper understanding of what you must've felt. It's unbearably frustrating."

"I've asked Doc to let you come and stay at my place…well, Alexander's, so I can take care of you. It's a lot closer to the hospital than your home."

"You don't have to do that," she protested.

"I don't have to, but I want to," he said, and placed a kiss on her cheek.

She smiled and kissed him back. "Amazing how good it feels that we don't have to hide our feelings from everybody."

"It sure does."

"Will Doc entrust me to you?"

"He's going to run a couple of more tests on you today, and if everything checks out, there's no reason why you can't stay with me. Sarah said she'd go by your house and pick up whatever you need, just give her a list."

"Boy, what a difference recovering your memory makes. You're not married; no one is waiting for you, you can stay here in your new home and—by the way—who was that woman you believed was your wife?"

"No one important. An old memory from my early teens."

"Odd then, isn't it, that you'd remember her?"

"Yeah, I guess. My memory came back in bits and pieces, with the biggest blast coming back when we were in the mine. I'm still sorting it all out."

"I wish I'd been conscious to hear all of that. Sarah's something else, isn't she?"

They'd made their way around the garden several more times when Elisabeth slowed.

"Do you need to sit down?"

"No, I'm fine. It's odd that Pitman left you his entire estate. Why would he do that?"

Daniel shrugged. "He had no one else, apparently."

"I find it hard to believe. I wonder if—"

"Whoa, Sherlock, there will be plenty of time for you to sleuth around once you're fully recovered. For now, let's focus on you."

She smiled. "Okay. You're sure there's enough room at his—at *your* house?"

"It looked big from the outside, right?"

"Yeah, but sometimes the inside is—"

"The inside is as big. Don't worry."

Connie, one of the hospital nurses, approached them with a broad smile that lit up her face. "Okay, you two love birds, time to part. Doc's ready to run those tests. Daniel, you can wait if you like, or I can call you when she's done."

"I'll wait, Connie, thanks. I'd like to find out when I can take her home."

"That's fine. Doc's waiting in his office along with Dr. Baylor."

Two days later, Elisabeth was finally released from the hospital. She insisted on packing her own clothes and toiletries. Sarah fetched her from the hospital and drove her home to gather some things. They picked up Conrad, and he drove them to Daniel's home.

As they entered the clearing where Alexander's house stood, Elisabeth shivered. "I got so scared when the Sheriff drove by, and we hid. You should've seen us. I was shaking."

"You guys were very lucky fools," Conrad said.

"You're so right," Elisabeth giggled, gazing up at the house. "It's quite a place isn't it?"

"It's *beautiful*," Sarah said. "I never imagined Alexander living in a place like this when he first introduced himself to me."

"You'll have to tell me more about him and that movie. I'm all right now, so there's no need to tiptoe around me anymore."

As they pulled up to the house, Daniel raced down the porch steps and greeted Elisabeth with a big hug and kiss. "Welcome, my love!"

Embarrassed by his enthusiasm, Elisabeth blushed and giggled.

Beaming, Daniel hugged Sarah and kissed her on the cheek. "Welcome, Woman of Many Talents." He shook Conrad's hand effusively. "And welcome to you, Conrad."

"What, no superlatives for me?"

"Sorry." Daniel laughed. "But I only have eyes for these two beautiful ladies."

"Fair enough," Conrad said as he popped the trunk open.

"Let me get that," Daniel said.

"No, you escort the *beautiful ladies* inside. I'll bring Elisabeth's things in."

Holding both women by the elbow, Daniel did as he was told.

"Boy." Elisabeth sighed as she stepped into the house. "This foyer is beautiful. Look at the workmanship on that staircase."

"Daniel," Sarah said, "I can't help but notice that it smells delicious in here. What have you prepared for us?"

Daniel smiled. "A Spanish *tapa* of alioli with mushrooms and clams in a potato parsley sauce. A typical Spanish meal to welcome Elisabeth home— well, the home that belonged to Alexander—a man who loved Spain. And also in honor of your heritage, Sarah."

Conrad stepped into the foyer with Elisabeth's suitcases. "Where shall I put these?"

"The first room on the right at the top of the stairs. Thanks, Conrad."

"Alexander lived in Spain?" Elisabeth wondered. "Is that where he wrote his novels?"

"Mostly he painted portraits while he lived there. In fact all the paintings here are his. Come on, I'll show you the library, unless you'd like to unpack first."

"No need," Elisabeth said. "I'm dying to learn more about this mystery man."

"C'mon, then." Daniel marched to the library and proudly swung open the door.

Elisabeth stepped in and glanced around the room, her eyes full of curiosity until she noticed the painting of a young Daniel hanging on the wall and froze. She stared at it in amazement, turned to Daniel, gasped, and fainted.

Sarah grabbed her in time to break the fall.

Daniel rushed over, and together they eased her onto the floor as she came to.

"Elisabeth, what happened? Are you all right?" a concerned Daniel asked as he caressed her face and supported her head.

"You're Danny," she whispered.

"Yes, I'm Daniel," he said as he glanced at Sarah, puzzled by Elisabeth's statement.

"No, I mean, you're *my* Danny, from home."

"What do you mean?"

She reached up and touched his cheek. "Charlevoix. You're my Danny from Charlevoix."

Daniel paled as he slowly grasped her meaning. "You…you're *Ellie*?"

She nodded as tears flooded her eyes.

He pulled her to him in a fierce embrace, both sobbing uncontrollably.

Conrad entered the library and found Sarah sitting on the floor while Daniel and Elisabeth wept in each other's arms. "What happened?" Perplexed, he helped Sarah to her feet.

"They just realized that he's Danny and she's Ellie," Sarah whispered.

"They didn't know?"

Sarah motioned to him, and they quietly went out, closing the door behind them.

Daniel pulled Elisabeth up and wrapped her in a delicate embrace. He softly wiped her tears away. "Ellie. My Ellie. No wonder I fell for you so fast and so deeply," he whispered. "I never stopped loving you."

"Really?" she said in a small voice. "I loved you so, and yet, you dumped me. You broke my heart, Danny. What happened?"

"It's a long, sordid story, which I'll tell you—actually, you can read all about it. Alexander wrote our entire story in a book and a screenplay—the very movie that played in Sarah's head."

"You're kidding. He wrote about you and me? How did he know us?"

"That summer of '76—that's when I met him."

"That's the friend you were secretly meeting?"

"The very same."

"Oh my God. That's why he left you this house?"

"And his millions."

"Millions?"

Daniel nodded shyly. "Millions."

Elisabeth kissed him softly. "You don't have to be a chef anymore to earn a living?"

"No."

"Darn it, I was so looking forward to visiting foreign lands with you."

"Well, would you be terribly upset if we start with Paris?"

"Why Paris?"

Daniel paused for dramatic effect and smiled. "That's where my home is."

It was his turn to kiss her, only this time the kiss penetrated deep into their souls, reaching that place where they had first found love so many years before.

"Ellie," he whispered, his lips not far from hers, "will you marry me?"

Elisabeth's eyes filled with tears, and with a sob of joy, she murmured, "Yes, Danny."

They kissed and held each other, reclaiming the lost years.

"You live in Paris? Why didn't you tell me?" Elisabeth asked finally.

"I wanted to surprise you. Actually, I own a small restaurant and—"

"They must've been horrified all these months not hearing from you."

"They were worried, but they've managed in my absence quite well. They were glad to hear from me and are eager to meet you when we go home."

"Boy, oh boy! Paris, and your own restaurant. Wow!"

"C'mon," Daniel stood up and reached for her hand. "Let's give them the good news." They rushed out of the library and into the living room where Sarah and Conrad were examining all the art and artifacts strewn about.

"We're engaged," Elisabeth announced and hugged Sarah.

"That's wonderful. You'll both be very happy," Sarah said as she turned to hug Daniel. "I didn't expect you to get engaged so quickly."

"Why not? After all, they've been in love for years." Conrad said.

"This calls for a celebration. I'll bring us a good bottle of champagne. Elisabeth, please get us four flutes. You'll find them in the china cabinet to the right of the dining room," Daniel said as she rushed off.

"Let me help you," Sarah said as she followed her into the dining room. "I can't wait to see what you'll do with the place."

Elisabeth chuckled as she fished out the flutes and handed two to Sarah. "It'll be fun. But I'm really looking forward to Paris. Has he told you he lives there?"

Sarah nodded. "Billy found out from Alexander's estate attorneys, and he, in turn, told us. How about that?"

"A whole new life."

"Jet-setters." Conrad said.

Elisabeth giggled. "Far from it—kinda fun, though."

Daniel returned, champagne bottle in hand. He expertly opened it, filled the flutes, and passed them around. The two couples raised their glasses.

"Congratulations," Conrad said. "We wish you as much happiness and love in your marriage as we have found in ours."

As each finished their glass, Daniel refilled it. "I'm not sure the appetizer I prepared goes well with champagne, so I've opened a nice bottle of red wine from Rioja, if you'd like to switch."

"How about both?" Conrad suggested with a grin.

"To friendship," Elisabeth toasted. "To Sarah and Conrad, the best friends in the world."

"Hear, hear," Daniel said, holding out his glass to each of the others.

"So the town you lived in is called Charlevoix?" Sarah asked.

"Yes, it's a small town between Lake Michigan and the western end of Lake Charlevoix. Alexander changed the name to Amaray, to avoid any recognition or embarrassment."

"But he used everyone's real names."

"I assume he felt that by locating the story in a make-believe town the connection wouldn't be made. Anyway, if you'll go into the living room, I'll join you there in a minute."

They settled around the living room table as Daniel returned with the mushrooms on alioli *tapa*, saying, "I used your recipe for baguettes, Sarah. It's a good one."

"Thank you, Daniel, but the real credit goes to my mother and my nana." She took a bite. "Oh my goodness, I love the flavor, and the bread didn't get soggy. How did you do that?"

"Ah, that's because the alioli prevents it from seeping into the bread."

"These two are going to be impossible together," Elisabeth teased Conrad.

"As long as they keep making great food, it's okay with me. So, how did you become a chef, Daniel? Despite everything we've learned about you that question hasn't been answered."

"Well, after my father's death, I needed to get as far away from home as I could, so I enlisted in the Navy. I figured that traveling the world was as good a way as any to help me forget. Anyway, my first job turned out to be in the kitchen. I had a knack for it, especially baking, thanks to my mom. We were deployed in Asia for a while, and with every shore leave, I made it a point to learn about their different foods. Then I lucked out and ended up in Europe for a while. When my last tour ended, I headed directly for Spain and stepped in as sous-chef for a well-known restaurant in Madrid. By then I knew that the kitchen was the place for me and that the more I learned the better things would get. So I tried my hand in Italy, Argentina, and, after that, Mexico. One way or another, I always managed to land a job with the best chefs. After a few years I made my way to Paris and eventually started my own restaurant. Somehow, I seemed to always be in the right place at the right time. Things always worked out for me."

"Alexander," Sarah said.

Daniel gave her a puzzled look.

"He told me he kept a watchful eye over you. He followed your every move. He looked after you, and when you repeatedly turned him down, he decided to help you from afar."

"You're kidding."

"Why did you refuse to have anything to do with him?" Elisabeth asked.

He considered for a moment. "I blamed him for my father's death," he said.

"How? Why?" she asked.

Daniel glanced at Sarah and Conrad and back at Elisabeth. "Might as well jump right into it, I guess." He gulped down his glass of champagne in an attempt to bolster his courage. "Remember Mrs. Foster?" he asked his new fiancé.

"Humph. Do I ever. She's unforgettable."

"Yeah. Well, the fact is that she seduced me that summer. That's why I couldn't bring myself to be with you when you returned from visiting your grandmother. I was ashamed. It happened while you were gone."

"She forced you to have sex with her?"

He shook his head. "No, I did it more than willingly…encouraged by Alexander."

"But you were fifteen," Elisabeth protested. "How could she do that to you? And how could he spur you on?"

"Well, they both did. But that's not the worst of it." Daniel hesitated before continuing. "That summer I discovered that my father was sleeping with her, too. We shared the same mistress. I felt betrayed by both of them."

Stunned, Elisabeth reached for Daniel's hand. "Oh my God, Danny. How awful!"

He cleared his throat before going on. "Alexander suggested that I needed to…confront them. So I did. My father killed himself the next day." After a couple of deep breaths to regain his composure, Daniel continued. "I was devastated. I blamed Alexander for everything, for losing you, for ruining my life. I was convinced that I'd caused my father's death."

"My God." Elisabeth embraced Daniel as tears streaked down her cheeks. She kissed him softly. "How much you've suffered."

"It's all in the past," Daniel said, kissing away Elisabeth's tears.

"You never knew that Alexander kept tabs on you?" Sarah asked.

"No. Never. But now that you mention it, I wonder—" he paused.

"What?" Elisabeth asked.

"Shortly after my father's death, my mother received a letter from a legal firm in Chicago stating that my father had left a trust for us. It didn't sound like something Dad would do. He didn't have any money to speak of, so for us to get a significant monthly check from a trust felt pretty extravagant. But the money came regularly. We kept waiting for it to dry up, or for the lawyers to realize it was a mistake, but the checks kept coming until my mother passed on."

"Did they come from Alexander?" Elisabeth asked.

"It's not impossible from the sound of it," Conrad said. He turned to Daniel. "If you set your mind to it, I'm sure you'll be able to find out. After all, you now have control over the estate and all of Alexander's affairs."

"I might do that," Daniel said softly.

"What about your mother? Did she find out about Mrs. Foster and your father?" Elisabeth asked.

"Never. After I enlisted, she left Charlevoix and bought a small home in Saint Joseph where she'd grown up. Thanks to the money from the trust, she enjoyed a comfortable life. She volunteered for several organizations and had many friends. She loved to travel, and once my tour of duty ended, she'd visit me for long periods of time. Paris, of course, was her favorite. Several years ago she died peacefully in her sleep. She was home with me when it happened. I was very thankful for that."

"I'm glad she never found out," Elisabeth said as she kissed Daniel on the cheek.

"So am I."

"And your feelings toward Alexander now?"

"I'm at peace with him, Sarah. Since I moved in here, I've gotten a sense of his devotion to me. It's clear that he felt guilty about what had transpired between us. After reading the screenplay and the book, I understand not only what happened that year but Alexander himself. I have no resentment whatsoever. Actually, I'm quite moved by what he did and who he was. I regained my appreciation for the man who wrote *Rainbow* and what that book meant to me."

"Is he here now?" Elisabeth looked around the room.

"No," Sarah said with ease. "I haven't felt his presence since we left the mine. He needed to make sure that you were safe before moving on. Your wellbeing had been such an important part of his life that he couldn't leave until he knew you were all right."

"So he's gone now?" Elisabeth asked shyly. "Really gone?"

Sarah smiled. "Yes, he is."

"I'm glad. I couldn't live with him hovering over Danny day in and day out. Yikes!"

"I propose a toast." Conrad raised his glass. "To the long-awaited happiness and love of Ellie and Danny."

"And to Alexander who made it possible. May he rest in peace," Daniel added.

"To Alexander!" They said in unison.

"Sarah," Elisabeth asked, "when did you realize that I was Ellie and he was Danny?"

"A few weeks ago when I walked into the library and saw Alexander's portrait of Danny, I knew he was our Daniel. With you I sort of had a feeling, but I wasn't sure."

"You recognized Danny from the painting? How?"

"The movie that Alexander played in my mind."

"Wow," Elisabeth gasped. "He played you the movie, and you saw us the way we all looked in 1976?"

"I did."

"That's not all," Conrad added. "She's seen my grandmother in her teens, and the folks who built our houses back in the early 1800s."

"That's quite a gift you have," Elisabeth sighed. "Does it frighten you?"

"Not anymore."

"Okay," said Conrad, "I'm ready to try Daniel's clam dish."

"Let's do it, then." Daniel rose and held out his hand for Elisabeth.

"Can I read Alexander's book about us?" she asked.

"By all means."

"Will you ever finish writing the story?" Sarah asked.

Daniel turned to her and winked. "I might, Sarah. I might."

Bonus
Sarah's Recipes

Sarah uncovered her mother's cookbook, a small three-ring binder that contained all of the recipes she'd collected over the years, a devoted collection of recipes she'd learned from Sarah's nana—those they had advanced together as well as the many they had invented. Over the years, they had improved upon them, and as a result, most recipes had little notes here and there indicating what they had eliminated, added, or altered.

Each handwritten note revived the memories of the two of them and the feeling that somehow they were alongside Sarah as she created each meal, baked each loaf, or crafted delicious desserts.

Now this precious homemade compilation has Sarah's own notes and alterations and has become a three-generation cookbook that also incorporates Daniel's creations.

To view Sarah's and Daniel's recipes, please visit our website: www.2authors.com.

V. &. D. Povall

A HUSBAND AND wife–writing team that has authored and published nonfiction manuals and articles as well as written four short screenplays, six full-length screenplays, three women's fiction novels, the first installment of a murder-mystery series, and a science-fiction epic.

Between them they possess a doctorate and years of practical experience in film, theater, and television. Thanks to their rich international-family backgrounds, they bring to the page a wealth of experiences and points of view. They have lived in different cultures, are multilingual, and bring to their writing a broad understanding of human nature.

This is the second installment in The Perils of a Reluctant Psychic suspense-mystery series. The first, which introduced Sarah and her remarkable psychic powers, was *The Gift of the Twin Houses* (2015).

The third book in the series *"Jackal in the Mirror"* is slated for publication in 2017.

For more information, please visit their website at www.2authors.com.